Rackle's Tub

Rackle's Tub

Dorian Martin

black rainbow books[TM]

Los Angeles

www.blackrainbowbooks.com

Dedicated to

 B. G. Martin

(1939-1997)

"Walking in the dirt"

Physicist, writer, comedian and my dad.

Contents

PART 1

Point

Punch Is No Name For A Girl

It was bound to happen now. There was no escaping it. Her stomach tingled in that uneasy way before you get into a fight. A backyard party, fueled with rage and its adrenaline stench had cut through the fumes of burnt fat from a dying BBQ. It was all closing in on a girl named Punch, who wanted no part of the drama. A slightly pudgy, drunk, Mexican girl, Monica, would not let up her fury. She slammed the sliding glass door shut behind her and crushed a red, plastic cup of piss beer as she made her way towards Punch.

"Fuckin' bitch...!" Her mouth was on auto pilot. English words that easily rolled off the tongue when intoxicated. A loop track from her reptilian reasoning. People, already loud with whistles and 'cat fight!' shouting, only encouraged Monica to keep her course. "I'll fuckin' kick your ass bitch! You damn fucking whore! Come here you fuckin' bitch!!!" Punch, without a word, turned away and looked to Chris, the skinhead boy she came with letting him know with a nod it was time to leave. She headed towards the termite-chewed side gate. Chris pulled his black hoody back, revealing his crown as if it were a shiny trophy for the winner. Monica was now on Punch and smacked her face before someone pulled her off. Punch slid into her jacket, but Chris wouldn't let her leave. He grabbed her arm spinning her to her assailant.

"You could take her," said Chris. Punch shook her head.

"I'll wait in the car," Punch spoke softly.

Monica broke free from her friends. "You stupid bitch! Come here, you chicken shit!" Profanity as available as pennies. Punch turned, beer splashed onto her face. Chris's chin quivered. Monica smashed another cup to Punch's head and grabbed her hair.

The crowd intensified their tribal chants..."Yeah! Woohoo! Don't stop! Grab her! Do it! Knock her out!..."

"Let go of my hair," said Punch in a guttural voice. Chris just watched as others pulled them apart. With an air of composure Punch took off her jacket and threw it at her boy. The crowd vomited high volume when she next pulled out a hair tie to collect her brown, wavy, wild stallion. Her cute freckles, fine, pointy nose with concavity from the tip up to her hazel eyes, and a slim, athletic frame; Punch looked more like the thinking sort and not one who would get tangled in fights. Monica hit her cheek as Punch flinched.

"You fuckin' bitch. You little shit--!" Monica's words intensified her hits. This intimidation didn't work on Punch. Cell phone cameras flashed like a red carpet event. Monica now was swinging blindly, like an out of control windmill hitting the sky. Punch was in fight mode, moving like a Brownsville brawler blocking hits. She didn't yap when beating someone's face purple and raw. She went straight to work and shoved Monica back into the arms of her friends who almost dropped her. And when the hissing Latina charged, Punch landed a bull's-eye blow to the temple sending her cold to the ground. She didn't get up. This fight was over. Everyone gathered around Punch to love her. Some of the men fell to their pathetic knees and proposed to her. She winked at a video camera to her face and proceeded to leave without Chris.

"Get out of the way!" the camera man yelled at the crowd. His YouTube movie star was already past the gate. Chris followed Punch now like a shadow's shadow. He threw the jacket over her shoulders and squeezed.

"I'm not a pitbull. I want to be loved," said Punch.

"I love you," he laughed. "You fuckin' showed that bitch. You owned that motor-mouth cunt... put her in her place!"

"You're a little boy to me. Why would you encourage me to fight? Why did you push me? She was drunk."

"You destroyed her."

"I have no place for you in my life anymore."

"What do you mean? You represented!" He tried to get in front of her, but she pushed him aside.

"Don't follow me."

"What, you're gonna walk home?" He stopped, but this didn't bring her back, so he followed.

"Don't be a cunt. Leave me alone."

"You callin' me a cunt?" He ran up to her, grabbing her arm as he was accustomed to doing with past girlfriends. "You're not leaving me. No. Fuckin' cunt."

"I don't think you understand. I don't want you." She fixed her eyes on his to make sure he received the message.

"I don't give a fuck. That don't mean shit. I'm taking you home." His car was curb side. His grip slid to her wrist as he aimed her to the door.

"You want to bump titties with me?"

"Get in the fuckin' car." He beeped his door unlocked. She spit in his face and punched him in the gut quick and hard. He fell to the ground. She unbuckled her belt, dropped her jeans, squatted over his skull and rained on his face.

"I'm letting you off easy," she said. He coughed and covered his face. She buttoned up. "Thanks for everything. I think I've got it from here on out." By the time he rose to his feet, she was gone. What stock of woman was Punch? She was a champion in the guise of a tomboy, the girl next door who seemed unaware of exactly how stunning she really was. Her education went beyond any university, and her only teacher? Time.

Meet The Clocks

Time was the most powerful thing, more powerful than money, and everybody obeyed it and there was no escaping it. The Clocks, a dart team, functioned smoothly like clockwork. They operated like a well oiled machine, whose part and piece had a purpose or function. They were the individual gears, wheels, spindles and brackets fitted together as one good power team of players. To remove a part would be to have a clock that didn't work. The Clocks were four young, free-spirited men. The Marx Brothers on coke. The Rat Pack on Steroids. Bomb diffusers with the ability to grab a room with their silence and turn it into a good time. They were quick-witted, charismatic jokesters. A blend of joy and anarchy and easily the guys next door. They were the kind of men you wanted to follow. Easy to warm up to, and when they departed, made you feel a little lost. They're not from Los Angeles, but they've made a home of it. The boys were in their early twenties, Shard McEra was the leader of the group; James O'clock, the team's top weapon; Aster Day, the dirty blonde neurotic;

and Ticktock, a British chap like James, but unlike James, he was clinically insane.

A sunny afternoon. Shard was on his way to pick up his teammates in their team car, a 1965 Cadillac Coupe de Ville. Cockily patting the red leather interior, he drove as though his whole purpose was just to show off the car's shiny black exterior. That and the slightly off-center team logo - a giant white-faced clock - painted on the hood. A clean, small bullet hole at the driver's window was never fixed. Shard loved the hole like some women love a scar on a sexy man. The hair trigger of Shard's lustful mind was engaged by a young woman bringing her bike to a stop at a crosswalk. Her legs and ass bulged through the thin skin of her garments while she waited for the light to change. That lucky bike seat! As he drove down the boulevard, every woman he saw he wanted to fuck the living shit out of. He wanted to get out of his car, grab them and have a violent quickie and then off they'd go. His jaws hurt, he wanted to fuck so bad. He understood why men stared and whistled, shouted and pulled over because God-damn, sex made people lose their heads. It's in our nature to screw. Fuck. Eat. Sleep. Repeat. That's what being a man was all about. Everything else was cosmetic if you really broke it all down to its core. Money, career, dreams, etc. These ambitions set us apart from our cousins of the same kingdom, but damn! The animalistic urge to fuck, fuck, fuck is so strong.

Women, women, women- a tribal chant in Shard's mind- some women wore tight spandex while walking their insect-like dogs. Or tiny, ass-hugging shorts as they jogged with their lucky iPods, licking their ears with music. Or mini skirts while they chatted on the phone, leaving an audition from a casting office, leg muscles ripped to such tight poetry. The curves of a woman, bulbous and ready to eat. If Shard wasn't getting it from his gal, or even if he was, he'd still pulverize his penis into a spitting fountain when alone at home. A quick elbow to the horn and Shard found his smokes in the jacket pocket of his sharkskin suit. And in the pocket of his lavender shirt, he pulled out the matches. He lit up at a red light. Crossing the street, another woman in jeans. God this town is full of them. He loved tight jeans on a woman, the way they stretched over the contours of her legs. It was like a denim wrapper, ripe and ready to be torn open to bite the juicy fruit underneath. Luckily she made it to the other side, safe. The light turned green.

* * * * *

James O'clock was born in Greenwich England, blessed to be both handsome and intelligent. Slender, a little under the athletic side, shaggy dark brown hair and a perfect profile from every angle.

Shard pulled up to the Brevoort Hotel. James, in a dark, thin suit and thin tie, waited while a young neighbor gal, sitting on the edge of a retaining wall, stared at him lustfully. She didn't have to speak when her eyes did all the talking. James carried a box that resembled a cigar case. Inside, the tungsten darts. He jumped in the car. They drove farther east. James kicked his feet up on the dash board. Black boots with Cuban heels. Shard gave James a look and he brought his feet down.

"A letter from the New Yorker! Just got it." James pulled out an envelope from inside his jacket. "Haven't opened it!" James opened it.

"Drum roll."

James read and then looked out the window.

"They didn't like it?"

"They didn't like it." James returned the envelope to his pocket.

"Sorry. Well to your credit, the LA Weekly liked your stuff. And what about your doodles hanging in the coffee shop?"

"All returned. Nobody wanted it."

"I thought one of those actors from the AA meetings over there bought one."

"No. A director trying to kick a coke habit stole one. The blooming lout."

"All the famous cartoonists have had a butt-load of rejections. Bugs Bunny was originally a cockroach named Bugsy and Warner Brothers said fuck that, so he then became an aardvark and again-"

"A roach to an aardvark. Really? Hmm, every bloody animal until they decided on a rabbit."

"Same thing with Woody woodpecker, an adult cartoon at first."

* * * * *

The boys used to be called the 4 Brandos! Each member would dress up as Marlon Brando from one of these four early films. James was *Viva Sapata* Brando, with the fake mustache and sombrero. Shard was *Street Car* Brando, Aster was *Waterfront* Brando and Ticktock was *The Wild One* Brando. Then they became the Sensational Tungsten Darts! Or Shard's Tungsten Darts! The S.T.D.'S! Shard loved the double meaning, but soon its novelty wore off and the name changed to the Sundowners and then changed once more to the Clocks.

Aster waited with a briefcase big enough to hold all his disinfectants and other antibacterial supplies. The cartoonish white gloves on his hands made him look like Mickey Mouse, although of course, each of Aster's hands had all five fingers unlike Mickey's three.

"Greetings my fine fellow dart players, this is a fine day to-"

"Get in the car." Shard interrupted. Aster climbed in the back seat.

"While I was researching Nadar and Green party advocates, I stumbled over a new kind of diet." Aster buckled up.

"Are you still a vegan?" said James.

"Not anymore. No sir my fine English friend. Balance is key!"

"Good for you mate. I applaud that."

Finally, Ticktock. Tattooed on the top of his forehead was the Roman numeral for twelve, beneath his boyish, brown bangs. On his right hand, the Roman numeral for nine and his left hand a three. Rumor had it, a six was tattooed below the belt in his pubes, but no one cared to venture down there for a look. He wore black slacks, white shirt, black suspenders and a black derby. He must have been born with sugar in his veins, because hyper drive was the slot his gear was jammed in. His backpack over his outfit didn't look right, but then neither did the first car. Its basic purpose outweighed its aesthetic appeal. Ticktock stood in the middle of the street waiting for them. Never mind that there were cars honking and swerving to avoid him. He didn't budge until Shard's sedan turned the corner, then he ran, at full speed, head-on, towards the car. Shard picked up speed. So did Ticktock. Playing chicken, especially when it's man against car, is not a game for the light-headed. James sat upright, looking to Shard, then back at Ticktock.

"Slow down," Aster said, his eyes transfixed on Ticktock speeding towards them.

"He can't hear you." James said.

"Seriously. Slow down." Aster didn't see the humor.

"I'm banking on him turning left and I'll swerve right," Shard interjected.

"It's not funny." Aster's eyes enlarged to the size of 50-cent pieces. Shard slammed on the brakes. Ticktock smashed into the car. He lay on the ground convulsing.

Shard rolled down the window. "Excuse me," said Shard, "could you show me how to get to the Hollywood sign?" Ticktock pointed upward. Shard looked up. "Oh is it up there?" Ticktock cracked a grin. "Thank you, son." Shard dropped a shiny nickel on Ticktock's chest and then turned the car around. Ticktock still lay on the street, body shaking of its own self-induced quakes. Anyone watching would have thought it real. That's how these cats rolled. Through the rearview, Shard watched as Ticktock pulled out a cigarette, lit it, and let it stand erect in his mouth. The gesture reminded Aster to break out his ChapStick and smear his own lips. Shard pulled over and Ticktock ran to the car. He took off his backpack, tossed it in and dove, head first, through the back window, scurrying over Aster's lap.

"The New Yorker mate!" exclaimed Ticktock. "Yea or nay?"

James pulled out a wallet-sized, leather-bound logbook, where now the envelope was inside, and handed the whole thing over. Ticktock grabbed it and opened the letter. After a moment...

"What?! The fuckin' bastards!" He crumpled the page and stuck it in his mouth for a good chewing. "Well, keep yer pecker up. We'll sort this out." Ticktock leafed through the pages of the log book. "What's your fascination with ants? I never understood it." James held his hand out to collect his journal. Instead, Ticktock placed the wet wad of paper from his mouth in James's palm. Ticktock flipped to another page and read out loud. "The carnage was everywhere. Two little black ants hung on for dear life to the legs of the bigger red ant, who at this point was missing both of her antennas and one left, hind leg. Jennifer Los Feliz. Take Franklin to Western... make a left... buzzer outside the gate is broken." Everyone laughed. He handed the leather-bound journal back to James.

Shard cranked up the music. *All Day And All Of The Night* by the Kinks opened the barrage of music artillery that would be their tournament battle cry. They were all passionate about good old rock and roll. Especially the variety that was produced in their parent's generation. Sixties rock. Garage punk. Raw sounds with real blokes playing real instruments. What they didn't like about a lot of current music was that it was so overproduced, it lost its humanity. All this overproducing, in the end, will kill a song's soul. Music needs to move you. Music should vibrate the body and spirit into a shamanistic, out-of-body explosion. Heavy drums, banging guitars, melodic vocals and harmonies, wavy bass lines, catchy tunes that, when put together, added to a higher sense of euphoria! Once a week, they would gather at Shard's apartment to listen to music. Music night. He provided the drinks unless someone wanted to share a new ale they'd discovered. They arrived bearing their favorite music from their collection and introduced it to everyone else. They would sit back and let the music wash over them. They often pretended to listen to favorite tracks, as if for the first time, to see what had drawn them in.

Aside from the obvious heavy hitters like, The Beatles, The Rolling Stones, The Who, The Kinks, The Animals, Paul Revere & The Raiders, The Doors, The Byrds, The Hollies, Cream, The Dave Clark 5, The Zombies, The Turtles, The Sonics, Blue Cheer, Pink Floyd, The Easybeats, Gerry and the Pacemakers, Mamas and Papas, Simon and Garfunkle, Jimi Hendrix, James Brown, Otis Redding, Herman's Hermits, Bob Dylan, The Monkees, The Yardbirds... they listened to obscure bands like The Monks, The Seeds, The Standells, The Creation, Love, Os Mutantes, The

Troggs, The Small Faces, The Pretty Things, Fire, Q'65, The
Masters Apprentices, The Smoke, The Thirteenth Floor Elevators,
The Outsiders, Them, The Avengers- *Be a Caveman*, The Blues
Inc.- *Tell Me Girl*, The Wee Four-*Weird*, Sons of Fred, The Ways
and Means- *Breaking Up A Dream*, Dave Dee, Dozy, Beaky, Mick
& Tich, Thane Russal & Three- *Sercurity*, Blues Magoos, The Beau
Brummels, The Leaves, The Knickerbockers, The Electric Prunes,
Honeybus, Manfred Mann, The Zakary Thaks, Los Shakers, The
Mops, The Haunted, The Mascots, Love Sculpture, The Downliner
Sect, The Twilights, The Guess Who, Mouse & The Traps, The "E"
Types, The Gestures, The Mojo Men... some of the contemporary
bands they enjoyed, Nirvana, Beck, The White Stripes, The Hives,
The Vines, Kings of Leon, Elliott Smith, Tom Waits, REM, The
Muse, The Strokes, Mr. Bungle...

Just to name a few.

Watford, England 1890

The attic of a prestigious school house was the perfect place to
fuck because no one ever ventured up there. John Rackle pounded
a woman from behind, a rag in her mouth preventing an operatic
reaction. He gazed at his time piece. Class will start in five minutes.
Yet, in this instant, nothing would get in the way of his orgasm. He
stopped to rest, briefly enough, so when he continued, he could
recapture the brilliant sensation of when he first inserted, which
carried him to an even heavier crescendo. This elephantine faculty
member loved John's penis as it ballooned, strangely, like a cobra
inside her. She, too, taught at the school. Music classes in the south
wing, a muffin girl on the down slope of 30. Heavy in all the right
places. As for Mr. Rackle, he seemed to understand his mental
quarks better with age. He had his split personalities down to a
science. After their quickie, the recipient to John's thrusts staggered
and pulled lint from her tongue. She made her way down the hall to
the south wing while adjusting her knickers.

A full classroom of 10-year-olds waited without a professor.
The doorknob turned and Professor John Rackle made his way to
the head of the class. After he settled in and took attendance, the

lessons were underway. Choosing the heaviest child in class, he set
him to running around the room as though chased by a phantom.

"You can't move at the speed of light. And your massiveness
makes you easy to localize," said John from his desk top, perched
against it. The class laughed at the exhausted boy. "Come. Have a
seat." John walked to the chalk board. "Let me offer a mathematical
demonstration to illustrate the possibility..."

"Arrest that man!" The school's principal and the police burst
into the classroom. Was it possible someone discovered his affair in
the attic? John was puzzled for he was fastidious with the secret of
his lustful behavior.

"What is this?" John's hands were placed behind him. "Not in
front of my class."

"Mister Rackle. Your teachings are pure fiction. Fantastical,
hyperbole, nonsensical...you shall not poison these children's minds
with your theorems of ghost atoms, particles, or whatever fairy tale
your queer mind indulges," said the principal.

"A bit extreme isn't it? I am teaching physics. Theory. Harmless.
Just harmless theories." John was escorted to the door.

"I beg to differ, Mister Rackle," said the principal. He leaned in
close, "And there are other matters."

"Very well then. I need my satchel and papers." The principal
nodded to the police and they let him collect his belongings. John
looked up to his students. "Class. It has truly been a pleasure. Do
not be afraid to dream." The police took hold of his arms and
pulled him. "Take heart in your learning. These are magical times,
understanding the beauty that is of our universe..."

"Class!" The principal chimed in like a foghorn. "Pay him no
mind. Mister Rackle is suffering the effects of a head injury he
acquired in his youth. He does not speak good sense. Therefore,
every lesson from his teachings from day one shall be erased
from your little memories. I apologize for the wasted time. Our
screening process will be of much further scrutiny from now on. I
can personally assure you all of that." John's applauds and whistles
could be heard from the halls. As he passed classroom after
classroom, he pretended to lead a marching band, his knees kicked

high. With sociopathic eyes, and his voice at different octaves, he hummed the British National anthem, *God Save The Queen*.

* * * * *

A tavern nearby calmed John's nerves. Unemployed, but not near any breakdown, his stout state brought his gaze to a bathhouse next door. Standing outside the steamy entryway -an older woman. He stared at her as if her shoulders would rest his tiredness from afar. She was a thick woman with pillow-soft sensuality. Bosoms, upright and shiny. Fingers, wrinkled white and peeling like an onion. Mother sat down with another round of beers. John continued to study the woman from across the way. She has curvy hips, like Mother's, John thought. He got up, his eyes still on the strange woman.

"Sweetie," said Mother. She noticed the other woman. "She can't help you any more than I can." After handing him the mug, she took him by the arm and he begrudgingly followed. She kissed him on the lips. He looked away. His cheek scratching a second kiss from Mother.

Colorado 1891

Many girls began coming home with black eyes, busted lips, a frazzled ear or two and bones with hairline fractures, mapping out new roads under fleshy skies of fat and skin. The residual from a hush-hush, brutish society starting to show itself to flummoxed and angry husbands. Proper was a woman's place. The comedy in all this was the clever means of trying to explain away their injuries. 'I was busy feeding the chickens when I stepped on a rake, and the handle stood to greet me like a soldier at arms.' Makeup didn't hide the scratches or puss-oozed gashes very well. And just as a man's day of labor left him spent as is, this added concern drank even deeper from his confidence when his wife brushed the seriousness of the wounds off as simple accidents around the farm. Every week, new wounds. Husbands soon began fearing an affair had gone violently sour. The truth of the matter, someone had orchestrated a women's Victorian boxing faction. There was one cause for all these strings of indecorous behavior in women's athletics. Her name was Punch. Not short for the black masked, hooked nose, boastful Punchinello of the 17th century in Naples: inspiration for the famous puppet show, *Punch and Judy* playing all over England - you know, the one where Punch strangled his children and beat his wife to death. No. Not the same Punch publication as the London Charivari based on the puppet. No. They called her Punch due to her bone-breaking hits. She founded the women's boxing club in her husband's barn.

Punch rushed into the building, dressed in Victorian garb - her hair in a bun, corset over her bloomers - then started stripping. Nearby farmers, gamblers, miners, ranchers and perverts had already gathered inside in a reserved madness of thrilling delight. A homemade, ranch style boxing ring was placed together quicker than the strike of a coiled snake. Forming the sides of the ring - ropes off a naval ship. And the four corners - haystacks, each corner four haystacks high.

"Guard the door." Punch said, as her dress dropped to the floor. The bloated, fence-post of a man at the door nodded. He sat, perched on an old wine barrel, staring at her, but when Punch caught him looking, he hopped off his seat to shut the door. A pre-drilled eye hole opened, where he nestled his right eye like he would his butt to a toilet seat. Light shot out of the carpenter bee-sized hole when he pulled away to sneak another peek at the punishing angel in knickers. Another man handed her a pair of boxing gloves. Already in the ring and being fitted into her gloves was a behemoth of a girl. There were no weight classes and other fighters always outweighed Punch. She was 5 feet 7 inches tall and somewhere in the neighborhood of 130 pounds.

Punch challenged most every whore and barroom wench in the local area. One saloon girl died, but it was days later and believed not to be related. Or, so Punch convinced herself. While in town, a man accosted Punch for sex and began the act without her consent. With a right-handed blow to his left temple, she fractured his skull, sending him thrashing on the street like a wild salmon on shore. He grabbed his left eye with both hands and picked himself up and staggered away. At the nearest bar, he sat alone until a cerebral hemorrhage killed him some hours later.

As Punch entered the ring, the two took note of each other. Punch winked at her. The other girl spit black bog water from her chew. It caught on the side ropes, where it hung in a slow motion drip. She then hit her gloves together as a means of intimidation. A squirrelly man brought both women to the center of the ring.

"All right ladies. The winner gets a silver butter dish," he said.

"I don't want another one," Punch replied. "It's hers, regardless of the outcome."

"I want a clean fight," the man continued.

"I don't want the dish either," her opponent said, "All I want is her teeth. Make a necklace for my pigs to wear."

Punch smiled. "Don't speak so harshly of your family. Unfortunately, I do not have enough teeth to wrap around that fat neck of yours. You may have to borrow the ones I'll hand you from your own mouth." She snorted like a pig. The other girl lunged for Punch, looking like she had every intention of killing her.

The referee pushed her back. "To your corners," he shouted. The girls walked back and waited. At the sound of the dinner triangle, the two girls met in a dance, center ring. Punch dodged a couple of obvious swings. The crowd cheered. Then, Punch zeroed in on her opponent and began the punishment. With quick combinations, she opened up on the unlucky woman's right side, each hit landing squarely. Punch made contact with her jaw. Then the ribs. With every jab, the girl's heart must have thought cannons were firing upon her walls. The calcium rich structure rattled with every blow. Punch snapped her punches like firecrackers. But before she could lay on the thick assault, the battle was over. Her opponent dropped. A broken tooth rode her tongue like a raft over the red falls and out onto the floor. The ref just stared, only shaken from his stupor by the screaming crowd.

"Yeah don't bother counting," she said. "She's taking her sabbatical." Punch watched as roses were thrown at her feet.

"And the winner by knockout." The ref grabbed her wrist and held it up high. "Puuuuuunch!" The crowd loved her.

Later that night, upstairs in the barn counting money, Punch sat amongst the men. She was also the accountant in charge of the earnings. After all, it was her enterprise. A big cigar, like a swaying mantis, stayed to one side of her mouth. The dim light of the lantern hid the dirt and sweat hugging her skin. No one dared to cross her path. Even in business, she was a force not to be tangled with. She collected the money from her opponent's manager.

"Bring her back again, when you feel she's ready," she smiled. He was quickly escorted out by one of Punch's henchmen. "All right boys. We did well tonight. We have come out double from last time." The men treated her like fine crystal on the outside, but she was still a hard diamond whenever inside the ring. She had her husband, in part, to thank for that.

* * * * *

Both Punch and her drunk husband, Michael, were seated at their dinner table. He was slightly older and fussy as a child.

"You know," he said, "the women in Europe know how to dress." Michael downed the rest of his wine. "La Belle Époque. Everything is beautiful over there."

Punch paused before cutting her meat.

"They have etiquette," he continued. "The French, in particular. Unlike the American woman."

She took a sip of her wine.

He tapped his empty glass with his pudding spoon. She got up. "Indecent..." Michael threw words out to entice a reaction. "Crude. Uncultivated..." She poured him more wine from a small decanter. He stared at her fingers. "Look at your hands. Those aren't the hands of a fine lady. Those are working-class hands. No elegance. The only saving grace is that ring I bought you."

He slapped the wine from her hand, knocking the glass to the ground. He grabbed her shirt, yanking and ripping at it as he now stood. "Stop-" she cried.

"Your clothes...fucking rags. Any random whore bears finer linen than you! And you're my fucking wife!"

Her face flushed with the pain she tried to hide. "You're so cruel," her voice barely audible.

"You've made a mess. And an ass of yourself."

Punch bent over to pick up the glass. "Please teach me how you wish me to be," she pleaded. "And I swear to you, I will..."

"No." He shook his head and laughed before he drank from the decanter. "You can't teach a rowdy whore about the finer things!"

"Please...I'm not a whore. I'm sorry you find disappointment in me. I love you. You asked my hand in marriage. It is my duty to make you happy. There is nothing more that I wish for. I am more than willing-"

"Hopeless!"

"-to learn." He couldn't even look at her anymore. After a moment, she got up and ran out of the dining room, crying.

The Crompton Brewing Co. U.S.

Nearby, a newly built brewery hid secrets unrelated to the making of beer. The overly wealthy Crompton & Roy built the large factory with many hidden chambers in which to safely store poppy seed pods. Opium trade was its one secret. The place had yet another.

England 1891

John Rackle was spat upon in the most formal of places, the Bank of England. The bank manager got up from behind his rosewood desk and motioned for the guards to come quick.

"A tub for orgies?!" he said. "How dare you! You will get no funding whatsoever from me, nor any bureau, in all of England. And I will see to it, you filthy swine!" He grabbed John's notebook of plans and threw it at him. The guards lifted him over the seat and left the room, dragging John's heels on the rug. They tossed John outside the bank, his sketches sprawled, like his limbs. He picked himself up and gathered what he could of his work, some of the pages taking to flight at the idea of another round elsewhere. A sketch was caught at a couple's feet and deliberately stepped on. People passing offered no help, only smug stares, and at that, they were brief.

Mr. Rackle labored, day after exhausting day, knocking on doors, asking for financing, only to be bounced back into the

English streets. His search for funding found him as far north as
Scotland. On an overcast and rainy day, at a local farm opened
for auctions, John stood before a small crowd seated on hay
bales inside the barn. Not even five minutes into his delivery and
the group of prospectors laughed at him outright. Perhaps it
was the clumsy sketches of a man and woman in a large double
slipper tub. The various sketches of tub styles always had a couple
pictured together, with expressionless faces, while in compromised
positions.

"That's a whore trough!" one Scotsman yelled amongst the
laughter from the other farmers.

John spent that night drunk in a bathhouse tub, his Mother
scrubbing his back with a soapy cloth, as he lost clarity from the
steam that thickened around him. An angel bared her ass and then
spread her white wings. The Heavens were laughing at him, too.
His vision turned out to be an elderly man, naked, drying his legs
with a white towel.

"Mother, I have to leave you." John's eyes fixed on the design
of the adjacent tub.

"Nonsense, dear. You need me now, more than ever." She
planted a kiss on his wet shoulder.

"Mother, please."

"Who loves you, darling?" Mother got up to her feet. "What
you need now is a good, hardy supper. Followed by a good night's,
sound sleep." John looked at her. "Get up now. Let's dry you off."
She reached for a white towel, as John shielded his groin. "Don't
be bashful, darling. There is nothing I haven't already seen."
John grabbed the towel and covered up as he stepped out of the
lukewarm water.

* * * * *

In 1873, a New York company, Mott Iron Works, manufactured
the first porcelain, enameled bathtubs. They were considered too
expensive to transport and install. The tubs were later discovered to
cause lead poisoning.

The Atlantic ocean was a large bath, drawn. The ship, a bar of soap on a dish, near to cleanse oneself of the old world dirt. The American continent, the towel. Her sun-warmed streets offered the clean slate from the turbulent wash. The cruise-liner was packed with many European immigrants. John sat with his traveling companion, a trunk large enough to transport a small boy, made of England's best leather and shiny latches. He leaned against it, taking in the salty, crisp, cold air. Bells and gulls, wind and creaking wood, helped drown out the spatter of foreign tongues. Hallucinations in the sky that drifted upward, until he looked elsewhere, put him to slumber. A paperboy was making his rounds. Not wanting to shout, John waited until he got within range of his dinner table voice.

"Paper, please. English." The boy pulled out the day's read, while John fished a coin from his vest pocket.

John kept to himself for most of the journey. He would sit with his morning tea, notebook out, writing math formulas and taking a moment's detour to sketch out bathtubs. Getting lost in one's work offered a tinge of euphoria. He enjoyed ripping his map, smashing the compass and diving out the window, wayward into some wandering between the cracks of his intellect. He had always maintained that vigor of childhood curiosities. Most men's view of the world in his twenties may carry a lot of hope, while learning to ground himself, overly so, with social practicalities. Once he reached his thirties, he viewed the world with doubt and cynicism, as he adjusted to dreams forgotten or considered unattainable and settled with priorities better to sustain himself. John was not fighting to find the magic in the world. Magic that seemed so apparent to him in younger years. He was now downright certain it was out there. He based this on a series of successes, that confirmed, little by little, his direction, which in turn, quietly comforted his confidence. Upon arriving in America, John, having introduced his soles to New York cobblestone, found refuge in a cafe with outdoor seating. A newspaper, abandoned on a table, grabbed his eyes. One might think it was the typical words of a muckraker. The headlines, bold and inviting.

Brewery Shut Down! Opium Smuggling and Mass Suicide!

The brewery was a nice piece of property, John thought. Now available for purchase somewhere in Colorado. Nobody would touch it because of the double negative, which John saw as a positive. He didn't care if people blew their brains upward on the ceiling and walls, or jumped out of windows with the sharp dislocating pain of broken bones hitting hard streets, or any of the illegal activity under the guise of ale making. Superstition was not a road blocker for John, like it was for many others. He wondered why people would stop their pursuit, in terrible fear of something that doesn't even exist. If you crossed a black cat or stepped under a ladder, would that really alter existence? A cat is a cat. Pigmentation of fur color holds no unearthly reach to shape one's future. It's a cat. All these things could be broken down with a little logic. Some of the wisest people would suddenly turn into crying children when asked to confront a superstition. Folding the paper, John slid it into his case and left the cafe. He took a train westward and never gave New York a chance. What John loved about America was that everything was so spread out. The vast areas to put up a shop of your own. To start a life of your own. The land, as endless as the ocean.

* * * * *

The Crompton Brewing Company was empty. The realtor pointed out the large spaces and high ceilings to John, who nodded as he followed.

"The previous owners were filthy rich," the realtor said.

"Why did it go under so quickly?" John was curious about details the paper may have left out.

"You have the perfect location. The owners went to extremes searching for the right spot to build. But they knew nothing of brewing. In fact, Mr. Crompton never touched his tongue to a pint of anything in his entire life!"

"How could you make such an absurd statement? Were you with Mr. Crompton all his life? You think the news of this shutdown stopped at just the local papers? I read about this available real estate all the way from New York, for Christ's sake."

The realtor continued his walk with deaf ears. "The big rooms are perfect for your bath company."

"I'll take it."

The realtor turned to face John. His hearing restored, a sense of relief and delight on his face.

"Perfect choice, Mr. Rackle."

"But, I want you to show me where the opium kitchens were, and the rooms where the mass suicide took place, and all the hidden nooks and crannies..."

The realtor became ghostly unsettled. He gasped for air. John hesitated at his terror.

"...I just want to make my peace with it and have it done with, my boy, before I dare venture forth in business. If you please," John reasoned. "Surely you can understand that."

"What are you talking about? There was no such tragedy. I don't know anything about kitchens or suicides..." The realtor wiggled as John threw the paper at his feet.

"I find your reaction staged. Unless you are a complete imbecile, how can you not know about this double catastrophe? If the papers are truthful, is it not you whose shoulders this rests upon, to dutifully and tastefully disclose the incident for your patrons in the marketplace? Please. Indulge me," John said. The realtor picked the paper up off the floor, giving only a quick glance at the headlines.

"You know how troubling this place has been to unload?"

"How troubling could it be, as to any other place, when it's fresh on the market?"

"Yes, but, still, no one wants it. At one point, the bank wanted to give it away right when it became available." The realtor wasn't making sense to John, so he decided to let it be.

"Free real estate? Well, I'll reason with that price, too."

"Well, actually, the bank does need some compensation. Still interested?"

"You just sold it. The deal is done. Let us sign the papers, shall we?" John shook his hand.

John found no problem in securing a small business loan from the bank for being "brave" enough to take the property off their hands. It wasn't long before John's dream of a bath company was up and running. And in 1892, he opened for business.

Behind The Clock

James thought every generation suffered from retrospection. This was a compliment to the movements, styles and thoughts of the past, but only a healthy one if used for learning what the previous did and adopted and applying it to the forward motion of his own generation. Placing the template on solid foundations. Given enough time, one became retro for their own generation. Having this hindsight, when others were completely vogue in thought and execution of the present, could make one feel modern, and so different, that they appeared new. When, in fact, they were only mirroring a gesture not known by their contemporary counterparts because of its Paleolithic age. The Clocks had that nostalgic love affair. They had chosen to divorce themselves from modern day's, minute-by-minute updaters of unknowns, laying claim to high status by simply manipulating the various mediums to their advantage. These below-the-level-of-mediocrity people had no talent, other than promoting an otherwise empty product of self. They had nothing true to stand behind. They wanted the prominence without the work. Even longing for the troubles of stardom. The Clocks weren't Mods or hipsters. They were out-of-touch with today's trends and shallow standards, not haphazardly, but by a collective like-mindedness. They weren't above it all either. They simply preferred different things in life. They didn't find entertainment in everyone's 15 minutes. They didn't give a fuck about the reality TV, webisodic, polished version of home movies from lives of these attention whores.

It was a task to hold up an image and create a stamp. The Clocks took that old Cadillac to San Francisco, for a tournament. They were fortunate enough to have sponsorships: A local, underground, political/art magazine, a head-shop, the LA Weekly and an auto garage Shard worked for, the Cadillac's best friend. With gas prices what they were, a gas tank capacity of 26 gallons, frequent breakdowns, and parts no longer manufactured, the

Cadillac wasn't exactly the smartest way to go, but she did look fucking beautiful moving these boys from town to town. Chrome bumpers against the shiny black body and whitewall tires, a turbo hydra-matic transmission and the roar of the rebuilt 429 cubic inch V8 engine, couldn't help but inspire its occupants. The car was worth it to them. When you spotted the boys pulling into the bar's parking lot, you knew you were dealing with class. Suffering a couple of minor setbacks was well worth the aura they created. What woman could resist a young, well-dressed man leaning against his clean, classic Cadillac as he waved her over? And even if she had a boyfriend, what guy could resist it either?

"Two things I find difficult to peel my eyes from are classic cars and beautiful women," Shard had often said. The others all agreed. "Now, a beautiful woman driving a classic car... hello, Saint Peter!"

Most contenders in these dart tournaments never fussed about their own appearance. T-shirts with stupid logos, baseball caps, jeans or whatever clothes they threw on. Fucking boring. The Clocks didn't so much want to raise the bar as they wanted to have fun. When one indulges in the magic of presence, you need not say a word when you step into a room. Having presence required a full body involvement. You've got to feel it from your toes all the way up to your crown. It wasn't about being elite, but being in the now. What you radiated rippled your persona, like a long arm extending a handshake across the bar. And everyone's reaction said it for you. The same applied to musicians. When you're in a rock band, you never want to look like someone from the audience just got up on stage and grabbed a guitar. You want to add theatrics! It's part of what people pay for. It shows a little more effort for their dollar. The excitement it generates is contagious, spreading to all who want to do their part in uplifting life to a new aesthetic level. This is how to live, goddamn it! Whatever uncomfortable, hot layers of feelings develop, you transcend and focus on the game at hand. Then you drink it up. It's a self-induced high. No substances needed to trigger it. Artists know this feeling. To live the creative life is the highest life one can live. The Clocks were a theatrical bunch. They wore Chelsea boots, tight fitting, Cuban-heeled, ankle high, black, leather boots with sharp pointed toes that had a center seam stitch from ankle to toe and either elastic or zipper sides. They wore the 3 button, form fitting suits and thin ties. Their rock heros of the sixties wore them. They easily resembled a band from that era.

* * * * *

Shard sat at the bar with their shiny trophy. The Clocks had just finished another win. James sat next to him, both of their once immaculately white shirts and neck ties now untucked, slightly damp and wrinkled. The place had no air conditioning. Probably on purpose, knowing the Clocks always dressed in full attire. But that didn't matter. They were victorious.

"Aster tells me the ladies room is always cleaner than the men's," said James as he watched Aster, cleaning kit in hand, disappear into the ladies room. Ticktock grabbed a glass of water and poured it over his own head. He shook like a wet, summer dog and marched to the men's room.

"We're an eclectic bunch, aren't we?" Shard held up his glass of ale and James did the same. After they clinked bottoms, they drank it down. "No one should have to take care of more than one or two wackos at a time. I've met my quota with those two. I'm not a charity worker. I'm at my rope's end, and if I extend myself beyond that, I'll hit my breaking point. But you gotta love 'em though."

"Here, here...," James lifted his empty glass.

"Is your boy using the ladies room?" The bearded bartender flipped his towel over his shoulder. Shard and James looked at one another in silence.

The ladies room had a little vanity station when you first entered. Aster kept his eyes down, found an empty stall and slipped in, locking the door. Fitted with a pair of surgical gloves, he closed the toilet seat and with his boot, flushed for good measure. His cleaning kit hung on a coat hook and unrolled, open with displays of cleaning bottles. He lifted the toilet lid. Out came the bottle of rubbing alcohol, which doused the seat. A lighted match ignited the seat into a ring of fire. Another spritzer bottle put the blaze out. Everything he did was perfectly timed and with a smooth motion. The bottles went back into the bag. A large piece of toilet paper lay over the surface of the toilet water. Another on each side of the seat. The wax seat cover was carefully pulled, as not to rip. He placed it on the seat with its tongue hanging down into the water. Finally, he dropped his trousers to sit. And it was only for a tinkle.

Ticktock slammed open the door to the men's room. "Nasty in there. I'm gonna try me luck in the ladies-" The bartender pointed to him. Ticktock stopped. Caught! "Right. I'll wait in the car." Shard threw Ticktock the keys and he disappeared out the door. James thought it was a good idea to hit the bathroom before they hit the road.

Sitting on the toilet in the men's room, James had no need for magazines; the stall provided enough reading material for him. Aside from the typical profanity and gang references, there were some interesting pieces.

A drawing of a priest positioned between two choir boys labeled: *Missionary Position.*

Another drawing of two penises touching labeled: *Cock Fighting. Illegal in Colorado.*

And other things such as, *You're lucky. 2 stalls down, gay microbes on toilet seat wait for ass.*

But, it was a little armchair mystery that really caught James's attention.

He rode after her on horseback and that was the last Time we saw him. His horse returned without him. Not even a Minute and we knew something was wrong and we set out after him. We searched until the sun left. There were no signs of him anywhere. Days went by and still, nobody was found. It wasn't until the following Week when he was spotted many miles from where he had last been seen. Walking on the side of the road. A good Samaritan picked him up. He looked like he had aged 20 Years. His hair, now grey. White stubble, like a cactus, grew from his chin and cheeks. His eyes, like frozen gems with his cry for help, silenced and fossilized, said more than words. He spoke nothing of the past Week and when asked, he fell back into that paralyzed slumber, fighting to get back to the shores of humanity, clawing at the Sand as the tide slowly pulled him away.

What's broken James? Clock is ticking. Call little girl Punch.

.

James flinched upon reading his own name. A peculiar symbol shaped like a smile, along with a phone number, were written below the story. Although he had no inkling what that symbol was, he pulled out a matchbook and jotted the name and phone number. The area code was unfamiliar. This must be a joke, James thought. He tried to smudge his name, but it was dry. It was so like his mates to play around, but this was different. Strange. Aster never used the men's room. Ticktock wasn't a writer. Shard had yet to use the men's room. Maybe it was an opponent? After all, the Clocks were well known in the dart playing community. But how would they know which stall to write in? James didn't even think he would use a stall. Was there a story in every stall? Maybe it was just a coincidence. James was a common name.

Creepy.

The stall next door received a new visitor. He saw the trophy set on the floor. James finished his business and after a flush, snatched up the trophy.

"Hey," Shard, no doubt paralyzed by an outgoing shit, shouted. "Not funny." James held his breath and brought the trophy to the sink to wash his hands. "James. That better be you." James dried his hands, straightened his hair in the mirror, grabbed the trophy and left. "Fine. I'll just win another one."

Rackle's Tub.

As man expanded west, so did his lust and need for brothels. And brothels were the main buyers of John Rackle's specialized tubs.

"How did the tutoring go?" A worker collected John's coat.

John felt good returning to his factory for the evening.

"If I keep to simple science and arithmetic, I shouldn't have a problem losing students." John grabbed the mail, sorting through it. One letter in particular caught his attention. "Ah! Denver!" He opened it and read. He folded the letter back into the envelope.

"Well?"

"Let us ponder our reach at the moment; Chicago, San Francisco -"

"- New Orleans -"

"Right. We've acquired clients in New York, and now my fine dolt of a friend, we have our very own Denver in the orgy tub business!"

"Yes Sir!"

"This should help pay down the debt of our mortgage. I don't care if they use the tubs as hog scalders, this calls for a celebration!"

As their jaunt around the factory to inspect operations continued, they made their way to a couple of his men retiring for the evening.

"Hey, we're gonna go watch a fight. Why don't you come along?" said one worker.

"Boxing? Really?" John put his time piece away. "All right then. Let me lock up." He fetched his coat.

* * * * *

The barn looked desolate in the sprawled countryside. John's carriage came to a complete stop just short of the ranch. Hidden, in dark paths between oak trees, were many carriages parked away from the view of the road. John and his coworkers stepped out of their transport and began the trek to the barn. The sky of burnt sapphire had darkened to midnight blue. Already, there was a line of people to get in. A large curtain, hung so as to keep light from escaping the building, had to be moved aside to enter the arena. A fight was already in progress. John was overrun by the shock of seeing two women glove to glove. Many states had prohibited prizefighting. Women's boxing was outlawed in England, so John was a bit surprised to find it here. He knew this was an illegal operation just by the secrecy with the parking. The men headed to the back to find their seats.

"This isn't boxing, it's a freak show!" John protested. "I'm a perverted chap, I realize, but I have to draw the line. To watch these poor sweaty, three hundred pound spinsters beat their ape heads in is not entirely appealing. In fact, not appealing at all."

"Wait 'til ya see this girl they call Punch," said the first worker. "Cute as all hell. She has stars at the end of her fists. So say those who've received them."

The fight ended and once a winner was declared, the two girls left the ring. These matches were not vaudevillian acts. And these weren't saloon brawls, where women fighters would kick, maul, scratch and tear into each other like a couple of bobcats. This was boxing. Women wore gloves.

A bookie approached John and his two workers.

"Would you care to wager sir? The next match up is our dear Punch and Long Legs Sally. Put your bets down now," the bookie said.

"Punch!" the other men were already well aware of her reputation. "Put me down for Punch!" They reached into their pockets to pull out their day's earnings, money John had given them, now to be thrown at a fight. No doubt these men had earned it well, but, he admitted, it carried a slight sting.

"Yeah. Me too!" said another man nearby. John hesitated. The bookie looked to him. A third man placed money for her opponent, Long Legs Sally. She also had a reputation of hurting other fighters.

"And you sir?" The bookie waited for a brief moment before turning away.

"Yes. I'll, ah..." John scrambled for his cash. "Put me down for Punch as well..." He counted the money before handing it over. "Here."

The squirrelly ref returned and took center ring, where he raised his arms for silence. The crowd quieted down. "Ladies and gentlemen. Now, on to the main fight of the evening. The one you've all come for! Two of the greatest fighters in women's boxing will come head to head! Tit to tit! To duke it out for your enjoyment and their dignity! These two ladies have never met until tonight! So place those bets! This is going to be a real show!" The crowd started up again.

Long Legs Sally entered the ring with her trainers. She's a negroid, John observed. Tall for even a man. His eyes were quickly drawn to a shorter white girl, already in gloves. No, this can't be! That foolish, little school girl is going to fight that big machine of a woman?! John felt outrage spreading like a bowl of molasses poured thick over his back. As the ref flagged them both to the center of the ring, John fixated on Punch. The poor girl is going to die, John thought. After the ref finished going over the rules, both girls touched gloves before going to their respective corners.

"This is cruel!" hissed John.

"In this corner, respectively with no mention of weight, from the banks of the Mississippi...LONG LEGS SALLY!" She raised her gloves to a not-too-supportive audience. "And in this corner, our very own, homegrown... PUNCH!" The crowd jostled and cheered as she turned to them. She raised one glove and smiled, dimples and all. "All right, ladies! Are you ready?" They both nodded.

At the sound of the triangle, the girls exploded into action. Center ring and already blows delivered from both fighters. Because Punch wasn't a big girl, she had to be quick in everything she did. The crowd turned mad with noise. John's hair stood all over his body, as his dear Punch showed to be worth her weight in fury. One solid hit to Sally's lowered head shook Sally's body off -kilter, but her long legs kept her up. Another body-rattling hit sent Sally to the ropes. Recovering, she sent a long-reaching connection to Punch's eye. Surprisingly she took the hit, and yet still stayed in the pocket for her own safety. Both girls pummeled each other with close-range hits. Punch threw a wild left; Sally shoved Punch back into a tumble and onto her ass. The crowd was desperate. Punch hopped quickly to her feet, glove raised to penetrate a block - only to meet Sally's punch upside her head. With another fist to her opposite side, Punch kept in the defensive position. At first it seemed that these girls had met their equal in each other. But as it stood now, Sally's hits had turned into a domination over her rag doll opponent.

Poor girl... John turned to his employees, head shaking bitterly. They all shouted for her as if she had a chance. Are we not watching the same fight? John thought.

Keeping light on her feet, Punch decided against any infighting, remaining outside of Sally's reach so she could regain energy. And it was enough to delay the beating before the round was over. The triangle sent both girls back to their corners. The walls of that barn had never housed such excitement.

John shouted to Punch. "Stop the fight!" His gangly legs trembled, and as the triangle screamed for round two, his ass slid off the seat.

Both girls took their time, sizing each other up. Again, Punch took a hit to the eye. Sally delivered a couple more jabs, and when she opened to hit, Punch countered in a beeline to her nose. The tower of a woman was sent sprawling backwards. Punch fans rose to their feet. John, for the first time, realized Punch had what it took. Her quickness and agility reminded him of those of a mongoose and a cobra. The fight continued. Punch followed up with more hits, but Sally's defense was up and working again. Punch continued to test it, and weaken it, only to receive an offensive Sally move to her jaw. This sent Punch back, staggering, and Sally moved in on her, unloading a couple of artillery rounds, most deflected by Punch's quick glove work, even with her eye swollen shut, purple as a plum. The fighters moved steadily in a circle, never breaking focus. Sally dispersed some swings, but they were diffused by the time they reached their intended target. The rest of the round proved to be a standstill. Sally had the advantage of height and long reach. Punch, the smarter fighter, had the advantage of her right hook. Once she landed that, no matter who it was, the fight was usually over. The triangle rang, and yet again, brought the girls to their corners. John got up and left his friends to stand ringside, shoulder to shoulder with the others.

"Punch! You can do it, my love!" He pushed his way to her corner. "Punch!" For just a moment, her good eye looked at him, but then her gaze returned to her trainers.

Other men asked him to step back, but John kept his focus. Punch swooshed a mouthful of moonshine and spit it out. Some of it splashed down onto John's face; he felt baptized. The triangle rang out again! Round three! Both girls shot up and danced around the platform, their defenses tight. The entire round was served in this manner, the boos and hisses inevitable. The triangle returned them home for more pampering.

"This is the longest I've seen her fight!" said a farmer standing near. "She usually puts it away in the first or second round."

The triangle signaled the start of the fourth. The girls joined at the center. Quicker than a blink, Punch dispatched a right uppercut, sailing like a bullet past Sally's closing hands into the bottom of her jaw, through the tongue, cracking the teeth and into the brain. Sally's knees buckled, and she crashed to the ground. Like a short fuse to dynamite, Punch ignited instant applause. Sally tried to get up, but found she couldn't win against her aching joints and her head, now perilously losing clarity. It was a sensation of a million needles pricking and spreading from ground zero to envelop her body like a throbbing, underwater wildfire! Punch kneeled to the ground, concern in her one open eye. When the ref was finished with his countdown, she spoke to him, her voice winded, yet authoritative and...caring. John took in every detail of the moment. The blood dripping from Punch's eye, her hair stuck to her sweaty face and neck, and still- compassion for her opponent. Sally's trainers collected her. The ref grabbed Punch by the wrist, raising it high.

"THE WINNER BY KNOCKOUT! PUUUUNNNNCH!"
The crowd rushed the ring as John's blood rushed his heart.

* * * * *

The next morning at work, John was checking inventory when he heard the bell at the front door jingle. John saw a man and woman, presumably husband and wife, standing in the display room of the lobby.

"Hello. Welcome," John said. Drawing near, he saw the woman's face and her bruised eye. As if on a trampoline, his heart bounced, then lodged itself in his trachea.

"We're looking to purchase a tub for our newly added guest room, upstairs..." Michael noticed John looking at Punch. He hadn't meant to stare, but Michael just assumed it was the shiner that had caught John's attention. It was painful to look at.

"My wife, she's a little blunderous. Accident prone."

"I sleepwalk sometimes," she interjected.

"Please sir, whatever thoughts you may entertain... a cruel husband, I never beat her. I do not want that judgment on me."

"It is quite true," said Punch. "I foolishly bumped into our fountain in the courtyard last night," she winked her good eye at John, "while my husband was away on business. Although I have suspicion it was more of an excursion." Michael laughed through his nose and shook his head.

"Women are so frivolous at times." Michael parted ways to look at floor models. John smiled, so as to stay neutral.

"Well, like they say, 'a fountain in the night, may hinder thy sight,'" John said. Punch snickered. Michael examined the larger tubs most peculiarly.

"Who said that?" Michael's eyes never left the tub.

"Nobody. Until now," said John. He leaned close to Punch. "I won a pretty penny with you last night. I say, what a fight."

"Thank you. Sally was a tough cookie," she whispered. "I knew if I didn't act quickly, she would have taken me."

"You were wonderful to watch. Most beautiful!" John glanced over her lowered head to Michael, then back to the bashful Punch, her dimples showing again in her smile.

"Thank you, sir."

"Please. Call me John." He extended his hand to her, while she lifted hers to his. He didn't let go, but instead held her fingers as if they were precious pearls that he polished with a kiss.

"Mary Tabitha Lilybell. But, you may call me Tabby."

"Getting acquainted, are we?" Michael shouted from across the room.

"Or if you wish, you may call me Punch." John had the inkling that her husband didn't know what went on in his barn. She turned to Michael.

"No, darling," she shouted back, "what sort of salesman would he be? Like they say, 'a salesman in thy night, would cast thee buyer such a fright!'" John snickered.

"Mister Rackle," he said. "Have you no tubs of smaller dimensions?"

"Smaller? No sir. These tubs are only designed for multiple people," John explained.

"Multiple people? Are we saving water?"

"Well, that would be a splendid way to look at it I suppose," said John.

"Who takes baths with multiple people?"

Then John realized, Michael didn't know what kinds of tubs these were. "Well sir," John tailored his response, "you and your lovely wife could now share the tub experience..."

Michael drew closer. "Are you fucking mad?"

"To share the tub with your wife causes such an alarm?" John realized he needed to be frank about his product. "They're orgy tubs sir." Punch struggled to hold back her building laughter. Michael grabbed her by the arm.

"This is outrageous!" At closer inspection, Michael's eyes widened as he suddenly spotted the details he had easily overlooked, details that clearly indicated these tubs were for uses other than bathing. The faucet was in the shape of a penis; as were the water blasters at the bottom of the tubs, the drain a vagina. Handrails on both sides for back and forth action. A *hot* tit and a *cold* tit. Drink holders big enough for champaign bottles. Large colorful feathers in decoration.

The bell at the front door jingled again. An overly dandified man and his entourage of women entered the shop. Punch laughed outwardly now, tugged away by her embarrassed husband. John loved that he had been able to make as much of an impression on her as she had on him.

* * * * *

John had turned one of the rooms upstairs into his new office. It had been the study where Roy, of the Crompton Brewing Company, had supposedly fallen out the window to his death, opium pipe still warm in his hand when the cops found him. It was uncharacteristic for an opium smoker to jump to his death, which intrigued John ever so slightly. What could have possibly caused a man feeling euphoric to leave his room by way of window? Next to John's desk, a normal, clawfoot bathtub was filled to the brim with books. The last of his belongings had arrived from England, and there were still many he had yet to unpack. Most of his wooden trunks he put into storage above his office, in the attic.

Upon his desk, under the light, a new magic was being realized. In the realms of his own secrecy he could have the full freedom, unscrutinized, to explore his bizarre postulations. Such as coextensive universes. The time was ripe for one science to replace another. John scribbled equations, taking a moment here and there to draw the contours of a bathtub, so simple in its elegance. They reminded him of logarithm curves and spirals. Then he would return to his numerical riddle-solving. He would bite into the hours, all day and all of the night, with theoretical physics. He wanted his equations to have that same simple elegance. He played with the indefinite integral symbol by laying it on its back, stretching it in the shape of a bathtub. Then, he placed numbers and theorems inside the "*tub*". This created manifold effects that performed several functions at once. It was a bathtub full of ethers, where particles converted the intangible into tangible. He had to create new physics to explain his theories. John glowed brighter than his light at this new perspective of problem solving and understanding the universe. He had invented a new mathematical symbol. Like his factory, he called it *Rackle's Tub*. And his world would not be the same again.

All the while, floating above his head, close to the ceiling, an atmospheric knot, tightly shut, began to loosen her labium majus.

He didn't know how long he lay in the dirt, but John opened his eyes to a factory worker pulling his arm. Sun shone brightly.

"Mr. Rackle!" The worker sat him up against the Bedford-limestone wall. A smidgen of dry vomit was on his chest. "Mr. Rackle, are you all right, sir?"

John took in his surroundings, then nodded.

"Yes, yes, thank you." He stood and brushed his clothes with a swat of his hands. "A tad too heavy on the bottle, I say."

"Sir, what's Purgalapudlia?"

John looked at him a bit puzzled. He walked back to the factory.

"You were talkin' in your sleep."

Home

Charles E. Toberman, who built the Gruamann's Chinese theater, had also built James's home, the Brevoort Hotel in the heart of Hollywood. Although converted into low rent apartments, it was still, technically, a hotel. The bulldog of a manager kept a watchful eye at the front office. He was an old New Yorker who worked and partied with the best of the art/film world of his day and now ran the hotel very much like Al Swearengen ran the Gem Saloon. A framed shopping list on the wall of his office read: cat food, bread, heroin, milk.

The Brevoort was home to many varieties of people finding refuge from high prices. With the lobby's peach-painted walls, red carpet and coffee table with built-in ash trays, the place had more of a feel of a halfway house once its occupants gathered, bumming cigarettes from each other and talking about painkillers, conspiracies and politics. At best, it was a place for transition. It was where one went to reinvent himself, recover from debt, then, make his mark on the world. Or, it was where one went to die.

Across the street was an Armenian-Christian church. A couple times a week there would be a hearse parked out front. Men in black suits and close-cropped haircuts stood outside like bouncers to a club. They nervously smoked and patrolled the sidewalks in packs. Over a million was spent in the extravagant remodeling of the church, the yard, and underground parking. Flowers lay strewn about the sidewalks after the funeral services were long over. It made for a colorful stroll to El Pollo Loco down the block. The sidewalks required attention to avoid stepping in vomit and human shit left there the night before. Homeless people and bar patrons trafficked by frequently. The *oh-wop* sound from the blades of a helicopter circling the building and sirens crying like a cat in heat were weekly rituals. The Bliss Cafe held AA meetings in the mornings and open mic in the nights. Around the corner, Crispy Crust Pizza made the damn best pizza in the area. James would frequent there as he followed a young, hispanic couple, cute with the aroma of weed drifting behind them. Near the Brevoort, Freddie Roach's Wildcard Boxing Club trained some of the world's best fighters. When James craved damn good Mexican food, he walked to the Cactus Taqueria. Because he didn't have a kitchen at his place, when James was jonesing for homestyle cooking, he would hit up the Cat & Fiddle restaurant and pub for some good old English fish and chips.

Many of the street performers, who dressed up as famous movie stars and comic book heroes in front of the "Mann's" Chinese Theater on Hollywood Boulevard, had made a home at the Brevoort also. Rain or shine, superheroes gathered on the boulevard for the hustle. They worked for tips. Many tourists got their pictures taken with their favorite icons. Some of these characters were made worse for wear. A droopy-eared, hot-tempered Batman, and a Spiderman, who at times rivaled a homeless man in stench, surprised James with how they managed to collect money in such conditions. Spiderman's uniform was stained and ripped. His hairy gut hung out like a greasy bathroom mat. Of course, there were more than one Spiderman, as there were more than one of each character. A thousand Captain Jack Sparrows, some big, some small, some short, some tall, spread between two Darth Vaders for a little piece of the sidewalk to call their own, while a drunk Elmo found moments to be rude. James would listen to their stories when a few gathered in the lobby. There was always a character that flipped out and demanded tips and became intrusive with other character's photo opportunities. Charlie Chaplin (the good one), Shrek and Freddy Kruger knew how to engage their audience. Sometimes the disgruntled character would place a foot, head or groin in the other character's shots and felt in his right to request a small percentage of the administered tips. It was a cutthroat occupation working the boulevard. Many stores didn't like them "panhandling" in front of their building. At first, one wanted to laugh at these people, but then cry because there seemed to be an undercurrent of sadness in what these quick-aging characters put up with. Some were failed actors, coming to Hollywood from all over the world with big dreams. A Polish Joker stood next to a French Marilyn Monroe for a photo. They looked nothing whatsoever like the characters they portrayed, but they had found a spiritual connection to that entity. Some had confessed to James that they did this out of the pure joy of becoming a character and interacting with the public. James related to that with his dart team's own "costume".

James thought that artists, being inspired by the success of other artists, and rightly so, was all they would come to expect of their own endeavors. They tried to map their lives to theirs, but the painful truth was that very few made a difference as the likes of the said "successful" artist. The factors and variables were ignored, for example, the context of time, the hustle behind the flow, the peculiar circumstances to that individual, having a plan, etc. They became blind and deaf to the countless stories of artists who had failed, and that number was far greater than those who had succeeded. It wasn't always a healthy measuring stick for your own growth, comparing yourself to others. As there were many roads to Rome, one could argue that you shouldn't kill someone's dream. After all, every success was inspired at a time of obscurity before new ground was broken. The definition of success and failure were vague terms to begin with, with many areas and degrees of both in the personal struggle. The various outcomes as varied as the artists themselves. James toyed with the idea of giving up his passion as a cartoonist and getting a "real" job. He even thought about returning to England. But for now, he wanted to duke it out here in Los Angeles. James came to the paradoxical conclusion to inject reality checks into your dreaming. James believed the theory, an illusion, once it reached its end, had two possible outcomes, it would either be recognized as something unrealistic to obtain and therefore painfully dropped, the person then, fooling themselves no more, or it might transform into reality as the illusion hardens to fact. In that instance, the loss was not painful. However, in the end, a loss of illusion yielded a better outcome. In both cases, one moved on with life.

* * * * *

James had an apartment on the second floor with an interior courtyard view of Spanish styled bungalows from an era he found familiar through movies, postcards and books. For it was well before his father's sperm stabbed his mother's egg that such places were an everyday norm in Los Angeles. Early afternoons filtered through his bathroom window with yellow and warm green hues reflected from the large leaves of the towering banana trees. A large Union Jack hung on one wall of his room. A dart board hung outside the bathroom door. Some people had indoor plants, James had ant farms. Three on a small table. One large one with red harvest ants, and two smaller ones, each with yet a different species. There was something meditative about watching them go about their day. Some of his art work, framed, leaned against the wall in stacks. The plaster on the walls and ceiling looked like the white frosting of a cake, smoothed out with a dull knife, leaving little strokes of mini mountain ranges in half-circle paths. His magazine drawing for the cover of the New Yorker depicted several people standing together, their bodies looking like skyscrapers and their heads facing the sky. The bustle of city life, tiny at their feet.

James emptied his pockets on his night stand, the matchbook from the last tournament flipped open, revealing the phone number fortune in its underbelly. The teeth of the matches pointed to Punch's name. James felt a little quiver in his gut before picking up the matchbook. He dialed the number. After a moment, the purr of the other line ringing sent the quiver up through his chest.

Ringing.
Ringing.
Ringing.
Then, Beep! Silence. James's breathing echoed on the line before he killed the connection.

1892 Visionary Provokers

John Rackle, businessman, ex-professor in mathematics and now, the weekly sponge for the exciting Girl's Victorian Boxing Affiliation. Or, in other words, the Punch Fan Club. During and after a hard day's night, John's head inflated with thoughts of her. She laid an entangled stronghold on his cerebellum. He was given a special seat in the back row, overlooking the ring high above at the barn owl elevation. During fights, he pulled out his penis and with his pulsating grip he fought to maintain facial composure while he felt the quick tickle of vibration as his prostate coughed out the gravy. On one occasion, an onlooker below mistook his friend's newly decorated shoulder splat for the gift of a passing swallow landing on a beam above.

Punch had just finished off a gal from New York who was carried away in a wheelbarrow. She now stood center ring, her eyes on Mr. Rackle. Without a slip of a word from her lips, the hysteria from the newly fought match silenced. To John, up on the rafters in his special box seating, what was once a view of hairy heads and hats became a blinking sprawl of faces. Through the factory windows of her eyes, anyone close enough could see workers assembling a mischievous proposition, sealed and ready for delivery.

"Mister John Rackle," said Punch. "I have a favor to ask of you." John perked up. "Come down from that insipid box I placed you in." He didn't react. "Come down. I know you are not the bashful sort, given the line of work you're in." He stood from his sweaty stool. "Come join me in the ring for a contest."

"What contest?" His voice, a whisper. One bystander shouted.

"She wants you to get in the ring with her!" Another chimed in with, "Yes!" John shook his head and made his way down.

"No! I am not fighting anyone." John climbed down the ladder, feeling everyone's eyes on him. He made his way ring-side, hands slapping his back as he passed. His pride and sense of self had not noted such frailty in a while. The audience was on his every stiff and awkward-bound gesture. When he had a single twitch, it would gyrate his body as if a ghost crept up behind him and blew into his ear.

"Mister Rackle runs a unique bathtub company here in town." Punch was all giggles as her crowd cheered. John smiled when he turned to face the audience and nodded to them for their support. She lifted her hands. The silence drifted over the crowd like a newly washed blanket landing, parachute style, over the bed. "Mister Rackle. Come up here with me."

"Why? Don't be silly, girl-"

"I want your bath company, Mister Rackle. And I'm going to fight you for it."

The audience, like a million moth larvas, shredded the blanket of silence.

"No," he said. "That is ridiculous. Of course not..."

"The winner of the fight gets Rackle's Tub!"

"It is not up for contest-"

A couple of field working brutes grabbed John and carried him into the ring. "Let me go! Please. Please, please! Stop...!" With one heave up, John became airborne and landed in the ring. Punch walked up to him, gazing her eyes on his uneasy stare.

"I want you to remain bare knuckled and hit me as hard as you can," she commanded.

"No. I am not going to hit you..."

She slugged him in the gut, he dropped to his knees in search for air.

"You better do something to stop me, Mr. Rackle. Because I am about to come at you with such punishing imprecations-"

"ENOUGH! GODDAMN IT! I am not fighting you!" He wondered if getting up would unleash another offensive reaction. "You understand?!" The crowd became disappointed in John. He curled up like a baby on the floor and changed his voice to that of a crying child's. "Let me be... you, you bad girl. Bad, bad, bad!" His thumb went into his mouth. Punch was confused by his behavior. He crawled around on all fours. "I'm just a lil' bunny rabbit. I wanna go home to nibble on my carrots." The laughter from the audience and John's little boy behavior kicked in her maternal instincts. She ripped a glove off and lowered her hand to help him up. His voice returned. "You have humiliated me here. I shall never come see you again. You are a fucking bitch!" His words carried a sting that her opponent's jabs lacked. Now on his feet, he turned to the crowd. "I will not strike a woman!" They continued to berate him. He spotted two of his employees embarrassed for him, faces red. "If she chooses to punch me, I shall not fight back. So you see, no contest here. A contest must have willing, amicable contestants to participate." After everyone settled down, John found more of his scattered confidence and began to lay them back, brick by brick. "Buy my tubs!" He turned to Punch, one hand still gloved. A trainer began unlacing it as she looked to recover from the word *bitch*.

"Sorry, John."

"As well you should be. American cunt!" His verbal blow left more of a bruise than any of her black eyes. She turned her head.

"I was promoting your business. You do not...there is no need to become nasty with me," she wiped her eyes with her free hand. The trainer, finally through with loosening the threads, pulled off her glove. "I am still a girl."

"You are a woman. Act like one."

He found that he couldn't move. It seemed the banter between them had liquefied the leather from his boots and cemented them to the floor. If he were to leave, it might prove awkward enough to rob him of sleep for a week. And thus, he wouldn't want to ever show his face here. If he stayed, he would surely be made a buffoon. Which, again, would lead to replay this event in his mind, night after night. He extended his hand.

"Punch. Allow me to escort you. Please."

She looked at him, shyly nodded and took his hand, transforming back into the polite Victorian she had raged against in her own inner civil war.

She looked into his eyes, and he embraced her. He rested his cheek to her head.

"I'm sorry for my poisonous mouth. I am mad for you, darling," said John.

The audience stood and clapped as the two stayed embraced in the ring. With sponsorship like that, more business was brought to the bathhouse. John realized the genius in Punch only retrospectively in regards to her marketing. The girl really was a born leader.

* * * * *

Punch arrived in a carriage to John's factory on a morning made beautiful not for the weather, but for the visit. Her business finery offset only by a huge cigar. Once inside, John and Punch sat at his table, he with his tea and she with her coffee - black.

"As you must know by now, I'm not one to take up millinery or dress-making or child rearing," she took a puff from her stogie. "Work with the needle or whatever apron-wearing task may seem respectable, but it is not for me."

"It is your choice of athleticism that's at question," he said.

"Happy boys, they have their games of all sorts. In England, playing fields for cricket. Here it's football. And what are girls supposed to do? Slide down the kitchen stair-rails? Hoops? Hide and seek? Silly games of marbles? What drudgery to scamper about with these droll contests."

He took a sip of tea. "You have brought to light your point. I do agree. But there is always tennis."

"Sure. I just needed a manner in which to address this simmering, agitated state of mine. My husband goes away on long travels. Has affairs with all these worldly women, while I have stayed true. Present company excluded. Despite his penis for a compass."

"I do not understand why he would seek another's affection, unless you challenge him in the ring," he said. "All that is beauteous sits right here in front of me. You are both the Virgin Mary and the devil. Every man, in his secret heart, desires both attributes in his woman."

"I am surprised my vulgarity hasn't chased you away. But, thank you kindly for that wonderful...way with words."

"Perhaps it is the boxing that keeps him looking elsewhere."

"No, he has no knowledge of it. Though he has his suspicions. These barnyard brawls are what I've been hiding like an affair." She took note of a gathering audience in John's workers from a small distance. John noticed them too.

"You see? Any one of these men would gladly give their earnings for a chance to be with you."

"Let me make it clear. I am no tart, despite my adventurous behavior."

"Yes, yes I understand, and I did not mean it in that capacity. Forgive me."

She smiled, "All right then. They may keep their earnings. I am independently wealthy because of these fights."

"You are quite the entrepreneur," he said.

"And that is why I am here."

"You are sadly mistaken. I am not selling my business."

"Nor am I buying it." She leaned toward him. "I wish to go into business with you."

"In what capacity can you serve the business?"

"Please, let's cut the fluff. You know damn well in what capacity. I could be a benefactor. With my name alone, do you not see an increase in sales? I endorse your product, and it will become gold! I could also do the books, help balance the budget, handle payroll. I am an irresistible, tenacious businesswoman!"

"I do love your capricious nature. You have to have one to start a business like mine."

"Or mine."

"Yes. In addition, I find your company makes me all the more whole," he leaned toward her. "You know, I have been to every one of your matches since I arrived from New York, and I found that I have become totally entranced by you."

"So kind of you. Now, listen to this assessment. You already have the reputation with your tubs. Everything is in place, John. We just have to expand and show the world what we can do. I admire you, despite the silly theatrics in the ring and even though you did not strike me, I still find you... striking."

John gave her a quick smack across her cheek.

"There. I did it. Let's have no more talk of this."

She took a puff and blew the smoke into his face. Then she smiled.

"And your husband? Will he know of your employment here?"

She shrugged. "I really do not care."

* * * * *

Her mother had been a dancer and played drums for a private school before strengthening her back in the labors of the cannery industry. She gave birth to Punch in 1869. Her dad was a barroom fighter. She took up boxing as self-defense, honing skills she had already developed in fights after school, terrorizing bullies and quickly deflating their egos. Her classmates saw her as a hero. The self-defense was later brought out again, with her abusive husband. On one rainy September night, Michael's violent behavior reached its pinnacle. He struck her, and she, without a thought, laid him flat. This was to be a new beginning in her marriage. On another occasion, being a creature of habit, he hit her again and she then tenderized his guts so quickly, he was bedridden for two days.

"You should try not to hurt me like that," she would explain afterwards while bringing him soup. "I'm a human being." And that was the last of the beatings.

Punch never sized up the opponents she was about to fight. At least this was the impression she gave. She was difficult to solve. Although right-handed, she was ambidextrous in the ring. One round, she would take the stance of a south paw, the next, a classic, balanced stance. The clock in her head put out such odd timing, it confused the hell out of the other fighters, which made her extremely dangerous and unpredictable. Add speed and she became deadly. She turned into a machine and knew exactly how to break down her opponent and disperse them efficiently on the spot. She had lost fights before, but now, ever so rarely. Pound for pound, she was a force. She was between a lightweight and at the very most, a light welterweight. It was unusual for someone of her build to have the power of knockouts, but she instinctively knew the physics behind what it would take to deliver the result. One viewer described her opponents as metal heads, and her gloves as magnets. One thing was for sure, she had most certainly earned her name.

The Shaman, The Wildcard, The Fool And The Pretty Boy

All of which belonged to every one of the pendulum partners. One trait might show itself at a greater percentage than the others, but these spices were all present.

"I always held on to a rule about not shagging birds who live in the same building," said James. "Sometimes, I admit, it's very challenging to resist when you've got this fantastic bird and she comes on to you." Their San Francisco trophy was between him and Shard in the front seat.

"Have you ever?" Shard gently turned the Cadillac's power steering with the over-all steering ratio of 18.2 to 1 and 38.5 degrees turning angle for fast response and short turning diameter.

"No. I tend to learn my lesson through other people's mistakes," said James with a wink to Shard.

"Yeah. She was a nightmare," Shard admitted. He looked in the rearview. Aster and Ticktock were fighting sleep. The deep-cushioned backseat of a Cadillac could sometimes have that comatose effect.

"Sex is such a turn off," Ticktock yawned.

"Turn offs during sex, for me, would be food, blood, farting and comedy," Shard said. They laughed.

"You're not into whip cream on a girl's twat?" James asked him.

"No. I don't like the sticky mess."

"You're starting to sound like our boy Aster over here," said Ticktock who then hung his arms over the seat, making them appear gorilla-like.

"The bottom line is, hair in food grosses me out. Like I don't want to lift my bun to find my cheese going through puberty," Shard said. "It's gross."

"I had this girl where I wasn't totally sure she was a girl," Ticktock volunteered. "She was cute, but there was something about her. Maybe the square shoulders or deep voice. I mean, all the red flags were there. And I would just ignore them, cause she was so cute. First flag, Adam's apple. And I dismissed it as, 'oh, she had a throat accident.' Second flag, her calves were a hell of a lot bigger than mine. And I thought, she doesn't have a car, so she probably does a lot of walking. The next flag, while I was feeling her, there was hair on her upper thighs above the knees. And I thought, nah, she must of been one of those French hippie chicks. Maybe she was in a hurry to meet me and didn't have time to shave that high. And then the flag of all flags. I grabbed her hard-on and I still found a way to dismiss it. I thought, it must have been a juiced up clit, you know? Maybe she was an athlete on steroids."

"That would explain the calves," James said.

"Right. So, I ended it," Ticktock said.

"Shit. What if it *was* a girl all along?" Shard asked.

"What do the girls look like where you come from?" James asked.

"And you just passed the best sex you would've ever had?" Shard said.

"Oh, I didn't pass it up," Ticktock laughed. "But what pissed me off was when she started calling me by some other bloke's name. I mean, we're fucking and she yells, hell, she's screaming the other guys name and I'm like, 'my name is not Rape. It's Ticktock. Who the fuck is this Rape fella? Shit. Talk about a fucked up night."

"Aren't you two related?" Shard asked.

"Shard, no comedy hour during sex?" asked James. "How do you expect her not to laugh when she pulls your pants down?"

"Comedy hour? I'd be happy if I lasted that long. But when I'm pounding her, you know- in the moment. It's not funny. I'm focused. I'm silent. I don't like to talk. It's serious business."

"I know when I'm shagging the twelve year olds, I always ask how school was before I give 'em a mouthful. You know what I mean?" said Ticktock. They all laughed at the crudeness.

"That's terrible," Aster replied.

"Yeah," said Shard. "You should start them at thirteen. At least. No preteen shit. Not cool."

"Well, you know," Ticktock said. "If you go out to international waters, it's legal. Just three miles off the coast and it's not breaking the law."

"What if you bring them back pregnant?" James asked.

"She could press charges, but the law is the law. They can't touch you," Ticktock must have done the research.

"There you have it," James with his radio announcer voice, "Free legal advice from the law offices of Ticktock."

A pop sound outside soon became evident of a flat tire. "Fuck." Shard pulled over.

Rear suspension: Four-link drive. Rear springs are helical-coil type. Rubber bushings for quieter, softer ride. See your Cadillac dealer today.

* * * * *

"I don't understand why you don't want to go out when it's just the two of us." Aster, in his apartment, had his phone clamped against his shoulder with his cheek. "Why does the whole group have to be there?" A mini fridge rested on the bottom of a sagging shelf hanging from the wall. The screws holding the framing in place were ready to pop out. He opened the fridge and looked in before closing it.

"But hey, that's cool. You should read my latest blog on dating etiquette. I've had over ninety hits -- hello?" He looked at his phone and re-dialed. Straight to voicemail. "Okay."

His 3 vacuum cleaners were also stored on the flimsy shelf next to the fridge. One vacuum had a label on which he used a sharpie to write "carpets", another vacuum labeled "furniture", but it was the third for bathroom and area rugs that he grabbed. He dialed his phone again while sucking up some lint from his area rug. He placed the vac back. On top of the fridge was a microwave oven and on top of that, a toaster oven. He pulled out the crumb tray and emptied it into an all chrome, bullet-shaped trash can with a push-in lid. It was lined with white trash bags that were frequently tossed out before they reached the halfway point.

"Hello? Hey I think our connection was lost."

All of his furniture was black. Aster pulled open the drawers of his dresser. Clothes are neatly folded. Socks in one drawer, divided in 3 sections: black, white and other colors. Underwear, also divided. Briefs, boxers and boxer briefs.

"No, I agree! I think a woman needs her space. It's very important." He grabbed his lint-sticky roller and rolled it over the clothes already folded in the drawers. "She needs someone to listen, and to be there for her, to protect her, to vanquish obstacles that may prevent her from succeeding..." Once he finished a drawer, he shut it and dropped to the open drawer below it. "...And I have to say, I have all those traits that women so desire. I make 'em laugh, I can satisfy them in other capacities, if you know what I mean?"

His big television sat on the shelves, which had a dvd player on top and a stereo on top of that.

"For sanitary reasons, I'm going to rip out the carpeting here so the hardwood floors show. Yeah, you could say I'm a handy man too. I'm good with tools. Girls like that."

Bathroom was white, chrome and spotless. It reflected nicely when Aster flipped on the lights. Everything buffed to a shine. A paper towel dispenser hung over the sink. A box of surgical masks and gloves were neatly stationed at every room, all two of them.

"...So Friday, let's go watch a movie. They play classic films down the street...oh? Hmm, how about Saturday? Your staple-machine is broken? All weekend? That's a bummer. What brand stapler- oh, of course."

Aster sat on the plastic covered couch. "No that's fine. That's cool, that's cool. I totally understand. Well let me know when you want to go out then. I'll leave it up to you. The ball is officially in your court. I just lobbed one over. Hello? Hello?"

He closed his phone.

His black laptop open and a box of tissues near, Aster went to YouTube. Among the videos on the front page being viewed at this hour, was '*Unknown girl wins by knockout!*' He clicked on the link. It was a home video of a backyard brawl. The camera was a little shaky. A white girl with long, loose, curly hair tied back, stood with her fists cocked as she waited for a Latina girl to charge her. Once she charged, a cold clock to the temple sent the Latina down. The camera zoomed in on the face of the unknown white girl. She winked to the camera before disappearing out the side gate. The camera next, zoomed in on the other girl, now asleep on the grass. The video had generated a lot of hits, a few million. The punch was so quick Aster had to play it again. His little, one-eyed friend came out to join him for the screening.

A Scoop Of The Annie Oakley Of Boxing And Two Pinches Of The English Devil Of Physics

What a business team Punch and John had become! There was an increase in orgy tub sales. Brothels and private buyers from all over the country were making purchases. Punch was hoping to leave her boxing hobby for this new one, but her reputation had put up walls overnight. She couldn't keep her fighting a secret any longer. She was finding it difficult to deal with the law. Mobsters were yet another problem which proved harder to elude. Jefferson Randolph "Soapy" Smith, known for swindling people through sales of soap, and the overlord of Denver's underworld and the entire west for that matter, wanted to regulate her and the fight league, but she was beyond his control. "Soapy" Smith had a female boarding house on Market Street in Denver where he would bring women to become soiled doves, but he knew Punch was a different kind of girl. He was intrigued to the point of romantic interest. Punch always managed to stay one step ahead of them, but one step was proving to be too close. Especially when she made fools of them. On her first encounter, she had an associate inform the pressing "Soapy" Smith gangsters where the next fight would be. They showed up at an abandoned farm, where Punch sat on a wheelchair in one corner of a pig pen pretending to be mentally challenged, and at the other corner, another gal sat with crutches nearby. Round one never started. "Soapy" Smith and his men were extremely disappointed and left. After all, he was a charity man, despite his long criminal record and found handicap boxing vulgar. The following week Punch's charade was discovered by one of the

gangsters. She broke his nose in an altercation. And when he came
gunning for her, she hid out as a scarecrow. Rather than admit
to his friends he was beat by a girl, he blamed another gangster.
Sometimes Punch would disguise herself as a man when she went
into town so she wouldn't be bothered.

Punch had become an adept accountant. She liked to work
with her backside to the sun, her leg curled around the table's. The
accounts book sprawled open and enjoying the tickle of her pen on
its belly. She looked up at John's approach.

"Your husband is out of town?" She nodded and continued
working.

"France," she said. He handed her the order. She grabbed it and
placed it on a small pile of papers.

"I think you should take a look at that one now. Personally."
She stopped to pick up the page. Her husband's name was on it,
along with the destination for delivery. A residence, not her own.
She handed it back and picked up where she left off. John stood
over her, folding the page, and turned away. He was out the door
when he heard her get up and run. The log book held her place of
time with a teardrop, expanding on the page, smudging the wet ink.
Punch braced herself against a tree behind the factory. John drew
closer. "I am not fulfilling his order," he confessed. She stopped
crying.

"These are tears of joy," she smiled.

"Of course," he said as he reached out for her shoulder.

"I brought this all onto myself. It is a little imprudent of me to
suddenly become astounded."

"Well yes, I suppose. He answered your plea. I'm sorry.
Mother too, would be upset with him." She embraced him to cry
her face into his heart. He kissed her crown. "Nevertheless, this
might brighten things. I want to show you something...a sort of
mathematical discovery." Punch lifted her head. "I've been having
these dreams, of the same place, every night. As if they were
consecutive chapters in a book. I wake up exhausted and sick. I
can't help but think there is a relation between my work and my
dreams."

"Oh, yes. That did brighten things."

* * * * *

Change in the noon breeze sounded like a fast-moving carriage ripping the gravel road. Yet, the true sounds of change came from the gullet. Gurgling stomach acids brought on by electrical impulses from the brainstorms of anxiety, fear and rage. Michael was coming home a day early. Or, did Punch have her boxing club a day late? Either case, it was time for brass tacks. Michael had already drawn up the papers needed for divorce. Such papers were his bullets, filling the interior chamber of his attaché case, ready to unload on his spouse. Just. Sign. Here. Bang. Bang. Bang. His newfound French cuisine awaited him at a Denver Hotel, uptown. The carriage, now at the dawn of the ranch, found a daunting obstacle... where to park? His ranch was packed with carriages beyond anything he had ever seen.

"What in the Lord...?!" Michael pushed open the cart's door and jumped out while it was still in motion. To come upon such a populace of strangers in his home was past infuriation. This all confirmed what he needed to do. Jealousy jumped on his back as he marched to the house. The front door required no key, for it was already open, wide. He turned towards his coachman. "Go fetch the police!" If the driver understood, or not, Michael did not know because he was making his way in at that moment. Surprisingly empty when Michael entered, he made his way down the hall to the study. "PUNCH!" His liquor cabinet was cleaned out. He reached around his desk, pulling out a drawer. A pearl-handled, chrome pistol laid covered under a single sheet of stationary, waiting. Barging out the front doors, Michael turned to the barn. A strange man leaned against the wall of the barn, rolling his face to it, dropping his trousers and watering the weeds. Michael wanted to crush his skull, but as he approached the building, he heard the muffled, colosseum-of-a-sound coming out of its closed doors.

"Hey!" Michael addressed the irrigator. He didn't respond, instead he fell to the ground, slurring a love poem for Punch, pecker in hand. Michael grabbed the handle to the barn door and struggled to open it. Someone's eye from behind the door peered.

"Open this goddamn door! I demand you!"

The eye's laughter fueled Michael's fire. "Full capacity," the eye said. Michael struggled again to open the door. "FULL CAPACITY!" Michael pointed his pistol at the eye.

"This is MY BARN, you lead-brained SHIT!" The man behind the door anticipated the trigger pull and jumped to the floor, keeping his eye, but losing some hair, as the bullet zipped through the hole and embedded itself in a beam.

"HOLD IT! HOLD, HOLD IT!" The guard opened the door. Michael, gun drawn, pushed past the guard. The place was packed. Michael's banker, dripping, bloody, sweaty and winded, sat in one corner - his wife Punch in the other. The banker had donated proceeds to Rackle's Tub in exchange for a fight with her. They had been fighting fisticuffs, bare knuckled by his request, so he could grapple with her. He was already regretting it. Michael stood in disbelief. To have an unexpected visual before you, crossing into the surreal and back, surreal and back again, like the pendulum of a grandfather clock, the concentric point of the two worlds overlapped and Michael understood the truth of the present moment. He shot the gun in the air. Twice. The crowd silenced.

"PUNCH! What the fuck are you doing?!" Michael climbed into the ring. "What, in God's name, kind of vulgarity is this?!!!!" He grabbed her arm and brought her to her feet, pulling her out of the ring. "How dare you engage in such a beastly, devil-hearted, betrayal of your womanhood!!!!" He turned to the audience, "Everyone, out! This is MY BARN! AND MY WIFE! The sheriff is on his way!" Punch knuckled him in the gut. It triggered a roar of laughter.

"You have been fucking another woman. Again."

He straightened up. "We need to talk. In private. This is not a public affair, and none of their business."

"And this is none of yours. So who is she?"

"I will not discuss it here."

"Is she French?"

"She is far more woman than you will ever be."

"How long has this been going on?"

"I have the papers for our divorce."

"And a divorce you shall have," said Punch. "How long have you two been seeing each other?" She remained calm in her questioning. Michael, on the other hand, was distracted by the audience closing in on him.

"What...? I want a divorce. This is a private matter!" He hoped his words would act like a fly swatter. Unfortunately, he had chosen to swat at an abattoir. Punch shook her head.

"I shall grant you the stupid divorce. Just tell me, how long has this affair been going on?"

"Four months. Around, about. Off and on. Maybe longer."

"No matter. You broke my heart a long time ago. Now, all that remains is scar tissue for you." And with that, Punch disappeared into the shuffle of people. A man punched Michael in the gut, another shoved him to the floor.

* * * * *

One might say Punch looked sexy behind bars, while still cuffed at the wrists. The bailiff leaned his shoulder against the bars to study her. He wanted to drink up these last moments before thumbing through the keys till he found the right one.

"She's the prettiest jailbird I ever laid eyes on," he inserted the key. "A shame to see her leave." He opened her cage. She held her wrists to the bailiff while staring at John, who had just bailed her out. "I'm gonna miss you, my spring daisy," said the bailiff as he removed her shackles.

* * * * *

John replaced the shackles with a wedding ring, sliding it onto her finger. The ceremony was held at a Protestant church. The two had become more agnostic than anything, but it was close by and Punch taught the minister's bastard son how to box. Punch glowed in her bridal gown. John was in a black tuxedo and top hat.

"I can't believe Mother didn't show," John griped.

"I'm sorry, John. We shall have to go visit her then, won't we?" The two kissed.

* * * * *

John placed his face to a large, copper kettle. A remnant of the factory's brewery birth. He covered his eyes and began a countdown. Punch, without shoes, but still in her wedding dress, tip-toed up the stairs. She held up the front of her dress, so as not to step on it.

"You have to count to one hundred!"

"Ten. Twenty. Thirty...," he counted.

"No!" she laughed. "You've got to start at one. Two..."

"...Three. Four..."

"No cheating!"

John smiled. "Five. Six. Seven..."

Punch continued to climb the stairs to the attic.

"...Seventy-eight. Seventy-nine. La-da-da. One hundred! Ready or not, here I come!" John made a dash for the stairs, his shoes loud against the floor. He stopped to listen for Punch and quietly pulled his shoes off, setting them aside. In the first room he dropped to his knees, searching under a desk. No Punch. He got up and opened the closet. Empty. He left the room and continued up the stairs. John approached another room down the hall. He quietly laid his hand on the knob to a closed door. Fingers wrapped the handle and with terrifying speed, opened the door.

"If you are in this room, consider yourself caught!" The room was piled with tubs and machinery. It would take awhile to comb. He waited a minute before shutting the door. He climbed another set of stairs to yet another hallway. A door already open, John set off to explore. It was a sparse room. Only a bed. He peeked under its skirt. Nothing. Room after room soon brought on fatigue. John removed his jacket, tossing it on a nearby chair.

"All right, my dear. I surrender!" he shouted. "Meet me in the kitchen for a celebratory drink!" He made his way down the stairs. John sat alone at the kitchen table. Two glasses, his and hers, were out. He laughed. "You are victorious, my sweet! Come hither and have a little sip of your reward!" He poured himself wine. "We shall have a toast!" He held his glass up before bringing it to his lips for a sip.

* * * * *

The wine bottle empty, John's face lay buried in his arms. With a jolt, he awakened to the still empty, and now darkened, room.

"Punch." The silence became a physical pain, heavy and cold. Her wine glass... untouched. He got up and left the kitchen. "Punch? Where are you?" He headed for the stairs. "Punch, my dear." He turned on lights. After clapping his hands and calling out, "Punch. Punch! My silly girl! Enough of this game," he listened for her. Still nothing. "I don't want to play anymore!" A thin root of panic curled over his heart, tapping his blood.

Outside the factory, John expected a missing carriage, but it was right where it always was. Parked in the same spot. He looked back at the factory. The only lights were the ones he had turned on himself. He ventured to the stables. All horses accounted for. She must have run away then, John thought. But why? He ran back to the factory. John climbed the stairs.

"Punch! Come on!" Another moment followed. "Punch...!" He entered his study, turned on the light. He kicked his desk. "Punch, damn you! Show yourself!" He leaned against the wall. "I...do not... want to bloody play anymore, okay?! Punch, please!" His tears hit the ground at the same time as his knees. "Mother, I miss you. You're right..." He curled into a ball, crying. His voice changed into that of a small child. "You told me no one is good enough. You told me." He got up and sat, moving his body to and fro.

"Mother. I need my milk. Mother, I need my milk. I'm in pain, mother. I'm in pain..."

The next morning, the deputy sheriff's carriage was parked outside the factory.

"Unfortunately, I've seen too many of these runaway cases," said the sheriff. "Couples rush to get married, and moments later come to the realization that it's not for them and then, poof! Off they go. Into the night. Never to come back. Were there any arguments, any sort of rift between you?"

"No, no. We were playing hide and seek, and she took off," he explained.

"Clever. Of course. Under the cloak of a game," reasoned the sheriff.

"We loved each other. I mean, perhaps we did rush things. She was coming out of another marriage. I felt I had to act quickly. She was getting marriage proposals already."

The deputy sheriff nodded. "It's starting to come clear. Oh, and ah, I will speculate kidnapping as another possibility. After all, her fame, has no doubt, brought her fans and foes alike, some wanting to kiss her, while others, knife her. I'll see what I can do. If a wedding gown turns up, we'll find her. Good day." And with that, the deputy sheriff parted. Good day? Hardly. A heavy heart hindered it. John had grown so used to her company he didn't realize she was his breath. And now that she was so quickly and cleanly gone, his mind spun trying to find the clarity of an answer. Maybe she went back to her ex-husband. Maybe she'll return. He could speculate all day, trying to mathematically make sense of it, so long as the outcome wasn't zero.

Peripheral Dancers

We are bombarded daily with these visitors. Little squiggly things that disappear when looked at head-on. Similar to a piece of lint, stuck on film, while watching a movie. We don't think much of it. Many are unaware of them. These visitors had been following James at greater frequencies. It was enough for him to take serious note, fearing it to be symptoms of a stroke.

Why did girls always want to keep a piece of his clothing? James pondered this as he drove up the curvy road of Laurel Canyon in his two-seater convertible M.G. He'd lost many good shirts because of this. He guessed that, for them, it was a token of him. His fragrance still on the shirt. He supposed it was the same with guys collecting trophies of women's knickers. But he had never been much of a collector.

Interrupted, he whipped around in reaction to something. Not there. Another peripheral distraction.

James would frequent an older woman's house in the hills from an offshoot of Laurel Canyon. Her name was Cheryl. Driving up the confusing and cramped streets excited him. It was a delight knowing someone who lived among the stars. Like many in the area, Cheryl had done her fair share of movies and TV, but had since moved on to unrelated interests. These cottages in the hills had character and history. Well, if you wanted to call the last eighty years history. L.A. years were like dog years. She aged differently than a mid-west city or the suburban sprawls of elsewhere. She was constantly reinventing herself. And by doing so, changed expeditiously. For better or for worse. A face lift here, tummy tuck there. Buildings, people, trends, the counterculture... Thankfully, there had been movements to preserve Los Angeles. Laurel Canyon felt like it was operating in a time zone all its own. The hills were far from glamorous. Markets, banks, post office, everyday conveniences were all at the bottom of the hill, either on the Hollywood side or the valley side. The wear and tear on the brakes going up and down the hill must get expensive. In the neighborhood, there were no sidewalks. People's driveways were more like small turnouts. The narrow roads, like deer trails. The cars, parked curb-side, had their side view mirrors turned in like a boxer's ear folded over with cauliflower. The houses were yard-less and cramped right on top of each other. Some were hanging off the edge of cliffs or built right into the sides of mountains. Thin, wooden support beams, looking more like the legs of an arthritic old man, kept some of these homes from sliding down the face of the mountain onto a house directly below. The damp, slate hillsides deteriorated rain after rain. Eucalyptus branches fell during high winds, blocking roads. And during heavy storms, the flooded streets turned into raging rivers. Power outages were commonplace. Construction trucks, gardening pickups and plumbing vans blocked the streets when parked. One had to be careful of speed demons taking the blind corners. Property taxes were high.

There was a mixed group of people who lived in the hills. Some were pretentious personalities, which, when broken down to their core, revealed a pseudo intellectual, business class. The type that would buy a wonderfully bound classic book, not to read, but to adorn a shelf. Then, in contrast, there were the artists, musicians, actors, writers, free spirited-personalities, eccentric and true to themselves. These canyonites were as distinctive as their homes and no two homes looked alike. James had gotten to know a few people living in the hills because of Cheryl. He loved the bustle of city life, like in London or New York. He was also torn evenly in the opposite direction. The quiet solitude of country living felt beautiful to him. Los Angeles, so spread out, had a little bit of both.

He made his way over the uneven road to Cheryl's home. His stomach had a tingle that spread to his dick at the thought of fucking her. As soon as he parked, he got out and climbed the steep stairs to her already open back door. A single daisy in hand, he entered the kitchen. She greeted him in her tight, shiny yoga pants and sports bra. He held up the daisy. She laid the flower on the granite kitchen counter. No time for a vase. Fucking must begin immediately. A handful of ass, he squeezed her and with the other hand, grabbed her shoulder while they linked lips. Like two wrestlers locked in a death grip, they bumped against the counter, then the table, and finally the couch, where they plopped down on a couple of remotes. She made noises like he was fucking her with a nail gun, but he had grown used to that by now. James's phone rang. An unfamiliar ring tone. It went to voicemail. After he reached orgasm, a flash of cobalt blue fizzled quickly across the room. But he made nothing of it.

* * * * *

Shard's apartment was located on the Hollywood side of the hills. James got out of the elevator and noticed a young woman down the hall, carrying an armful of boxes while pushing a box on the floor with her foot. James rushed over to her rescue.

"Let me help you with that."

"Oh, thanks," she said. James now used his own foot to keep pushing the box, rather than picking it up.

"So, what's your name?" he continued to carefully boot the box. "How far are we going?"

She laughed at his box kicking, but avoided his questions. "Thanks a lot."

"Sure," he winked at her, while his hands slipped into his pockets.

"This is me here," she pointed to a door with her nose.

"Good," he dribbled the box to her door and picked it up.

"Just set it down," she said. He placed the box back down.

"Which pocket are your keys in?" he asked.

"Left one."

He dived his hand into her pocket, while avoiding eye contact and then fished them out.

"It's the silver one," she said. He unlocked her door, then turned and gave her a quick peck on the cheek. She blushed. "Thanks."

James dashed to Shard's door. Shard pulled James inside with such a force, he left his shadow behind, outside.

Shard's pad was simple, with a bachelor's sense of order and priority. It wasn't the college decor of bikini posters, rock bands and school banners. His place had more of a Dean Martin sort of sophistication with a touch of the rebel yell and territorial pissings. His roommate wasn't home. James, Shard, Aster and Ticktock were all seated at the kitchen table. In the center of the table sat James's cell phone. It was switched to speaker phone. James pressed the voicemail function and upped the volume. Two saved messages.

"James, you need to move in with me. This fuck and run... I'm not complaining, but I need..." James ended the message frantically, the others laughing.

"Shit. Sorry," he said. He found the next message. "Sh. Listen."

It was a woman's voice, a younger one this time. "Welcome to the greatest dart tournament ever! All dart players, pack your bags. With a grand prize of one million dollars, this is a tournament you do not want to miss. Even if you suck eggs, you do not want to regret passing up this opportunity. So come on down to Rackle's Tub and --"

The message was cut off. Everyone at the table turned ghostly white.

"Is this for real?" said Shard.

"It's the number I got off the bathroom wall from the San Francisco tournament. It's a Colorado area code," said James while he grabbed the phone.

"If it was written on the bathroom wall, we might have already missed it. That could've been an old recording," said Shard.

"Call it back!" Ticktock screeched.

James hit redial and put the phone to his ear.

"Put it on speaker phone," Ticktock kept going.

James maneuvered a button and now everyone shared the suspense of the simple sound they'd all heard a million times on their own phones. The phone continued to ring.

"This is killing me," James said, pacing the room. Aster pulled out his ChapStick and layered his lips. Shard looked at Aster and puckered his lips with a dozen kisses. Ticktock faked a full body seizure. The phone beeped. "Hello? This is James. I've gotten your message regarding the dart tournament. I'm very much interested and would like some information. Please give me a call here at three-two-three..."

The phone beeped.

"What? Hello...?" James turned to Shard. "The line went dead. How do you like that?"

"I don't," said Shard. "Maybe they'll leave you another message."

"Yeah. Funny," said James.

"Let me give 'em slags a call," Ticktock got up from his chair, knocking it over behind him. James handed the phone over. He called again. This time, the three-tone alert sounded.

"I'm sorry. The number you are trying to reach has been disconnected. If you feel you have dialed this number in error, please hang up and try again."

"What? Blimey!" Ticktock handed the phone back. "You sure that's the right number?" James searched his phone and dialed the number. Again, the disconnection tone came on.

"Yes." James collapsed his phone shut.

"Look it up online," Aster said.

"YEAH!" Ticktock exploded. "Google it. Google Rackle's Tub!"

Shard opened his sleeping laptop and did a search for Rackle's Tub, but the search turned up nothing.

* * * * *

James entered his Lexington Avenue hotel/apartment. The jingle-jangle of his keys was silenced with a thud when he tossed them on the tabletop. He kicked off his boots and headed for the sink to wash his hands. Hands must always be clean when handling the "tool". He grabbed a roll of toilet paper and brought it to the bed. After he climbed into his sweats, he depleted his mental Roledex of ex-girlfriends trying to conjure up a hot moment. None were stimulating him. He lay in bed, "tool" in hand, trying to muster up a moment to jerk off to. The days when he would buy porno magazines and keep them under his mattress were gone. Yes, internet porn had saved many trees. Though James didn't have the energy to fire up his laptop and do all that searching, and he most certainly didn't want to deal with a booty call. He couldn't just nod off either. He was stuck in the land between sleep and awake and needing to spew. His ritual every morning and every night.

Right before dreams began to drag him by the eyelids, James remembered an infomercial girl in a tight, aerobics outfit, laying her groin over a large, inflatable, exercise ball. The commercial became clearer. The product was called *Amazing Big Balls*. They were blue, and this sexy girl would demonstrate all the uses with the ball to get the best workout. With her crotch still on the ball and while keeping her arms up with hands folded behind her head, she would roll back and forth and in circular motions, her toes planted on the ground in a pivot. That girl hit him just right. Her legs sprawled out like a spider as she continued to rotate on her twat and inner thighs. Now, James imagined her naked. Still working the ball. His phone ringing jolted him awake like tiny globules of toothpaste flicked into the eye from the bristles of the toothbrush, stinging. It was an unrecognizable musical tone. He staggered to reach his phone, which displayed a blocked number.

"Hello?" James greeted.

"James?" The young woman's voice on the other end sounded a little nervous.

"Yes."

"Hi. I received your message regarding the dart tournament and-"

"Oh yes! I'm very much interested in participating."

"Great..."

"I'm part of a team already. We do the circuits and um, would love to join your..."

"Good. Good..."

James looked to the open matchbook on his nightstand. "Are you the bird they call Punch?"

"Tweet-tweet. Yup. That's me."

"Funny thing, I don't... how am I going to say this...? I don't mean any disrespect at all, but you don't know where I found your number. It was written on the wall of a bathroom in San Francisco. And here I am in Los Angeles."

"Really? I don't believe you."

"I swear. And it's not like me to call up numbers I find in restrooms, you know. I was curious about your name and the little story attached to it."

"Did the wall say I was a good time slut?"

"Well, not a good time."

"Great. What an introduction. We're off to a fine start, aren't we?"

"I'm still amazed by this phone call," James added.

"Yeah, well, back to business then," she reminded. "This is a real tournament. A million dollars to the top team. You haven't missed the deadline to join. So I'm going to go ahead and fill out your application, James. Your last name?"

"O'clock."

"James O'clock?"

"Yes. Funny, I know."

"Okay. Just bear with me." He could hear her heavy typing, as if she were playing Beethoven on the computer's keyboard. "I'm going to need the names of your teammates."

"Sure. Shard McEra." He heard her slap the keyboard once.

"Yeah. Got it. Go on."

"Right. Um, Aster, Day." Again, all he heard was a slap to the keyboard. "You know, there are more than one letter to these names."

"What? Oh. I'm a fast typist. He's in there. Next."

"Okay. Ticktock." He listened. There was no typing sound. "Did you get that one?"

"Yeah. Ticktock." She typed and typed, her fingers dancing all over the keyboard for a long minute or two. "Tick..." she continued typing. "Tock. Interesting names."

"It's a theme."

"Timeless. Okay, James, give me a couple of seconds while I finish up here." She continued typing. "Oh. You're already in the system. The Clocks." She typed again.

"That's right. How did that happen?"

"We send people to scout around for talent, but that's strange how you got in here."

"Funny."

"It's just a database of information. It says here you're from England." She laughed.

"Wow, Punch. You're brilliant." She typed some more.

"You're all set. I hope you're ready for a road trip. The place is called Rackle's Tub. We're in colorful Colorado."

"Great! What if, through some strange, twist-of-fate or cosmic event, you become the love of my life? That would make for a great conversational piece, wouldn't it?"

"James. It's a dart tournament."

"Right. Yes."

"But I do look forward to meeting you."

PART 2

Barrel

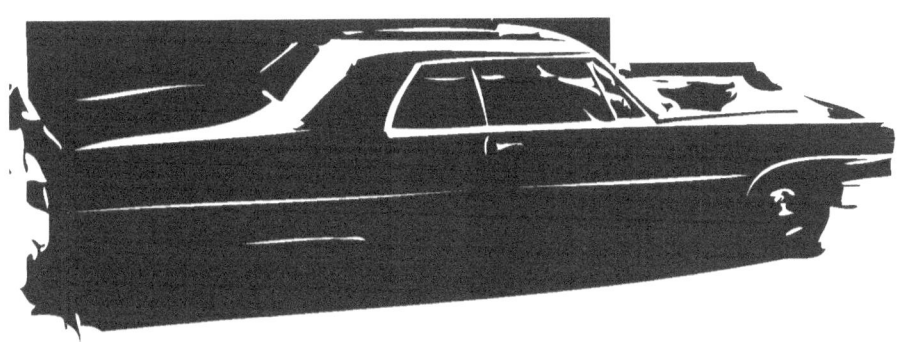

The Collector

Feet tangled in her garments. Darkness, blurred vision, increased salivation, delirium and a troubled respiratory system. Punch felt a thud to her skull like nothing she'd ever experienced before. The blood stung her eyes as it raced down her crown. She managed to get up. Some sort of fire inside her shot through the disorientation like a bolt, screaming for help. Her voice was gone, but the fight, though barely hanging on, was still in her. She swung her tight fists into the air. She was surrounded by molesters. A tall, well-formed man with no detail to his body, but eyes the most aggresive. Everywhere on his skin, eyes. Wings, large and feathered behind him. Each attacker was different. Some were hideous. Yet they all had multiple eyes. The tall attacker swung his club again. She blocked it with her funny bone. It laughed up her entire arm as she tumbled over. Her eyes widened, trying to understand what was happening. Tears, with their emergency escape plan, bailed down her cheeks. He charged her. She kicked her feet like a netted animal, her wedding dress tangled in her legs, and felt another sharp, shocking thud to her thigh. Punch was not going to take this anymore. She scrambled up and pounced on her attacker with death in her heart. Hit after hit, she sent her attacker plunging back, his wings flapping like a caged rooster. She delivered a right hook to his temple, nearly knocking his head off. He stumbled to the ground with her right on him, locked in the fight. The kill had taken up full volume in her brain, and there was no shutting it off. She beat him so hard, hits went straight to the ground. Bloodied knuckles kept the violent momentum as his blood, like battery acid, shot into her mouth, teeth and tongue; its bitterness ran down her throat. She bit into him when she could no longer feel her hands. Under the strength of her legs, his life was leaving him. She threw up on him, and nearly choking, grabbed the club and destroyed his skull. She blindly swung at the others, who backed away. She tried to run, only to discover the ground beneath her feet was no longer there. She fell into blackness. As she came too, she found herself lying in a bathtub. Being carried off by a new group of men. Looking at her without looking at her. Closing her eyes, she passed out. The work had to be done quick. Punch was brought to a room with gray shadows for light. The door was shut and locked. What was left of her wedding dress was abraded. The remainder of it was ripped off. She was drenched in sweat. But what made her slippery to handle was the blood. She felt it all over her body. They carried her to a large, metallic chair that reclined and strapped her in. Sounds were not registering uniformly to what she was seeing. And the things she was seeing- the dead body of her attacker lying on a table and pushed against her chair. She recognized her vomit mixed with his brain matter in his caved-in cranium. The smell made her stomach gurgle with gases. Double vision- she closed her eyes. Thirst was powerful. She gasped as a wet sponge was used to wipe her down. She couldn't form words easily. "What's -going on-?" She finally spoke as she struggled against the straps. But whatever verbal response they made was lost. Her mind became loud with reptilian urges. A pain in her bones forced her eyes open, the pupils expanding over the entire iris, forcing the iris to expand into the sclera and causing a blue halo effect around the edge. Her tears turned red and her skin drained of color, almost to a blue-grey tint. Her paleness caused a slight glow. She noticed a tube was connected from the body of her attacker's to her own. His blood went into her arm. Her swollen knuckles pushed out sharp, bony ridges that blackened into claws. Her canines grew slightly, the enamel coming to a sharper point like that of a carnivore. Her appearance drove some of her captors back. She put the straps to their absolute test. Body convulsing in fits of rage. Her voice returned as she growled, moaned and cried. The others stood by, waiting and waiting. Until, helpless, she realized she was spent. Morning made things better.

"She'll be a detriment," a voice said from somewhere. Punch, tucked in bed and wrapped in gauze, turned to one side, eyes open, her poor body throbbing from the abuse of the night before.

"Or an asset," another voice responded.

"How did she do it?" spoke the first voice. "How did she kill her collector?"

"John...?" Punch called out. "John. Where am I?" She tried

to focus on a figure in the room. The figure stood still, yet there appeared flashes of motion, like another body moving behind and in front of him. She shut her eyes. Needed rest was pressing her.

The days and nights crept by her bed like quiet little children, off for some midnight sweets.

Yeah, Yeah, Yeah!

Fossil fuel filled feast for a first-class fucking four wheel framed fetish with front flagrant fenders, followed by fine-farrant fins, flagged fans on foot of this fantasmo force, which fired frothy fumes, F-f-f-f-f- FOOM! The black Caddy in the black night pulled to a stop to pick up a passenger. Black, shiny boots climbed into the car. The car sped off. The wheels mean and the headlights angry eyes. The speedometer needle swayed from one end to the other. It trembled to the motor's music. Shard's hand was on the wheel with a cigarette between his fingers. He pulled over to make another pick up. Again, another pair of boots climbed into the back seat. The song *Boss Hoss,* by the Sonics, blasted out of the speakers. The car pealed out and got back onto the main street.

At a diner not too far off, Ticktock watched the clock above the kitchen door. Once the minute hand hit its mark, he screamed, "YEAH!" and ripped his apron off, throwing it over the cook. He dashed for his time card. A collision with the head chef ignited an explosion of flour and outrage. Ticktock apologized, clocked out, grabbed his bag and pushed through, bumping into people... waiters and busboys. Pots and pans with people's orders were knocked to the floor by accident. The chef chased him.

"You fucker. Come here," said the chef. "You're fired!" Ticktock smiled when he looked back. The patrons seated in the dining area became distracted by the noises and yelling from the kitchen. Like a powdery-white cannon ball, Ticktock blasted out the door, where he jumped a counter with a mad chef and waiter at his heels.

Outside, motor running, the boy's Cadillac waited to receive its own. This metal, two ton capsule was Ticktock's saving grace for now. At his age, he could afford the risk. Without opening the door,

Ticktock leaped through the rolled down window. His bag smacked Aster in the face. The car left the lot, its value appreciated.

"You crazy, English bastard," said Shard.

"Fucker," Aster said as he shoved the bag back to Ticktock's laughing face.

James too, looked over from the front seat. "You've got white stuff all over your face," he said.

Ticktock swabbed his face with a finger, and after inspecting it, covered one nostril with the other hand and snorted the flour off his finger.

"I know, I know. Its gotten out of control." He brushed his face and then, like a wet dog, shook his body free of the flour. Then, frisked Aster's shirt for a smoke. "I'm so fuckin' pumped about this tournament," continued Ticktock. "I quit me bloody job! That's how confident I am."

"Or stupid," Aster said.

"Ticktock. Keep your cool. You're English, remember?" James winked.

"James Dean, Bogart, Steve McQueen, they were cool and they were Americans," Shard said. Ticktock lit his smoke.

"They're actors, Shard," said James. "If you read their script, the directions said -act cool like an Englishman."

Ticktock laughing in the background, slammed his back to the seat.

"Yeah. How cool would they be if they had a thousand Zulus charging them?" Ticktock said, cleaning his face of the powdery mess.

"Oh, you think you wouldn't piss your pants 'cause you're English?" asked Shard. "I just saw you run from one chef."

"Yeah, we kicked your ass in seventeen seventy six," said Aster. "And then we had to come bail you out of both world wars. Or else you'd be speaking Deutsche!"

James reclined back in his seat in amusement. "Ah, Churchill had it under control as he puffed away on his La Aroma de Cubas and sipped his brandy," said James.

"Well who won more fucking wars than any other country?" asked Ticktock. "It wasn't you Yanks, I'll tell ya that much."

"Touché Ticktock," James said. "And if it wasn't for us colonizing you guys, you'd all be speaking French." James found another track on the stereo of an English band, The Creation, "*Making Time*" to punctuate his statement.

In an exaggerated French accent, Ticktock teased... "*Oh ho-ho! Oui, oui, merci, croissant ah, de Jerry Lewis and de Inspector Clouseau... I like little boys.*"

"We gave you America because we were busy with our imperial progress on the rest of the world," said James.

Shard looked over. "Well, what good did it do ya?" he said. "You ended up giving it all back."

"In the end, all that bloodshed for nothing," added Aster. James looked over at the two Americans.

"We had to make English the universal language. Mission accomplished, I say," and with that, James ended the debate.

A sign off the highway read, Las Vegas: 180 miles. In the darkness, the desert could have easily been either an ocean or the sheer drop off of a cliff's edge. Looking out the window, it was so solid black for miles out that anything could have been out there.

"A million split four ways is two hundred and fifty thousand!" exclaimed Ticktock. "Say it! Two hundred and fifty THOUSAND!"

"Yeah," said Aster, looking out at the passing nighttime desert.

"Yeah?!" Ticktock unbuckled his belt.

"Oh no..."

"Yeah...?!" Ticktock repeated. "That's all you've got to say?" He jumped on top of Aster to shake him.

"Stop it. You're giving me germs. You never even washed your hands."

"You have germs on your face right now." Ticktock got off him and sat back down. "Everybody does, Bubble Boy." He buckled up.

"No, living in a bubble'll make his immune system weaker," said James.

"You should live in a padded cell," Aster told Ticktock.

"I have," Ticktock looked away. "It's all in your mind, mate."

"It's not his fault he has some germ phobia, neurosis, disorder, syndrome, retardation, paranoia, or whatever the hell it's called," said Shard.

"Shut up! It's not funny. I came to the conclusion that you guys had accepted me for who I am. I guess I was wrong." Aster's comment silenced the group's laughter. "My loyalty to you guys, and all I hold most dear, has never wavered. I never doubted your good intentions, and I am now deeply crippled by these shenanigans." He pulled out his ChapStick, popped off the lid and moistened his lips.

"You're not a pussy licker, are you?" Ticktock asked. Aster looked at him. "You need to lighten up. Of course we love you. Just havin' a laugh."

"At my expense. Well my friend, the currency is high," said Aster.

"What's that mean Aster? Your words are clumsy. You speak in prose and riddles," Ticktock said.

"If you can't figure it out--"

"Does anyone have a water bottle I can piss in?" Ticktock unbuttoned his pants. "A woman's place is on my face..." He searched under the seat. No empty bottle could be found. "Shard, pull over. I've gotta go." Aster was relieved to hear the request.

* * * * *

James's journal entry:

Polyergus breviceps, or more commonly known as slave raiding ants, can not survive on their own. They use other ants to raise their young and to nurture the queen. They almost always conduct raids at 4 o'clock. They rush into the nest of some unfortunate F. argentea, kill the adults and steal the eggs, looking like peeled potatoes clutched in their mandibles. Then, they carry these eggs back to the nest, where they hatch into a new generation that will look after the colony.

* * * * *

It was morning at a desert rest stop. Off the trail, a war was raging. Raging for ants anyway. Red ants, not usually early morning risers, were fighting the tiny, imported Argentine ants. These were

the black ants so typically found everywhere in southern California
and the southwest. They don't hurt when they bite or sting, but
they do have the numbers. James stood over them, notebook out,
watching the battle. Hypnotized by the tiny, silent movements
of ground that blurred into a kinetic carpet. The red ants were
harvester ants. They were being trapped in their own home. Two
lines of Argentine ants flowed into the hole of the harvester ant's
hill. They had traveled a good distance to get to the enemy's nest.

*As a child, I'd cling to the leg of my dad, sitting on his foot, and ride
him across the kitchen into the living room,* James noted in his journal.
*The small black ants were doing the same thing. Three ants, each attached to
a leg of the one larger red ant, riding her away from the nest, their mandibles
clamping away like a right-handed child using left-handed scissors. It takes
many bites before the dullness of their jaws becomes threateningly real.* As
James wrote, a leg fell off, the black ant with it. *Like over sized-shoes...
when I was a child, I'd wear my dad's shoes around the house, which were like
two boats on my feet. Lifting each foot, careful not to drop the shoe, caused me
to walk funny. This red ant shared a similar style. She wore shoes of black ant
leather. But, she clearly preferred her feet bare.* James sketched some ant
cartoons.

"William Wallace has lead his army of Scotsmen straight
into the heart of the English colony..." narrated James to Shard.
The two were accompanied by the others who had taken in
his enthusiasm and tried it on for a fit. "I have to record this.
Otherwise, what has transpired here will never be known. And
these lives would have all been lost for nothing. They have no
scribe of their own, you see. These ants are wiping out our native
species," said James.

"Dork," said Ticktock.

"Do you want some alone time?" Shard squeezed his shoulders.

"Oh look," said Aster, "that's cool. They're truly not getting
along."

"Yeah, it's politics gone wrong," Shard lifted his feet as they
began to crawl over his boots.

"I think, with the economy being the way it is, and with the super radicals laying their slant on the major populous that you often see in the news, these ants are right wingers..." Aster muscled his way for respect in an awkward form of a political comparison to ants. It failed.

"Which ants are the right wingers?" asked Ticktock. Aster didn't respond.

"Who is opposed to radical change?" James asked Ticktock. "I think the red ones. They are content where they are. They only have one queen, a dictator, and they will fight other harvester ants. The black ones have several queens and they all get along fine with each other. They're looking for new opportunity."

"Left wing bastards," Shard said.

"Stick your penis in the hole," was Ticktock's bullet fast banter of absurdity. "Let them bite it. Feel the pain. Absorb it. Develop the immunities. Let it swell to twice the size. Get it hard. Lube it. Find a ho. Bag it. Stick it. Pump it. Release it. Pay her the Benjamins. Wash it. Call it a day." And with that, Ticktock parted from the battlefield.

"Just put down the black ants won," Shard left. James and Aster were still at the mound.

"You're right about ants and people being a lot alike," said James as he patted Aster's shoulder and closed his notebook. "Let's get."

Transcendental Hole in the Wall

Since the disappearance of Punch, John immersed himself in solid work hours around the clock. A book by William Kingdon Clifford, *Elements of Dynamic,* was opened to a chapter on *"Kinematics"*- a term coined by the author defining 3-dimensional dynamics in the 4th dimension. John was a follower of his colleague's work and truly believed Mr. Clifford found a unified field theory, but sadly, at the age of thirty four, died of consumption before he could disclose it. Under the light of his desk lamp, John had been writing equations and dipping them into his own new theorem, *Rackle's Tub.* No one wanted anything to do with his theorems, and so without the intention of publication, he explored them for himself. Euclidean and Non-Euclidean geometries, played along with theorems for electromagnetism, added flavor to John's strange brew, getting closer and closer to that fantastic sensation of satisfaction. Like a boy discovering ejaculation for the first time, there was an exhilarating pleasure to solving the universe.

A 4-dimensional, hyper volume, bounded by a 3-sphere, once inserted into a Rackle's Tub, created magic. It opened doors.

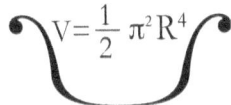

$$V = \frac{1}{2}\pi^2 R^4$$

John worked on spacetime theories before Hermann Minkowski.

$s^2 < 0$ Time-like interval

$s^2 > 0$ Space-like interval

$s^2 = 0$ Light-like interval

(Spacetime interval between two events)

$$S^2 = \Delta r^2 - c^2 \Delta t^2$$

Indeed, there was a parallel to John's dreams and the math work. John had been visiting a place tucked somewhere between his dreams and time. He'd been visiting often enough that he soon established a residency. In his dreams, someone ordered him to draw up plans and to have them ready. Behind him, a room full of what looked like electrical currents were indeed, the peripheral dancers. They had a fleeting moment of underwater grace. John rose to his feet and dimmed the light. He rolled up his plans and stuck them in a leather bag. With his head through the loop of the strap, he secured the bag to his body. He moved away from his desk and reached for the ceiling. Hands opened wide, fingers stretched out, he used gentle Tai Chi-like movements. His hands moved in circular patterns through the air down in front of him. He paid no attention to the flashing moments of electrical brilliance fizzing out nearby. His fingers tenderly rubbing the clitoris of this floating vagina. The doorbell to the portal. Her lips opened. He closed his eyes and breathed her in.

Welcome To Purgalapudlia

The fourth dimension took a visual adjustment. There was a dissolution of the 3-D form. Things were seen from all sides at once. Very much like Cubism. Pablo Picasso must have visited Purgalapudlia when he painted such works as *Portrait of Ambrose Vollard*. It was comparable to wearing someone else's glasses when one had 20/20 vision. One would feel dizzy, but then, would look normal again. A dormant portion of the brain is triggered which has the capacity to see in other dimensions. John followed several Purgalapudlians (*also called Purggies, Purgy, Purggy, Purgals*) down a busy street, under a thick, gravy sky. The architecture all around was a unique and balanced mixture of Art Nouveau and Cubism. A similarity to the Victorian style at home eased John's transition between the two worlds. Multiple noses, misplaced eyes, faces on the back of their heads, everyone, an abstract version of modern man. John braced himself against a wall to vomit. The others stopped and watched. They've seen John do this before. Bluet, the Indift, which was another name for king of Purgalapudlia, patted John on the back. He was a jolly, heavy fellow with tiny eyes and swollen fingers. Bluet was a man with no point of view. His indifference to feelings was expected, that's why it was such a surprise that he recruited John Rackle for an important task. There had been an energy shortage and it was expected to get worse.

"Come now, John. Soon you won't have to show us the diary of your gut!" Bluet pulled out a rag, damp from past nose-blowing and used it to wipe John's mouth. "You may keep it." John kept it. Cloth from royalty was a kind gesture. John's eyes kicked in, as night vision would, and soon everyone appeared like normal humans.

In Bluet's chamber, John had his blueprints opened for display to a small audience. He stood before them and pointed to the drawings.

"It works in similarity to oil drilling. The idea being to pierce the brane of the third dimension..."

John was distracted by someone with urgent news who just entered. "...This mortal girl just became immortal...!"

"What? Excuse me, wait, what is this talk of a mortal girl?" asked John. He feared Punch may have come up here. Which meant she didn't run away... John's mind raced. Suddenly it became clear. It wasn't like what Mother had said. Punch wasn't like the other girls- full of disappointment. Mother was wrong.

"Sorry, sir. Sorry to interrupt."

"No-no. Show me!"

"What?"

"Please."

"Now?"

"Yes! Take me to her," he rushed over to the young man. "Did you get a name, boy?" Bluet yawned as he waved the two off.

* * * * *

John followed through a field of black wheat. The horizon was interrupted with large towers, resembling giant windmills, about one per acre. They stood taller than a lighthouse and had crowns with large rotors. These four arms moved in a steady, circular motion. At the end of each arm, a large cup collected the sought after energy of airborne souls. Hence, the name soulmills for such buildings. The rotors were vacuum tubes to bring in the souls once collected from the soul catcher on the end of its arm. Between each arm was another smaller arm. These were called soul magnets, to attract in souls close enough to be scooped up by the soul catcher. Once the soul was captured, it was brought into a room directly below the crown called the energy cap. This room was made of tungsten to endure high energy from soul compression. Tungsten in Purgalapudlia seemed to have taken a stronger form than elsewhere. Below the energy cap were the living quarters. It was the only floor in the building with windows, long and narrow ones. The rest of the building was cold and walled in with brick, minus a set of doors at the bottom.

John marveled at the sight of such soon-to-be dinosaurs. It was an old system, long overdue for a change during what is now becoming the brink of an energy revolution.

Soulmill: red-black-red-white-black, was the color code above the doors. The immortal girl was stationed inside. John followed the Purgalapudlian into the daunting tower. The fragrance of aged dust and powdery perfume oil caused John's vision to flutter between third and fourth dimensional sight. The interior was dark, with an iron spiral staircase ascending through each bare-bone level, all the way to the top. The elevator was out of commission. As John climbed the stairs, the painful memory of his honeymoon numbed his brain. A defense mechanism that cold-heartedly shut out feelings of love. He would not allow himself to experience such a loss again. His body reflected his mental island of desertion. He became less enthusiastic of the reunion and now each step was an affirmation of Mother's voice. Punch must have come here on her own. She wanted to get away. John struggled with how to play his emotions as he climbed closer to the door. How was a healthy-minded human supposed to react when reunited with a lost love? Based on the books he'd read and the plays he'd seen, he knew he could mimic a behavior pattern. They arrived at a door. He plastered his hair back with the sweat from his palms. The door was unlocked. Inside, a family of Purggy workers were busy preparing food and cleaning machinery of large iron wheels and brackets. Punch, with a bandage wrapped around her head and her hair tied back, sat at the window, peering out. John was caught up with such a sensory overload, it took him a moment to speak.

"Punch." She turned to him. They stared at one another as if sight was delayed in its delivery of information.

"John!" She tried to run, but limped from pain. "It's you! You found me!" She fell into his arms.

"Look at you, my sweet." He embraced her tight.

"John..." she cried.

"I found you. I found you." He looked into her eyes. "Welcome to Purgalapudlia." They both laughed. "Funny name, you know."

"It's your turn to hide," she wiped the tears from her face. "I'll start counting."

* * * * *

They rode in a mobile bathtub. No wheels, the clawed feet walked on their own as if they were riding on the backs of lions. Punch lay against John, in his lap, incredulous at the idea of self-moving tubs.

"I still can't believe they have brought animation to your tubs..." She sat up.

"This was something I was preparing to show you -a surprise, if you will," he said.

"Surprise? No, no, this is more of a... an attack of... astonishment!" She gripped both sides of the tub. "To all my senses." She turned to face John. "I thought I was dead." Her eyes glossed. "I was brutally assaulted by these monsters."

"Those weren't monsters. They were angels."

"No."

John nodded.

"Angels are supposed to be beautiful, with glorious white wings. These beasts had eyes, all over-"

"For multi-dimensional travel. You, my dear, I have just learned, have accomplished a feat that has not been achieved in recent memory for these Purgalapudlians. You killed your collector. That angel you speak of. And from what I understand, this makes you immortal. I have yet to face mine, so why was yours expecting you? Why did it attack? There is a lot of violence that has surfaced due to this energy crisis."

Punch felt faint and lay back down in John's lap. He inhaled deeply the scent of her scalp. "This place is truly... like nothing I've ever known. I still don't understand the laws out here. I will take you to my new headquarters. Another factory, John Rackle Industries. A unique name -I know. You may unwind and get some rest there. I will look after you." He noticed she had fallen asleep. He kissed her wrapped head. "My poor girl."

J.R. Industries was a spacious place. John held his scotch while his Mother, also holding a scotch, stood near him. They watched Punch, wrapped in a blanket on the couch.

"She's a simpleton," said Mother. "I cannot believe you had eyes for her. Sure, she's cute, but she is beneath you." Punch turned over and emerged from her chrysalis of sleep.

"Hello," Punch pulled the blanket off and set eyes on the place for the first time. "How long was I out?" She noticed the other woman. No one responded. "So, this is your new factory?" John made his way to the bar.

"Scotch?" he offered.

"Maybe a little," she got up and joined him. She nodded at the sour faced woman. "I am so sorry. I have not had the pleasure." She walked to her with an extended hand.

"Oh, this is Mother," John poured Punch a drink.

"John has told me all about you," Mother said shaking Punch's hand. John handed Punch a glass.

"Did he?"

"You know, I thought I lost you," said John. He avoided eye contact as he made his way to his Mother's side.

"But you found me, John," said Punch.

"I didn't know what happened to you. You left me. Abandoned the marriage." John sipped his drink. His tone caused Punch concern.

"What? No, I--"

"The idea of marriage was too overbearing. You ran away from me!"

"No, John. Where did I go?" She made her way closer. "I didn't know what happened to me either. Are you blaming me? I would never do such a thing to you."

John grabbed his Mother's hand and brought it up to his lips for a kiss.

"Please believe me, John. You're all I have. If I did not want to be your wife, I would have told you so at the start." Punch watched him kiss Mother's other hand. He ignored her and found the cruelty in doing so fed his quiet, perverse satisfaction. "John, love, we can be a family now." Punch rubbed his shoulder.

"My time is for her now," said John; his eyes never left Mother's.

"My duty as a wife is not to lessen your affection for your mother. Quite the contrary, I encourage it..." Punch was distracted by John's waving hand to a servant who suddenly appeared behind her.

"Could you draw us a hot bath?" The servant nodded and left the room. "I believe a hot bath for us all would be just what we need for some clarity. Don't you agree, Mother?"

"Perhaps, my dear son," said Mother. "Give Mother a kiss." The two kissed, lip to lip. "That a-boy. Again." They kissed once more, on the lips.

"Are we still married?" Punch asked.

"I'll explain everything," said John.

"What is there to explain? It's a simple yes or no question."

"Please," John wrapped his arm around her, then Mother, as they left the room. "I'm going to need you more than ever." Down the hall, in a large bathroom, the orgy tub awaited.

"Well, you were rather quick to start another life since I last saw you," Punch griped. John ignored her and furthered his silent insult by whispering into Mother's ear. Mother laughed with even more emphasis, now that there was an audience.

"I love this place," said John, "we love this place. Political ambitions aside, the people of Purgalapudlia know to leave me and Mother alone. No ridicule from them. They are indifferent to my relationships and they recognize the importance of my mathematical theories. Which is more than what I can say for the people back home."

The three entered the steamy room. Three robes had been laid out. John was the first to remove his clothes. The two ladies hesitated to follow suit. John, naked, walked into the hot water slowly so as to not burn himself.

"I promise, the tub won't move," John smiled. Both women stood still. "Mother. Come now, darling..." Mother removed her dress and knickers. She crawled into the hot tub, naked. She kissed him on the lips again. Punch shook her head.

"This is repulsive. Sickening behavior--" Punch was finding her clarity all right. "Your moral demeanor is absolutely obliterated."

"Punch, my dear. Please join Mother and I as one happy family." He grabbed Mother's hand and kissed her lips again.

"Sure. I'd love to join Oedipus in a good fuck fest with Mother."

"How dare you talk to my son with such cruel words," screamed Mother.

"And my moral demeanor is obliterated," said John as he got on his knees to kiss Mother elsewhere. "Funny words from a fighting, gambling, cigar-smoking, trash-talking, criminal-minded whore!"

"I shall not share bath water with this cunt!" Mother ordered. "I did not approve of the marriage then. And I certainly don't approve of it now!"

John's voice changed to that of a child. "Baby needs milk, Mommy," he said. She hugged him and held tight. Punch became dizzy.

"Now, now," Mother patted John. "Look what you did to my boy. Can't you see he's not well?"

Punch fled the room. The walls were leaning in on her.

* * * * *

It was back to the soulmills. Punch disappeared from John a second time. John searched for her, but to no avail. He resented Mother for planting the distrust with women in his adolescence, which now bloomed into a sad and twisted psychosis. He was still mad for Punch. And, he wanted to please Mother. The soulmill workers already disliked John for the development of a new soul-obtaining system. John had created machines that didn't require Purgalapudlians to run them. For generations, families would live and work the mills. It was a profitable way of life. They caught the souls' that angels and other collectors missed. These portals, once as numerous and undiscovered as prairie dog mounds all over the great western plains, were now so overly watched by collectors it was time for something different to compete.

Punch sat turning a wheel with a nub, while peddling in the same fashion as an old sewing machine. The device made noises like a paper press. It was attached to the wall, where large, tungsten tubes resembling those of a pipe organ connected to the darkness of the ceiling. This generated the soul extraction. Near Punch was a dashboard-looking setup with ivory ball knobs that pushed out with steam pressure. There was a whole panel of them and Punch would push them back in and flip a switch next to the knob only to repeat the process with another knob elsewhere on the grid. She clamped on a metal gear from the machine and shifted down causing the pipes to bang overhead. Then she shifted back up and turned the wheel again. There were a couple variations of these machines in the room. The sweat was part of the job at these work stations and the faint aroma of the perfume oil stuck to them.

An explosion nearby brought everyone to their feet. Another boom and everyone rushed to the window. A raiding party of angels, some flying by the use of their own wings while others on the ground, approached in mobile bathtubs with cannons mounted on the front. The cannons fired at a neighboring soulmill. Like stepping on an ant hill, Purgies were soon escaping the mill with urgency. Some of the mobile tubs gave chase, tufts of earth sent airborne as the clawed feet pulled the tubs into such a terrifying speed that they easily ran the Purgies down. The only thing faster was bullets wizzing through Purgy flesh.

"We need to do something," said Punch.

"There's nothing we can do." said an older Purgy, who turned away.

"Nothing?! We can't just stand here-"

"Get back to work."

"Work? While our neighbors are being slaughtered?"

"Your labor at this moment is far more important!"

"More important?! Your priorities are fucked! What if that was happening to us? Then what?" Punch was furious.

"Well it's not, is it? Let it go. It's one less strain on our backs."

"What-? I don't understand."

"With that soulmill out of comission, we have less competition, and therefore, more souls for ourselves to collect. The angels will come again, sure, but the odds of them striking our mill are slim."

"Does everyone here feel the same?" Punch looked around the room at the neutral expressions. "Huh?" They all shuffled back to work. Their reaction, or the lack of one, shocked Punch. She was now the only one at the window. She looked back out at the horror again. The angels had finished their work of stealing all the souls from the neighboring mill. Most took to flight. Mobile tubs galloped off, loaded with souls. Only three angels remained. They had more than soul-snatching in mind. A young Purgy female had provoked a tickle in their groins; the weight of their growing cocks guiding them to the female. They grabbed her arms, one wiping his knobbly penis on her leg. Punch pressed against the window, her breath fogging it. She shook her head, words blocked by her pounding heart. An angel yanked the Purgy female's hair and another ripped her clothes away from her pussy. A third one jammed his cock into her mouth with stroke after stroke, while smacking her face. Punch, helpless, banged on the window, screaming. The rape from multi-eyed monsters unleashed her bitter memory. The other Purgy workers got up from their work stations and pulled Punch away from the window.

"NO-!!!" Punch, reliving her nightmare, swung at them as they trapped her arms. "LET ME GO-!!!!" Her eyes flashed a moment of discoloration with a sharp brightness. The workers staggered back in fear of this strange occurrence. But Punch just stood there, catching her breath, and looked once more out the window. One of the angels broke the Purgy female's neck with his savage hands. Her limp body dragged on the floor before it raised into the air as the angels flew, carrying her and then tossing her on the roof of the neighboring mill.

In the silence and solitude of her chamber, Punch cried her heart out. She was devastated, homesick, lost and heartbroken. As she wiped her cheeks, she noticed something as deviating as Apollo's silver bow, or Aphrodite's charm, or Dionysus's blue hair. She wept tears of gold. She feared it to be blood at first and rushed to the broken mirror in her room. The tear came out clear and soon darkened. She collected it in her hand and found it to be so beautiful. She softly pressed her finger into her palm, scooping the gold tear, bringing it in for a closer inspection and became mesmerized. She rubbed her thumb over her finger, feeling the moist texture. She cried again, blurring her vision. She couldn't help but think of John. God, she missed him so much despite his unacceptable behavior. She wondered what he would think of her bizarre ability, but then feared it would just be another reason not to like her. Punch didn't suffer any of the symptoms of toxicity that gold would have on a normal human, like the inhibited enzymatic activity and suppressed bone marrow function. But then, this gold had a bio-friendly element because of its origin. When she awoke the next day, the exposure to the open air caused the tears to harden, rock solid, on her pillow. She bagged them and stuffed them in her mattress. She might have been naïve, but she was no idiot. She started to collect her tears. After the angel assault, Punch's soulmill was as voiceless as a monastery. The Purgies have always been subservient to angels. Punch awkwardly climbed into her work station. She could feel the eyes of her coworkers, as the sounds of machines stopped operating long enough to add weight to her discomfort. They didn't want to risk aggravating her and they didn't like her interfering with the angels' affairs. As soon as Punch started up her machine, the others followed suit.

* * * * *

The first contaminated soul Punch had ever seen came through her mill one rainy morning. Souls resembled a small papaya in shape once they entered into the Purgalapudlian stratosphere, but then they defied description, for they glowed with the intensity of an electric fire, yet they weren't hot to touch. They had a heaviness, but could take to air. You could feel their surface and then they could be as transparent as steam. Depending on the soul type, some were white, some blue and others red. But when a bad one comes in, we all know what that looks like. The contaminated soul was dotted black. As a precaution, the mill had to be temporarily shutdown. Panic and paranoia then blossomed in the idle minds.

By the seventh hour of downtime, a conspiracy theory spread amongst the workers. It seemed the timing was too perfect. Was this contaminated soul planted? Punch doubted it. She had heard of a celestial virus causing problems elsewhere, but nothing grand enough to be alarmed over. She found disgust in their overreacting to the soul virus and their lack of response with the angel attack. Punch left the mill with her bag of tears. She journeyed away from all the soulmills and out into the black fields, not knowing how long she would be gone or if she would ever return. The sparkling glitter of souls winked at her from high up in the dark, crying sky. She could feel droplets of rain on her cheeks. Punch imagined, as she gazed at the twinkling sky, that every soul out there belonged to someone who was now deceased. It was a bittersweet spectacle to behold. These were the souls that got away. No soulmill or angel could catch them now. Punch wanted to get away too. The souls reminded her of the stars back home.

Punch approached what appeared to be a disheveled vagabond, and next to him, a rickety old machine made of wheels, pulleys and other various odds and ends. He stared intently at the ground before him, jumping when she cleared her throat to let him know she was there. She waved at him. He quickly pulled a sheet over the bathtub beside him, but not before Punch saw it was filled bright with souls. He was obviously a Purgy who had gone the route of a freelancer and this was one of his private portals.

"It's okay," she affirmed. "I just needed to walk for a bit."

Sensing she was not a threat, the old Purgy nodded and tended his machine, which was set up to fish for souls at a portal that appeared to Punch to no longer be there.

"Did you make that?" She drew close to the machine. "Fascinating!"

"It does not perform like it first did," said the stranger.

"Any luck with the fishing?" she asked.

"This spot... when it's good, it's good."

She noticed a tarp forming a canopy on the other side of the tub. It was his tent. A pillow and blanket lay neatly folded inside. Everyone older who worked the soulmills had a certain smell. It was impossible to describe, for it was neither bad nor good. He had a faint version of it. Punch too, wondered if she had that smell. It was the smell of compressed souls. She heard about these guys, the ones that the soulmills spit out. He became the unfair victim that such soulmill infrastructures brought on.

"Would you like a place to stay? With this rain, you may catch a cold." Punch thought he could take her place back at the mill. The portal opened wide and bright under her. Lightening struck the portal, bull's eye and Punch was swallowed whole. The stranger, hidden now behind his tub, peeked at the ground where his new friend had stood only a second ago. She was no longer there. His fishing machine, like a horse with rigor mortis, crashed to the ground.

Colorado 1964

An unsteady hiccup of cobalt-blue currents clothed Punch as she lay on the floor of John's study at Rackle's Tub. She picked herself up, eyes trying desperately to adjust to the three dimensional perspective. The disillusion caused her to throw up. Unfortunately, unlike her tears, her vomit had no marketplace value. Stomach slosh from Purgalapudlian grown grubs. She decided to lay there until normalcy returned. It didn't take long and the details of the room became clearer. Dust was thick everywhere. A moth, long hollowed-out of its moist body, now just a shell. The entire floor was a junkyard of roach shells, moth wings, dead skin and fly heads. Her blue, electrical aura had now disappeared. Home again, she rose and made her way to the window. She coughed, sending dust particles airborne. Spiders had taken over the interior decorating all over the window, making it hard to see through. She wiped the surface clean with her sleeve.

"Oh, no...this is not my home..." she left the room.

Punch stepped out into the chilly, Colorado evening. One must have thought she was dressed for a costume party with her Victorian meets Purgalapudlian dress. Peering through an iron gate that wasn't there before, but clearly had weathered the years, she became stock-still. Outside, roads were no longer dirt, but paved black. Lots across the street that were once empty fields, had now grown tall, healthy buildings. There were no horse-drawn carts, but four-wheeled, metal machines parked all along the curb and rumbling down the street at high speeds -steam coming out from little pipes at the back with an oil-like smell. A few people walked about in peculiar clothing. She coughed from the thickness of the air and looked back at her own building. Tears dripped from her emotionally squeezed eyes. She opened the gate and shuffled to the sidewalk. Street lights, telephone poles, billboards, street signs -they all looked so...different. Even the trash looked...different. To an inhabitant of the 20th century such trash as fast food wrappers and soda cups, cigarette butts and the sun-burnt gum, now a black dot on the sidewalk was common place. But to Punch, even the air was a new kind of foreign.

"I'm lost," she said. After she wiped her face, the gold on her fingers added to her dementia. What the fuck am I? She thought. Her reaction to a changed home triggered a heavier panic than her stay in Purgalapudlia. Disorientation laughed madness into her ears and tempted her to run. She braced herself against a parking meter and with a collection of deep breaths, she returned to Rackle's Tub. To run amok wouldn't solve a damn thing. She had to be wise in her new home, as she had been in Purgalapudlia. Fighting in the ring had taught her the importance of having a cool and disciplined mind. A passing airplane caused her to duck low. She had never heard thunder like that.

Punch, at first, ventured out into society in small increments of time, exhausted from the bombardment of the 20th century. She took notes of her discoveries, terrified, yet thrilled beyond her senses to absorb her new world. She had the entire factory to herself, helping ground her. In the study, she made another important discovery. On the desk, under a layer of dust, was a folder with her name. Opening it, she found the deed to the property. John had signed it over to her. Intentionally leaving the date off.

* * * * *

Her first year was a hypersensitive one. The various different smells, sounds, technology, styles, manners and attitudes were a little overwhelming. Punch had the advantages of youth, intelligence and immortality to help her adapt to this transition. A less hardy woman would have perished by now. In the privacy of her many rooms, she cried. The sounds bounced off the walls in the hallways of her factory. It was time to relearn language. Her America had become a foreign country. Blessed with beauty, Punch found acceptance into most social circles, but remained a private person. No boxing. Men were completely enamored by her and women were jealous. She used her awkward charm to smooth over disputes. She came across as manic to some, because everything modern thrilled her. Even disposable ballpoint pens and electric can openers amused her. A societal sponge, Punch sat in cafes, listening to conversations. The new sounds from 1964 coming out of a jukebox was a challenge for her to restrain from crying. She stood, hypnotized by televisions playing at storefront windows. An entire day was easily spent watching TV. People passing didn't find it too unusual, but the salesman did. When he closed shop and turned off the power, she snapped out of her trance with the box. She looked at the salesman, the night sky, and back to the TV before making her way home.

She *loved* the idea of girls wearing jeans. Clothing was so much easier on women than it had been in Victorian times. Which led to another obstacle she faced within the first month of that year. Money. Inflation. Most of her money was exactly where she left it in 1892. The format of cash had changed in the last 72 years. She had Treasury Notes with Chief Justice John Marshall on them. She also had silver and gold certificates of various amounts, but in 1964, silver certificates were no longer redeemable for silver dollars. And the Gold Reserve Act of 1934 forced owners to sell their gold to the U.S. Treasury. The value of gold had gone up since 1892, but had remained immune to inflation for most of the 20th century at thirty five dollars for one troy ounce.

Punch collected her tears in glass tubes and rather than taking it to an assayer, she decided to test it for herself. She grabbed a dish and placed a shot glass in the center. She filled the dish with water. The shot glass filled with sulfuric acid. She carefully placed the gold into the glass. She cried her way to the Federal Reserve Bank and opened an account. Her tears were now in the form of little gold bullions. She also vaulted her gold overseas with central banks and sophisticated investors. She made herself cry by any means. Movies, TV, music, self-inflicted wounds, funerals for children, weddings and memories. Physical pain proved to be much more difficult to weep over than psychological pain. Anxiety over the new world helped. It wasn't long before she produced a small fortune. In her purse she carried a tear collecting kit of glass tubes, a chrome funnel-like device that fit over her cheeks and under her eyes, cork caps for the tubes and a cloth to wipe up. She carried it in a small, black leather case which resembled a men's toiletry bag.

* * * * *

She took the opportunity to travel. Her wealth attracted the attention of undesirables: Irish gangs, Italian mobsters, and local criminals. Her cleverness in hiding, and her chameleon-like abilities, allowed her to move within such dangerous enemies. A good game of hide and seek was always welcome, and having dealt with troubling people all her life, she was good at it. On the flip side, when it came to Punch...they had no idea who they were dealing with.

Punch toured the country under an alias. She marveled at the idea of flying. Terrifying, yet incredible. Imagine, all that weight of steel and passengers, such a mass, defying gravity, lifting higher than any bird! And feeling the powerful roar and speed of takeoff, planting her against the seat as they ascended into the clouds was so exciting, she crawled over another passenger's lap just to look out the window at the shrinking earth and large, shaving cream, clouds!

New York 1965

A young Johnny Cash type, sat behind the wheel in his black Cadillac Coupe de Ville, parked in front of a clothing boutique. He bit into a large sandwich that he held in his left hand, while his right arm stretched over the top of the passenger seat. The wooden door to the bar nearby crashed open. A young woman ran out and into the clothing boutique joining several mannequins in the store window. She grabbed a hat and struck a pose. In a matter of seconds, two pimps, soaking wet, flew out of the bar. One bled from a broken nose, which he painfully pinched to stop the bleeding. The other ran to the Cadillac. The "mannequin" watched them with anticipation from the corner of her eyes. In order to pacify his laughter, the Cadillac driver took a huge bite from his sandwich. The pimp bent down to his eye-line from across the passenger side.

"Hey. You see a little brunette woman run by?"

With his mouth full, the man in the Cadillac nodded.

A saleswoman approached the new mannequin and tapped her on the leg. In perfect mannequin form, she didn't react. She tapped again...

"Excuse me..." the saleswoman had no inkling of the danger Punch was facing outside the window. "Can I help you...?"

The Cadillac driver pointed the opposite direction down the street. The nose bleeder, already faced that way, took off running.

"Hey, thanks pal," the other pimp said. He joined his friend in the pursuit. Punch watched them leave. She looked to the man in the sedan, who waved her over. As she stepped down, the saleswoman grabbed her hat. The man in the sedan started up the car. But, before the pimps got out of view, they spotted Punch getting in. The driver stepped on the gas and cranked up the Beethoven. She giggled and looked back at the two, who had given up the chase.

"Thank you so much," she said. He smiled and looked into his rearview mirror.

"I'd say you got yourself out of a pickle. What the hell did you do to get two pimps riled up?"

She examined the red interior of the car, all the gauges, steering wheel and violin music coming from the speakers...

"What?"

"They looked pretty upset. What did you do?"

"Oh, you wouldn't believe me."

"You're certainly not dressed for hustling."

"I'm not a prostitute," she said.

"Yeah, I didn't think so."

"I've got a lot of people after me. I make mittens. His didn't have thumbs. He was upset."

"Okay." He stared at her, trying to unwrap her oddness, while taking quick road checks. "You're a kooky girl. Cute, but kooky. So where are we headed?"

"I don't know. I'm not driving." She pulled out a cigarette.

"Coffee and blueberry pie."

"Lovely. But let's go uptown."

"You got it."

"I got what?"

"What?" he asked.

"What do I have?"

"I don't follow."

"Well of course. You're driving." She broke into another giggle.

"Hey, Kooky, what's your name?"

She lit her cigarette and blew the smoke from the side of her mouth. "Glendora."

"Well Glendora, I'm Kipling. Pleasure to make your acquaintance," he shook her hand. "How long you been in New York?"

She put on a pair of large Jacqueline Kennedy sunglasses from her small purse. Her incognito look. "Not long. And you?"

"Just long enough to visit this colored friend of mine. He's the best piano man I've ever heard. And also to break the car in. Brand spankin' new."

"I've never been with a colored man," she volunteered.

"Neither have I."

She laughed. A red light brought them to a stop.

"What is kooky?"

Clean through the window, a bullet pierced his skull, which laid his head to rest on the car's horn. The adjacent sedan was opening doors. Mobsters lept out of the nearby sedan to give chase to a now, long gone, Punch. Her sprinting legs ripping the skirt at the seams.

Medicine Of Solitude

Too many enemies to be comfortable, Punch returned from her travels, back home to her red-bricked citadel. Rackle's Tub was the one place where no one bothered her. She decided to remodel the place. The factory remained shut and locked from public entry. Lights were always on during the night. The gates and surrounding walls, overgrown with vines and bushes, were impenetrable obstacles for prying eyes. Fortunately, most people didn't take interest in old buildings in that part of town, they were everywhere. Year after year, bills were met with a call to the bank. In some sort of fluke in the system, Rackle's Tub escaped the radar in paying property tax for years. It was as if the place didn't exist. Squatters and vagabonds never considered entering because the place felt like it was busy in a quiet sort of way. Gardening services piled their flyers and business cards like little insults. But, it took only one thunderstorm to wash them away.

Meet The Zeros

"Every man, gay or straight, has had a crush on Marilyn Monroe at some point in his life." Shard would often begin road trips with such absolute statements. The car pulled into a gas station, thirsty. A high price for its cocktail of octane and tonic.

Traffic slowed. A road flair dropped to the ground. The lights of both highway patrol and the paramedics flashed. Covered bodies were rolled away in gurneys. No survivors.

"That looks pretty bad," Aster spotted the mangled car.

"It's an older sedan," said James.

"Yeah, you're right," Shard strained to look from his disappearing angle. The axle and underpinnings of the sedan looked familiar. Comfortable in the back seat, Ticktock was out. Picking up speed, the boys marathoned it all day through state lines. The deserts turned into grasslands that turned into foothills, then became mountains.

Welcome to Colorful Colorado.

The Cadillac zipped past the sign by the road, Shard the only one to witness the entry to the state, smiled. The rest of the boys were dream-drooling.

The Cadillac finally pulled into the parking lot of a hotel. Shard dropped off James at the lobby and parked. A slammed '98 Honda Civic, so lowered it looked like it slid to a stop alongside the Caddy, subwoofer rattling the teeth in everyone's head, caused Shard and the boys to look. With Japanese script decal on the sides of the car and a large dart board spray-painted on the hood, the car shined in its ghetto flair. One of the guys inside got out and made his way to the lobby. The driver, Steve, a slender Japanese American, spiked hair, all smiles, got out of the car.

"The Zeros," Aster said. Shard got out.

Steve recognized the boys and their signature car. "The Clocks. Shard, what's up man?"

"Steve. Hey, what's shakin'?"

The booming bass volume lowered and the other two Zeros got out of the car. These guys were the Young Ones, Tokyo style. The Punk, the Raver, the Playboy and Mr. Hip Hop. Three of them were Japanese and the fourth, a *Krazy* Korean.

Steve, the leader, looked like a dark raver in his black trench coat, black jeans and the tons of hair product he used.

Clean, calculated and comfortable, without being anal about it, Jeff, the playboy, dressed in pin-striped suit vests with matching slacks, chain watch and proper hygiene to the fullest degree.

Toto, in his red-plaid pants and suspenders, the punk, had bleached hair, more orange than blonde, shaven on the sides. Lips pierced and body, slender with a cat-like form. His soft-spoken nature contradicted his loud-mouthed wardrobe.

Wes, the hip hop Korean wore expensive, baggy jeans, high end T-shirts with brazen logos and a pristine ball cap, turned sideways.

He, like Ticktock, was hyper as a wolverine on the prowl.

Aster got out of the car and joined the others. Wes and Toto walked around the Cadillac as if it were a museum exhibit. Ticktock inside the car sent Toto spinning away with laughter. Wes continued to stare at him, shaking his head. Ticktock was naked.

"Shit. Is there room in that back seat for two?" said Wes.

Ticktock stuck his head out the window. "Hey, you beastly brute!" He got out of the car, holding his shirt over his groin. Everyone winced except Shard. "Shard! What are these bloody bastards doing here?"

"We're here to win the million, mutha fucka!" Wes slapped Ticktock's ass. He bent over for more. Wes grabbed his thighs and thrusted.

"We should've gotten them their own room," said Shard.

"No," said Steve. "We should've left them home with food and water."

Ticktock jumped back in the car.

"What?!" said Wes. "He was ready to go. And when you put a hole in front of me, my instincts kick in, you know what I'm sayin'? I'm like, Hell yeah. I'm pluggin' that shit."

"I'm riding shotgun," said Aster.

"Where's James?" asked Steve.

"He's checkin' us in. We just drove from Los Angeles," said Shard.

"Shit. In that thing? And it didn't break down?" Steve teased.

"Hey. This is a classic...thing," said Shard.

"Well, we were on the road already," said Steve. "We've been doing better on the road than home. How did you guys find out about this tournament?"

"It was an accident for us," Shard said.

"Yeah, it was the funniest thing," Steve explained. "We come out of playing slots at Rio in Vegas and I found this parking ticket on my window. I was pissed, because I didn't park illegally. But when I opened it, it was the invitation to the Rackle's Tub dart tournament."

"Really?"

"Yeah. Isn't that weird?"

"Yeah. That's... different. Wow."

"A million bucks. We're there," Wes injected.

"The Zeros! Grrrr! My bank account!" James and Jeff joined the group. "Let's meet at the pub tonight," James suggested.

"Let's do it!" said Steve.

"Have you guys been there yet?" asked James.

"We drove by it. It's fuckin' crazy!" Wes said. "There's a huge fuckin' bathtub hanging on the front of the building. You can't miss it. The building is old as fuck, you know? But, it's like big and shit!"

From the back seat of the Cadillac, a clothed Ticktock held out a bottle of vodka. "Let's do it baby, yeah!" said Ticktock.

Toto grabbed the bottle and took a swig. "Don't give it to the Korean," said Toto.

"What the fuck?!" Wes made his way over and grabbed the bottle, wiping it before drinking.

"He's a lightweight," said Toto.

"I am," agreed Wes. "Plus my face turns red. But I'm gonna get shit-faced tonight, mutha fucka!"

"Yes!" agreed Ticktock. "Especially during the tournament. I heard you play better drunk."

"Fuck you!" said Wes.

"Guys..." James jerked his head toward the security guard watching them. Everyone got into their respective rides and quietly rolled to their rooms.

* * * * *

Welcome to Rackle's Tub, tournament of darts! was stamped on the breast of a rubber ducky. There were a total of four. Two per bed. Next to the TV was a wet bar and fridge. Shard explored the little bottles of liquor in the bar. A rubber ducky sqeaked as it hit him on the butt. He ignored it, nose still checking inventory. Ticktock jumped on the bed.

"Be careful!" said Aster. "There could be bedbugs." He put on a pair of surgical gloves and lifted the bed spread.

"Must you start that again?" Ticktock got up.

"You'll thank me later. In fact, I wouldn't lay on the bed spread.

You'll find fecal matter, blood, harmful microbes, semen..." he pulled out the sheet and dropped to his knees for closer inspection. Ticktock lay on the other bed.

"Room service." James was on the hotel phone as he unbuttoned his shirt. "Yeah, I'd like to order dinner." A rubber ducky hit him on the head. Ticktock grabbed another duck and threw it at Aster, but Shard blocked it with a punch, redirecting its flight to James. When Aster finished inspection with the bed he went to the other one.

Dinner arrived. The four were seated around a small, crowded table eating. Tiny empty liquor bottles were piled amongst the plates of food. James pointed with a wad of fries. "I think from that wall to that bed is about seven feet."

"Yeah, we'll hang the board up on that wall," Shard agreed. Ticktock walked over to the wall to examine a painting, an abstract, sponge-painted pastel, '80s style decor. He examined the frame.

"They fuckin' nailed this picture to the wall!" Ticktock said. "How daft is that? Like someone is gonna steal this shit of a painting."

After dinner, Shard pulled out a flat, black case and lay it on the bed. Inside was a dart board. After placing a protective matt on the wall, he hung the dart board over the picture, securing it with suction cups. James pulled out his dart case. Inside were four tungsten darts with sponsor's and team names printed on the flights.

"Tungsten. Ninety percent," said James as he pulled out one of the darts. He looked to the board and gave Shard a nod. Shard handed Aster a bandana in which he used to blindfold James. James brought his arm up, aimed the dart and threw it. Bull's-eye! They let out a cheer. James pulled off his blindfold, smiled and shot Aster a wink. Ticktock pulled out his zippo and lit up a smoke.

"Can I see the light?" Aster reached for the zippo. Ticktock gave him the cigarettes too. "No thanks." Aster grabbed a chair and set it under a fire sprinkler up on the ceiling. He stepped on the chair and opened the flame in the zippo.

"NO!" everyone shouted. Ticktock jumped on the chair and grabbed the lighter.

"How do we know if it works?" Aster reasoned. "I don't want to die in a fire."

"Well bloody Christ, are you fuckin' kidding me?!" Ticktock pushed Aster off the chair. "You fuckin' looney bastard. You start that shit, we'll leave ya in the car."

"Come here, son," said Shard to Aster. "We need to gel and look after each other. Those sprinklers, by law, have to be inspected periodically. Don't waste energy on that shit. All right? This competition is going to throw many distractions at us. So we need to maintain that sharp focus we do so well. This goes for everybody." Ticktock jumped down and returned the chair. "Don't expect an easy win here," continued Shard. "That would be foolish thinking. You guys know from here on out, we'll be going up against the best. If the Zeros are here, you know it'll be a challenge already. But, at the same time, we are more than capable of putting this tournament away. It is within our grasp. We have the manpower to destroy."

"Yeah," said Ticktock.

"Shut up," said Shard. The others nodded. "And also, just as important..." Shard raised his empty, mini-whiskey bottle. "Let's enjoy this opportunity. Let's have fun. These next couple of days will never come again. Here we are, fuckin' Colorado! In a dart tournament! For a million dollars! With your best friends. I mean, fuck. If this isn't a moment to remember..."

"How many bottles did you have?" James interrupted. Everyone laughed.

"I lost count at five," said Shard.

"That was a good pep talk," said James.

"Yeah. Thanks," said Aster. Shard nodded.

Industrious Neurotransmitters

Her Victorian world was forever gone. Not that Punch was looking to go back, but Purgalapudlia would be the closest thing to it now. Punch locked herself into the factory for peace and for a better understanding of who she was and what she had become. Not only were her receptor sites working overtime with environmental stimuli, she was also becoming aware of her new self. She acquired an unusual craving that couldn't be satisfied so easily or obviously. It was a hunger for something and when she ate until her belly was full, the cravings didn't go away. It was strangely parallel to her first sexual arousal from womanhood. It bothered her enough to keep her up at night. Maybe she was lacking a vitamin that her new diet wasn't providing. It was an unfamiliar sensation growing from the primitive temporal lobe and limbic areas of her brain.

A large pad of paper had architectural sketches that Punch busied herself with one night in her study. She broke off the tip of the pencil on her page...again. Why was she pressing so hard? She put her pencil down to rub her eyes and her temple. She pushed away from her desk, arms still sprawled out in front of her while her head dropped to her lap. She clawed at her desk, the page snagging under her nails. A violent and savage blood, boiling, brought her to her feet, her body fighting to restore equilibrium. It was an intense desire for something unknown that she never fed and was now voicing itself with an uncontrollable tantrum. It tasted of metallic anxiety, and her flesh became a placid gray. She acted as if she was handed a new mouth, one size too big. She adjusted her jaws for a fit. Teeth, sharper, by evidence of a cut tongue. The blood of which, drove her frenzy into a downward spiral of instability. What felt like numb scabs or warts on her knuckles, grew outward and sharp, becoming claws. Her denim, blue shirt and jeans tightened as her body required more oxygen. She could feel the little tugging from her claws and teeth, pulled farther out from the bone with pleasurable growing pains. She killed the desk lamp with the swat of her hand. Every fiber of muscle puffed with an ache as if she'd been lifting weights. The discovery her halo eyes made next was a doorway -floating near the ceiling. It became visible to her for the first time. It was the same color as most of the glow-in-the-dark toys you find anywhere, but intense. She reached for it as it collapsed like an open flower welcoming her in.

No collector awaited on the other side. She was strangely disappointed. The Purgy skies were still grey. Hidden in the black grass, a couple of Purggies rose. They were itching for a fight until they noticed she was looking and feeling a little monstrous. They backed away at her approach.

"Oh, fuck me-" she turned to one of the Purggies. She braced her hands over her knees like a tired basketball player, head down. "I don't know what's happening to me," she said.

With a nod, one of the Purggies produced cuffs. "You have claws-" He cautiously grabbed her wrists and brought them behind her back.

"What are you doing?"

"Just for our safety. Then I'll take 'em off."

"You think I'm going to hurt you?"

"I really don't want to take a chance. Please." He put the cuffs in place and led her to a parked bathtub close by. The others joined them.

* * * * *

A bazaar-like establishment was the perfect place to quench her hunger. Punch faded in and out as she was escorted now by foot, down a busy street. Sweat coming out of her in buckets. Her temperature rising, she became acutely aware of multi-eyed angels watching her as she passed. She was brought to an alleyway, where her captors uncuffed her. On one of the buildings, a badly dented, rusty, steel door appeared out of nowhere. The Purggies knocked. A large angel opened the door.

"What business do you have?" he asked.

"We've brought a contender," the Purgy said. The angel looked over Punch, whose sweat was now glistening from her face. He laughed.

"She can hardly stand," he said.

Punch grabbed the angel and ripped into his neck. The Purggies ran as if rockets were tied to their feet. The angel wrestled her to the ground, he couldn't stop her from shredding him apart. Eyes scratched out. Blood swallowed. She tore open his rib cage and shoveled his oyster-like softness into her mouth, the pearl of his soul, glowing in her throat like a musically sweet fruit in all its pastel flavored electricity. This was an alpha male, rich in souls. Punch sat on her knee, hunched over, bloodied and satisfied. No one else seemed to have noticed, for this alleyway was further darkened by the dreary weather. Punch relaxed. She studied her hands. Claws were gone and with it, the desperate element that drove her to attack. Rain poured down as she slammed her back to the wall. She took advantage of the shower to clean the debris from her face.

A couple bathtubs rode past. Occupants carrying supplies for the marketplace. Purgalapudlia didn't escape change, although not to the extent of back home. It was heavier populated. And it had a run-down appearance. Many shops and buildings were without light. Perhaps it was true about the energy crisis. A statue in the center of the town square had a strikingly similar appearance to John. As Punch drew near, she had come to find it was John. The plaque below his feet read:

Hail to John Rackle! The Indift of Purgalapudlia!

Already the statue had been vandalized -paint splotched on his groin. How appropriate, she thought. It was now time to pay John Rackle a visit. She vaguely remembered where John's factory was and headed out that way. She crossed through fields and scattered forests, the hike much needed to clear her busy mind. The city behind her soon became a faint glow. Punch squeezed the sore muscles in her arms as she walked. Just up ahead, a new machine resembling a spiral shell, sucking from the ground seemed so out of place. They were everywhere decorating the barren lanscape. These machines, unlike anything she had seen, were attached to pipes that traveled along the ground for a mile or better. Every so many yards of pipe was stamped with a logo -*J.R. Industries*. She ran her fingers over the name. A sharp vibration kicked at her hand.

Another thud followed. A comotion just a hundred yards off was loud enough for Punch to peek over the pipe for a better view. Two bathtubs were parked near and several Purgies were swinging axes down into the pipe. She didn't know if she should confront them or leave. But it was too late. She was spotted. The Purgies stopped their work to watch her. She crawled under the pipe and out the other side to show herself while delicately waving at them.

"It's Punch!" cried one of the workers.

"Yes -it's me!" Surprised, Punch made her way over to the group. The group gathered closer to one another as if they were about to be attacked. The Purgies with axes held them up with both hands. Punch noticed they were her fellow soulmill workers.

"Hey. I'm alone." Punch didn't want to get too close. "You can put down your weapons," she nervously giggled. "What are you guys doing?"

They put down their axes. The elder Purgy of the group stepped forward. "We're taking what's ours." He nodded for the other Purgies to continue chopping.

"Vandalizing property?"

"We've been vandalized! Because of these machines, we are out of work and out of home." The chopping caused Punch to cringe with every hit. "We are now forced to live like nomads. I've already lost half my crew-" Light shot through the cracks of the tube. Other Purgies gathered near with large bags ready to collect the source of the light. Punch's eyes sparkled, the colors moving like fast clouds at the sight of the eminent illumination.

"Stop it -" Punch said under heavy breathing. "I'll talk to John Rackle. Maybe I can help you-"

"Her eyes!" shouted one of the Purgies.

Punch looked at the Purgie questioningly. The others stood back. She hid her face with her hair, then decided it was best to leave.

* * * * *

John Rackle sat clasping a glass of whiskey with both hands, while his eyes, still open, were out of business. His chair faced a dying fire in the fireplace and he stared at the pulsing embers. A noise at his window was dismissed as wind and rain. But a draft slapped his cheek shaking him awake. Punch stood in the room, clothes dripping wet and her eyes reflecting light as if they were polished marble, black with a white dot in the center of both.

"Miss me?"

John dropped his glass and stood panting with whiskey breath. "Punch!" He stepped forward to greet her. "Me lady. Look at you, my love-"

Punch didn't move. "I'm not someone you want to love anymore."

John slowed his approach. He smiled as her eyes returned to normal. "But you are." He embraced her. "Welcome back." He guided her away from the window. "Let's get you dried off you poor little pussycat."

Welcome To The Extraordinary World Of Rackle's Tub

The Cadillac turned into the main strip with the Honda right behind. Blaring out the Cadillac's windows was the song, "*My Generation*" by The Who. The Honda boomed with a trance-techno dance beat. The town resembled Carnaby Street, London, 1965. There were many fashion boutiques, music bars, little bookshops, art galleries and a vibrant nightlife. Gorgeous young people drinking coffee at cafes, smoking, shopping, eating outside in the patio of diners. The strip was alive with artists, poets, musicians, bohemians, lovers, gypsies, all with a youthful energy regardless of age. An old town with new blood.

"This is fuckin' fab," James said while looking out the window, trying to take it all in. "How did we never come here before?"

The boys were looking their best in traditional, three-button suits.

"There she is!" announced Shard.

They approached a large brick building on the corner. Hanging on the front of the building, above the doors was a car-sized bathtub, surrounded in blinking lights. Over the tub, in large scarlet red letters, the name...

Rackle's Tub.

Their articulation, stapled by their thoughts caused a moment of silence. Outside the building, a line of people waited to get in.

"This is more surreal than I imagined," Aster said. Ticktock gave Aster a loving pinch. A man flagged them in to a cobblestone driveway. Up ahead were two tunnels, side by side, that went through the building to a large courtyard on the other side. It was as if the car were air particles inhaled by the building's nose. A plaque, with the Rackle's Tub symbol, emblazoned in gold, hung between the two tunnels like a mighty crest. The Honda followed them to a packed parking structure in the back. Men with green-lit flashlights directed them to empty spaces. The Zeros and the Clocks gathered outside their cars and found another, shorter line in the back, under an ornate awning. The sign above the door read:

Welcome to the bathhouse. Your baptism awaits. Leave your faith at the door, along with your coat and hat.

Behind a wooden podium by the door, a tall, slender greeter, dressed in the Edwardian-style with his long black jacket and black stove pipe hat checked people in. The Clocks and the Zeros, as well as others in line, were unusually quiet, as if they were entering a library or a church. Perfume, with an aged, yellow dust and machine grease, faint as it was, silenced them further. After the greeter checked them in, the wooden, ship-deck doors opened on their own accord.

Inside, a cool breeze carried faint notes from a Hammond B-3 organ. It had a sick, faraway circus sound. The boys entered the dimly lit hallway, the doors closing behind them. Marbled mirrors on red velvet walls gave a stereotypical haunted mansion ambiance. At the end of the long hallway was where the magic began. The restaurant.

When the Clocks and Zeros entered, their senses had been annihilated for new ones. In the center of the lobby, a giant pond with rotating, floating bathtub booths felt like a dream. Overlooking the pond were balconies with more bathtub seating. Everything was bathtubs. The salad bar was a tub filled with ice. Some tubs held cold drinks and at the bar was a tub with several different faucets, each for a different draft of beer on tap. There

were people everywhere. A man, dressed as a jester, was feeling
the walls as if he were reading Braille. Before words could be
vocalized, two cute hostesses, in white shirts and black skirts, split
the two teams, taking them to different sections of the restaurant.
They could only wave goodbye to one another before finding their
respective seats. Both teams had their own private bathtub booth,
larger than normal bathtubs, lined with cushioned red leather seats.
Each booth had its own shower curtain for privacy. Chrome shower
racks, soap and sponge holders held ketchup, mustard, salt and
pepper. Napkins hung from towel bars. One tall shower head was
used for a light over the table, while another was used as a coat rack
and hanger. The hostess passed out menus that looked more like
comic books.

"You are free to order drinks now," she told the Clocks.
"However, the food, I would advise you order after the
inauguration and short tour." They nodded continuing to absorb
their surroundings. "Your waiter will be here shortly. Welcome
to Rackle's Tub! Enjoy!" And with that, she disappeared into the
bustle of people.

All over the walls and high ceilings were pipes. Some chrome,
some brass, copper and some white. The walls were painted with
murals and poetry; magazine and newspaper clippings. Quotes were
written on the walls. Every generation had left a stamp of their
reflections. Movie posters, political propaganda advertisements,
band photos and legendary album covers. Some of the table tops
were carved with initials and vows of love from as far back as 1966.

James got the impulse to hit the bar. "I'll be back with drinks,"
he said as he got up and left.

Near the bar, a small live band played a Victorian era concerto.
Punch watched James grab a seat at the bar to listen while he waited
to order. It was linked up to another bar stool. Punch quickly made
her way over and sat on that stool, their shoulders uncomfortably
touching. James looked at her as he pulled his seat away from hers.
She looked down at his seat and back at him.

"Are you afraid of me?" she asked. He nodded and winked.

"I saved that seat for you," he said.

"How do you know this isn't already my seat?" she shot back.

"Because, I reserved the entire bar a year ago for this date. And that included booking the band," answered James.

"I fucked the band. Every player up there."

"Not every player," replied James. "I play the triangle and I've never had the pleasure."

She laughed. "You know, you can order drinks at your table."

"Oh, I wouldn't have bumped into you then."

"You would have sooner or later," she said.

"I prefer sooner."

The two locked eyes and James was hit by a hurricane. Her hair was tied back, white sleeves rolled up, she nervously kicked one foot, over and over against the bar as a school girl would have done. She smelled of a thousand wonderful things.

"I gotta go," said Punch as she got up. James couldn't speak. She bravely kissed his cheek and left. His skin flushed.

"What the fuck?" he cleared his tightened throat and breathed in the last of the fragrance that lingered of her. He closed his eyes as he still felt the lips of that strange girl.

Upon returning empty-handed to his booth, James, with zombie eyes, slid into his seat.

"What did you do?" asked Shard, "Drink it all on the way over?"

"Huh? Oh, yes. Shit. Sorry. I met a fantastic bird at the bar."

"Must have been a thirsty one," continued Shard.

"She absorbed me in an instant."

"And the drinks," said Ticktock.

"Should we be worried about you?" asked Shard.

"...She was devastatingly beautiful."

"Yeah," Ticktock responded. "We got a problem. I've never seen him gaga over a girl this bad."

"No. I'm fine. Let's have a drink." Everyone paused.

"What a fuckin' brilliant idea!" Ticktock exploded. "Why don't you go get us some? Goddamn it."

"Don't get caught in the tender trap," reasoned Aster. Everyone looked at Aster. After another moment... "How would you describe her?"

"No, no! Shut the fuck up!" shouted Ticktock. " Forget her. Drinks, let's go! And I'll get the next round. Jesus, bloody Christ." Everyone laughed. James got up.

"Come on boys," said James, "Since when have you had to worry about me?"

James made his way back to the bar. As he waited for his order, he glanced down at the bar table. He found a quote which read:

For while I gazed,
In transport tossed,
My breath was gone,
My voice was lost.
My bosom glowed:
The subtle flame,
Ran quick through all,
My vital frame...
        -Sappho

He lifted his head and looked over his shoulder and then across the bar to see if Punch was anywhere, then carefully carried the drinks back to his booth.

* * * * *

James, warm from a good scotch buzz, entered the bathroom. The sound of cascading water relaxed him further. He hit the first urinal and began business. Written on the wall, in front of his nose, Emerson:

The surest poison is time.

As James finished, something caught his peripheral. A giant man who must have been nine feet tall was doing his business. His shaggy, caveman head, stuck out of the stall, looking as if he were wearing a metal suit. His name was Og, which also happened to be the initial sound people made when they first encountered him. Og! James froze. The cascading water stopped. Then it poured out again. It was Og's piss and it sounded more like a hail storm. Og flushed to prevent it from flooding over and shot James a look of indifference. James washed his hands, pulled out his black, plastic comb to fix his hair a little. He looked back at the pissing Og and nodded. Then he left.

* * * * *

The dart players gathered for orientation in a large ballroom. The room was packed. The Clocks and Zeros stood together. On stage, a man attached a camera to a tripod. He approached the dark oak podium and spoke into the chrome bullet of a microphone.

"Hello... can we get everyone together for a shoot?" the camera man politely ordered. "Just squeeze together for one minute." He positioned his camera, looking through the viewfinder. From backstage, Punch ran to the front of the group right as he clicked. Flash! He shook his head.

"Perfect!" Punch shouted. "Now let's get one more, with a jolly cheer!" Everyone shouted, with raised drinks in the air.

The photographer clicked his camera. "Good!" he said. Punch ran backstage again, curtain swaying.

"My God, I saw her on YouTube!" Aster realized. "She knocked some girl out."

"Really?" asked Ticktock.

"Thank you! First dart tournament!" said the cameraman. The crowd cheered. "We'll hang this in the lobby." The cameraman looked stage left and then stage right. "Where did she go? Punch -? She was just here-- the curly hair. Did you know she was a boxer? It's how she got her name." Punch now stood stage left, behind the curtain. "Oh here she is."

She shook her head. "Don't stop. You're doing a good job."

"Did I mention she's Hell on wheels?" He stood aside and pointed to her as she approached the podium.

"Thank you, for that." She looked to the audience. "Hello everyone and welcome to Rackle's Tub!" The crowd cheered again. "Those of you with drink in hand, hold 'em up high!" Everyone shouted with their drinks to the Heavens.

"That's her!" James prodded Shard. "That's the crazy bird at the bar!" The boys didn't know what to make of her.

"She's cute," said Shard, eyes never leaving her.

"As you know..." she continued, "My name is Punch and I'll be your hostess. I want everyone to feel at home here. If you haven't already discovered, our bar is stocked with every beer, stout, ale ever made. Foreign. Domestic. Micro. Regional. Macro... in other words..." she untied her hair and let it all hang down after a shake. "God damn. If alcohol is a weakness, I don't know what to tell you." The crowd hooted and howled with drinks in the air. The cameraman rudely grabbed the microphone from her.

"I found um, I found our house special. It was a bottle of Crompton and Roy--"

Punch gently shook her head. "That's not beer." She covered her eyes a moment before turning to him. "Did you really drink it?"

"Yeah."

She looked away, embarrassed for him. "Oh no, why?"

"I mean it wasn't the greatest tasting..."

"Well, for varnish remover, it tastes great!"

The audience laughed.

"What?"

She gently pulled the microphone from his fingers and placed it back in its holder.

"Those bottles have been sitting upstairs by a window for about... a hundred years."

"Well you had them by the bar-"

"On the floor. Next to the trash. Do you randomly pick up strange bottles and drink from them?"

"No. I saw the label and just helped myself."

"So you didn't even pay for it."

He became flushed and awkwardly shuffled to the edge of the stage, shaking his head.

"Where are you going now...to have another bottle?" she said. She sensed his humiliation and felt cruel for teasing him, especially when an audience backed her up with laughter. "Wait. Come here." He stopped and turned. She walked over to him and embraced him. "I'm sorry Mr. Cameraman. I'll get you a twelve pack of whatever you want."

"No, all right. Okay," he assured her with the shrug of his shoulders.

"I can be a real bitch sometimes. *Hell on wheels.*" The audience clapped. "I'm sorry." She returned to the podium as he took a seat. "Oh, fuck me. Okay. Did I mention I'll be your warm and friendly hostess for this tournament?" The crowd laughed and screamed, whistled and cheered! The ones without drinks applauded. "Don't ask me how I gathered you all here. But, through an act of fate, I've collected the best dart players from all over the land. Feel privileged. If you are standing before me, it means you're great! With the exception of a couple filler teams, I won't mention who, you guys and gals are second to none. The winner will receive... you're all here to win, right?!" The crowd exploded with stadium-like noises. "The grand prize, a gift certificate to Denny's. All you can eat!" The crowd booed! "All right, fine." She looked to stage right and signaled to someone for approval, then nodded. "Okay, here's what we'll do... I just got the thumbs up... Two, gift certificates...to Denny's." They chuckled and booed at her. "Oh God. You know, there was a vicious, cruel rumor of a million dollar prize..." The crowd interrupted with Yeah! "Okay. Fine. A million it is! The winner of this tournament will receive a check for one million dollars!"

The audience started shouting... Punch. Punch. Punch. Punch...

"Listen. One million!" they silenced. "Now that's a lot of fucking money, for some bar-fly to swing his arm at a wall. But then there are those who toss balls into baskets and make ten times as much money. Am I right?" They clapped. "And the winners... on a serious note, will take me out. Maybe the first night, and yes, there will be more than one night, we could go horseback riding and a picnic. The rest of the week, I'll leave it up to you." The crowd loved her. Punch. Punch. Punch. Punch... Her smile was frame-able. "This is our first tournament. Thank you for being here. It is my honor, truly. You want to do this again next year?" The crowd had out-of-control volume. "Good luck!" She blew a kiss to them and with a wave, left the stage. The crowd continued to pulverize the sound barrier.

James was a little shook up by her presentation. Oh wow, she's a handful he thought. An all-girl dart team made eye contact with the Clocks. The boys finally noticed. James winked at them, but then looked back to the stage, as if Punch had never left.

* * * * *

The dart teams had been broken down for the tours. One hostess per four teams. The Clocks were fortunate enough to have Punch as their tour guide. The Zeros had someone else lead them around. They parted ways once again.

Punch took the group down a hallway. "All the tubs in this place were made by Mr. Rackle. In 1892, John Rackle founded Rackle's Tub. Once a short-lived brewery, it was then turned into a bathtub factory. Roll-rim, claw foot tubs. Those were the standard tubs of the day. But what really made him famous was his main line of tubs. He was a real playboy. Those huge tubs most of you were sitting in for dinner are his famous orgy tubs. He was rejected in England for the idea, so he came to America to fulfill his vision. And that's why I celebrate this place."

"Bathroom?" a player asked.

"No, it's bathtubs," she said.

"No, where's the bathroom?"

"Oh, shit. Not here. Obviously. On your way to the front lobby you'll see it. Anyone else? Good." She led the jovial group once again, minus one player. "The only real competition Rackle's Tub had was from Mott Iron Works with some of the first porcelain enameled tubs. While they made tubs for the White House, John Rackle made tubs for the whore house. Now some believed this factory was merely a distraction or even a cover up for John's true passion. Physics. He spent countless hours problem solving with the use of equations. Unfortunately, his theorems were so ahead of their time, he was violently and shamefully attacked causing him to suffer nervous breakdowns throughout his life." She stopped, turned and walked the opposite direction, cutting her group in half as they got out of her way. They followed her. "How are we all doing?"

The response was positive. The group was eager to learn more. She stopped.

"I'm not lost, in case you're wondering," she said. She turned around once more and cut through the group again. James delighted in seeing her right up close. He breathed her as she walked past. A quick poke to his ribs broke his trance. She was fast, no kidding, he thought. She took the reins of the group and continued the tour.

Ticktock giggled behind James. "She got ya mate," he whispered. James smiled. He was thankful it wasn't a real jab.

"Welcome to the hall of darts!" With the turn of both handles, Punch pushed open the doors. "This is where it happens. For some of you anyway."

She brought everyone through, into an expansive room the size of a Vegas casino, the extremely high ceilings were painted blue and white to look like the sky. There were many dartboard stations, each looked like a carpeted bowling lane, roped off in red velvet. A bar was opposite all the dartboard stations. Above the bar was a level of balcony and seating. It was an elegant setup. No tubs here. Instead, Victorian chairs and tables.

"I need a volunteer."

Leaving no time for a reaction Punch grabbed James by the arm. "You. What's your name?" Behind him the boys giggled and whooped.

"James."

"The triangle player," said Punch.

"Yeah..."

"Okay. I need you to go to the bar and get me a dark and stormy." He nodded and as he left... "Wait." He approached her. She pointed to her cheek. "Right here." This was too perfect, James thought. He kissed her cheek. Everyone clapped. He blushed as he scampered backwards to the bar. It was a battle to maintain composure. He loved that she singled him out. She looked to her crew. "Before I dismiss you for dinner, I need to tell you a tidbit of important information. So listen up. The tournament starts tomorrow night at 8pm sharp! You will get your schedule of who you'll play against and at what station you'll play them at and where to go afterwards. You'll note it is very self-explanatory. So, there will be no need to ask questions. However, should you have a question, you will soon find, you... no, you don't have one. There will be question voids. At each station. That will suck it from your head. And stuff you with knowledge. For example, did you all know that alcohol frees impulses already there. It does not create new ones. So if you see me wanting to rip someone's head open... Oh and ah... did you know a porcupine's quill swells when it enters the victim, due to the heat and moisture of their body, and every movement of the victim's muscles, pulls against the barbs, forcing the quill in deeper, until it penetrates, a vital body organ or two. See, I didn't know that!" She looked at James on his way back. "It was planted in my head by these damn question voids." Her group laughed. James brought Punch her drink. "Thank you sweetie." She took a sip. James pointed to his cheek. She kissed it.

* * * * *

At their booth, the Clocks viewed tomorrow's schedule.

"We've seen these guys, the Pointers," said Shard. "Beach Boy lookin' group. Remember they had those orange striped, barber shop shirts?"

"Oh yeah," Aster remembered.

"I think they're brothers," said James.

"Their mum still dresses them," joked Ticktock. He took a swig of scotch.

"The Zeros are up against that hick team, the Bull's Eye," noted Aster.

"Wannabe hicks," said Ticktock.

"Yeah. They're not real cowboys," said Shard. "They're from Long Island."

"Straw hats. Denim vests. Fuckin' gay bastards," said Ticktock. "Backstreet Boys gone western. The Zeros will kill 'em! Tokyo style!" He sliced the air with a samurai sword. Nobody laughed. Shard, crunching on ice from his swig of drink, brought everyone back to strategy.

"The Pointers' strong lead man is Ryan," noted Shard. "I think if we play a clean game of five-oh-one, we should be all right."

"Any bloody game we play with them we'll be all right!" assured Ticktock.

"We're at station seven," noted James.

A waiter dressed as a jester approached their table. He was just putting away his scientific calculator, his "Jew fro" compressed under his hat.

"Hi. I'm Gus Dillard. And I'll be your server today." He was a slender man with intelligent eyes and a James Dean kind of cool about him. "Dillard is short for Dillardmanbergerstein."

"How much do they pay you to wear that outfit?" Shard asked.

"What outfit?" Gus said. They noticed his extra large cod piece with a pointy nose.

"A little modest down there, aren't we?" said Ticktock.

"How would you know my business down there?" Gus shot back.

"Well, I don't," said Ticktock, "but, you're standing over there and I'm still getting poked in the ribs."

"Then turn around," Shard quipped. "Give the guy a break and let's order."

"Just get me another one of these." Ticktock held up an empty old-fashioned.

"How do you like working here? You're probably used to it," said James as he put his menu down.

"This place is new. Open once a year, believe it or not," said Gus.

"You're kidding," said James.

"No. I mean, it's open for like a couple weeks of the year and then shuts down. I don't know how she can afford it--"

"She?" James was all ears.

"Yeah. Punch. It's her place. Her concept. It was just a piece of property. An abandoned factory. And she thought to transform it into something like never before. Got to give it to her. This is the most fucking, amazing place I've ever worked. She took me in when my van broke down and lets me stay here rent free."

"Well, you pay with your labor," Aster reminded him.

"No, that's what's fuckin' cool man. She's payin' me to work here too! She's a little genius wrapped like a sweet piece of candy."

"Mother Teresa as a centerfold," said Ticktock.

"No, you mean Mother Teresa, in a *body* of a centerfold," corrected Aster.

"Well, I knew what you meant," said Gus. "So what'll it be my friends?"

Ticktock grabbed a fork. "For starters, I'll have the...cod." He licked his lips and leaned in towards Gus's groin. He poked the nose with his fork.

"I'll see what I can do," flinched Gus. He looked at Ticktock, then at Shard. "Should I be careful with this one?"

"He's harmless," said Shard looking at his groin. "Just let him play with your penis a little bit. He'll get tired soon."

"You guys are already making my first night... unforgettable," said Gus.

"They're just testing you," said James. "Although, I did see cod on the menu." He opened the menu and pointed to it. "So spit in their food, not mine."

"We charge extra for that," said Gus.

Aster looked at the guys, then at Gus. "You don't really spit in the food, do you?"

"No. But I can make an exception," said Gus. That only made them laugh harder.

Get Ye Darts Ready!

At the hotel, the Clocks spent all morning practicing darts. Anticipation for tonight was another contender to deal with. They sat around all afternoon, trying to take it easy. James read the paper in bed. Shard and Aster watched TV. Ticktock paced the room.

"Time is going so fuckin' slow!" said Ticktock. "It's still only 3:30! This time yesterday, it was 4:30!"

"Save your energy son," Shard pulled out a cigarette. "Save your energy." He lit his smoke.

Tournament Night was now upon them.

Finally.

The hall of darts was packed with players. At station seven, Og and a referee, dressed in a dark, Victorian suit, stood between the Pointers, who did look very much like the Beach Boys in their striped, short sleeve shirts and the Clocks, who were dressed in their black, 1964, British Invasion suits. Both teams shook hands.

"The game will be eight-oh-one," announced the ref. "Will the representatives from both teams, please step forward for corking."

Both teams start with 801 points. The winner is the first team that reaches zero, exactly zero with a double. Double is the first ring on a dartboard. Any score exceeding zero ends the turn, returning the score to that of the last dart.

Ryan and James both stepped up to the line. Ryan hit the twenty five ring with his dart. The rest of the Pointers cheered. James stepped up and hit the bull's eye. The Clocks kept their enthusiasm quiet. Og walked to the scoreboard.

Shard was up first. In a synchronized fashion, the Clocks removed their jackets and hung them on the back of their chairs. Shard stepped up to the line with his tungsten. He threw a triple twenty on his first throw, a double twelve on his second throw and a double seventeen on his third shot.

Ryan, next, stepped up to the line. The ref placed his hand on his chest to stop him until Shard had safely collected his darts. Og wrote the score. After Shard took a seat, Ryan threw an eight, an eleven and a double five. After collecting his darts, Aster was up. He stared intently at the board with his arm cocked. He threw a triple fourteen, a double nine and a triple nine. Og wrote the score as Aster collected his darts. The next Pointer was up. His first throw bounced off the board. Ryan buried his head collecting cuss words into his hands. This mistake set the pace for the Pointers and they were never able to recover. At the end of the game, both teams shook hands.

"Nice darts," said James to Ryan.

"Nice darts," responded Ryan. Og gathered the Pointers.

"Congratulations! The Clocks!" said the ref as he shook their hands. "What a splendid performance indeed. Ye shall move on

to the next level of the tournament." They noticed Og leading
the Pointers away through a door at the end of the station. James
pointed at them.

"And where are they going?"

The ref smiled and disappeared into the crowd.

"That's the one I saw in the bathroom pissing up a hailstorm,"
continued James.

"He was almost a distraction," said Shard.

"Every station has one," noticed Aster. "I think they're just
people walking on stilts."

"No fucking way," answered Ticktock. "Those are real,
abnormal people. Did you see the size of their heads?"

"Mechanical probably," Aster theorized.

"Your brain is *mechanical probably*," mimicked Ticktock.

"No, that's your brain."

"Gentlemen!" said Shard. "Has it escaped you that we are
one step closer to winning the million! So what does it matter
who's head is mechanical? We move on to the next match! Hello!
Beautiful job tonight boys. Let's get a drink."

* * * * *

At another dartboard station, the Zeros had zeroed in on their
opponents, the Bull's Eyes, with Pearl Harbor accuracy. These New
York rednecks had already begun bickering amongst themselves.
One of the players had thrown his straw cowboy hat to the ground
and stomped on it. Sweat poured off their bodies in gallons. The
Zeros on the other hand, were cool. With every winning shot -
and they were all winning shots, Wes erupted with impudent self-
congratulatory outbursts. "*Yeaya!*" and, "*Whoa-whoa-whoa, call the
police, hurry hurry, yo hurtin' someone this bad is a crime*," while flexing his
muscles and doing the robot dance. The ref penalized him a point
for bad sportsmanship prompting the Bull's Eyes to shout insults
at Wes, who retorted, he could give them all his points and still kick
their ass. The Zeros restrained Wes as the ref deducted another
point. Jeff was up to throw. He wore the matching pin striped
slacks and vest, light blue shirt, rolled at the sleeves. He checked his
chain watch as if he was bored of the game. He shot all doubles.

It was Steve, dressed in black, who put the game away with a triple fourteen and a triple twelve reducing the score to zero. The team jumped and embraced. A giant escorted the Bull's Eyes away. Had he not, a fight would have ensued.

* * * * *

At the infamous bar, four high ball glasses sat filled with 2 ounces of Gosling's Black Seal Rum and 3 ounces of Barrit's Ginger Beer. The Clocks had all ordered a dark and stormy for their celebratory drink. A salute to Punch. Shard pulled out his wallet, but the bartender shook his head and told them the first round was free for the winners. Then, as one four headed beast, they swiveled around in their bar stools in unison to watch the game at the station across from them, an all-girl match. The Bush League Bitches defeated the Fix Me Chix. The giant escorted the Fix Me Chix away. The Clocks saluted the Bitches with raised drinks. The Bitches smiled at the boys.

* * * * *

The Clocks and The Bush League Bitches squeezed into a bathtub booth.

"How 'bout those Giants?" asked James.

"Oh -I know!" said Michelle, the pretty blonde who'd already attached herself to James -her shoulder pressed against his. "They're kinda freaky!"

"Bouncers? Scorekeepers-?" said Shard.

"They better not lay a finger on me," said Roma, the dark haired Bitch. "I'll cut their balls off."

"That's the spirit," Ticktock took a sip.

"You guys musicians too?" asked Betty, the hefty blonde with black roots and torn fishnets.

"Yeah, from the '60s!" Michelle said.

"No," said Shard. "We're poseurs."

"It's true," said James. "They're poseurs."

"I'm a musician," Ticktock answered.

"Really?" Michelle asked.

"I play the clitar," he said.

"The clitar?" asked Roma

"It's a wind instrument. It makes a sort of moaning sound. Very beautiful to the male ear." Everyone laughed but Roma.

"What? Is that like a sitar?" she asked.

"Sure," said James as he winked at Michelle. She reached over and grabbed his drink and took a sip.

"Wow. What is that, rum?"

"Yeah. It's called, light and sunny," said Ticktock.

"No, dark and stormy," corrected James.

"You know, first drinks are free for the winners," informed Shard.

"Really?" Michelle delighted. "Free." She turned to her team. "Well, girls? Let's take advantage of this. Are we winners?" A unanimous YEAH! But no one got up to get a drink.

"Ah, fun fact," Aster entertained, "did you know the humpback penis has a ten foot whale?" He struggled with charm like a child with a loaded gun. "I mean, the whale, has a ten foot penis... that's big."

Silence ensued from the crowd until James jumped in. "How about them drinks?"

"I think the question void sucked more than a question from Aster's head," said Ticktock.

A reminder of Punch that pinged James in the stomach.

"Huh?" Cindy, the sandy-straight-haired Bitch didn't have Punch as her tour guide.

"Where did you pull that whale penis fun fact from?" Shard asked Aster.

"Where do you think he pulled it from?" Ticktock responded.

"Fuck you." Aster buried his face in his drink. "It's an interesting fact. Look it up!"

"I don't know if I want to spend my time with whale penis research," said Shard.

Gus approached the table dressed...as an astronaut.

"Hello." He opened his mask. "I'm Gus. I'll be your waiter."

After a moment of silence -laughter.

"Goddamn son," said Shard. "What theme are you trying for that you keep overshooting? Last night, the middle ages. Tonight, Buck Rogers--?"

"Are you just picking up shit and putting it on?" said Ticktock.

"What the fuck? Whose closet is that?" Shard pressed. "I mean, no one else is an astronaut tonight."

Gus stood still, blank expression on his face.

"We're sorry," said James. "We really like it. It takes a cool bloke to pull it off, you know." Gus looked to James and the girls. James turned to the others. "Am I right, guys?"

Gus lowered his head, dropped his note pad and pencil and as he slowly turned, the girls all vocalized pity in a *Ahhh...* He then turned and faced them all with a crazy smile.

"Like a Band-Aid over my wound, a cigarette would heal me quick! May I bum a smoke?" The boys reached into their jackets and pulled out cigarettes. Gus collected them all. "Very kind of you guys. Thank you." He bent down to collect his notepad and pencil. "Okay. The girls want drinks," said Gus.

"I'll have what he has. A ah..." Michelle glanced at James. He took the cue and ordered for her:

"Dark and stormy."

The Bitches were cute, but James couldn't keep his mind off Punch. The witty banter at the table continued as James drifted in a dream about Punch. Her fragrance and kisses to his cheek settled him into a lovely goose-bump feeling. James's eyes searched with the circling arms of a radar on screen for the *warm and friendly hostess*. She could be anywhere, he thought. He felt a little light headed, as if she had punched him. Michelle gave a nudge. He awoke from his open-eyed dreaming.

"Well, what do you think?" she asked.

"Yes." He wrapped his arm around her and squeezed, though he never caught the question. Gus had served the girls then joined them at the table.

"You guys hear about the dart team that died on the way up?" said Gus. "Car crash wiped out an entire team."

"Really?" said Aster.

"Yeah," said Gus.

"Where did it happen?" asked Shard.

"It was out on highway 70," answered Gus.

A man dressed in a suit, stopped at their table. He handed an envelope to Shard. The team name was written on it. The man produced another envelope for the Bitches.

"I'm afraid I'm gonna have to give you girls the boot. Gus," Shard said. "You too." Michelle hugged James and Betty hugged Ticktock goodbye. Shard tore open the envelope and pulled out the folded paper that revealed their fate. The boys crowded around to read.

"Oh no," said Aster. "We're playing the Blackbulls."

"So?" asked Ticktock.

"They're good," Shard gave the list to Aster.

"The Zeros have to play the Blitz," read Aster.

"They're stuck with the fascist team and we've got the other end. The fuckin' socialist, Black Panther machine," said Ticktock.

"Well my brothers, it's all good," Shard assured them. "We're fucking blessed to be here. I mean look at this place! The excitement. The opportunity. The women. The whole Goddamn process of it all. So let's not forget or overlook the moment to moment thrill of being here and playing the best, Goddamn game of darts ever!"

"Amen to that sermon," said James.

"Yeah," replied Aster.

"Group hug!" Ticktock extended his arms.

"That's a moment we can skip," Shard joked.

* * * * *

Out in the parking lot, James watched as Aster cleaned the Cadillac, purple pharmaceutical gloves and the roll of paper towels under his arm. From the shadows, Punch approached James.

"Is that your boy over there?"

He turned to see her. His heart tripped over a blood vessel like an untied shoe lace.

"Punch. Hey. Yeah, me mate. He's got this thing with cleanliness."

She nodded.

"You guys played a really good game."

"What are you, um... were you watching our game?"

"Yeah."

"Thanks." His eyes were caught in her stare. He looked to the ground for safety. "We're looking forward to the next one."

"I hope so." She still stared at him.

"So, you own this place?" He looked at her and back to the ground. She didn't answer, but watched, waiting for him to lift his head. After the silence, he finally did.

"Am I making you nervous, James?"

He shook his head, pulled out a cigarette and then nodded.

"You're my triangle player." She lovingly hit his shoulder. His left ear went deaf. A button from his coat popped off. He lit his smoke and offered her one. She declined.

"What are you doing tonight?" he boldly asked. The old James found his footing. Hearing restored. She bent over and picked up his button. "I'll let you keep that if we can have a drink or a huge bowl of pasta. I'm famished!"

"Come here." She smiled, wrapped her arm around his. "I'll cook you a little something."

"That's very sweet of you, thanks," he said. The two marched towards a back door. Punch stopped.

"No. Let's go through the kitchen," she said. Still locked arm in arm, they changed direction and walked to another door, farther down. "Let's wave goodbye to your friend." The two, still attached like conjoined twins, circled over towards the car. "What's his name?"

"Aster! We're going in," he shouted. "See you inside." They circled around back and disappeared into the building, giggling.

* * * * *

Shard and Ticktock remained at the bathtub booth drinking. A little tipsy, but still coherent, they welcomed Gus, without his astronaut suit, to join them.

"There's no such thing as souls," Shard said.

"Yes there is!" Gus shot back.

"Bullshit."

"How much do you weigh?"

"About one sixty." Shard took a swig.

"What do you think is making one hundred and sixty pounds of meat, of flesh, move? Think about this. What really gives it life?"

"Heart pumping oxygen into the blood," said Shard.

"Right. But what causes this system to operate? What causes the body to function, the heart to beat. The lungs to take air? What really gives a pile of flesh animation? To move?" Gus pressed.

"Beyond oxygen molecules, I don't know," Shard confessed. Ticktock listened.

"It's your mind. Or in other words, your soul. What triggers the neurons in your brain to buzz and make your thoughts buzz which triggers your body to work like a machine? It's your soul. Without it man, you're just a pile of lifeless meat." Gus took a moment to take a drag from his smoke. "The human is made of two different things. The body and the soul. But we can't really see the soul because it doesn't take up space."

"Aha!" cried Shard.

"Aha what, man?"

"Nothing," said Shard. "I just thought I'd throw that in there." Ticktock laughed. "Continue."

"You're a comedian. Are you hiding a pain?"

"Just dealing with it, until it stops talking."

"If you want me to shut up, just ask directly," said Gus.

"Actually, I don't. I apologize. I'm genuinely interested in your soul theories," said Shard.

"Me too," Ticktock finally spoke.

"He hasn't said a word in ten minutes," Shard brought to light. "That means you're very interesting to listen too. So please, we want to hear you or you wouldn't be sitting here." He slapped Gus on the shoulder.

"All right. Showing a little alpha male. I'll play along. I'm not trying to be a threat to your ego or anyone's. I subscribe to the theory... I believe the soul is a substance, but it's not something you can physically handle. It's aetherial. Its behavior is thought. It's like a dream. It is free will."

"How do you know it's there?" said Ticktock.

"Well, the soul is like a Wednesday or like Mozart's 25th symphony. It doesn't exist in space, but it exists. So where does the music go when it's not played? It still exists. Where does Wednesday go when it's Friday? They hold no place in space."

"They physically exist on paper," said Shard after another puff from his cigarette. "And air currents every time you play it. It's a short-lived life."

"You destroy that paper, burn it up and it still exists. That is what a soul is like," Gus said.

"If a generation destroyed that sheet of music, preventing future generations from learning it, it will only exist in the memory of that last generation, and die with them, therefore, not existing," said Shard, staring into his glass. "Out, just like the dodo bird."

"A short-lived life then. But if later discovered, it would be as vital and alive as when first written. Maybe it was dormant all these years. Look, my illustrations might not be an exact translation of what a soul compares to, but I know you've got the idea behind it. I think someone holds a threatened ego with this nitpicking. Don't take it personally."

"All right. Well you just blew my ego to pieces," Shard confessed.

"Sarcasm, of course."

"No, but seriously, you've said some interesting things I didn't..."

"You have a great poker face," said Gus.

"Thanks, but my cards are out on the table." Shard finished his drink. "My *ego* doesn't factor into it."

"You sound like the fuckin' Matrix. The red pill or the blue pill?" said Ticktock.

"Well, you're a very passionate man, Gus," said Shard while putting out his smoke and grabbing a new one. He popped it in his mouth. "And that's a beautiful thing." He lit it.

"Thanks. May I have another cigarette and I'll entertain you all with my theories on horse shit."

They all laughed. Shard tossed him the pack.

"I think we just heard it," Shard shot back. Gus and Shard pointed to each other at the same time. "Ooooh!"

* * * * *

James and Punch hid in her study. The room with the portal next to the ceiling. The couple sat on an area rug. Scattered around them, large ornate pillows in various colors of bourbon and port and scarlet. An old claw foot bathtub stood guard on one side of the room. The lamp from the desk was placed on the floor to create a cozier environment. James refilled their glasses of red wine.

"You wanna hear something gross?" she asked.

"No."

"Well, I'm gonna run you over with it anyway," she smiled. "This is a true story. It happened here. Okay. One of my workers, a religious man, takes a shit--"

"Oh no..." James covered his ears.

"Listen!" she pulled his arm away and laughed. "He goes to wipe his ass and as he looks between his legs, into the bowl, like we all do, he sees the strangest sight! A miracle! His shit looked like...... like the Virgin Mary."

"What?!" said James.

"I shit you not. Pun intended." Punch continued, "The guy felt so blessed. That is until he was done wiping. He had discarded all the used toilet paper into a nearby trash can as to not crowd the fecal matter. Then he became horribly torn. To flush or not to flush?" She noticed James looking away.

"That is the question," mumbled James.

"I'm not very lady-like, am I? You're disgusted with me, aren't you? I can tell." She sipped her glass.

"No love, you're quite civilized."

"I'm just so fucking rude and vulgar sometimes..." She hung her eyes to the floor. Then, she slapped her hand with self punishments and bit into it like a dog.

"N-no," said James, grabbing her hand from the abuse and kissing it. "No you're not. Well, ok, maybe a tad vulgar, but what does it matter really? Besides, I have to see this story to the end."

"Are you sure?"

"Yes."

"It gets graphic."

"Oh, you mean it hasn't yet?" said James. "I'm gonna need another drink." He downed his glass and held it out for a refill. Punch took a sip herself before grabbing the bottle, clumsily pouring too much into his glass.

"Oh, sorry!" They laughed. "Okay, so as the guy finished wiping his ass, he decides to keep his caca floating. So, he guards the toilet. No one can use it. I'm talking for two days! He wraps the yellow construction tape around the stall."

"So this was one of your employees?"

"Yeah, one of the bus boys."

"Wow."

"So, I had to take a look for myself," she said. "When I pushed aside the yellow tape and peeked, I swear to God, it freakishly, really did look like the Virgin Mary... holding baby Jesus."

"Baby Jesus was there too?" said James. She laughed again. James thought her dimples and perfect smile were a betrayal to the conversation, they didn't match her tongue. Such a beautiful thing should be chatting about clothes and shopping, fine foods and cosmetics. Not shit floating in toilets.

"Yeah!" she said. "A piece of corn was his head."

"Damn that's blasphemous. You're gonna burn in Hell." James grabbed her hand again and squeezed it. "Funny thing about corn. I guess it has no nutritional value because it always comes out in one piece."

She spit her wine, laughing.

"Sorry love." He kissed her hand. "So then what happened?"

Punch wiped her mouth.

"Sorry. Well, the poor guy was right about his shit. So I supervised as he scooped her out of the toilet, dripping and falling to pieces. Prior to that, he had people coming in to take pictures and to pray at this porcelain alter. It got to the point where there were just too many people coming in for his shit. Now when I was a Christian, I too would've knelt down for a prayer."

"To the shit?"

"To the shit." Silence...

shattered with more howling laughter.

"I can't believe you got involved in the handling of it."

"I had to. I couldn't open for business with this shit taking place." More laughter. "After he placed it in a ziplock bag, he took it to his church and had it blessed."

"Holy crap!" cried James. Punch fell over into his arms. After their shits and giggles, a pleasant, subdued moment settled their smiles, a serene elegance drifted and landed on them, feather light. She looked up into his eyes and warmly reached her hand to the side of his neck. Their eyes closed as he leaned in to kiss. They both stopped to look at each other. They kissed again. Violently grabbing each other, while their wine-wet lips stayed glued. Her exhales turned him on. She smacked his cheek bone causing a moment of building tension before their tongues made their introduction. A welcomed invasion past the white fences, into the moist yard of each other's mouth. He grabbed her breasts and her ass while she rolled her body on the ground, knocking over the wine. She lifted herself to her knees and ripped her shirt open. Revealing an old skeleton key she wore around her neck. The sound of ripping garments awakened a monstrous appetite to fuck hard. She tore her own sleeves off and handed one to him.

"Here," she panted. "I need you to gag me."

"Why?"

"I have thin walls."

He brought the rolled sleeve around her mouth and tied it at the back of her head. She ripped open his shirt as he took his pants off. Her pants, also off, revealed a black, silk g-string. They were smooth to his thumb as he rubbed over her crotch and the other hand, pinched her nipple to stand tall as if he was tuning a radio. His lips nestled over the other one. Licking and softly biting it to rise all pointy. Her moans further rushed the blood to his now throbbing penis. They wrestled. He squeezed her jiggling, bubble butt and bit it. She made more womanly noises. The kind that drives men crazy. Her muscular legs shot open and like the

Venus Fly trap, wrapped tight around his waist, melting him with her pussy juice. She was wet for him. A small, copper box, velvet interior, tipped over, spilling a couple of condoms. James grabbed one and tore it open with his teeth. He gripped her legs, as if he were a blind man feeling every part of it, down to her blushing, beautiful toes and back up to her inner thighs. He brought his nose between her legs and yanked her panties aside and with his tongue, pulled back the clit's hoody and combed its bald head with soft, rhythmic lapping. His tongue dove deeper into her vagina and back out brushing upwards over her clit. It didn't take long for her legs to spasm with the intensity of orgasm. He could smell her cum as it came tunneling out and cascading over her shapely curved landscape. She dragged her stretched legs and crotch to the tub gripping its claw foot as another wave of orgasms rattled her. He pulled her close and slowly inserted into her flooded canal. She gripped the side of the tub to transfer some of her powerful, raw, energy. Light specks of gold collected around her eyes which looked like heavenly sweat, glistening. He built into a heavy thrust, slamming hips to hips. Pubic area to pubic area.

"Fuckin' punch me!" she growled through the fabric. Before he could respond, she slapped his face. He grabbed her by the back of the hair.

"No! Fuck that!" he told her.

"In the gut!"

"No!" He slammed her harder with his hips, over and over. The intensity, climbing, climbing...until the light exploded in the room like a hot flare in the night sky! Exhausted, they collapsed into each other. She tore her gag off to suck in more air.

Out of breath, "Oh God James..."

"Fuck, you're good..." he could barely get the words out.

"I concur..."

"You're a lil' firecracker, aren't you?" he said.

"Kaboom!"

Punch looked so delicious naked and wet. James was still hungry for her. He got up to dispose of the condom. He felt silly having it still on like a snake trying to shed its skin. She rolled to her stomach, the sweat and wine on her body, the perfect marinade. But first, a warm shower. Together.

* * * * *

Afterhours at Rackle's Tub was comparable to a lucky child who had Disneyland all to himself. James got off the phone with Shard. Punch sat at the closed bar. A fresh bowl of salsa and a bag of chips were on the counter.

"I always get the after-sex munchies," she said with her mouth full, crunching. He kissed her head and joined her in the snacking. "I really feel like I was born in the wrong century."

"You don't like this one?" he asked.

"No. I do!" she replied. "I love it! I mean, what I meant to say is, I feel like I was born in the 19th century... kind of."

"I sensed that about you," he said. "Wise beyond your years."

"Really?"

"I don't like the hitting shit. Where did that come from?" he asked.

"I don't know. Something primal in me I suppose."

"I'm not into that," he reached for a chip. She shrugged her shoulders.

"I'll eat to that," she scooped salsa and held it. He followed suit. They bumped chips and swallowed. "We should be a little discreet about our affair. Do you agree?"

"Good point. My friends already know about you though."

"It's going to look like I'm playing favoritism, should you win."

"What if you wear a mustache?"

"Perfect! We'll be faggots together." She held up her chip to his. While they both laughed, James was quick to learn that she had a peculiar offensive mouth, which came across as strangely naive for someone who seemed so comfortable with people. But James wasn't a stranger to odd behavior. He had his dart team to thank for that. "To the furry upper lip!"

"Cheers," said James. They both crunched. "Hey, did you know the humpback whale has a ten foot penis?"

"Are you staying the night?" she asked. "It's already 2:30."

"If it's okay with you."

A State Of Reciprocated Limerence

James had fallen asleep in the bath. Only, it was flooded with pillows and blankets. Punch, naked with him, under the covers, watched him sleep, content to soak him up with her stares. He had cute curvy eyelashes, she noticed. It took all of her restraint not to kiss his eyelids open.

During the wee hours of morning, James, not sure if he was awake or in a dream, found himself alone. Beside the closed door, a lot of shoes of various sizes and types, mainly men's, were scattered as if removed in a hurry. He thought it odd.

* * * * *

James made his way to the hotel late that morning. The rest of the boys noticed something different about him. It could be blamed on a lack of sleep or a hangover. Shard was acutely aware when their Clock was off. But they'd never seen James in love.

"It's not in my nature to worry, but you realize we're playing against a damn good team tonight," said Shard from the bathroom, while shaving. "We'll have plenty of time to live it up."

"Yeah, sorry," said James. "It's just that... that Punch... it tickles me that she is such a... I don't know... such an amazing bird."

"Be careful. For all we know, she could be rooting for the home team." Shard rinsed his blade and shut off the water. Ticktock was sleeping off a hangover while Aster was in bed, lost in his reading.

"No," replied James, "she seems genuinely genuine... I don't know. She is crass though, but charming as hell."

"Women can pull you away, so easily from your priorities. They can sap your brain time if you're not watching," continued Shard as he finished up in the bathroom. "You shouldn't fuck her."

"Yeah, yeah... you don't need to tell me this," said James. He brought himself to his tired feet so he could crash on the bed. "I know about women... at least I think I do."

"I'm just making contact with you." Shard entered the room with a towel around his shoulders. "Glad you made it back safe. We kind of need to look after each other out here. We're talking a million dollars. The closer we get to that goal, the more enemies we may acquire. People have killed for a lot less."

"Yeah. Back in the twenties, when a shiny nickel could buy you four acres." Ticktock rubbed his eyes. "What's for breakfast?"

Shard threw his towel at him. "I don't know, but you're getting it," said Shard.

"I'm trying to read," said Aster. "Now-now James, over here, is in love. It might be advantageous to have him dating that girl. It's her tournament. It's her place. Let's let things simmer, okay?" Aster disappeared back into his book.

"Thanks," James mumbled with closed eyes. "Not in love."

"Hey, I'll have a grapefruit with whole wheat toast and one tofu sausage," ordered Aster. Shard grabbed a pen and wrote it down on hotel stationary.

"Okay...one bowl of Wheaties."

"What?"

"They're not gonna have tofu sausage."

He wrote his own order next. And looked to James.

"James? Cornflakes?"

"Sure."

"I'll have eggs, bacon and waffles," said Ticktock.

"Good..." Shard tossed the list, fluttering through the air, at Ticktock's head. "Go get it."

"I can't-"

"Yes you can. And you will." Shard kicked his bed.

"-But-"

Shard and the rest of the boys gave him a look.

"Shit," protested Ticktock. As he pulled the sheets off. "Okay. You asked for it." Once Ticktock rose from the bed, it became clear why he should have remained under the covers. His tiger skin thong worked its magic as a friend repellent.

* * * * *

Tournament time! Night two and players were getting testy. Some people rub you the wrong way before they even open their mouths. Hating them is effortless for whatever reason.

The Blackbulls took their place at station 16, wearing black turtlenecks and black leather jackets. Two of them had black shades and black felt hats. One slender player, Jerome, carried an afro as big as a moose head! He walked with a polite arrogance, almost slow motion with its smoothness. These boys were a class act. The Clocks approached the board at station 16, in their black, 3-buttoned suits with thin black ties. Except for Ticktock. He was dressed in white tights tucked into large black boots and white jacket without lapels, white suspenders and a black derby like Alex from *A Clockwork Orange*. The teams sized each other up. They shook hands and the ref signaled for the corking to begin. James first, he threw a dart straight into the bull's eye. Jerome next, he hit the bull's eye mark also. After collecting his dart, he spun on his heels and did a little James Brown shuffle, his finger pointing to his team. He slapped them all a five and took his seat. Aster threw and hit the triple ring. Sky, the leader of the Blackbulls, hit just outside the twenty-five ring which was closer to the bull's eye than Aster's triple ring. He slapped his teammates five because his hit brought them up first to throw. A hard, brute-force of a man, Sky's reasonably sized fro and eagle-wing eyebrows, made him appear angry twenty four seven. Jerome spun, clapped and approached the line pinching his dart like a fat doobie then hitting a triple eighteen, four and a thirteen. Shard stepped to the line and threw a triple twelve, nine and seventeen. Sky threw nothing but triples. The scoreboard soon showed the two teams neck and neck.

Another close game pitted the Zeros and the Blitz at station seven. The Blitz were the bad kind of skinheads. Punch's old skinhead boyfriend, Chris, from the BBQ, was bouncing his legs everywhere while he sat. She wouldn't have recognized him. His weight loss resembled that of a Holocaust prisoner. Unbeknownst to her, she had reduced him to this desperate bag of bones. His motive for being there was not in his team's best interest. His head turned to every corner of the hall searching for his lost love.

Steve was up to throw. A triple seventeen, a twelve and a nine. He gathered his darts. As he sat, the next player from the Blitz was greeted with arms in the air. The Nazi salute in unison, "*Sieg Heil!*" Punch's ex-lover's teeth rattled when he shouted. They did this every time one of their players went up to throw. The Blitz were a good team, despite their extreme political and social views.

The red-laced Doc Martens, bleached blue jeans, wife beaters with red suspenders, heavy tats on the arms, hid deep-seated fears and inadequacies.

"I'm gonna propose to her after we win," rattled Chris while looking everywhere but the game. "Gonna get her back." Tom, the head Blitz member, leaned his face into his and smacked him. He dared him to hit back, but Chris knew better. Tom marched to the line. With a deep breath in and out he hit triples, Hitler salutes in the air.

The Blackbulls threw their closed fists in the air. Toto, the bleached haired punk won it for the Zeros as did James against the Blackbulls. The ref announced the Clocks as the winners. The teams shook hands.

"Good game," said Sky.

"Thanks," said Shard.

"You cats are a'right," Jerome said. Og escorted the Blackbulls away.

At station seven, another giant escorted the Blitz away. Chris took off running. He had the Charlie Manson eyes and his jealous heart screamed at him, knife her! KNIFE HER! A pocket knife, blade out, slipped in his sweaty grip, but still caged in his fingers. He collected himself at a bar, blade in his pocket and eyes spinning in their sockets like a slot machine. He slapped the counter...

"Hey!" Chris slapped it a couple more times before the bartender came over.

"What can I get ya?" said the bartender.

"You know where I can find Punch? I need to talk to her."

"Last I saw, she was with that James fellow-"

"James?!"

"The guy in a suit-" The noise level at the bar was on the high side.

"Zoot- what?"

"Suit."

"Zoot suit. Is he some kind of boyfriend? I fuckin' need to talk to her. It's kind of important."

"What's your name?" the bartender asked. Chris shook his head as he backed from the bar and dashed into the crowd.

The next day proved to be more intense, matches all day long. As soon as a team won, they moved on to a different station to play the winning team from a previous match and with only fifteen minute breaks between the games. There was a lunch break at noon for two hours. Then, back to the grind. The Clocks and Zeros by the end of the day, though victorious, they were spent. They had yet to cross paths.

* * * * *

Gus, wearing a long sleeved, jailbird shirt from Andy Warhol's closet, carried a birdcage into Punch's study. The Clocks followed. Gus lifted the cover off the cage. A dove, as white as a fly maggot on a raven's wing, sat tightly in the corner of the cage. Gus sat the cage on the ground and walked over to the room's window to make sure it was shut and locked.

"Some rooms have a sort of energy," explained Gus. "That's due to a vortex in the room. An angel's doorway." Without touching the walls, Gus ran his hands back and forth in front of them.

"If you can find termites that way--" Aster hit Shard on the shoulder to shut him up.

"Yeah, that would be lucrative," agreed Gus. "Some rooms in this building have a unique energy, but I feel it strongly here."

"Are you trying to find the doorway?" asked Shard. Gus nodded, still focused on his search.

"Yeah. Do you guys feel a complete easiness in this room?" said Gus. The others looked to each other. "I used to have this dog that always took a shit in the pantry room of my mom's house because the energy was so soothing. In fact, I feel like taking a shit right now." He unbuckled his belt and unbuttoned his trousers. The boys watched.

"Where are the girls tonight?" Shard asked Ticktock.

"You're supposed to stop me and say, 'No Gus!'" he buttoned back up and chuckled. No one found him funny.

"What are you?" asked James. "We're tired."

"Just call me a naturalist." Gus bent over the birdcage.

"Gus, the naturalist," said James looking around, reminiscing his moment here with Punch from the other night.

"That's me," Gus said.

"Punch doesn't mind you being in here?" James pulled out a cigarette.

"She's cool like that," said Gus. "I'm gonna show you something that'll blaze your brain. And trip you mad. Like a fish that's gone a fryin' when your heart's a dyin'..."

"What's he talkin' about?" Aster asked. The others shook their head.

"At Berkley I studied chaos and quantum theory."

"Really?" asked Shard. "Were you working on your doctorate?"

"Oh, no. I got kicked out," said Gus.

"That's crazy! How did you get fired from janitorial services?" Ticktock humored.

"How does that make you a naturalist?" said James.

"I lingered in bio too," said Gus. He looked into the cage. "Actually my grades weren't that good. Money was tight. Oh, and I was smoking weed in the attic of the physics department." The boys laughed. "But I loved biology and physics. I learned about these moody doorways that exist throughout the world and universe. Kind of like black holes. What's behind the door?" Everybody looked to the door of the room.

"No. Not, not that door," said Gus. "The vortex! What can we expect to find on the other side? A Level IV Multiverse perhaps? A parallel universe that differs in every way... laws of physics, location... exists maybe outside of space and time?"

"Oh, come off it," said James. "You don't really believe in all that stuff do you?"

"I'll show you," said Gus. "This room has only one window." he pointed. "And it's shut."

Ticktock crawled to sleep in the bath. James felt a little bothered by this.

Gus continued, "Now, I need everyone to go out to the hallway." Gus opened the cage and grabbed the bird. With an upward toss, the bird flew around the room. "Don't let it out!" The Clocks opened the door and with Gus behind them, left the room, quickly shutting the door.

"Why did we leave the room?" asked Shard. "If you wanted us to see the miracle, shouldn't we be in there to see it?"

Gus smiled. "Well... in the off chance that we're not allowed in there."

"You see?! I don't feel right snooping around in her room without her," said James. "I think this whole thing is daft! How do you know about this room and its shit inducing energy?"

"Well, I've thrown this damn bird in pretty much every other damn room."

"Did Punch ever take you up here?" James asked.

"No. But she does let me have my run of the place. I have a room upstairs. Why are you so agitated?"

"Because he likes her in a big way, hee-hee..." volunteered Ticktock.

"Geez! She's an element," said Gus.

James, now self-aware, realized his overreaction was unsettling. No woman had ever extracted such harsh, jealous feelings from him. And he'd only known her a day. "Sorry," he mumbled.

"You guys heard of the scientist Schrodinger and his hypothetical illustration with the cat in the box?" Gus asked.

"I only know of the cat in the hat and his hypothetical recipe for green eggs and Canadian bacon," offered Ticktock. Gus smiled.

"Hmm, never studied that one." Gus sat on the floor and pulled out a cigarette and lit it. "A fired electron hits the target. Now, it can go leftwards or rightwards. But, until an observation is made of where the electron is going, it is logical to suppose that two ghost-worlds or ghost electrons coexist in a state of unreality. Now, the instant you observe the direction of the electron, one of the ghosts disappears. And the other one becomes reality from its former state."

A hall light flickered. The rest of the boys sat on the floor like kids around the teacher for story time.

"Now," continued Gus, "is the universe split into two parallel realities? You place the cat in a box with a cyanide ball and close the lid. Ball may break or not depending on the radioactive decay which will trigger the release of the poison. Before you open it, there is that fifty-fifty percent probability that the cat will be alive or dead. But until it is observed, the cat exists in two realities. And once observed, one of those realities disappears and the other one shows itself."

"Yeah, I've read about the cat in the box," said James. "It's tired."

A blackout in the hallway brought the boys to their feet. They went back into the room where the light was still on. As they entered, they noticed the dove's wing fall from the ceiling, flapping, bloodless, on the floor. It was a clean cut. The rest of the bird... gone.

"Shit!" exclaimed Gus. "This is it! This is the room--!" He licked his fingertips and stretched his hands out, extending his arms, feeling a couple inches away from the wall. He scanned as far as he could reach up the wall. "Did you see that?! Somewhere, where the wing fell from, is the vortex! The cycolinas doorway. Gate of Saint Peter. It's here! Fuck! It fell from the ceiling." He laughed, "Now am I crazy?"

The boys searched the room. The window was still shut. There was no evidence of the bird, other than the broken wing, which at this point, ceased its flapping and fell asleep in the arms of rigor mortis.

Outside in the hall, the sound of people approaching sent the boys scrambling to return the room to its previous condition. Gus opened the cage and threw the wing inside and plopped the cover on the cage. He placed his finger to his lips and cracked the door for a peek. The hallway lights were back on. The group piled out into the hallway. The boys passed several men and women in waiter uniforms, headed the opposite way.

"What kind of bird do you have there?" one of the waiters grabbed the cover to look. Gus pulled the cage away, hitting the wall with it.

"He's sleeping. It's a dove," said Gus who pushed onward.

"Its wings have been clipped so it can't fly away! ...haheehee," shouted Ticktock as the group made a turn towards the stairs.

The lights went out halfway down the stairs.

"We're almost to the bottom," said Gus. When the lights turned back on, Punch, who it seemed had fallen out of the darkness, grabbed James by the lapels and slammed him against the wall.

"Hi," she said, with a wide smile. Startled, Gus dropped his birdcage and it rattled and rolled down the remainder of the stairs. She looked to the cage. "Please tell me that was empty." Gus nodded and ran after it. She grabbed James by the arm.

"Are we in trouble?" asked James.

"For what?"

"I, I don't know... nothing." He kissed the back of her hand. "You scared me."

"I scared you?! The lights came on and suddenly five men are running towards me..." she reasoned.

"Yeah, of course," he said. She pulled out an envelope from her pocket and handed it to Shard.

"Congratulations, boys." Shard opened the letter and read it.

"We get to sit out this next round." Shard gave the schedule to Ticktock.

"Yeah!" said Ticktock as he read who was playing tomorrow. "Oh looky-looky! The Zeros are playing the Bush League Bitches tomorrow night! Wow! Bloody Hell!"

"Really?" asked Aster. Punch and James grabbed hands and she led him back up the stairs.

"I need a moment with your boy here," she said.

"Yeah, sure," smiled Shard.

"I'm okay with it," said James.

"*Are you okay with it*?" she mocked.

"It's up to Ticktock, actually." James pointed to his mate.

"It's true. I test out all his women before he takes them on, to make sure they're safe to eat," surrendered Ticktock. Punch gasped into laughter.

"Ah, yeah, let's go, love," said James, now quickly leading Punch up the stairs.

"What?!" cried Ticktock. They watched the two run off like lovers do. "Lucky bastard. They take the high road and we take the low road." They headed out to the main floor.

"I say we hit the bar, fellas," ordered Shard. "What's that? Aster is buying?"

"Yeah, Bubble Boy!" Ticktock grabbed Aster by the shoulders and shook him. "Is that true?! Huh? Huh?"

"You'd have to physically carry me to..." Aster's words were still on deck strapping their parachutes when Shard and Ticktock hoisted him up on their shoulders.

"Onward! To the Bar!" commanded Shard.

"Aye, aye captain!" said Ticktock with Aster's ankles on his shoulder. He slapped him on the butt. "Yeeha, mate!"

* * * * *

"You're surprisingly strong for a girl your size," said James as they stopped in front of the door to the study.

"Oh yeah?" Punch had sweetness in her eyes. "Well then don't make me angry. Simple."

"Right. Simple."

He leaned in for a kiss. She closed her eyes. The lights shut off. The two stood but a moment in total darkness. She laughed and opened the door. They entered.

"Gus was telling us about a doorway in here. Not the one we entered, but a vortex."

"Really." She made her way to the tub and folded blankets.

"Yeah. And I don't know how he did this, but he took a bird, the one that was previously in the cage, and he threw it in here and suddenly, it disappeared." Punch smiled tight lipped, dimples filling with restrained laughter. "I know. Silly. But what I found to be so shocking was, the bird's wing! Somehow, broke off. And we all saw it fall, as if out of nowhere. And the bird... completely gone! Vanished! Bloody crazy you know."

"Could you lock the door?" She emptied the tub of its bedding.

"What's the matter with you?" asked James, noticing a peculiar sort of amusement on her face.

"Just lock the door, sweetie." He turned the lock. Her face lit up and she nervously hit her knuckles together.

"What's going on?"

While she paced around the room, she bit into her knuckle and then faced him. "He's right. He shouldn't have been in here, but he's right."

"Okay."

"That's why I've brought you here," she said, still anxious.

"I don't follow..."

"James... this is gonna sound stupid... do you believe in angels?"

"What?"

"Um... celestial beings...?"

"What are you driving at?"

"Angels."

"Yeah, I um, I don't know. Why?"

"I don't know how to say this or prepare you for what I'm about to show you, ah..." her caution-filled laugh eased her.

"Just say it, you crazy bird!" James laughed. "You're a different kind of girl altogether aren't you?"

"Yes. Different." She slapped her hands to her thighs. "James. I'm an angel."

"See? That wasn't so hard, was it?" He took her hands. "You're the most beautiful angel I've ever seen." She shook her head.

"Fuck! I have to show you what I'm talking about. Fuck it! I have to warn you... shit! Okay. Sorry. I'm going to take you to a place like nothing you've ever seen! Ever! But there's no need to be scared. You can trust me James. It's just that it's a different sort of world..." She noticed she was losing him. "And wait. No, it's not drugs, or anything like that either. James?"

"I love your enthusiasm. Okay. Take me to Wonderland. I'm yours girl."

"Okay. Good attitude. Open-minded and all that shit. Love it. I'd offer you a drink, but I don't want to hinder any moment of this experience. You will want to have a clear head to absorb it all."

She kissed him quick on the lips and then walked behind the desk and unlocked a drawer, pulling out water pipes that she laid on the desk top. On the floor, just below where the vortex slept, a piece of hardwood was removed to show a drainage screen. A section of wall was opened and Punch, assembled a water pipe into another one already inside.

"You're a plumber too?"

"I need you to help me move the tub over here, so it lines up," she pointed to the pipe in the wall. James got behind the tub. He waited for her to get the other side. "Just a little nudge." As he pushed, it began to slowly walk.

"Whoa, what the--?" James looked at the feet. "How does it do that?"

"That's nothing. Trust me," she said while she connected a faucet to the pipe on the wall and as the tub lined up under the faucet, she placed a plug into the tub's drain. She turned the knob and hot water cascaded into the bathtub.

"Give me your cell," she said while opening another desk drawer. He handed it to her and she locked it up. "Okay, you can get in." He took off his jacket. She stopped him with a hand to his arm. "No."

"You're kidding?"

"No. You're gonna need your clothes."

"Are we taking a bath?" He put his jacket back on.

"Only a spiritual one."

"Do we need soap for that?"

"You can leave your shoes here," she smiled. As soon as he removed his boots, he stepped into the bath. She peeled off her black boots and stepped in front of him. They both sat down. Their clothes reflecting new colors into the water. The water was already to their waist. Steam clouded the room. She looked back at him and leaned for a kiss, to make sure he was still with her. The light in the room flickered off and back on. "I know what you're thinking. I'm the craziest bitch you've ever met." She faced forward, her back to him now. "And you're right."

"Punch. You have offered a fresh prospect every hour I've known you," said James. "We just met and already I'm... I'm..." He wondered if it was wise to express his true feelings. She turned her head to the side for a better listen. "...I'm close to losing myself to you. I don't know." Too late. He let her in on his heart.

She twisted around, the water swooshing between them. "Thank you for that. Me too." She tasted his lips. The lights went out. He noticed electrical currents on either side of his peripheral vision. The room had become a sauna. Punch faced forward. With the water, up to their chests, she shut off the valve. "Hold on."

The vortex glowed a green hue as it opened large, down to the floor in front of them. A wind blew at them, refreshing. Water sprayed James's face. He cleared his eyes and with a falling sensation, opened them to find they were no longer in the room. They both grabbed the rim of the tub. He felt his body pushed and pulled from every direction, at once. It looked like he was trapped in a Cubist painting. All around, a crystalized blackness. He couldn't make anything out. Punch was no longer in front of him, a blue electrical current had taken her place. Then she was back. His own hands became two-dimensional. Punch turned to him. The loud sounds of water falling caused Punch to shout.

"Don't panic, James! You'll be okay! It's just a little bumpy!" She looked like a broken mirror...either that, or his retina split into pieces. Her nose, two dimensional. Ears, one dimensional. Eyes, three dimensional. Hair, four dimensional... everything was shifting into various dimensional shapes. Sounds were lost and found. The water in the tub changed properties, becoming like a jello-cushion before the tub faded away. James now looked to his cartoon-like arms and feet, which were there and gone and there and gone. Toes became overly huge and then small. She grabbed his hand and the two swam up through some brush and crawled out from a hole in the ground. Punch and James stood dry under a dark and cloudy sky. A breeze drifted by.

"Welcome to Purgalapudlia. The fourth dimension," she said. Nearby, a few Purggies rose from hiding.

"It is our dear Punch!" cried one of the Purggies. James bent over and vomited. Punch used her hand to wipe his chin.

"You'll get used to it soon," she assured him. She wiped her hands clean on her pants then waved at the others. "I've brought someone dear to me. It's his first time here. This is James."

"Hello James," one said.

"Hi James," the other said. The greetings were met with a wave of his arm in the air as James was still bent over, ready to hurl again.

"Sorry," he told them. He threw up and collapsed to the ground. She knelt down beside him and stroked his hair.

"It's okay, sweetie. Your eyes will soon adjust." The others huddled around him. Two new ones gathered. They didn't look human at all, not to James. Two of them had wasp wings from their shoulders down the length of their body. "Could you go fetch some water?" she asked one of them.

"Yes. Right away." He left.

"Keep your eyes open. It's the only way you'll adjust," Punch said.

James looked up at Punch and the others. From his perspective, they were all multi-faced and multi-limbed.

"It's called the Picasso effect," Punch continued. "We all look like one of those abstract, multi-angled paintings."

James sat up.

"We just came out of a multidimensional forest. Tightly woven forests of infinite number of dimensions."

"Ok, I'm feeling better. Yeah, I think. What the fuck is this?!" He looked around. "Where are we?"

"It's the fourth dimension, good sir," answered one of the Purggies. "You two traveled through a pierced brane. A portal. Connecting our two worlds." He looked at Punch. "Does he know about such matters?"

"Well, now he does," she joked. The Purggie who answered was an athletically built fellow. James got up to his feet once the other returned with water.

"Are you the pit brawler of the bunch?" she asked the athletically built fellow. He knew exactly where she was going with this.

"Yes, Punch," he regretfully said.

"Let's play the portal. You and me!"

"No. I will not fight you."

"Come on. I want to show James a sample of a Purggie contest around the portal."

"It is illegal, now."

"Don't bullshit your way out of this! Come on. Bare-knuckles."

She and the pit brawler were surrounded by a ring of watchers, James included. The two fighters stood in the center with the portal. It resembled a school yard fight the way the two faced each other and circled around the portal. With the music of an elated group, cheering and jeering, James remained quiet.

"What's your name?" she asked.

"Michael."

"Come on James!" Punch shouted. "Let me hear you!" Her eyes never left the pit brawler's.

"Go Sugar Tits!" yelled James. She looked over, distracted by his choice of words.

The pit brawler threw a blow which she caught with her shoulder. Punch immediately spun a hit to his temple. As he stumbled back, she followed him with a blow to his nose and down he went, through the portal. Everyone threw their arms in the air.

"Sugar Tits! Sugar Tits! Sugar Tits...!" they all shouted. Her face became red. James was all smiles and she hid her face in his chest.

"Sugar tits?" she asked.

"I'm sorry sugar butt," he said as she lifted her head to his. "Damn proud of you luv."

"Kiss me then."

"Which pair of lips? You've got three," teased James.

"Try the one in the middle you fucker." As the two kissed, the rest of the Purggies clapped. They were honored to have her.

Michael crawled back up from the portal with his nose bleeding. A friend lifted him up.

* * * * *

Punch and James rode in a mobile bathtub into town. The desolation of the place was a clear sign that the celestial virus had in fact real consequences. Lights out everywhere, abandoned bathtubs sat broken. Although it was day, the overcast weather caused Purgies to carry dim lanterns.

"It used to be a popular sport to fight me over the portals," she said. "I've lost a few matches. But now they don't want to fight me."

"Michael looked scared," said James.

"Maybe. You know, Michael is a common name for angels. But he's not a true angel. I call everybody up here angels. True angels look more like monsters, with eyes all over their bodies. It's rather disturbing." James looked around at the landscapes. Things were finally starting to look normal again for James.

"I'm sorry. I'm still floored!" James saw the passing buildings and a few mobile tubs traveling up alleyways and Purggies walking about. "I see it all and I still can't believe what I'm seeing. This is crazy!" said James. "I mean, look at you. And what you've done. And this place!"

"It is overwhelming!" she agreed.

"I mean, just having portals. Alone. You read about these sort of things in science fiction. Or you see 'em in movies. You never think it's real. And yet, here we are. It's fuckin' real as shit!" James couldn't sit still. His head bounced around as if his neck was a spring.

Vast fields with soul drilling rigs filled the landscape. These machines, up close, were similar in design to the Apollo Lunar Landing. From a distance, they looked like a virus with its spider-like legs supporting a large red casing that stuck straight into the air. Each of these pylons had a specialized drill pipe, drill collar and a bit for brane piercing. This device pulled up souls from the third dimension. Another kind of soul rig, spread out in fewer numbers, resembled a large snail shell attached to a large plate on the ground. A pipe ran from this "shell" through miles of ringed stumps. These devices pumped souls from the third dimension and then piped them out for use in the fourth dimension. James reached his hand over the rim and pulled up some of the plants in passing. The leaves, flower and stem were black in his hand. Punch looked at the plant he collected.

"Let me see that," she feigned concern.

"Interesting isn't it?"

"Shit James! That's the... fuck! Of all the plants to handle, you had to grab our only poisonous one!"

"What?!"

"That's the famous black poison... planticus!"

"Oh really? Now if I heard you correctly, you said plant a kiss."

"Yeah. You heard correctly."

"Mmhmm. I thought so." He tossed the plant over.

"So what are you gonna do about it? Sugar nuts!"

"Oh, sweet!" He closed his lips on hers. She opened hers and closed them on his. They were like two kissing gouramis.

"That plant wasn't really-?"

"No."

He looked back out at the countryside. "So all those rigs out there collect souls?"

"James," Punch hesitated so as to collect her thoughts. "I don't know how religious you are. But there are some cold, hard facts I'm not sure if it would be right for me to share."

"I'm not religious," pushed James. "I want to learn. Would love to learn the truth."

"Are you sure, sweetie? Because it rocked my world when I first found out. But I lived in a time when... I mean. My parents were very religious."

"No. I understand. It is what it is and I want to know what it is."

"Mortals don't come up here," she said.

"This is the afterlife?"

"When someone dies, there is no Heaven or Hell. No redemption or damnation. Just dimensions." James was on her every word. "Souls travel naturally through various portals from the third dimension to the fourth where they are collected and used, very much like gasoline is used for cars."

"Really?" A blanket of chills wrapped him. "Souls are just a source of energy?"

"Yup. It is sexless. It's neither good nor bad. If Hitler's soul was in Moses, he'd still be Moses," she explained. "There are different types of souls just like there are different blood groups or I guess, an octane number on gas."

James looked out at the fields. She placed her hand on his.

"I'm sorry baby," she said.

"Wow. No, it makes sense. They're no different up here than they are down there."

"Yeah. Greed is universal." She looked out at the passing countryside. "Am I being selfish bringing you up here? Maybe it was unfair of me."

"No-"

"Do you want me to take you back?"

"No. You kidding me? Love it!" James scooted closer. "I love the fact, that of all the people, I was chosen. Actually, why did you choose me to share this with?" She smiled and searched her fingers on her lap. Her delayed reaction was based on an indecision to bestow a heavy truth.

"Why? I think I like you, James." She picked her thumb until it bled. Eyes on her wound. "Is that okay?" She stuck her thumb in her mouth to lick it clean and to nip off the hanging skin.

James waited for her to look at him. Now, she was nervous and blushing. He wrapped his arms tight around her.

"Not good enough. Punchy. Does that make you my guardian angel then?"

"Yeah."

"Shit. So you're not a human are you?"

"No! I am a human. I'm not an *angel* angel. You shoot me, I'm gonna die. I'm from Colorado. I just happened upon some very unusual circumstances. And honestly, I'm feeling a little weird bringing you here."

"Well, it's too late for that now, isn't it? I'm here. With you." He winked.

"I want to show you something." She took James up to a stone wall that guarded a fetching little two-story country cottage. It sat partly under the shade of a couple large trees. The yard was sizable enough for horses. James thought it looked cozy and inviting. She slowed the tub so the two could better admire the place. "I'm gonna live there someday."

"It's nice, isn't it?" said James, not sure if living here was a good idea.

"Yeah." She stared as if to commit it to memory. "One day."

* * * * *

They rode through another town. This town was grander than the last. The buildings looked like they were dancing. Shapes tipping backwards and forwards, looking beautifully deformed rather than formed. Almost an optical illusion without simple horizontal-vertical designs, but more of a positive-negative, motionless movement. The windows were like points of crystallization. The gloomy weather gave the city an older mystique.

"This is the capital of Purgalapudlia. Pearley," she raised her arm.

"Look at this place. It's all twisted-like."

Past the town square, a statue of John Rackle stood, now headless and painted over. *Damnatio memoriae*, in mild form. Across the street, newly erected, was a statue of Punch wearing oversized boxing gloves.

"That's you!" James cried as they rode closer. "You're some sort of leader around here aren't you?"

"I organized their first police force and now, army units." James was in awe. He looked over at John's statue.

"The other fellow... they don't care much for him, do they?"

"That's their king."

"Really?"

"He's actually a brilliant man. His machines took away jobs and that's why all the protest. I'm taking you to meet him right now."

"What's his name?"

"John Rackle."

"As in, Rackle's Tub?"

"Yup."

"But I thought that was like a hundred years ago."

"It's, yeah, right. Um... time, is a little weird out here. He's still alive and kicking." A squadron of Purggy Police rode past in ten mobile tubs. Across the front of each tub were three lines painted-black, white and red. They all wore gypsy-blue tunics and a fixed stare straight ahead. At once, they all looked to Punch and gave her a salute as they passed by. She smiled and embarrassingly waved them off.

"Look at you," he said. "You're not kidding. I am in the company of royalty."

"Please..."

"Please? Why are you blushing? You're so humble. And the most unassuming girl. Listen to you. 'Oh I saved humanity. Not a biggie.' Come on. Own up Punchy."

"They probably do that to everybody," she smiled.

"Yeah." They looked back at the fading squadron, and the fading town. "How does any man measure up?" He turned to Punch. "Right? I mean, you must have a hard time finding a man who is really worthy. That won't be threatened by your accomplishments. You're not bashful. I knew that when we met at the bar."

With her back still to James, she nestled her mouth into her shoulder, eyes watching him. James knew now what Gus meant when he called her an element. She was lost in thought, her eyes looking to the floor, and then back at James. The tub had left the capital and entered the country. He watched her, then looked out at the scenery. She turned and firmly grabbed his hand.

"Shut the fuck up! James... O'clock!" She reeled in his hand and bit his knuckle. He squirmed. She let go. "If I fart, there's no escaping it. You'll be forced to breathe it in. You're kind of trapped back there. That's why I always sit in the front."

James gave her a bear hug. "I've never met anyone like you," he laughed.

"Don't squeeze me too tightly-"

"I bet your farts smell like Chanel number five."

"You're willing to take that risk?"

* * * * *

J.R. Industries stood tall in the distance, a spacious ranch around it. Punch and James rode past the gate and sped by a herd of roll rim, claw foot tubs, running near them like bisons. The thundering of their feet hitting the ground was an impressive sound for James. At a hangar, big enough for airplanes, several Purggy guards, waved them in. Their tub slowed to a trot toward a John Rackle, who stood waiting. John lowered his head before Punch. Then looked at her, lending her a hand while she stepped out. Her fingers felt the greeting of his lips upon them. James stepped out of the tub.

"Punch my dear. So good to see you. Ravishing as always," said John.

"Yeah, hey thanks. This is James." John shook hands with James.

"So he's the one with the indestructible soul," said John, looking James over. "I've heard about you." James wasn't sure he understood.

"Hello," said James. "I've heard about you too, you know. Legend."

"Come now, I would be too modest to wear that cumbersome coat. Thank you, nevertheless." John turned his attention to Punch, who was walking off. "Of course he's handsome. English. You like them British don't you?"

"I'm hungry," she said and opened a door. Their tub joined another tub, sniffing its butt like dogs do. "How's Mother?" Punch asked but entered the building without them, not wanting to wait for an answer.

* * * * *

Inside, warm and comfortable. Punch, John and James feasted at the table.

"Everything here runs on souls," explained John. "Heating, transportation, lighting, food... an extremely sought after source of energy." He whistled at a nearby bathtub. "Here Spot! Come on!" The tub ran over to him, bumping his chair. He patted its rim. The tub searched James, lifted its leg and drained water on his feet. "Spot! No! Come here!" Spot walked over to its master. "Bad tub." He looked over to James. "It's just water."

"That's fine," said James.

"As I was saying, we have a pending problem with the energy crisis," continued John. "Simply put... a soul shortage. You see my boy, souls cannot be destroyed. Until now. For the first time in history, souls have fallen to a... oh, let us call it, a celestial, virus. Madmathix. It has spread like wildfire, destroying many souls. Thus, creating a panic of such magnitude, that Punch here, established the nation's first police force, which now has branched into the nation's first army. She has deployed them to protect portals in our district."

"These portals are like oil wells?" said James.

"And I own many," John downed what little scotch he had.

Punch rolled her eyes at James to make light of John's arrogant statement.

"There is one soul type that is immune to madmathix," said Punch.

"Mine." James assumed. She nodded.

"My boy, you have been blessed with a grade A soul!" John reached for a bottle. The trickle of scotch filling the glass caught James's eye. Its burnt amber reflection wavered on the darkened wood surface of the table. John tightened the cap and with a careful thud to the table, sat the bottle down.

"Soul type B positive to the infinitum..." John rose from his seat and rifled through a nearby table piled with rolled maps and documents. "Don't believe everything you've read about angels, my Christian boy. Guardian angels have had a monopoly over souls..." he unrolled one scroll and glanced it over quick before moving to the next one. "They are driven by greed. They've already purchased you, so as to keep a watchful eye over their property. Very much like a rancher keeps tabs on his livestock. They brand you. Waiting for your demise so they can collect that luminous fruit." He found the document he wanted and with a nod, brought it to the table, laying it out in front of James. The scotch bottle held one corner down, his glass held the other and James laid his arms over the bottom of the page to keep it from rolling up. "Here we go. The table of souls." The chart looked similar to the periodic table of the elements. "Although our universe is varied and vast, there is only a limited number of soul types," John pointed to the far left boxes. "We start with simple souls which include fungi, plants, flowers, trees. Then as we move further right, the simplified souls include invertebrates. Then fish, reptiles, birds, mammals. And that is where complex souls begin. Mankind." John pointed to the box with James's soul type. "And here you are."

"Fascinating." James studied the chart. The symbol for soul looked like the heart rate with a slash through it followed by a dot which represented a soul transcending. Various plus or minus signs were to the left of the symbol, while the lazy eight of the infinity was the exponent. "It would make a great tattoo." He looked to the boxes on the right. "And what soul types are these?"

"Those, also, are complex. They are celestial souls and unknowns," said John. He returned to his seat.

"Wow..." James scanned that area of the chart. The boxes at the very end were drawn in dotted lines. "So how did you know my soul type?" Punch and John looked at one another. Punch got up from the table and rubbed James's shoulders.

"You no longer have an angel looking after you," she said.

"Sounds like a good thing," he said. She kneeled before him and took his hand. "Right?"

"Right," agreed Punch. "I um, without realizing, have rubbed out your angel."

He laughed. "You killed my angel?"

"Yeah. And so your soul has become my property in a sense." She kissed his knuckle. "And that's how we learned your soul type."

"I don't know how I'm supposed to feel or react about this--"

"I mean, I don't *own you*, own you. You have free will. I can't control fate or see into the future. You can do what you want. Anytime." She got back up and bumped her thigh to his arm as she leaned in. "It's just that I'm going to be pissed if you think you can leave me for another. And if you tarnish that soul... so much as a scratch..." She looked away and with a deep inhale, cracked her knuckles under the tightness of her fists. She brought her face to his. "I will kill you." She looked right into his soul. James lost his breath. She smiled and elbowed him. He smiled and pointed at her. "Shit. Sorry. I kid. You can leave me anytime. No strings attached. But, seriously, I have been looking after you."

"No, that's ah, okay. Fine. I'm fine." James was startled next by a bear hug from Punch. John looked away and downed the rest of his glass. The page curled against the bottle.

"Don't be nervous," she whispered to his ear. He nodded.

"James," called John. "How about a little tour of my factory?"

"Would love it. Thank you." James got up and Punch returned to her seat.

"Are you coming, love?" James asked.

"No. You go ahead."

"Not without you, sugar butt."

She smiled. "Now, how could a girl refuse that?" She got up and slid her fingers into his.

John watched the two glow with mutual affection.

"Sugar butt?" John said. "Colorful."

* * * * *

Bathtubs were built in an assembly line sort of fashion. Purggies, their *wasp* wings buzzing, worked the machines. The warehouse resembled a Detroit auto plant in full swing. Technology, more towards the Ford, Model T, era.

"These tubs are built for military purposes," said Punch.

"Isn't it silly to be riding in tubs?" asked James. "Why don't you use tanks or cars and trucks?"

"Well, believe it or not, these tubs are better suited than any of those vehicles. These tubs can jump and climb. They have speed like any vehicle. They don't run on petroleum. They can stalk in absolute silence. They can go where wheeled vehicles can't." She knocked on the side panel to one of the completed tubs. "And they're durable." She turned to James. "I'm just glad he didn't make toilets."

"Cute," said John. "And durability comes handy in the Tub Wars. It's not just porcelain. It has an armor plating within the cast iron mixture." They followed John to another area of the assembly line where the tubs were completed. "What brings all these tubs into animation is the very essence that brings you and I to animation. Souls are harnessed into these tubs." He pointed to a chrome, overflow strainer, which in this case, covered a glass disc that housed a glowing soul. The greenish-white light pulsated, which meant it was at rest. When active, it stayed solid. "The Rackle tub has changed the face of warfare." On both sides to each tub were vents which resembled those on a 1967 Mustang. Seated flat over the vents was a chrome-cased glass unit that housed a soul magnet.

"This is a crucial time in Purgy history," said Punch. "We are taking a stand and showing the angels and diangles that we are now independent. And we will meet their threats eye to eye and vanquish them if pressed."

"What are diangles?" James asked.

"They are demons," said John. "With insect personalties. They lack souls of their own, so they conduct raids on those with them. They too have their own districts with wells that I've built and sold them. Unfortunately, all those rigs and tubs run on soul energy, so using them is at such a high cost, that they attack us and angels and others who have supplies. And thus, the first Purgy police force was born." John smiled at Punch.

"Purgy has become home to many unwelcome guests," said Punch. "Angels and diangles are from other dimensions all together. But, because we have such a rich supply of souls, they've settled in, depleting our resources. The native inhabitants have been left with the smallest percentage. One of these tribes brought the virus with them."

"Yes. Regrettably," said John. He glanced at his time piece. "Although I am the Indift, the King, politics has never been my strong suit. Punch, here has taken up the fight. She's my biggest client in regards to the manufacturing of the war tubs."

"Yet, he keeps making war machines for the enemy." Punch bent over to the foot of a bathtub.

"You could say I'm a businessman first. My sanction here has become a neutral zone."

"Switzerland," James added. John nodded. Punch lifted the tub's foot and spread its toes. John pointed to it.

"Our new models have webbed feet for aquatic warfare," said John. He and James bent down alongside Punch for a closer inspection.

"Like duck feet with eagle talons," said Punch. James touched the large, sharp claws. The digital pads under each toe were thick enough to allow the feet to plant itself flat, without touching the claws to the ground.

"Don't cut yourself!" said Mother.

"Mother." John embraced her. He pulled her to meet James. "Come. I want you to meet my guest. Mother, this is James."

"The boy needs a hair cut," said Mother.

James put out his hand and shook hers.

"Pleasure," said James.

Mother forced a smile.

"He's the boy with the good soul," John reminded her. Another mention of his soul made James uneasy.

* * * * *

Gus, Shard, Aster and Ticktock were seated at a booth. Drinks in hand. Aster sipped his through a straw.

"My two goals... to understand the world and to achieve recognition," said Gus.

"Our goal is to win a million," said Ticktock.

"Well, I'd say, you're on your way." Gus pulled out a smoke and lit it. "Whenever you get that feeling that something lingered in a room, like that room--"

"You mean how butt air lingers?" said Ticktock. He pointed to Aster. "His has staying power."

Nobody laughed. Gus sat motionless, blowing smoke out his nostrils.

"Well, I'm not referring to a room smelling like ass, but more of a sensation I suppose. It could be a remembrance of someone or something that happened years ago in that room. The sensation or energy, playing itself out, over and over -could mean it's trapped in that vortex, spinning. It's like, what somebody did in that room, with such high emotions, because of the vortex present, has left a print. An impression. They would have to be strong emotions to be *recorded* so to speak. You know, a celebration. Falling in love. A birth. A heated argument. A murder. If that makes sense."

"Oh abso-fucking-lutley!" Ticktock was drunk. "I don't know if it's the booze or your theories that's knocking me off my fucking bollocks!"

"If I find a place, that for no reason, makes me feel great, there's a chance a doorway is there, feeding off my energy?" asked Aster.

"A Peter's vortex. Yes something like that," said Gus.

"Peter's vortex?" asked Aster.

"They have many names. You know, Peter's gate..."

"Angel twat!" responded Ticktock, "floating snatch. Butt hole of thy demon..."

"To name a few, yeah." Gus humored him.

Ticktock continued. "What do you think would happen if I licked it?"

"You'll catch herpatitus," said Shard.

A waiter approached with another round of drinks.

"Could we have a bottle of Glenfiddich, love?" Ticktock requested. The waiter nodded and left.

"These doorways can be found anywhere, man," said Gus. "Up in the sky. Behind bushes or treetops. Their sizes range from a pinprick to a football field. And we found one here, man!"

"There's probably one in the Bermuda Triangle!" said Aster. He squirted his hands with sanitizer and fanatically waved them in the air to dry. "That would explain all those mysterious disappearances."

"Yes. That's very possible," agreed Gus.

"A wing lost its fucking bird! What the fuck?! You know what I'm bloody saying?!" Ticktock stood up. "It's fucking crazy! Where the hell did that bird go?! I don't know. It's another fucking world out there. Crazy, cuckoo, cuckoo..." He collapsed back into his seat.

"I know. Thank you!" said Gus. "It is unbelievable. Black holes of our atmosphere."

"Another name?" said Aster.

"He threw a bird in the room. It completely...poof! Disappeared. Gone. *What the fuck*, should be the question gentlemen," said Ticktock. "*What...?* -Say it with me, *-the fuck?*"

"What the fuck indeed?" said Gus. Ticktock snapped his finger and pointed to Gus as a nod of approval.

"So what is your theory?" Aster asked.

"I honestly don't know. I guess it's the result of something collapsing in on itself. A gravitational pull forming a vacuum of pressure that appears when currents are stressed... I don't know. It's brane, b-r-a-n-e, piercing. String theory. I'm going back. Further tests need to be done."

"Of course," said Aster. "It was what I was going to suggest. I want to go with you, if it's all right."

"Sure. You all can come. I want to set up a camera. See if I can capture movement in playback. Slow down the frames."

"Are you gonna use another bird?" asked Shard.

"No. I think I'll use air currents."

"I've got some air currents for you." Ticktock got up.

"No. No, don't..." Aster protested. "Just stand over there." As Ticktock climbed out of the booth, a trail of noises began its parade out his butt.

"Pardon me. Excuse me..." Ticktock stood away from the table.

"You fragrant fucker," said Shard as he waved the air away from the table. Ticktock rolled on the floor with laughter as more juicy noises shot out his ass. There was no escaping it.

"Okay, I'm changing tables," announced Gus.

"It's not safe to get up," warned Shard. Gus had already stood, then sat back down, his face turning green.

"Good God, that's horrible!" Gus, like the others with their own shirts, buried his nose. Meanwhile, Ticktock, red-faced, couldn't stop laughing.

"You know, you can't attract women over here doing that." Shard looked at an incoming waitress. Ticktock sat up. The smell, burned his nostril hairs.

"Right. Women." He agreed. The silence, interrupted as more gas permeated. The waitress walked by and after entering the death cloud, dropped her tray. Her name tag popped off. Her eyes stung shut.

"Damn it!" cried Shard. "They're gonna associate that smell with us!"

"Everyone farts," screamed Ticktock through a gut-wrenching laugh.

"Not like that they don't!" laughed Shard. "Your farts aren't human."

* * * * *

Shard gave Ticktock a piggy-back ride through the lobby while Aster followed, carrying Ticktock's unopened bottle of Glenfiddich. Two girls, one in form-fitting pants, the other in a tight mini skirt, walked past. Ticktock turned back to stare. Shard did the same.

"Pay them a compliment," said Shard.

"Hey, gorgeous!" Ticktock slurred. The girls turned around.

"Excuse me?" the girl in the mini said.

"Nice legs! What time do they open?"

"Fuck you, asshole!" said the girl in the pants. Shard turned to see her furious friend closing in, with her fist cocked.

"Oh shit..." Ticktock kicked his heels into Shard like a race horse. "Run...!"

Shard laughed as he tried to gallop away, but it was too late. As Shard ran for the door, he could hear the heavy pounding his friend was receiving on the back. Blow after blow, while finally at the exit, Ticktock jumped off Shard, mumbling *bitch*. The two girls walked away.

"Ahh, you suck. You need to be shot and turned into glue," Ticktock pushed open the door and left.

"I'm sorry," Shard laughed. Aster too found amusement in Ticktock's beating. "I can't believe they actually attacked us. Crazy," said Shard, looking back.

* * * * *

The parking lot of the hotel became a hangout for a lot of the participating dart teams, once Rackle's Tub closed. Shard, Aster and Ticktock scrambled to the lot. But the walk did promise to entertain with colorful shops, pubs and vistas through alleyways. The Zeros had just parked when they caught the Clocks shuffling in.

"Look at 'em, punk ass be-atches!" Wes yelled out the window. Aster and the boys looked over.

Ticktock walked up to the car and unbuckled his belt.

"I think I'll take a piss right here," he said as he unbuttoned his trousers. The Zeros got out of the car. Ticktock buttoned back up.

"Was up?" Wes reached his hand to Ticktock. Ticktock embraced him. "Yo, not in public."

"Hey there."

"You guys got an off day tomorrow," said Steve.

"Damn straight, you fuckin' porcupine," said Ticktock.

Aster held up the bottle of scotch. "Ah, do you boys want to, ah..." he jiggled the bottle in the air.

"That's me scotch you puddled, pillok, piss pants!" Ticktock tried to grab it. Aster had the advantage of sober reflexes. "Give it, you bubble boy bastard!"

"No. Let's get 'em liquored up!" Shard whispered loudly. The gang laughed and collectively headed to their rooms.

Chris spotted a group of dart players dressed in zoot suits standing near the Zeros' room. Chris looked and reeked as if he had been homeless and in his desperate condition, released stronger body odor, at the mere thought of killing James.

"Haha- James!" Chris made his way over to the zoot suit team. They smelled him coming and felt his ugly energy. "Punch tells me you guys are good. Which one is James?"

"You got the wrong team, homie," said one of the zoot suits.

"Are you James?" Chris asked getting into the zoot suit's face. "You think Punch is your girl?! Huh? Are you fucking her?!" Chris pulled out a gun which fired before he could point it. Another player pulled out a gun and shot Chris in the leg.

The Clocks and Zeros stopped at the scuffle as the zoot suits shoved Chris, punching and kicking. A crack in the sky... bullets blasting, Shard grabbed Ticktock and Jeff and pushed them in the opposite direction as the boys ran to his room. Shard nervously searched for his key and then opened the door, shoving everyone in and slamming the door shut.

Chris dropped dead.

The Clocks and Zeros stayed quiet in the room. They could hear everyone run in scattered formation.

"Where's James?" asked Jeff.

"He's still over there," Shard said. As they pulled out cell phones, they could hear shouts outside for the cops.

* * * * *

James sat in one of the finished war tubs, the long legs of the tub brought the brim up to the height of a man's shoulders. Inside, two wooden benches with padded-leather made for comfortable seating. The seat belts were leather straps with polished chrome buckles. Under the seats, metal springs coiled ready to absorb the shocks from the rugged terrain. Punch straddled the bench, James in her lap while she stroked his hair.

John pretended to be deep in conversation with a worker, but he kept sneaking glances over at the occupied tub. Bitterness of his glare made him cross-eyed.

"How fast can she go?" asked James pulling the length of the seat belt.

"Faster than a race horse," said Punch. James missed his mates, but didn't feel the need to reunite just yet. A group of Purgy diplomats entered. They bowed quickly to John before approaching Punch. She sat up from her lazy lean.

"What does a dart tournament have to do with all this?" said James when a diplomat whispered in her ear.

"Give me a minute James," she said following the group out of the warehouse. James stepped out from the tub, watching her leave.

"Urgent matter presses," John came close to James.

"What's going on?"

"My little fool," he shook his head. "She's not someone you fall in love with."

"We're friends," James muttered, caught off guard by the warning.

"Ah!" John reveled. "Then maybe your foundation is on solid ground after all! But, if you have fault lines in the heart, she will make them shift, unexpectedly."

Mother approached with a small biscuit. She placed it in John's mouth.

"Thank you, dear," said John while Mother slipped her hand into his.

"And what foundation are you built on?" said James after noting the peculiar overt affection.

"It's not your business to investigate," said Mother.

"Intrusive, unpolished manner, surprising from a prick of your age," added John. "But do take notice and remind yourself. Every night. Before you lay your pretty face to the pillow, of my benevolent caution to you."

"Caution noted. Thank you." The loathing undercurrent of hatred in John brewing at their introduction, now bubbled to the surface. James felt warned.

"Darling," said Mother. "Don't badger the plummy boy. I'm going to fetch you some tea."

"You care for some tea?" asked John.

"No." James found a work bench and sat, John's words ricocheting against the walls of his head, like an echo.

"Not for him!" whispered Mother. She left.

"Clever boy, aren't you?" John moved closer to James. "I can see right through the mesh linen you foolishly use to hide your heart."

"Is it that obvious?"

"As you and me standing here. She is exquisite isn't she? Although Mother doesn't approve. No one is ever good enough for her little boy blue."

"I'm sorry, I can't place the hostility... were you two a... couple?"

John, offended, "She was my wife."

Punch entered with an urgent sense of duty, her hair tied back. Took one second for her to read the look on James's dumbfounded face and understand the damage John had done while she was gone. John knew there was a glow about them. And it bit into his heart like the clamps of a charged jumper cable. Punch grabbed James by the hand and led him away.

"Are you okay?" she asked.

"You were married to him?"

"Yeah. What a nightmare that turned out to be."

She brought him back in her quarters outside the warehouse and shut the door.

"You mustn't let him get into your head." She opened a closet door and pulled out an unusual uniform, placing it over a chair. She unbuttoned her blouse. Her key necklace dangling.

"What's happening?"

"There's been a takeover at one of our soul wells by the same group of diangles I've warned to stay away." And just like that, her trousers dropped and she slid into a pair of form-fitting, black, leather-looking pants, grooved like muscle fibers. She pulled the pants up tight. James couldn't look away. She grabbed the red armor corset on the chair and wrapped it around her body. "I'm gonna annihilate them! Could you help me with the back?" She turned away from him and held on to a nearby pole. James reached for the laces.

"Is this bulletproof?"

"You can't have a gun fight against immortals." He pulled on the laces. "Tighter..."

"So how do you stop them?"

"You tell them, *hey... please stop this madness. Okay?* And if they don't listen, then you blast them with tungsten plated soul. But, because of the soul shortage, we're having to improvise."

"Am I going with you?" He finished lacing and she turned to face him.

"No, James."

"I'm going with you."

"No. I'm not going to risk losing you over a silly skirmish. It's not going to take long. I'll be boisterous and swift! They won't even know what hit 'em." She wrapped a black leather belt and holsters around her waist. After she fastened it, she grabbed him by the shoulders. "I want you to stay here. But, I need you to promise me, you won't let John get under your skin. He's a mother-fucker."

"Well, he seemed nice at first."

"No, really. He's a mother-fucker." She lifted his chin to fix her gaze to his. "Listen to these two words. Mother. Fucker." She nodded as James finally got her drift.

"Shit. Oh--shit! That's most foul! Fuck." She threw over a black cloak that buttoned at the neck. "Come on, really?"

Punch raised her eyebrows.

"I think I'm gonna puke," James genuinely felt ill.

"I actually did." She grabbed a black helmet with one large red plume. James followed her out the door.

"He told me not to fall in love," he said to her back as she strapped on her helmet.

She stopped and turned. "He told you not to fall in love with me?" She looked away. "Not that you would, but how dare he. That... that..."

"Mother fucker?" he laughed. She grabbed his hand.

"Yeah." Punch smiled and looked into his eyes. "That mother of all fuckers!" They laughed. Then silence left them idle in stares. Punch became suddenly serious, her pupils growing large. "Kiss me."

"No." James pretended disinterest.

"What?"

"I'm not gonna kiss ya," he said with a stony face.

"Oh, yes, you are..." She moved in for the kiss and he dodged her lips. "What? Come on. Please?"

"No."

"No?" She got down on one knee before him, on the cold, marble floor. "Please?" she whispered, her head down, the feather from her helmet hitting his face. He dropped down to his knees and lifted her chin.

"Of course I'll kiss you," said James with such comfort to melt the purr off a cat. They touched lip to lip and a tear of gold ran down her rosy cheek. She let out a sigh and wrapped her arms around him.

"I finally found someone who fills me with such...fucking delight," she said as James helped her to her feet. He wiped her cheek, but dismissed the strangeness of it.

"Oh yeah?" said James. "Who is that?"

"Ticktock, of course. Love that guy!"

"Me too." He winked at her.

"You're taking the fight out of me, James." She marched onward. "You can sleep in my room until I return. Help yourself to anything and if John fucks with you, I shall royally kick his ass!" A couple armed guards met her. One of them handed her an old detached, porcelain, single-handle faucet marked *Hot*. She checked the barrel, pulled the handle to one side and placed it in her holster.

James, at a safe enough distance not to be detected, followed them into the hangar. Punch addressed her troops. James approached a guard standing by the door.

"Hello. I, um, need armor to wear. A uniform like yours." The guard stared at him. "I think Punch said you would know where to..." And with the magic word, the guard stomped his foot and nodded.

"Sir!" He ran off and returned moments later with a helmet, different in style than Punch's and a cloak made from the feathers of angel wings.

Punch turned to find James buttoning the cloak. His helmet fell off his head.

"No, James."

"You have no choice." He was already in one of the tubs and grabbing the leather straps. "How do you... ?"

"Silcher!" She called to a nearby soldier. He snapped his body to her. "You will drive James here, at the back of our squadron. I don't want to see him up front with me."

Silcher stomped his foot and nodded. Silcher jumped in the front seat and fastened himself in. James watched how he did it. Punch brought one leg into his tub to help strap him in. She made sure his straps were secure.

"I admire your false confidence," said Punch.

"I've never seen a diangle before." James secured his helmet.

"Oh, you will." Punch kissed him, then slapped his helmet over his nose and departed for her tub.

To James the helmets resembled upside down plates with two round holes drilled out to see. The single red plume on top was less flamboyant than Punch's. The leather, square ammunition pouches hung inside the tubs on both sides along with a faucet handle gun up front by Silcher. Hundreds of Purgy soldiers jumped into tubs and loaded their guns. James reached in one of the leather pouches and pulled out a tungsten plated soul bullet. It rolled heavy in his palm. The casing had a decorative symbol along with the soul type, carved on the side. The hangar door slowly opened, the overcast weather on their faces. Punch led the tubs out of the hangar. A low moaning came from James's tub and the soul light shined bright and solid behind him. The tub jerked around, antsy for action. The tub marched out the hangar door. At the inside front of each tub, the gooseneck, British hand held tub faucet with 60" hose, porcelain handle and cradle resembled a phone resting on the receiver. Punch's voice, scratchy as an old phonograph, came out from a round chrome drain near the front. James only caught a few words... *testing new weapon, James, crash course...* Silcher picked up the faucet and spoke into it. He turned a brushed nickel supply arm for speed control and a swivel spout for steering. Silcher hung up the phone and turned to look at James.

"It's your lucky day!" said Silcher. "Punch designed a new weapon. And guess who's going to try it out?" James could see Punch bringing her tub in towards his until it bumped side by side. She unstrapped herself.

"Diangles have a weakness," said Punch as she gathered a different looking weapon. "Like a man's scrotum, they wear their hearts outside the body, otherwise it would overheat." She climbed into his tub with the weapon. "Let me see your right hand." He laid his arm down before her. She strapped a device onto his wrist which wrapped around the inside of his hand and fit the length of his forearm. "Their core body temperature runs extremely hot and thus important for the heart to stay cool. And that's where we hit 'em." She secured the arm weapon. It was surprisingly light. "Remember me explaining how a porcupine's quill works?"

"Yeah."

"Well it's the same principle here. Loaded in these tubes..." she pointed to the black tubing attached to his forearm, "is what essentially looks like a beefed up quill. This weapon... cock your arm back." James brought his arm back and forward. A silver, quill was placed into his hand from the tubing. "Relies on you throwing it at the target, exactly like a dart." She grabbed the quill and banged it against her hip. "It's completely safe and harmless, until, you throw it."

"Really?"

"Once it penetrates the enemy, it doesn't matter where, it digs itself into the body. Every time the enemy exhales, it gets further and further inside. The edges become barbed so it can't be pulled out. Once it sinks all the way into the flesh, it splinters into a bunch of tiny quills that swim around the body, piercing everything to pieces." She grabbed the quill and loaded it back in. "You never have to take it off. Just put it in lock mode..." She snapped a switch. "And you can still handle your gun."

"You designed this?"

"Yeah. When I was a girl, I rescued a dog that was smacked in the face by a porcupine. Since then, I was fascinated by how the quill worked. Oh, and... I love a good dart player." She smiled. "Silcher will show you how to use the gun."

"Thanks, love," said James as Punch stepped back into her tub.

"Be careful baby," she leaned over and kissed him. Then strapped herself in.

"I will." He watched her ride up to the front line of the squadron. Silcher handed him a gun.

"This is our gun. Hold it like this..." It rested in his left palm. "The chamber houses four bullets. You load them up the spout." Silcher loaded the weapon. "Turn handle to the left to load. To cock, throw the handle all the way to the right. To fire, aim and pull handle to center and back right again. Repeat."

Punch raised a short sword in the air. She then pointed it straight ahead and instantaneously, all the tubs took off at a high speed. James slammed to the back of the tub, the gun fell to the bottom and as he bent over to pick it up, his helmet fell off. He hung on to the handles on the inner sides of the tub. The wind blowing his cheeks, all he could hear was the thundering stampede of all the tub's feet, hitting the ground. There must have been a couple hundred war tubs, each with two Purgy angels, some with unfolded wasp wings. Their speed increased by the second. James picked up the gun and slid it into a holster, then placed his helmet back on.

Before long they had crossed the desert terrain. Punch raised her arm and the moving army split into two parallel armies. James watched Punch and her fleet separate from his. Another woman, non-Purgy, led his half. The sky, in different shades of charcoal, threatened of rain, but never delivered. Outcrops of rocky cliffs nearby pointed skyward. The split squadron grew farther apart. On the horizon were soul well rigs and a station. It was occupied by beings that resembled reptilian insects...diangles. They covered that station as ants would cover a carcass. They had tubs of their own. Punch and her fleet descended into the fields first. Once the diangles spotted her, several took off flying in their pterodactyl-like wings. The rest, in their tubs, turned to face Punch and her fast approaching army. They charged! James felt a level of confidence peel away like a flaky layer of garlic skin. The two armies of tubs ran in great speed towards each other and it quickly became all so clear that the diangles weren't giving up without a fight.

"Grab your gun!" ordered Silcher. James grabbed the gun. Shots have already begun. Overhead, in the sky, several winged diangles flew past. James aimed his gun, looking into a diangle's eyes that resembled the sound holes on a violin. They had abdomens like ants, pinchers like scorpions and long, pointy heads that opened to swallow souls with. They were gone before James could fire. Another caste of diangles had gripping hands to manipulate weapons and drive tubs. They pulled out pitchforks and held them out like jousts. Blasts from Purgy guns took out many diangles. Souls of the dead were sucked into the side vents of the tubs. The two enemy forces collided with an explosion of sound. Punch and her front line stood their tubs, belly up to receive the blows from the pitchforks, cracking diangle weapons in half. And the diangles that got hit in the heart with soul bullets, were killed on the spot. James's fleet attacked from the opposite side. Bathtubs running side by side, bumping each other and thrashing about with their claws, forming a large circle during the fight as the Purgy tubs ran the diangle tubs to the ground by grabbing the feet of the enemy tubs and flipping them over. Punch blasted away and after she ran out of bullets, pulled out her sword and began slashing diangles to ribbons. James was terrified, his adrenaline in full peak. He shot down one flying diangle that came too near.

"Nice shot!" said Silcher. James couldn't speak, so a quick head nod did the trick. There were diangles and Purgy soldiers on foot fighting one another. A Purgy soldier had his arm snapped off by a diangle's vice-grip pinchers. Punch leapt from her tub and landed her sword down the heart and chest of a charging diangle. James set his gun down and unlocked the weapon on his wrist. He cocked his arm back and forward producing a "quill". He selected a target and threw a bull's eye right to the heart of a diangle. He cocked his arm and hit another diangle on the gut. The beast leaped at him in sailing bounds, but stopped as a thousand, tiny needle-like quills emerged from within, all over his body. He dropped dead.

Wow, James thought. This is a deadly simple weapon. He could feel the heat coming from the enemy, as if he was fighting beings made of fire.

A small band of angels flew over the battle ground. Punch looked at them passing, the color in her eyes, the first sign that a change in her body was taking place, moved like a kaleidoscope with fire-like patterns. Claws slowly poked through the skin over her shiny knuckles, bleeding. She looked at James, too far away to notice her. A nearby Purgy however couldn't help but notice the changes. She pointed to him while she arched her back.

"Don't let him see me like this-" Punch shut her eyes when growing teeth forced her mouth open. "Fucking angels-!" She gripped both sides of the tub while her muscles swelled.

"Yes Punch!" said the nearby Purgy. "Of course!" He swung his tub for James and intercepted him and Silcher.

Without words, Silcher understood the urgency and took off for a large boulder nearby. Both tubs cleared the battlefield, yet James couldn't see any immediate danger.

"What's happening?" James said as his view of Punch was blocked by the standing Purgy in the second tub.

"It's just a precautionary step," said Silcher as he steered them behind the boulder

Punch leaped from her tub at a passing diangle. She struggled to pry his head open and once she did, she swallowed the souls that lay inside. A quick knee to its heart and it ceased its struggle. Soon after, Punch turned back to her normal self.

At last the diangles were completely wiped out. James felt no remorse for killing diangles. Perhaps, he was still caught up in the frenzy of the moment. Broken and cracked tubs lay about, some upside down, feet wiggling in the air. Purgy casualties were minimal. Punch gathered her army and they all stood in formation. Purgy medics tended the wounded and helped in the gathering of the unfortunate few. She rode up to James with another tub following behind her.

"Punch! That was incredible!" said James, removing his helmet.

"You were amazing!" said Punch. She took off her helmet and hopped down from her tub to embrace him.

"Let's do it again! Yeah!" James threw his fist into the air. "The new weapon... perfect!"

"I'm sending you home."

"What? No."

"It would devastate me if something were to happen to you." She pointed to the non-Purgy woman in the other tub. "I'd like you to meet Killaovski." The woman removed her helmet. Her blonde hair tied in a bun. She had beautiful features and stood taller than Punch and was physically bigger. "She will be your escort back."

"Hello." Killaovski extended her hand out. James shook it.

"Hello. James," he introduced himself.

"I know," her accent sounded Russian. "Punch and I are both imperial assassins of the highest order. You are in safe hands."

"Right." He unhooked the weapon on his arm. He looked to Punch. "So where are you off too?"

"I have more fighting to do. The diangles have a temple close by. I'm going to take it."

"Come James," said Killaovski. "You ride in my tub." He nodded and hopped down from Silcher's tub.

"Good job, James," said Silcher. "I was very impressed. Hope to see you again."

"Yeah. Thanks for everything!" James shook his hand and then handed the quill shooter to Punch. "Please be careful, love. I need to see you again."

"You will." She kissed him quick on the lips. James climbed into Killaovski's tub. She steered the tub away and they departed. James turned to look at Punch, hoping it wouldn't be the last time. She waved as he disappeared over the horizon. James found a melancholy fruit growing ripe in his heart. Killaovski wasn't a talker. She was cold as a car hampered in snow. The mysteriousness of her was all the more alluring. Or at least it would have been, had James not been in love with Punch. He couldn't stop thinking of her. She rang in his brain the way a loud concert rings in the ears the following day.

"Here we are, James." Killaovski's first words of the entire trip. They both unbuckled and hopped out. They stood over the portal, slightly covered in the tall grass. "Are you ready?"

"Yes."

And like that, they both stepped into the portal. Red currents of electricity guided James through.

* * * * *

It was late morning. A stack of black journals landed on the checkout counter of a drug store in town. A dazed James placed his cell phone to his ear. The clerk grabbed one of the books and zapped it with a laser gun.

"Morning. I'm on my way," he said into his phone. He grabbed a pack of pens and added them to his purchase. The clerk zapped the pens. He hit the total key.

"That's twenty-three oh eight," said the clerk. James closed his phone and pulled out his wallet.

"Here you go." He gave him cash.

"Out of twenty-five..."

A red flash in his peripheral vision came and went too quickly for him to acknowledge it ever happened. And it didn't help that he was sleep-deprived either. It appeared once more and James smiled. He waved at it, but it was gone.

The clerk waved back, wondering if this guy was stoned.

* * * * *

Shard read the paper while Ticktock poured himself a scotch in the bathroom. He gargled it and swished it in his mouth before swallowing. Aster polished his dart case to a shine.

"It looks to me, if I had to venture an educated guess, that we will play the winner of the Zeros, Bitches game," said Aster.

Shard turned the page.

"Which means we'll play the Zeros," said Shard.

The doorknob turned and James entered.

"Hello, one and all!" James placed his purchase on the table. "Holy, mother of God!" The boys all turned to James. "God Damn It! Holy shit. God damn it, holy shit..." He paced the room and laughed.

"What happened?" Aster inquired.

James stepped up onto the bed and down to the floor, pushing chairs out of his path and headed to the door and turned and walked over the bed again.

"What the fuck?!" Ticktock was amused. "Did we already win the million?!"

"No," James laughed. His stupor finally brought him to the ground where he collapsed. "My brothers," he said. His face to the floor. "I've met my angel! And she's turned my life around!"

"So...we won the million?!" Ticktock pressed.

"I don't think so," said Shard.

"Maybe we get a portion of it because we're finalists!" Ticktock reasoned. "Is that bloody true?"

"No-no. It's not the money." James sat up. "Remember when Gus let that bird fly in the room?"

"Oh scrikey!" Ticktock buried his head in the pillow. The others were intrigued.

"Punch took me through that doorway!" James jumped to his feet. "It really exists! And she's a fuckin' real angel. I swear it." He rolled onto the bed.

"You really went through?" Aster asked.

"Are you high?" Shard asked next.

"No. No..." James sat back up. "It was beyond... it was literally another world."

Ticktock got up from his pillow. "I want to pull it on like a wet sock." Ticktock demonstrated with hip thrusts.

"Now, I have to ask, does Gus know about this?" Aster wondered.

"No. Shh, no. Hahaha... fuckin' love her! Fuck!" James slammed himself back onto the bed.

"I've never seen you so taken like this." Aster noted.

"You look drunk, stoned, wired, caffeinated, in love and reborn, all at the same time," observed Shard.

"A high state of limerence," said Aster.

"You hit the nail on the head! You have no fucking idea what I've seen. It'll blow your mind." James grabbed at his heart. "I don't even believe it and I was there. It wasn't your typical dinner-and-a-movie kind of date, you know. She really gets your heart and head spinning with high emotions."

"But you just met her!" said Shard, "how can anyone have that kind of effect on such a short time?!"

"It looks like the player got played." Ticktock smacked James on the leg. James closed his eyes. Drained.

"What did this girl do to him?" Shard wondered out loud. James fell asleep.

"I don't know, but she really worked him good." Ticktock climbed off the bed and went for his scotch. Aster looked at James's purchase.

Deeper

Although he hid it well, Shard felt as if the underpinnings of his team were coming undone. Ticktock took to booze much more aggressively than before. He discovered gills so he could live in a river of rum. A sea of scotch. A basin of brandy. A gulf of gin. A lake of liquor. A pond of puffs. And an ocean of old fashions. James lived in such high altitudes, he no longer took in oxygen from the troposphere, but the lightest gases from the exosphere. Aster, on the other hand, appeared to have come out of it better. His obsessive cleaning and sanitizing were no longer at manic levels. As for himself, Shard, on the verge of an overwhelming anxiety attack, still presented himself as the captain in control.

Tournament night and the Clocks sat in a balcony above the bar, overlooking the matches, each with a round of stout. The Zeros were in mid-game against the Bush League Bitches. James had brought along one of his journals in which he obsessively forced the ink to translate his brain's rampant replay of his time with Punch. He hadn't seen her since the battle and constantly excused himself to the men's room only to wander in search for her. Shard teased him about having an enlarged prostate, but knew he was sick in the heart. Sometimes James sat on the hall floor, writing and waiting. On the wall he doodled a cartoon of Punch wearing one over-sized boxing glove on her right hand. The hall light hit it as if it were a museum display. After he signed it, he imagined Punch walking down the hall and spotting her cute caricature.

The Zeros were beating the Bitches. Michelle was up to throw. She hit a triple and two doubles.

"She's probably the best one on the team," Shard said.

"Betty is good," Ticktock defended. Steve was up to throw. He hit a triple twenty, a triple twelve and a triple sixteen. As he returned to his seat, the Bitches removed their already small, ass-hugging shorts to reveal thongs.

"Whoa!" cried Shard. "That's cheating! Look at that!" All the boys leaned in, knocking over drinks in the process.

"Shit. That would just take the wind out of me," said Ticktock.

"Even with a million dollars at stake?" Aster reminded him. "Well, truthfully, I think I could still manage a brilliant game. Of course, I can't do it alone, but a good mind cleansing ought to do the trick."

"What are you talking about?" Ticktock grabbed the tipped-over glass and set it straight.

"I'm talking about pure mind selective conditioning-"

"Well don't," said Ticktock.

"Goddamn!" Shard moved closer for a better look. "How can you not look at that!"

"Easy," said James, face buried in his journal. "It's just pussy."

"That's my Kryptonite," Shard confessed. He sat back down. "Who spilled my drink?" He turned his attention back at the match. "Look at Steve," Shard continued. "Now that's composure."

"He's a fuckin' robot," said Ticktock.

The girls bent over in front of the Zeros, ass in their direction, exposing the sliver of their thinly covered kootch. Even Michelle was in on it. Betty was up to throw next. After shaking her butt at the line she threw and missed.

"Shit!" Betty stomped her foot which made her ass jiggle. The Zeros clapped. Wes was dying. He fell off his chair.

"Fuck. This is bullshit!" Wes cried. "But not." Then he laughed. Jeff pointed to his own eyes with two fingers -focus. Wes nodded and looked away taking a deep inhale and deep exhale. He looked back at the girls who now bickered with one another, upset with Betty, who just couldn't make any good with her darts. Wes took off his shirt, revealing his six pack and pecks. The rest of the Zeros shook their heads.

"It's not the same," said Jeff. Wes put his shirt back on.

"Now drop your pants and we're talkin'," said Toto under his breath. He slapped Wes on the shoulder.

Betty threw a double one, her teammates cussing her under their breath. Michelle shushed them, but they kept bad-mouthing. Betty turned around.

"Shut up! You're not helping!" She yelled at her team. She then focused on the board and threw a double three.

"What the fuck is wrong with you?!" Cindy screamed at Betty. Then muttered under her breath, "Bitch."

"What did you call me?" Betty shot back. "What happened to team support?" She returned to her seat.

Cindy turned to the other girls. "She must be a fuckin' lesbian... bitch, distracted by her own team." Cindy wouldn't let up. Betty got up and walked over to Cindy.

"Well, if you wouldn't keep calling me a bitch, maybe I wouldn't have to be-"

"A bitch?" Cindy offered. She stood up taller.

"Yeah, keep callin' me a bitch...bitch! See what happens!" shouted Betty.

"You are a bitch!" Roma cut in.

Betty punched Cindy in the face. The two grabbed onto each other and then, swinging blindly along with hair pulling, the girls clinged to each other, desperate to deliver their frustrated rage in the most direct and unforgettable manner possible.

"Hey, cool it!" Michelle shouted. "Everybody!"

Roma kicked Betty. Michelle grabbed Roma and held her back. The Ref stepped in and separated the girls.

"If you ladies can't control yourselves, you will be terminated from the game!" he told them. "Is that understood?!" They all returned to their seat.

"Should they put their clothes back on?" asked Steve.

"NO!" was the quick response from the ref, the Zeros, the Clocks from above and everyone else around within earshot.

Steve buried his head into his hands. Jeff rose to his feet.

"I'm up," he said. He had to turn his face away to control his laughter.

"Just let it all out," Wes told him. "Or else you're gonna go crazy up there, ya know what I'm sayin'?"

"I'm good." Jeff calmed down and approached the line. Then, out of nowhere, he began to laugh. He stopped himself with a deep breath in and a long exhale out his mouth. "I'm good." Jeff nodded to his team and faced the board. From behind, his teammates saw his shoulders jerking uncontrollably as another round of laughter took over.

"Oh, come on!" Steve yelled. "Dude. Focus!" Toto and Wes looked at each other and started laughing. Steve was upset with them. "Fuck, guys. Let's close this out." Jeff couldn't stop laughing. The tears were coming out. "We need somebody else up there." Jeff finally calmed himself. He turned to the ref.

"Can I take a minute to collect myself? Just a minute?" he asked while high-pitched laughter rippled his words. "I'm sorry..."

"Granted," replied the ref. Jeff sat back down. The rest of the Zeros gathered around him.

"Dude, come on," coached Steve.

"Oh that'll help," said Wes.

"I'm good," said Jeff, wiping the tears dry.

"Are you?" Steve asked. "Cause man, this is getting old."

"No, I'm good. Really." He took another deep breath.

"You're our golden boy!" Wes hit him on the shoulders. Jeff nodded and stood, darts in hand. Victory in his heart. As he made his way to the line, the Bitches tried desperately to distract him. Cindy bent over right in front of him to tie her boot. He walked around her. The pressure got to him. He began to sweat. Roma spread her legs in front of him. The Zeros scooted to the edge of their seat, fingers crossed. Jeff stepped around Roma. The journey to the line felt like a long trek, in slow motion. The Clocks stood at the edge of the balcony.

"Oh, he's not gonna make it," said James.

Jeff bumped into Betty who plopped herself down in front of

him, spreading her legs to share every man's favorite, dam-building rodent. Jeff stared at it, hypnotized. Steve got up and smacked him on the back of the head. Jeff finally made it to the line. Poised and elegant, like a gold-winning Olympian, Jeff threw the first dart. Bull's eye! But then, it fell to the ground. Both teams watched his every move. His second throw hit the steel ring around the bull's eye and bounced off. He could hear his mates moaning.

"Focus," whispered Steve. Jeff stared at the board a moment, raised his hand and threw. Bam! It hit the bull's eye. And stayed! The Zeros jumped to victory, embracing each other. The girls put on their clothes as they argued amongst themselves.

"Now you can leave them off!" shouted Steve.

"Fuck YOU!" screamed Roma.

The Clocks, still standing, clapped and whistled at the teams. Michelle and Betty ran up to join them. Roma and Cindy began fighting. A giant stepped in and held the two apart. He escorted the girls away, while wondering where Michelle and Betty went.

Michelle hugged James, Betty hugging Ticktock. Shard and Aster looked to each other in mutual disappointment. Then Aster watched Roma and Cindy leave behind a door.

"Where are they taking them?" Aster asked.

"Don't know, don't care," said Betty. "After this game, we'll all go our separate ways anyway."

"Well, you girls certainly lived up to your name," said James. Michelle squeezed his arm.

"We hate each other." Michelle agreed. "Betty and I are cool, but Cindy and Roma have always been real bitches."

"I hate Cindy with a passion!" declared Betty.

"What's up with that stunt you pulled?" asked Shard, wanting details.

"It worked the last game we played," Betty sighed.

"Well," said Shard, "the Zeros are a gay dart team."

"That explains it," said Betty.

"The thongs are a last ditch effort when all else fails," said Michelle. "It was actually her idea." She pointed to Betty who shared a wicked grin.

"That's cold," said Shard.

"Poor Jeff was dying out there!" said Ticktock. "You almost killed the bastard."

"That was the point! Hello!" Betty teased.

"Yeah guys. Hello!" Ticktock echoed as he wrapped his arm around Betty.

"Did I say you could put your arm around me?"

"You did. You don't remember?"

"You owe me a drink don't you remember?" she suggested.

Ticktock looked at her blank and quickly kissed her ear, lips pulling her lobe. Betty smiled and squirmed. She pushed him back.

"What'll it be, honey bee?"

Michelle noticed James had dived back into his journal. "What are you writing?"

"Just ah... stories." James continued writing. The page also revealed some of his cartooning, flying diangles and jumping bathtubs.

"You're a writer?"

"You know...not really. But when I find inspiration, I try to act on it." He slipped his journal into his bag, fearing she'd sneak more than a peek.

* * * * *

Warm blood trailed on the basement floor. The only source of light came from side vents high up on the walls, giving the large copper kettles and dark room, a blue tint. An unnerving finality about the place drowned warm thoughts. Roma, alone in the most desolate of places, was injured and unsure of where she was hurt because her body grew numb all over and her mind on the verge of a coma. Maybe she sustained a hit to the head. She was close to naked though and it deeply disturbed her that she couldn't find the source of her bleeding. Her screams, messengers, working on her behalf, bouncing all over the kettles, up and down the aisles, searched for help. Help that didn't translate well into languages that spiders and roaches spoke. An extremely pale Punch emerged from the blackness, her eyes trying to swallow every source of light. She spotted Roma by the foot of a stairway, ascending.

"Hey baby, you look lost," said Punch with a tired, raspy voice. She made her way closer to the bleeding wreck. The basement, to Roma, was a labyrinth of these large kettles, now dull, dusty and inoperable. She sensed something disturbing about Punch as she untied her hair to let it hang loose.

"Stay away from me, bitch! Stay away!"

"I just want to help. You're bleeding everywhere." Punch kept getting closer and then had to lean against a kettle as she tried to hide the pain of her own muscles convulsing. The pain subsided. "It's Roma, right?" She made her way to her.

"What's wrong with you?"

"Let's go upstairs and get you cleaned up." Punch used the iron railing to help herself up the stairs.

"Just stay away from me!"

On closer inspection, Punch was so pale, she glowed an ash white with piercing eyes that resembled a cat's in the night. This terrified Roma. Her voice hit a temporary snag. Punch grabbed her arm. Her complexion returning.

"No-no. It's okay." She walked her to the top of the stone stairs. Struggling from her grasp, Roma renewed her scream. Silence came quick in the form of a damaging right hook to her temple, dropping her. She rolled, relaxed, down the stairs, dead.

* * * * *

The Clocks were comfortable with Michelle and Betty at their table. Of course drinks helped. Shard spotted Punch below and nudged James under the table. James stood as if fire ants climbed up his ass. Punch served a nearby table, her complexion fully restored. Michelle stopped, mid-sentence to watch James.

"She's also a waitress," said Aster.

"Yeah." James felt the blood rushing back into his face and arms. He could finally breathe. He watched Punch carry a tray of dishes into the kitchen. Michelle watched Punch disappear. "Actually, I'll be right back. Excuse me."

He left the table and made his way down the stairs, his heart pounding at the thought of bumping into her. Lights flickered in the kitchen. Surprisingly, not too many people present, James

crept through a narrow corridor which led into a large room with
polished, stainless steel sinks. He froze. His breath had been pulled.
It was there that he saw an *angel* washing dishes. The sleeves of
her white shirt rolled above the elbow, her hair tied back. Water
splashed out of a coffee cup and onto her leg as she carried it over
to the sink. She wore tight, black jeans and the fabric absorbing
the water was poetic. Punch didn't wear dishwashing gloves. She
worked fast and the flickering light didn't distract, even when it was
a blackout for a full minute. She kept working, scrubbing. When the
lights returned, James kept watching in silence. Watching her meaty
thighs press against the counter drove him mad. He wondered how
long it would take before she would notice him. As she put away
some dishes, she pulled the hanging hose and lightly sprayed him.
Then, she continued scrubbing.

"How long are you going to stand there?" she asked without
eye contact.

"I could stand here all night, so long as you're in front of me,"
he replied. She looked at him and smiled. "That was cheesy, wasn't
it?" He made his way over.

"Yeah." She looked for a towel. "But I've come to expect that
from you. You'd be in rare form if you weren't." She couldn't find
a towel so she dried her hands on her jeans. James embraced her.
She squeezed him and they kissed. "Miss me?" she asked between
kisses.

"Like the day misses the night," James replied. She laughed with
her gut.

"Further proof of my point."

"What, too cheesy?" he laughed.

"Shut up."

"I'm so glad you made it back safe," he said.

"Thanks. Yeah." She grabbed his hands. "I'm glad you made it
back too. I'm still worried about what you've seen."

"Oh, I'm better for it."

She kissed his hands. "I can't play cool with you anymore."

"Oh yeah?" he delighted in asking. She nodded. They kissed, fondling each other. He lifted her on top of the wet counter. She wrapped her legs around him, pulling him in, grabbing his head to make sure her kisses were well placed...

...when the lights went out. Right on cue.

PART 3

Shaft

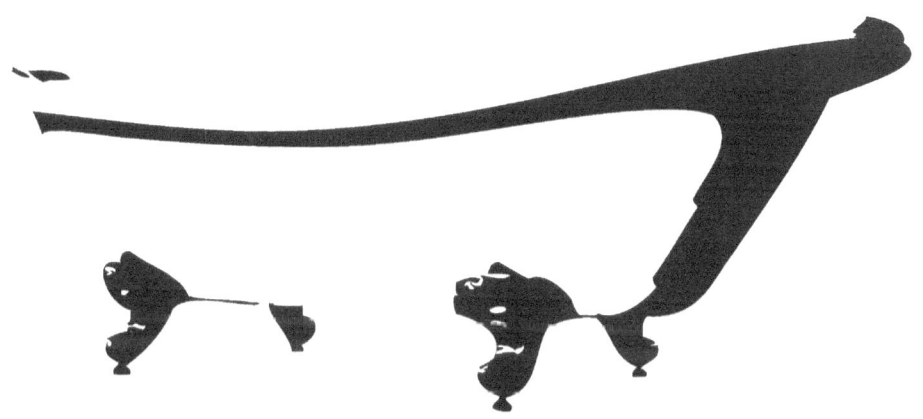

<u>Holy Cause Is Not A Crime</u>

Shard, Aster and Michelle sat together downstairs at the bar. Although it may have been obvious by now, Shard kept quiet about James and Punch. He didn't want to jeopardize whatever game plan James had with Michelle. Aster caught on quickly and avoided the topic. Michelle didn't want to come across as desperate so after asking once and getting the runaround she dropped the subject. Michelle knew when she was out of her league.

Irritation was around the corner.

"Oh good Lord," Shard said to Aster as Gus made his way over with his Army duffle bag.

"Hi there." Gus plopped his bag on the floor. "Tonight my friends, we record the portal. Who's in?" Aster raised his hand. Shard and Michelle looked to each other.

"What's a portal?" she asked.

"Good question. Let's go." Gus grabbed his bag and the three followed. "Where's everybody else?"

"Other business." Shard wanted to avoid a slip-up from Aster's knee-jerk reaction of telling the truth. "Maybe they'll join us later."

Gus turned to face Michelle. "Hi, I'm Gus. We never officially met. What's your name?" She shook his hand.

"Michelle," she said.

"*Pleased to meet you... won't you guess my name...*" Gus sang his response. "*...I say what's troubling you is the nature of my game.*" The other's grabbed their beer bottles as Gus rushed them to follow at his pace.

Punch's room was all theirs. Gus dropped his bag in the corner and untied it. He pulled out several large candles with numbers Sharpied on them.

"I threw the bird in this room," Gus said. "You saw it. Where did it go? There's a vortex, a portal here, my friends and we're gonna find it." He set the candles in strategic spots on the floor, numbers facing out.

"Should we tell him?" Aster asked Shard as Gus went back to digging through his bag.

"Tell me what?" He pulled out his tripod and opened its legs. Shard nodded to Aster and took a swig of beer.

"I can't vouch for the validity of his story. He's been acting a little weird lately, but James claimed he's been through the vortex," Aster said.

Gus set up his camera on the tripod.

"James tell you that?" asked Gus, half-believing, while looking through the viewfinder.

"Yeah," said Aster. "In this room. He said Punch took him through."

"How do you explain that?" Gus stopped setting up.

"You're asking the wrong guy," Shard said.

"Are you guys fucking with me, man? Because, I'm serious about this shit. You saw it!"

"No. Yeah, I'm serious..." responded Aster.

"You saw what happened to that bird!" Gus continued.

"No, we didn't," said Shard. "You had us wait in the hall. Remember?"

"Oh yeah. But man, I'm not a magician. I have no tricks up my sleeve. Or a pocket full of bird wings."

"No, I believe you," reassured Aster. "We're just telling you what James told us." Gus pulled out a lighter from his bag.

"There's a time for jokes... I'm serious man. In scientist mode now. Sorry if I'm a little moody."

"What's on the other side of this vortex thing?" asked Michelle. "Should we be worried?"

"I don't know." Gus bent down to light a candle. "I believe they're portals for divinity."

"You believe in angels?" Shard asked.

"I call them angels. Not by the biblical sense, but something like a divine energy."

"But you're a *scientist*," said Shard.

"This is a new kind of science." He lit another candle.

"It sounds like metaphysical stuff," Michelle said.

Aster took a swig from his beer. "James said Punch was an angel."

"You guys just don't let up, do you?" Gus lit another candle. "Punch is weird-" Michelle spoke quietly as if to herself. "No, I don't know-" Aster wiped his lips of beer. "What are the candles for?" Michelle wondered.

"They will show us the way." Gus lit the last two and got up, sliding the lighter into his pocket, then got behind the camera and turned it on. The flame on candle three was rising. "Kill the lights." Aster turned off the lights and a warm glow of candlelight engulfed the room. Gus filmed as the flame continued to stretch upward, until it was three feet long. The other three looked on in amazement. "That's it!" Gus zoomed out on the growing flame so he could get a wider shot. "That's the fuckin' doorway! Shit man! That's it!" The flame reached towards the ceiling. "Candle number three is seeing movement unlike the other candles..." he narrated into the microphone. "At least four feet and still rising." Suddenly the flames from all the candles, joined candle three's flame, shooting upwards, outlining the portal by the ceiling. It was visible for a split, fiery second before the flames extinguished. Aster dropped his beer. Michelle ran out of the room. "Somebody get the lights!"

* * * * *

Michelle waited in the lobby for Betty to pick up her call. Come on! Betty wasn't answering. She left a voicemail and closed her phone. Shit, I hope she's not already back at the hotel, she thought. The walk back alone was not a trip Michelle was looking forward to taking. And if she did take it only to discover Betty missing, then that wouldn't make her feel good either.

Betty heard her phone ringing from her purse on the floor, but she was too busy receiving Ticktock's thrusts while inside an unused janitorial closet upstairs, to answer. The cramped quarters of the place made the quickie more exciting.

Michelle, anxious, opened her phone again to text Betty when Betty, arm and arm with Ticktock, arrived. Michelle didn't need to ask what they were doing. She snapped her phone shut.

* * * * *

In the grand courtyard area next to the restaurant kitchen, Gus's Volkswagen van parked. Shard and Aster were inside with Gus.

"I thought you had a room," fussed Aster.

"I'm more comfortable in here," said Gus.

Aster tried to ignore the dirty clutter. "It looks like you haven't dusted. I mean who has time, right?" reasoned Aster. Gus looked at him with curiosity rather than feeling insulted. "Except there's colonies of dust mites multiplying all over your cushions."

"Dust mites are everywhere. You're now becoming a little moody for my taste," said Gus. "Just relax, man." Gus connected the camera to his laptop and played it back in slow motion as the flames outlined the vortex.

* * * * *

Punch and James, holding hands, heard a friendly gathering behind the closed door to her study, down the hall. She pulled James back.

"Shit. You told them about the portal in my room?" she said.

"Was that a mistake?"

"Maybe not. What exactly did you say?"

"Everything."

"James-"

"Shit-"

"And they know about us?"

"Sorry, love. It's become a little obvious I suppose."

Punch glanced away, her eyes catching the spot on the wall where James had doodled the Punch cartoon. He studied Punch for a reaction. She smiled while tugging his hand.

"I'll clean it up," he said.

"Don't. It's cute, James."

Michelle felt a little uneasy being back in Punch's study after seeing the candle tests. Luckily she wasn't alone. Betty held her hand. There was an exciting energy of anticipation and the method of letting off steam was through song. With his mouth, Ticktock made beat box noises for Wes, who was laying down a rap to Jeff.

"*I knew you were gay. Well you know that's okay. With technology being what it is today, and advanced medicine, on-the-way, you can live with it and rumble in the hay. Just listen to the words that I say. Mark your calendars for the month of May. That's when you'll have yourself a good lay. Hairy legs, sweaty sack for me, no way. I like the kind of partner with a face you don't shave. Show me a pussy and I will stay. I know you like the sausage docked in your bay. Your hookers all come from the streets of west L.A. I know, cuz you were askin' me to pay. When you spot the Adam's apple you shout, hooray! So, I ain't got no problem wit you being gay! Being gay! Just stay outta my fuckin' way!*"

Everyone clapped. Jeff hugged Wes. "That was beautiful," said Jeff. When the door opened, Punch and James were clapping too.

"Well done Wes. Well done." James winked at him.

Punch slammed the door and locked it. This netted everyone's breath. They stood silently staring at her back. She turned to face them, her hands behind her, leaning against the door.

"Well all right, how lovely and all for me. It looks like I found my super troopers. First, I need to warn everybody about where we're going. I don't know what James has told you, but this journey is not for the faint of heart." Punch walked behind the desk and unlocked a drawer. "It'll be a little turbulent at first, but once you get past that..." she pulled open the drawer, "...smooth sailing." The bathtub was already in place. "James. Could you draw the bath? Hot water. I want a cloud of steam." He nodded and turned the water on. "I'm going to need everyone's cell phones. Where we're going, you won't need them."

"I'm tired, I think I'm gonna go," said Michelle.

"Oh, come on-" Betty watched her head for the door.

"No -let her go," said Punch.

"Michelle, are you sure?" asked James. In Michelle's heart she was fishing for a reaction from James... and she got one. "Come with us. It'll be fun."

After a dramatically long pause...

"Okay." Michelle handed her cell phone to Punch.

"There we go." James hugged her. "That-ah-girl."

Punch placed Betty's phone in the desk drawer. Jeff, Ticktock and James pulled out theirs and handed them over.

"No, I'm cool," said Wes. "I'll hold onto mine." He sent a text message out.

"It'll get damaged," said Punch, her hand still in the air, palms up, to receive. "Better to keep it safe here." He looked at her.

"Where exactly are we going?" Wes asked. She just smiled and collected his phone, securing it in the desk.

"Could you hit the lights?" she asked him.

"Yeah. Yeah fo sho." Before Wes turned out the light, James climbed into the filling tub. The others watched. Puzzled by his behavior.

"What are you doing?" asked Michelle.

"James, you don't need to get in there," said Punch. James, wet, turned.

"What?"

"I just wanted you to draw the bath for the steam."

"Seriously?"

She nodded.

"Oh. Okay." He climbed out, dripping. "Do you have a napkin? Or a tissue?"

"I'm sorry," said Punch. "We only have towels." Everyone laughed.

"Shoot."

"James." Michelle grabbed a blanket and wrapped it around him and then kissed his cheek.

"Thanks, love."

Punch, amused, turned to the others. The steam had gathered thick in the room.

"It might be pointless in explaining. James knows. This will sound crazy. But, what's gonna happen next is, everyone will be riding in bathtubs." Punch also described the notion of going through the wall without touching it. She looked over at Wes, still standing by the light switch. "Wes. The lights." He flipped them off. James was startled to feel Punch's breath on his neck. He hadn't heard her walk over. "It's okay. I was kidding about the bath. Get in." She climbed into the tub and the portal opened, pale green and gleaming, the light illuminating astonished faces. Two empty bathtubs appeared through the portal and awaited their occupants. "Just climb into the tubs," she ordered. "And get comfy."

* * * * *

Three white tubs sat empty in a windy field of tall, black grass. The occupants sprawled on the ground recovering from a vomit session. Punch stood over them. James got up and wiped his mouth.

"You'd think it would get easier," he said. She pinched his cheek with her thumb and looked out at the distant horizon. "Are we safe?"

"Yeah." She kissed him and then tasted her lips. "Did you have peanut butter today?"

"Yo. Where are we?" Wes climbed to his feet. "...So fuckin' unreal!"

Ticktock got up.

"I don't like feeling drunk when I haven't earned it. Is this some acid trip? I mean, what the bloody fuck?"

Jeff rose catching his balance. James shivered, his clothes damp. He straightened himself and tried to stop the Morse code clacking of his teeth. After all, Punch was a bit damp too and not showing any discomfort for it. The girls stayed planted. Panic attacks started in a form of quick breathing for Michelle. Crying felt like the only option she had to stabilize herself. James watched Punch place her hand on Michelle's forehead, whispering quietly into her ear. Michelle relaxed. Punch waved James to come over and sit by Michelle. Punch got up and touched Jeff on the arm to make sure he was okay. She did the same with Wes before gathering the two to sit with her. The wind stopped. A placid, dream-sensation took over, comforting like warm oil on dry arms. Across their shoulders and stomach and back, down their legs and feet, the neck... the blur of reality, fuzzy due to the climbing connection of the conscious and subconscious; the surreal and the real from their perspectives. Cheeks blushed as Punch pollinated each with her caring words. They surrendered to the long wisp motions on their faces and arms by her fingertips. The moment reached its full growth as the first drops of rain released them from their trance. 4-D vision was on. Sickness was gone.

The group traveled by tub to John's factory. James briefed them of this new world. In particular, the nasty diangles. He pulled out his sketchbook from his pocket and began cartooning. He looked back at his mates, to verify his sanity. They had questioned it. But they too stared in wonderment. Their jaws hung unlatched to their skulls. Eyes, like bee larvae, wiggling to escape their sockets. Ears, sonar sponges, bringing in sounds, holding them hostage for the brain's work pile, stacked high. Then add Punch and everything she is.

Military escorts met them and guided them into the hangar. The escorts wore the plate helmets and plumage. Their long-legged war tubs stood taller allowing them to look down at the crew of dart players.

During a good warm meal and a drink of Purgy root wine, the group couldn't help but notice the lights flickering even more so than when they first walked in. Punch unrolled a scroll of the table of souls then took a bite from her dinner. Wes, Jeff and Ticktock slurped their soups. Punch pointed out from the chart while studying Ticktock's face.

"This is you, Ticktock," said Punch. "Type A positive to the infinitum."

Ticktock looked at the scribble on the page with a sense of pride. "That's me?" he said. "Haha, jolly good! My soul type is A plus!"

All eyes eagerly scanned the chart.

"What about me?" said Michelle. "What's mine?"

Punch avoided her eyes and pointed to the chart. "You're, A neutral-" said Punch.

"Really? How can you tell?" asked Michelle. "You don't know my month-"

"It's not astrology," Punch smiled. Punch looked up at the fading lights -the soul energy used to power them, draining away. James watched Punch become irritaited.

"It's getting worse here, I swear-" said Punch as she pulled the napkin from her lap and threw it on the table. Just then, two Purgy soldiers marched right up to Punch and stomped their heels once.

"Punch," spoke one of the Purgy soldiers, "Diangles have launched attacks on various soul-well stations."

"Prepare for deployment," said Punch. "The winged tubs."

"Punch." The Purgy soldier nodded and both marched out of the room.

"Yeah, let's fight some diangles!" said James.

"This isn't a game of darts," said Punch. She scooted her chair back and stood.

"But it's like shooting rabbits," James continued.

"Nooo," said Michelle. "I don't want to kill anything that looks like a rabbit."

"Me neither," agreed Betty.

"They're not fluffy and cute," explained James. "They look more like giant ants-"

"-That will shoot back at you," said Punch. "No- all of you will remain here. Safe."

"Hey, I'm down for a little action," said Wes.

"Yeah, let's do it." Jeff stood.

"Count me in as well. I'll bloody bite their heads off, I will!" exclaimed Ticktock.

"Yeah, I'll shoot something, sure," Betty downed the rest of her drink.

"Look what you've started, James," said Punch.

"Oops!" James skipped around the table and squeezed Punch with an embrace. "That's the point of being here, right? The adventure!"

The armory room had a changing-locker room area within. Punch had gathered everyone there to be suited.

"Diangles are stuck between life and unlife," lectured Punch. She was already in uniform. "They lack the ability to replicate on their own. I mean they have some genetic prowess to make copies of themselves, but can't finish the process without the use of souls." She inspected Jeff's uniform, fastening his back plate with a leather strap. "How does that feel?" She tugged on his armor.

"It feels snug," he said. She nodded and moved to Ticktock.

"Mine feels great sweetheart!" He reached over and kissed her on the cheek. She squinted, but couldn't help but smile.

"Good, Ticktock." She hit his chest plate before moving on to Betty, helping her fasten her bodice-style armor. Betty looked to the ground off her shoulder, for Punch was stitching her up from the back.

"Thanks," she said.

Wes managed to suit himself up with ease. He was a natural.

"Bam, y'all!" Wes did the fashion runway model pose and turn. "Check it! Samurai warrior!"

"So stupid," said Betty under her breath.

Michelle went to James for help with her uniform. He fastened her up. She was surprised to find herself aroused when he jerked at her armor. Silcher entered. With a stomp of his left heel and click of his boots, he stood at attention before Punch.

"Silcher." Punch smiled.

"Punch. War tubs are ready for deployment," said Silcher.

"Good, good... you remember James." She checked Michelle's gear. Silcher looked over and smiled.

"Yes. Of course," he said.

"Hello, Silcher," James saluted.

"James." He reached out for a handshake.

"These are me mates," added James. "They'll be joining the tour."

"At a safe distance, I hope."

"Yes, they will be," answered Punch.

"He's a good Purgalapudlian, he is," addressed James to everyone. "I was in safe hands with him and his unit."

"What do you mean by 'unit'?" grinned Ticktock.

"He means my penis," Silcher joked back. Punch could be blamed for this crass, dry, witty humor, which had become in vogue amongst her men. Before her arrival, humor, in Purgy culture, was saved for leisure activities. She blocked her laughter with puffy cheeks. The silence separated them for a short moment until Wes came to the rescue with...

"Are you serious? Cuz..."

"Yeah, he's serious, you fuckin' idiot!" said Betty. She was still a little sore from losing to the Zeros, in which now she had to endure their company far longer than she hoped.

"Hey! Excuse me! I was joking back, bitch!"

"Don't fuckin' call me a bitch."

"Hey! Don't call me a fuckin' idiot."

"I think they're ready." Punch tapped on James.

* * * * *

The crew gathered in the hangar with the rest of the army. Punch was away, talking strategy with Killaovski and others. Surrounded by guards, John Rackle and Mother approached Punch who ignored them as she listened to a commander mumbling in her ear. John waved to James and friends with a giant broad-stroke salute. Mother stared and turned away with a shuffle. She grabbed John by the hand and tugged. John reluctantly followed.

"We're flying in those things?" asked Michelle.

A new kind of Imperial tub made its debut. The winged tubs. The wings were tucked to the side of the tub when idled. Punch assigned the gang to their respective tub and explained the different fronts they would be involved in. Two per tub, with a Purgalapudlian pilot up front. Punch grabbed Wes by the arm.

"Because of your love rap to Jeff..." she guided him towards a tub where Jeff stood. "...you two will share a tub." Everyone laughed. Ticktock and Betty were placed together and Michelle, who appeared to be the most fragile of the bunch, was placed with James. Punch would be in her own tub, up front, leading the fight. Each dart player was schooled with the *quill* weapon. Each wore one on their wrist. James helped demonstrate. Then, each Purgy pilot, showed them how to use a faucet gun. A crash course, easily understood by the new students of war. They were nervous about suddenly being thrust into combat. A delayed reaction. Yet, there was an athletic exhilaration that pumped the blood. After they've been buckled in, the dart players looked at one another. At that moment, the tubs walked, single file to the giant open hangar door. Light coming in and the runway, paved in flat, blood-red stones, stretched out, lit torches on both sides. The tubs had faces on the front. As the tubs lined up for takeoff, they made a low, nonstop moan. The chorus of low moans from the tubs as their wings awakened from their fold was hypnotic and melded everyone into a single-thinking organism. The first tub completely unfolded its wings, so marvelously long, feathered and white and began to gallop down the runway, flapping its wings, picking up speed and finally, with a slight bounce, soared high into the air. The other tubs followed, one by one. The dart players grew pale in anticipation, their clammy hands held tight to the grips in the tub. When they were finally up for takeoff, the runway ahead seemed shorter than they hoped it to be. The run began. The moan turned into a scream. A sustained scream. The sensation of picking up speed on a rugged ride and the swoosh of wings outward, reflecting light in their eyes like the white foam of the ocean water on a summer day, when the wave returning from its crash and you're standing in the spume, as it relaxes back into the sea, offered a cloud-like sedation to the mind. The scream faded away -they were airborne.

James looked down from his flying tub. "Everything looks ant sized."

Michelle looked down and lost her breath for a moment.

"I don't like this. I don't like this-" Michelle shook her head. It wasn't long before the entire fleet was in the air, headed for enemy ground. Michelle embraced James and clung to him.

A small platoon of diangles in flying tubs of their own, were easily spotted, their tub's large, black, bat wings unable to reach the Imperial tub's elevation.

Michelle pointed at them. "What's that?" James checked for his weapon hanging from a leather strap on the side of the tub. "Who are they?"

"Bad guys."

Punch, leading her fleet, intercepted the "bad guys" in a dog fight. The war tubs clawed each other and ripped wings to ribbons. Punch's tub tore off the wings of one tub, sending it crashing through the dark clouds below.

"Hold steady!" yelled Punch, her sword in the air. At her signal with a slash of her sword the fleet of tubs peeled off formation and entered the dark cloud. The army then emerged from the cloud... a hailstorm pounding down on an unsuspecting fleet of diangle tubs. The collision was as mighty as a force of angry Gods, thundering. The dart teams, at the tail end of the fleet, had yet to fight. Michelle, terrified, cried and screamed. Gun shots sounded like popcorn popping from the distance, getting louder as the players closed in. Wes, Jeff, Ticktock, Betty and James, with a nod from their Purgy pilots, switched off the safety mode to their quill weapons wrapped on their forearms. Soon, the serpent tail of Punch's fleet joined the fight. Wes, Jeff, Ticktock, Betty and James edged up to the sides of their tubs, finding aim at their targets. Exactly where to lean in the tub proved to be a challenge when the tubs shifted from side to side and spiraled downward, clutched in death grips with other enemy tubs. James threw first, his quill landing in a diangle's throat. He cocked his arm back to produce another quill. Wes threw a quill, hitting the enemy. Jeff, disintegrated a diangle's heart with his throw. Betty's quill smacked against the enemy's tub and bounced off. She cocked her arm back and felt the weight of a new quill landing in her hand. She torpedoed it into the diangle's arm. The quills proved well for close-range fighting. The use of faucet guns were too tricky to use in such conditions. It was a weapon that required both hands to operate. Diangles shot back with guns of their own. Stolen weapons from Purgalapudlians and commissioned weapons from John Rackle.

No more diangles in flight, Punch led her group to rest on a cliff's edge, below. Across the way, separated by a ravine the size of the Grand Canyon, more diangles safely gathered on the opposite cliff. They crawled around in their war tubs, right up to the edge, glaring at Punch, who calmly glared back. Punch took the opportunity to survey her troops. Killaovski gave her a nod. The dart players shook from exhaustion. Punch noticed Michelle, snug in James's arms. He rubbed her for warmth and rested his cheek on top of her head. A large cloud glided between the opposing armies. Punch made a split-minute decision, waving Killaovski over.

"Escort the dart players," ordered Punch, "I don't want to risk their lives in this attack." Killaovski nodded and raced to the dart players. Punch and her well tuned army snapped to attention when she raised her sword and at her signal, they swan dived into the cloud. Killaovski removed the dart players quickly and quietly from the mission and brought them to the ground for safety. After the cloud cleared, the diangles swarmed with panic when the cliff across them suddenly appeared empty of Punch and her fleet. The diangles, like frantic lemmings, leaped off the cliff. At that very moment, Punch and her fleet, shot upward, right underneath them, smashing them into all directions sky high. The Imperial tubs hovered above the remaining diangles, briefly before dive-bombing. From the view of the dart players, the raining of soul-bullets into enemy tubs impressed James and his mates, yet again, stunned beyond words as the onslaught came to a close. The enemy squadron had been eliminated.

* * * * *

No rest. At the factory, John Rackle oversaw the assembly line as workers pushed out more bathtubs. Better ones. Bigger ones. Different varieties. Punch braced herself over a map on the table, her hair tied back and out of the way.

"It's time. A direct attack to the main nest will sever the remaining colonies and prevent future ones," said Punch, "take out their leadership..." She clamped her bottom lip with her teeth, eyes still on the map. "Simple."

Killaovski stood next to her, also peering at the map. "Then we pick off the rest," said Killaovski. "Attack, first thing in the morning-"

"No," said Punch, "we attack now. With full force. It will also be a soul raid. We'll bring the equipment for that."

"Good," said Killaovski. "John hired the best when he hired you."

Punch looked over at James, Ticktock, Wes, Jeff, Betty and Michelle standing nearby. They appeared a little lost.

"This is my world now," said Punch. She squeezed Killaovski on the shoulder before sending her off to prepare for deployment.

"I'll help you protect the souls," volunteered James.

"No, that's my job," said Punch as she put her helmet back on. "Don't get me wrong, I mean all of you were exceptional out there."

Michelle grabbed James by the hand. "I'll wait here," said Michelle. Betty also nodded. James kissed Michelle's hand before letting it go.

"I'm going with Punch," James secured his helmet. Wes, Jeff and Ticktock did the same.

"James," said Punch. "It's you I'm worried about." She scratched his cheek with her thumb. "Nobody knows yet... how *special* you are. Once they do, it won't be good."

"I won't tell anyone," said James.

* * * * *

Refueled with new vigor, Punch led a charge on the ground in a double-ended slipper tub with six, running, clawed feet and legs. The other dart players overruled Punch's decision for them to stay behind as well and they joined her in the charge. The army traveled at a high rate of speed, the ground rumbling. There was no secret of their approach. The wind pressed James's hair back as he traveled the fastest speed he's ever experienced in a tub.

So many diangles ahead resembled a massive cloud at first glance. These diangles required no tubs to fly. With pointy heads and pterodactyl-like-wings, they flew with a peculiar armful of something, heading right for Punch and her army. Punch knew exactly what these packages that resembled a black sow bug, rolled into a knotted ball were. Punch turned to her army, pointing up at the fast-approaching diangles.

"SOUL SUCKERS!" Her army spread out. Discs on the side of each tub spun, unfolding poles of spears which raised skyward and locked into place.

Like bombers unloading, diangles dropped the soul suckers upon them. Once they landed in the tubs, the balls unrolled into an embracing creature with a snout like the end of a trombone and arms lined with suction disks. Claws dug straight into the bone of the victim as if a ship was dropping anchor. Once immobilized the creature's tail danced hypnotically, very much like a threatened cobra. The dizzy pattern on the face of the tail, *coma guides*, along with a light buzzing resonance from hidden sound gills, gyrated the victim's body into a spastic, soul regurgitation. The sound caused the temple to vibrate. The snout blew a heavy sound through the chest to stop the heart and suck in the soul. After collecting a few souls the winged diangle would grab the soul sucker and fly them back to the nest.

By spreading out and keeping spears upward, Punch deflected many from her army. Quite a few of her men hoisted soul sucker shish kebabs at the end of their spears. However, several landed in deathly embraces with Purgy troopers. Seeing a poor Purgy in a death embrace, Punch swooped in and pierced the soul sucker with her sword, yanking it off the gasping Purgy. She grabbed the creature's nose, shoved it between its legs and chopped its head, clean off.

Grabbing the faucet gun, James blasted at an incoming soul sucker. Tentacles, out and reaching. As it fell, a claw hooked into his armor and pinned him against the side of the tub.

"Shit-" James grabbed the soul sucker's arm as it dug into his flesh. Silcher chopped the creature's arm in half, pulling the claw out from James. James stood back up and took aim at the diangle, hovering over his head. Ticktock blasted from his nearby tub, sending the beast dead to the ground.

"Are you alright, mate?" shouted Ticktock. James nodded and looked to the open wound on his deltoid. Having seen the altercation, Punch jumped from her tub to James. She peeled open his armor. The wound gushed profusely. She pulled a flask from her belt.

"Your throwing arm...," she realized as she unscrewed the cap. James noticed the flask.

"What's that?"

"Just a little something I picked up at Wal-Mart," she poured it on his wound right as he laughed. The pain numbed quickly. But just looking at her, James felt the pain go away. She wiped the wound clean with a cloth. "I knew this was a risk... maybe you should've listened to me, you dumb fuck." she looked up into his eyes and got stuck in his gaze, defusing her frustration.

"Hey, it's fine. I'm fine," he responded. "Really. Never better." He brushed her hair from her eyes. Ticktock watched them. Jeff and Wes rode close to check also.

"He's gonna be alright, then?" said Ticktock.

"Yeah." Punch wrapped his arm.

Some of the winged diangles opened their pointy heads to collect the floating souls that had escaped the guts of the dying soul suckers. The remaining diangles retreated, their soul suckers full. Back to the nest. Punch took the moment to regroup and address all wounds. With her relentless energy, she led her troops once again. Straight to the nest.

Night dropped like a prayer's knees. The diangle embassy lit up the darkness, making it easy to spot for the advancing army. Punch's tub slowed and crept up sideways, towards the strange, Art-Deco-termite-mound of a building; It was a bizarre mixture. A glimpse of infinity, doors and windows upon more doors and windows, upon more doors and windows.

* * * * *

James's journal entry:

The soul sucker's belly, puffed with souls, is brought inside and dropped into a chamber where it gets stabbed by the diangle's pointy head. The diangle collects all the souls but one. The stomach heals quickly, but the beast soon dies and its cycle of life begins with the last soul inside its body, taking refuge in the skull, essentially eating the brain, incubating, where it grows a new body and breaks out of the old one. That's why having a skull as a trophy is not always wise. It may house a soul, working its magic. The way to kill such beasts is to sever the head, while it's still alive. This would leave all souls within, to be airborne. This was the explanation I was given by both Punch and Silcher. The soul sucker's body was supported with cartilage rather than bone and folded itself tight, similar to a closed umbrella. Because they lacked legs, they depended entirely on their winged counterparts for transportation. They could crawl, but at speeds equivalent to a sloth's. Their purpose was to collect souls. They were living transports. One soul sucker could swallow 50 souls! A diangle, only a few. So it wouldn't be a rare sight to see several diangles tearing into one sucker.

* * * * *

Punch parked her army just south of a ridge top, out of sight from the embassy. Several bathtubs armed with what resembled a harpoon gun, stepped out and in front of the army. These soul-collecting guns got their inspiration from the anatomy of the soul sucker. Each gun fired a large tungsten arrow, with folded arms and a deflated casing attached to a line from a spinning spool. A plow anchor at the end of the line followed the arrow into the sky. Once the tungsten arrow flew over the rooftop, the folded arms, now like spider legs, unfolded. It landed on the roof while the plow anchor dug into the ground and secured the device from floating away. From a distance, these soul collecting devices resembled a weathervane. Instead of having directionals at the end, they were vacuum tubes that spun. Above it, the long arrow laid horizontal with a soul magnet riding on top. Underneath the legs was a loose, flexible sac designed to hold the souls gathered.

With her signal, all her troopers unbuckled themselves free and stepped out of their war tubs. James thought of the African driver ants raiding a termite's mud hut. Jeff, Wes, Ticktock and James gathered towards the back of the army. They watched Punch, sword at her side, gun loaded and without hesitation, leading her troops through the back door as if she lived there.

"Dude, she's something--" Wes couldn't vocalize his thoughts. He checked to see if his quills were all set to go.

"How's your arm?" asked Jeff. James carefully moved it in a circular motion.

"It's sore, but it's good."

"Like shooting rabbits huh?" said Jeff.

"Dude, this is like the perfect, dart thrower's weapon," said Wes as he cocked his arm back to pull out a quill. Ticktock did the same.

"It's scary how easy it works." Ticktock loaded his quill back in. Silcher hurriedly waved them in.

"Now," said Silcher, "stay behind me!"

They entered the building. The smell of the place made their eyes sting and tear. As they ran down a narrow hall, they were already stepping over bodies of both diangles and purgies. A barrage of blasting guns and clanging swords rang in the ears. James fought against the claustrophobic feeling when the walls and ceiling became narrow by another doorway. Through the door, and around the bend, the boys tangled with diangles. The beasts spread their wings outward appearing bigger. With a violin-like-shrill, the diangles charged. Silcher blasted his faucet gun. James and the boys shot their quills with bull's eye accuracy. The enemies, flapping their wings, finally dropped and curled into a stiff, arthritic-looking pose like a sun-dried carcass.

Silcher brought James and the dart players to a balcony surrounding the center hall. There below, the Ambassador and his guards were cornered by Punch, Killaovski and Purgy fighters.

"Wait here. It'll be safer." Silcher ran off to join others in the fight. The diangle guards stood taller than the regular diangle soldiers with maroon colored markings like tiger stripes and spirals around their pointy heads. The Ambassador was winged. His lower body more slug-like and his pinchers delicate; his hands slender as one would find from someone with Marfan syndrome. He hovered behind his guards, eyes looked like inward sixes. Punch got in a scuffle with one of his guards. James foolishly rushed to the stairs.

"What are you doing?" asked Ticktock. James was already down the stairs.

"I need to help Punch," his voice trailing as he descended the stairs.

"Ah, she doesn't need help," said Wes.

"And who's gonna help you?" Ticktock shouted, "JAMES! NO! Shit." The others watched from the balcony.

"Fuck. Maybe we can cover him from here," suggested Jeff. He leaned over the balcony, his arm cocked with a quill. Below them, James threw a quill into a diangle guard and kicked him to the ground -dead. Another diangle, slapped into the back of James's neck and into his right shoulder, trapping its pincher in his armor, digging deep through his flesh. Jeff, Wes and Ticktock were too far to throw with accuracy. They ran after him to help.

"No!" Punch, swam through hits and stabs and made her way to James's attacker. One punch and its heart exploded. It dropped, hanging from James by the arm like a rag doll, pincher embedded. Punch grabbed the pincher grunting as she yanked them from James's shoulder. James fell against Punch, pale and bleeding.

"James!" Punch looked into his fading eyes. She struggled to bring him to safety. Another diangle struck at him, but Punch used her body to deflect the blow. A deep lash spread across her lower neck and shoulder. One pincher burrowed deeper and another stabbed her side. Wes threw a quill at Punch's attacker, stopping it cold. With a back kick, she dropped the beast behind her, where it lay squirming. Jeff covered James's wound with his hand.

"Take him outside!" Punch ordered, as her eyes started changing. She could see James glowing, his soul on the verge of leaving the body.

They carried him away. Punch intercepted a diangle chasing the dart players, throwing a left jab to its heart, then a right to yet another, cracking her knuckles on their beetle-shell-like body tissue. She wanted to be with James and fought harder, burning her fists, vision blearily close to blindness from the strong aroma and sweat. She ripped into diangles, pieces of them shredded and pulverized, splatting out like fruit from an uncapped blender.

Killaovski pummeled through the guards and jumped on the floating Ambassador's tail. It lifted her from the ground. As soon as Punch saw Killaovski with the Ambassador, she ran to find James. She knew nothing could escape Killaovski once she had them cornered. She was a death machine. She squeezed her fingers into the Ambassador. He came down, flapping his wings upon her like the cymbal player for a marching band with his crashes. But that didn't deter her. She locked her arm around its neck and snapped it.

Outside the embassy in the fresh, open, cool air. Punch found James. Her eyes filled with golden tears. She had Ticktock help her carry him to a medic bathtub. She jumped in and frantically tore off his armor and grabbed some cloth from the medic to stop the bleeding. Another medic tried to tend to her serious wounds.

"Him!" yelled Punch, "help him! Not me!" She tore off her helmet.

"Punch, you need to let him take care of that," said the first medic. "You're bleeding bad. I've got James." He nodded to the other medic, who placed a bandage on her shoulder to stop her bleeding. She couldn't take her eyes or hands off James.

Silcher gathered the dart players and left for home base, following Punch and half the army. Behind them, floating straight up from a line to the ground like a string of balloons, the soul collecting devices, now full, were pulled in by Purgy troopers.

* * * * *

James lay in sickbay at J.R. Industries. He slept warm under the blankets of his bed. Michelle sat by his side on a chair, where the cushion sank from supports no longer there. Punch, still in her uniform except her helmet, entered the room. Her sweaty hair tied back and her wounds unattended. The blood on her arm glistened red, coming down over her breast. Michelle was a little taken back by her grisly appearance, especially the blood-drenched cloth on her shoulder. She thought she would have taken care of that by now.

"He's sleeping," said Michelle. Punch, in turn, was startled by Michelle, so caring and uncomfortably close to her James.

"Good," replied Punch. She felt the awkwardness of her pending question throbbing with her wound. "Can I ask you something?"

Michelle looked up at her.

"Yeah."

"Are you two friends?" Punch asked.

"We're an item," said Michelle.

Punch dropped her gaze to the ground with a nod.

Michelle felt her claim over James was too direct. "You're really bleeding a lot." Punch felt the blood cascade off her fingers, which she gently rubbed with her thumb and then wiped them on her thigh. Punch looked at James. She didn't care who he liked so long as he was okay. Michelle gazed at her sleeping beauty. Punch turned for the door. "You know... I think he likes you," confessed Michelle. Punch stopped.

"What have I done to him?" Tears pushed through. "Excuse me..." She shoved the door open and left.

Ticktock and Betty curled up together on a white, angel-winged sofa. Wes and Jeff slept on another sofa on opposite ends. Wes, eyes still closed, shifted over to Jeff's side, falling on top of him. Jeff awoke, with half-closed eyes, to Wes breathing hot on his face and drool threatening to connect with him.

* * * * *

John Rackle busied himself at his desk writing an equation that resolved itself. He neared to writing the answer when a drop of blood beat his pen to the page. Standing behind him, Punch swatted his lamp to pop blackness. Expecting to get hit, John sunk his neck into his chest and listened to Punch breathing above him. No words. Just her angry breathing.

Punch broke the silence with a calm yet trembling voice, "You will no longer sell tubs or weapons to the enemy. Do you understand?"

"Tubs... are just a means of transportation," John meekly spoke. "I can't ban a customer from purchasing."

"I've tolerated your tubs when that's all they were. A *stationary* product for fucking. But now it's different. They're mobile and being used as war machines. Against us." Punch grabbed John's chair and spun him so she could be face to face. "Don't make me come in here and tell you again. You and I both know how horrible I can become."

The silence afterwards took all of John's efforts to penetrate. "Of course," agreed John. Punch almost appeared like a statue in her stillness. She finally lifted her stare and walked out the door.

Punch was exhausted and burdened with sadness. She laid, sprawled over an outside balcony, arms hanging out, her chin on the handrail and the cool night air against her wet cheeks. With her wound properly treated, she had slipped into jeans and a jacket. Michelle approached her.

"Hey," said Michelle softly.

"Hey." Punch sniffed and wiped her tears as she stood up.

"I've got a lot of questions," said Michelle.

Punch took a deep breath and cleared her throat. "Of course."

"Wanted to ask about James. Um, you said James was special."

"He is."

"And you protect souls?"

"Purgies have always been terrorized by diangles and Angels. Both have been coming here to set up districts and ownership. Stealing souls."

"Sounds like a noble thing you're doing."

"There are plenty of Purggies who don't approve of me." Punch rolled her head to look at Michelle, "Some believe I have a hidden agenda."

"Do you?"

"I come here and offer change. Disrupt the natural order of things. And it scares them. They see me as another foreign rebel with imperialistic motives. All I was doing was creating jobs after John shut down their soulmills. I had no intention of leading an army and taking on their holy cause."

"It just sort of fell into place. You kinda got roped into taking charge," observed Michelle.

"The name for king here is indift. The indift! You know what that stands for? Indifferent. Impartial, apathetic... that's the attitude of the general populace. That's why they've been so easy to manipulate."

"You're very convincing. And pretty. It probably comes easy for you to manipulate."

Punch got up to her face. "Michelle, you don't like me. That, I can't manipulate."

Killaovski entered with two Purgy guards, Ticktock, Betty, Wes and Jeff.

"Killaovski will take your party home. James will remain here with me until he gets better. It wouldn't be safe to move him," instructed Punch. Michelle nodded and the rest of the dart players, still sleepy, hugged Punch goodbye.

I Know A Place

Gus had written the equation for the uncertainty principle on a dry erase board.

$$\Delta p \; \Delta x \geq \hbar$$

Shard and Aster sat in the van beside him. Gus handed Shard a bong made of bone.

"Uncertainty is the fundamental ingredient of quantum theory." Gus pointed to the first part of the equation while trying to hold his breath. He let out the remainder of his smoky exhale. "This is errors in position..." he pointed to the other half of the equation, coughed, "And this is errors in momentum. It is greater than, or equal to the h-bar." Shard handed the bong to Aster who declined. Aster couldn't sit still as he endured the lecture. "Because we can't measure both position and momentum of an atom. You can't ask an atom where it is and at the same time, see how fast it's moving. An atom is like a ghost, man. Look for its motion and you can find its speed. Look for its location and you can find the atom at a place, but you can't have both. It's interesting." Gus grabbed the bong and took a hit. He handed the bong back to Shard while holding his breath. "This shit will blow your mind." He turned to his laptop and hit the space bar to awaken it. "I've zoomed in the frame and slowed the speed down. Watch the corners..." he moved the laptop to their view. Aster stood up.

"Could we open a window?" said Aster.

"Yeah. Of course. Sorry, man." Gus reached over to a side window and slid it open. A breeze came in and relaxed Aster slightly. "Is that better?" After a protesting cough, Aster nodded and tightened his lip. He still felt uneasy, though ChapStick helped. He covered his lips. On the computer screen, a strange, scribble-like object peeked out of the portal for a split second before disappearing back in.

"Did you see that?!" pointed Gus. He stopped the footage and brought it back to the screen where he paused it. The freeze frame produced a blurry image of what looked like a peripheral dancer.

"What is that?" asked Aster. Shard scooted closer for a better inspection.

"An angel," answered Gus. "Theology has us believing that angels exist only on a spiritual plane. But, they can also travel into the physical plane, thanks to doorways like that. Since we are living in time, we can't see angels. For the most part, they are living outside of time. Just like God. Angels are like neutrinos... billions of them are going through you right now! As if you were transparent."

"Really? Angels or neutrinos?" asked Shard. "Does that mean we could see God too? If angels can show themselves through portals, why not God himself?"

"Wait!" Gus whispered. "Look!" He pointed behind Shard. Aster and Shard turned around.

"Oh, you missed him!" Gus said. "He was right there! God was standing right there. I swear to... God! I'm surprised you didn't feel his beard. I swear to all that is holy... he was right there! Sandals and all!"

Shard looked to Aster with half-closed eyes. "How did we miss that?"

"He was in a hurry I guess," Gus shrugged his shoulders. "It's cool, man. I mean, he knows when you've been sleeping."

"Why would he know that?" asked Shard.

"...He knows when you're awake and shit," continued Gus.

"Does he even know when you've been bad or good?" said Shard.

"So, be good for goodness sake." Aster finished.

Gus laughed before taking another hit from his bong.

"God and Santa both have beards," humored Shard. "A true fact. It's in the internet. Wikipedia it." Gus coughed and handed Shard the bong. Shard lit the end and inhaled.

"Quantum cosmology..." continued Gus, "Quantum theory of the entire universe is the best way to understanding celestial worlds."

"That or ask God," Shard exhaled.

"I hate math," said Aster. "I respect it, but I get lazy-minded about it."

"Yeah, addition and subtraction..." joked Shard. "I mean Jesus Christ! You can go nuts trying to wrap your mind around that stuff." Gus and Shard laughed.

"Don't be a dick," said Aster.

"Well, this is math of the soul!" Gus said. He grabbed a die from his desk and rolled it. "There is only one outcome here, right?"

"Right." Aster viewed the die.

"Wrong!" said Gus. "We are only seeing one fraction of the full quantum reality! All six have appeared my friend, but in this universe, this dimension, we only see the one outcome before us!" Gus grabbed the die and tossed it back.

"Right," agreed Aster. They both laughed at him. Again.

"So what are we waiting for?" asked Shard. "Come on. Let's go fuck that portal!" He hopped to his feet.

* * * * *

The three boys entered Punch's study. Shard stared at his cell before slipping it into a coat pocket. "I've just been getting his voicemail all night." Shard said. Aster closed his phone.

"Yeah, well James usually answers when I call," said Aster. Gus closed the door.

"Well if it's true, they were able to go through, then why can't we? We're all made of the same kind of DNA." Gus reached into the air just off the wall. He swayed his fingers and arms into a Tai-Chi motion.

"I want to go through," volunteered Aster.

"Let Gus do it," suggested Shard. "He knows more of what he's doing than we do."

"That's cool, man. We could all go, actually." Gus stood back and looked at the ceiling while scratching his chin.

"Did you lose your key?" Shard looked up at the ceiling too.

"I want to be the first one," said Aster. "Some people dedicate their bodies to science. I want to..."

"--Well James already went through, so you wouldn't be the first one," said Shard.

"Well, you're not my father last time I pondered the notion," Aster looked up with a shallow grin. Shard laughed.

Father? What the fuck was he talking about Shard wondered. "Tournament," Shard reasoned back.

"Tell that to James," Aster said.

"Well that's a good idea," said Shard. "Why don't we just wait for him? And Punch. Then, they could tell the bouncer to let us in."

"You guys crack me up," laughed Gus.

"What if you don't come back?" Shard said to Aster. "You think the germs in this universe are bad, you have no idea what's waiting for you out there. All that cosmic cooties and angel shit, floating around."

"Funny," said Aster. "When my mind is made up, there's no... manipulating this infrastructure." He pointed to his temple.

"You don't need to prove anything to validate yourself, amongst us." Shard patted Aster on the back.

"I'm not. This is--- I'm doing it for myself."

Gus grabbed a chair and slid it over, just below the spot. "To open the door, you must feed energy to the vortex."

"How about the doorknob?" Shard asked.

"You know, your dry wit is starting to get a little drenched," Gus stood on the chair.

"He always does that," said Aster. "He thinks everything is funny. It gets really annoying." Shard threw his hands in the air and turned away.

"Let's change our energy into a collective, positive force." Gus reached above his head, over the wall. "No more arguing." His hand bumped the edge of the doorway and the portal showed itself as it rippled like water. Gus flinched, falling off the chair. "Fuck...!"

The boys stared in silence as the portal returned to its invisible state. Aster quickly stood on the chair, reaching his hand over the area, tapping it to a ripple.

"Shit!" After he recoiled, he inspected his hand, "I can feel it!" Aster said.

Aster bumped it again. Harder. The entire doorway showed itself, remaining in a constant state of motion.

"It feels like solid water, but not ice," said Aster, "It's more of a jello-like texture or, or..."

"-fake tits?" said Shard.

Aster looked at Gus for some ready comprehension, but Gus stood stoned silent. Shard shook his head.

"Ha-!" Aster placed his hand into the portal. "Whoa!" Aster pulled his hand out. He reached in again, both hands, and pulled himself up. His body broke up molecularly, sucked into the void like a vacuum inhaling sand off the floor.

"ASTER!" Shard ran to grab what had been his foot, but too late. He turned to Gus. "What the fuck happened to him?!"

"Holy shit!" Gus couldn't believe it either.

A record player, from the room next door, started up in mid-song. A female voice singing about putting on your best...

...and wear a smile. Just to come along with me a while, cause I'll tell you, I know a place where the music is fine. And the lights are always low.

I know a place where we can go...

"Where did he go?!" Shard got as close as he dared to the doorway, fearful of dissolving. The portal, now invisible again.

"He's not dead," speculated Gus. On what basis, he hadn't a clue. Except for the idea that James had done it. The two ran out of the room, down the hall to the next room where the music played. Gus knocked on the door. No one answered.

"Hey! Could you open the door?" asked Gus with his forehead pressed to the door. "Anyone home?!" He grabbed the doorknob -locked. He pulled out a set of keys. The two entered the room with the song loudly proclaiming...

I KNOW A PLACE...

They discovered the old Magnavox record player up against the wall, opposite the room next door. Gus lifted the needle off the scratchy record and stopped the turntable. The room was otherwise, empty.

"He broke up molecularly..." Gus was thinking out loud.

"What does that mean, exactly, for him?"

"He could be anywhere and everywhere."

"Sounds kind of painful."

* * * * *

On one of the upper floors, the dimly-lit chandelier hung from the ceiling, lighting the floor just below this one where Killaovski and the dart players walked with feet made of pillows and murmurs, soft in their ears. The clarity of returning home came soon as they followed Killaovski down the stairs to a better lit hallway.

* * * * *

A lamp, in funeral-ash color and leaves carved on both sides, sat in the main lobby downstairs providing light for a woman and her magazine on a leather sofa. The light flickered.

"...Hey, help-- help me..."

The woman looked around, bewildered. She looked at the lamp and then at the people nearby, wondering if she was the recipient of some hidden camera joke.

"...I'm inside. Help me..." The lamp spoke again. Light flickering every time it uttered a word. Suddenly the lampshade folded inward as it drew in oxygen. The woman screamed herself off the sofa dropping her magazine. The lampshade expanded back out. "Wait! Don't go." The lamp pleaded. Another woman joined her.

"-Oh my God-" said the startled woman, giggling now to what must be, clearly, a joke. Her friend wrapped her arm around her.

A crowd gathered in the lobby. Gus and Shard cut through the audience.

"What's going on?" Gus asked.

"A talking lamp," a man replied. "I've got to get one for the pad."

Shard grabbed the lamp in his arms like a baby. "Aster, is that you?"

"Yes! Help me, Shard," said the lamp. Shard pulled the plug but the lamp remained lit. He carried the lamp through the crowd.

"A social experiment!" explained Gus. "Thank you for participating!" He followed Shard back up the stairs.

A man in a stove top hat and a Dickens style suit descended the stairs right for Shard.

"Shard McEra," he said as he pulled forth an envelope, sealed with a red wax stamp. The initials on the wax, R.T. and written on the front,

Divisional Championships. The Clocks.

"Congratulations. Tomorrow will be a bye-day and then the next round begins the day after." He placed the envelope in his hand. "Good luck."

"Thank you," nodded Shard as the two parted ways in opposite direction. Shard handed the envelope to Gus while he wrapped the dragging chord around the base of the lamp. "You mumble all kinds of rhetoric about science, but you don't know shit!" hissed Shard. "Look at him! What the fuck are we gonna do?!"

The lamp flickered its light off the walls as it spit words out. "If you knew so much-- why did you-- let me go through?"

"Shut up, Aster. Bastard. If you would've only listened to me." Shard made his way down the hall, Gus behind him. He looked to Gus. "What if we put him through the doorway?"

"No good," Gus said. "You'll further complicate things."

"Further complicate things? I'd say we've already reached that point! Wouldn't you say so, Aster?" Shard arrived at the door to the study.

"He'll need an angel to escort him through the doorway," said Gus. "Only then, I believe, with uncertainty, his molecules will reassemble separate from the lamp's." Shard opened the door and carried the lamp in. Gus followed and closed the door.

"Just admit, you don't know shit about what you're talking about." Shard set the lamp on the floor.

"I don't, man." Gus looked to where the portal was. "But think about it, if you were to place the lamp through the doorway yourself, you're in danger of mixing his molecules and the lamp's molecules into another object. Hell, maybe it'll shoot him to another part of the world or galaxy! Or what if he disappears into another dimension? Then, he would be lost forever." Gus walked over to the portal area and stared. "I think we're lucky we've got a lamp. It has definitely shed some light on the situation."

"You didn't just say that."

"What? Oh fuck. I'm sorry."

Aster laughed, the light flickering to his chuckle. The lamp shade contracting and expanding.

"So we just wait for a divine one to swing by and pick up the lamp and take it with them?"

Gus looked at the lamp. "Aster. Did you say Punch took James through?"

"Claimed she was an angel too. Now, I'm a believer," flickered Aster.

"Her cornbread ain't cooked in the middle, if you know what I mean." Shard opened the envelope. He pulled out the folded page and read. "Oh, beautiful..."

"What?" shined Aster.

"We play the Zeros." Shard folded the envelope and letter, dropping it. He pulled out a pack of smokes -only to find it empty. He threw it at the portal; it missed and smacked the wall. With his hands tucked in his back pockets, he walked over to the area and stared up at the ceiling. From inside the desk, a couple cell phones went off. Shard and Gus gave each other a puzzled look. Shard pulled open the drawer and found a cache of cell phones. Shard picked up the ringing phones when...

The door burst open. An angry Steve and Toto barged in holding their phones out to match up the ringing from the phones in Shard's hands.

"You fuckers." Steve grabbed the two phones from Shard. "What are you doing with Wes and Jeff's cell phones?"

"In the desk," said Shard, pointing.

"Okay. So where are they at?"

"I don't know, but James and Ticktock are with them too." Shard pulled out their phones from the desk.

"Are you tryin' to sabotage our team?" demanded Steve in Shard's face. "It so happens we're playin' you next."

"Easy there, cowboy," said Shard holding his ground. "Too many crazy pills?"

"Callin' me crazy, fuckin' shit head?!"

"At this point, yeah." Shard looked over at Toto. "You got any smokes?"

"Not for you," Toto answered.

Steve pushed Shard back.

"Hey, hey guys. You want to be disqualified?" Gus jumped in. "Knock it off. We don't know where they went." Steve didn't let up.

"I don't give a fuck." He pushed Shard again.

"You better fuckin' stop that." Shard got into his face.

"Oh yeah? What are you gonna do about it?"

"Not much. But it will be quick and painful."

"Oh yeah?! You think you can kick my ass?!"

"There's nothing to think, I know I can---"

Steve rammed his head into Shard's gut. Shard grabbed Steve's back and rode the charge until he was slammed against the wall. Shard placed him in a headlock and the two shoved each other around the room.

"Break it up!" shouted Gus.

"Aster!" Shard shouted. As Gus grabbed the lamp, Toto tackled him thinking he was going to use it as a weapon. The lamp shattered to a million pieces!

"NO!" Shard pushed away from Steve and dived for the lamp, sweeping it together with his sleeve. "ASTER!" Shard screamed at the pieces. "Are you there...?" Steve kicked Shard under the arm. "You little fuck nut!" Shard tackled Steve right as he raised his knee to his gut. Toto continued his assault on Gus and the two wrestled to the ground. The door opened. Wes, Jeff, Ticktock, Betty and Michelle entered with Killaovski.

"What the fuck?!" said Wes. Ticktock, Jeff and Wes separated the brawlers.

"Where were you guys?!" demanded Steve. Wes and Jeff looked to each other. "What the fuck?! I've been lookin' for you two!"

"Dude, we're right here," said Wes.

"We play these guys next and then you disappear with them. You fuckin' ditch your phones! Fuck! A million fuckin' bucks is at stake here!" continued Steve.

"Calm the fuck down," said Wes.

"We thought... or he thought, you were kidnapped," said Toto as he pulled out his smokes and offered one to Shard, who was too busy picking up pieces of the shattered lamp to notice.

"Aster was --inside the lamp."

"What are you talking about?" asked Ticktock.

"It's crazy, man," said Gus. "But Aster was sucked into that portal and then he appeared in the lamp. I don't know, man."

"He was inside the lamp?" Betty asked.

"Now he's gone," said Shard. Killaovski walked over and knelt beside him.

"You're Shard?" she asked.

"Yeah."

She nudged the pieces of the lamp. Then she stood up and looked in the direction of the portal.

"Aster is not here, anymore," she said. "His spirit was collected when the lamp shattered in front of the vortex."

"What does that mean?" Shard stood up. "Is he okay? Can we get him back?" She made her way to the door.

"I'm not sure what happened to him. But I will try and find him." She opened the door and left, closing the door behind her on Shard's poignant questions.

"But the vortex is here. Where are you going?" He looked at Ticktock. "Who is she?" He went to the door, opened it to an empty hallway. "Hey!"

"That's Killaovski," said Ticktock. "I need to tell you about James."

"What? What about James? Where is he?" Shard grabbed Ticktock by the shoulders. "Is he all right?"

"Yeah. He's doing better," explained Ticktock. "He got injured. He stayed with Punch."

"Injured?!"

"Yeah..."

"What happened?"

"You wouldn't believe it."

"No. I think I would now," said Shard. "Did you not pay attention to what I just told you? Aster was sucked into that fucking hole and then thrown into a fucking lamp and now, a blonde stranger tells me he's fuckin' back in that Goddamn hole! Maybe gone forever. So what did the fuckin' bitch do to James?! Huh?!"

"She was looking after him."

"That's crazy," Wes said looking at the lamp pieces.

"He was in the lamp?" clarified Jeff. Shard looked over at Jeff.

"Yeah, Jeff. He was shot into the lamp. And shot out."

"Wow mate, that's--" Ticktock zoned out. "That's hard to..."

"I'm sorry Shard," Toto said. Shard nodded.

Steve gathered his team and left.

"Where's Punch?" asked Shard.

Steel To The Back-Bone Of Purgalapudlia

John Rackle stood at a podium facing a crowd. Behind him sat several high ranking officials, Punch among them, the only female on the council. While the others listened, Punch appeared distracted.

"We allowed the people's determination to have a voice," delivered John. "And spoken you all have, loud and brazen and clear as I am standing here before you. The monopoly these vilifiers have enjoyed is now broken. The vice grip in which they held our necks for so long has met a defiance alien to their tradition of oppression over us. They no longer stand a chance against what we have finally become. A new nation. The bright glow of our sovereignty is the bright glow of our souls within and out. Our principality will and has asserted itself once and for all. Their vice grip has cracked and fallen. We now hold the fists for the first time! Days are gone when we cowered in their shadows and allowed them to rape us. Today, my people of the fatherland, we have taken back what is rightfully ours!" John took in the admiration from the crowd. "We will not tolerate abuse any longer. We will stand a proud nation! Feel it, my friends. This is the feeling of steel in our bones. And fight in our blood. And freedom in our breath!" John looked back at Punch and then turned to the audience. "I give you, now, our visionary. Our sole reason we had a fighting chance--" The crowd's volume increased incredibly as all now stood at the mere mention of Punch. "She is our closed fist to adversity. The one who has crushed enemy after enemy after enemy all in the glorious name of Purgalapudlia! I give you now, your dear sweet patroness... Punch!"

She stood and waved at a crowd still voicing themselves with tremendous honor. She smiled and approached the podium after a handshake from John. She leaned against the podium, looking down to collect her thoughts. The crowd grew still and silent. She looked upon them.

"Wow. Thank you all for that wonderfully-warm reception and for accepting me into your magnificent world. A world that has become my home." The crowd applauded again. "Independence is something I've come to know as a companion, waiting and wanting to take my hand, but I was too afraid to reach out to it. Independence stood by me at all times, but I was never aware of its presence until just recently. I'm here to tell you, I have finally grasped independence, with both hands and made that leap over into its embrace. And what I have come to discover, my fellow

Purgy men and women, has burned away the layers of conditioned filth that I wore like an unwashed, ill-fitted, hand-me-down suit. Day after day. Night after night. Until my own stench sickened me and blinded me to fear. Deafened me to impertinence. Angered me enough to cause a stir I had not known within me. A healthy and much needed anger to engage in a face-to-face fight to the end! Size doesn't matter my friends. Strength doesn't matter. Look at me. It's what's right in here--" She hit her heart with a closed fist. "That cannot be restrained. That will not, and cannot be silenced into surrender."

Blood crept over her shoulder and down her breast. The audience murmured in concern.

"Our spirit cannot be compromised. Our values cannot be compromised. For it is our existence we are fighting for..."

"You're bleeding!" one pointed to her. A stage hand rushed towards her with a piece of cloth. She looked to her shoulder as she was soon patted down.

"Let's get you into care," said an escort, grabbing her.

She pulled free. "No."

With one hand she pressed the cloth to her shoulder.

"I got it---" she looked to the people, "It looks worse than it is," she continued. The crowd voiced their love. "Have I mentioned how important independence is? Did I go over that with you guys already? If I haven't, let me recapitulate... Independence. Got to have it!" With an exaggerated smile and thumbs up, she looked to her audience. An audience roaring with laughter. "Tastes great with milk. Try our new honey flavored Independence. Now with less suppression! Okay, I'm sorry. I don't mean to laugh off a serious concern for our future-- cheapen the cause with humor, but I have truly taken on your conviction of freedom and have made it my own. I've never been so moved, not even with my own people. The revelation of our revolution now rings a loud bell of truth! Throughout this land. Make no mistake about it, we are now a capable body of taking on any proposition against what we stand for! And delivering, with such vigor and mighty force, to any tyrant who dares put a hindrance to our growth and way of life!"

She grabbed her rag from her shoulder, now dripping in blood, and lifted it high.

"Let my blood, for all to see, speak, when my words fail. Heart!" She threw her rag out into the crowd and walked off-stage. A crowd of escorts surrounded her. She brushed them off with the wave of her arm as they followed, clinging to her.

Cocktails were served at the reception. J.R. Industries entertained lobbyists, diplomats and politicians as well as Punch supporters. Everyone was dressed in their Purgy finest, of suits in black and red, double-breasted and tails.

"...And she cried heart! The blood symbolizing the fuel for our soldiers," explained one diplomat to another, "...the lubricant to our nation's rigidity!"

"No, It's the one solid proof, beyond any word, of the absolute truth of her enterprise!" argued another diplomat.

Punch, with her hair down, appeared only briefly at the reception, but long enough to entrance the room with her beauty. Washed up, her battle armor discarded in favor of shiny skin-tight, black pants as if they were spray painted on her legs and to offset the extreme pants, she wore a crisp white, cotton blouse printed with simple, femine violets draping over her thighs. As she held a drink and spoke to admirers, she was something to look at. And look was what everyone did. Mother watched from the corner with scolding eyes. John thought Punch appeared pompous. Watching her forced smile and fidgeting gestures, John saw an impatient leader who didn't want to bother herself with the social formalities.

Punch slipped away to see James. It ate at her concentration being so long apart from him. James lay in dim-lit quarters, cozy in a twin-size bed. He awoke to the sound of the door closing quietly.

"How's my new scribe?" Punch made her way to him as he sat up. She kissed him and sat beside him.

"I guess I'm a lover, not a fighter," said James. He noticed how vibrant she looked. "Did you already go out?"

"I was at the victory party, but felt a little naked without you."

"You look... stand up. Let me take a look at you." She stood up and turned her thighs and back cheeks to him. Her muscles quivered under the restraint of her tight leggings. He breathed her in.

"You like?"

"You look absolutely, amazing, love. I mean perfect!"

"Thanks." She pulled out a hair tie and tied her hair back.

"I admit, falling for you is an injury you can't heal me from," James wondered if that came out right. "I mean..." She smiled and grabbed a canister of rubbing ointment.

"So, James... "

"Mhmm--?"

"I just have one little concern."

"Yes?"

"Michelle." She coyly avoided eye contact. She found the lid to the ointment the perfect distraction. "Should I be worried about her?"

"Look at me," said James. "Come here." She stood over him. "Wow." He shook his head, to clear his thoughts. "I need to set this straight. I am in love with you, Punch. Not Michelle." She ran her fingers through his hair. "I have no feelings for her other than maybe a brother would for his lost, little sister." She leaned in for a kiss. "I'm mad for you, Punch, and it does frighten me a bit. I've never been this in love with anyone." She set the canister down on the table, bedside.

"I'm crazy for you too, James."

"Crazy doesn't even begin to describe how I feel about you." He wrapped his arms around her legs and pulled her into bed. She squealed with joy. "I heard you gave a *bloody* good speech." She smiled and lifted her sleeve to show the fresh bandage.

"I guess it wasn't all the way healed," she said. He put his nose to it.

"It smells like fresh diapers."

"Diapers?" she said.

"God, you're so delicious!" Punch moved her body on top of his and wrapped a hand around the back of his neck. Part of her hair dangled over his face. They kissed. He bear-hugged her, pinning his crotch right up snug to hers.

* * * * *

John wasn't enjoying his drink. Mother by his side didn't help his agitated state any either. In fact, it fueled it.

"This party of supporters are here for her," he growled to Mother. "And she is off with the buffoon!"

"Let them be," she answered. "She is not worthy of the dirt you walk on."

A group of dandified men approached John.

"Excuse me," one said. "Do you know where we may find Punch?"

"No," hissed John. With a nudge from Mother, he answered with a touch more diplomacy. "Gentlemen, I'm afraid she left."

* * * * *

Punch and James were nude under the sheets, picking at each other's scabs. With the ointment rubbed warm in her hands, she grabbed his shoulders and slowly squeezed them; with a gentle crawling of her thumbs up his neck and into the back of his head, causing him to drop his head, limp. Their skin, lucent by lamplight.

She spoke softly, "You fought very well James."

"Thanks."

"I want to commission some work from you."

"Sure."

"A political cartoon for our national paper."

"Really?" James was inspired yet again.

James produced a black marker from the table's drawer. He pulled the marker out of its sheath and touched it to her leg. She lay still and watched him. He began to draw over the fleshy canvas of her legs. She closed her eyes to the comfort of the pen against her skin. It tickled her with a pleasant violation. She flipped to her stomach and he continued to draw all over her legs, and up to her rolling buttocks. Her ass gyrated as she gripped the sheets taut in both hands. This in turn caused all the blood in James's body to rush below his waist. Her lascivious breathing, caused her to flip over again, pointing her little furry muffin where ever his pen tip scratched. She raised her crotch to his face and he drew around it, circles. The feeling became frustratingly intense for her. Each stroke she surrendered despite the fact that she'd have a lot of work scrubbing it off later. This made it all the more welcome. And the love her heart incubated for James made it that much better. Breathing through her gritted teeth, James dropped the pen and nestled his mouth over her vagina.

* * * * *

A piece of soul, dotted in contamination sat inside a glass case. John looked at his scientists who busied themselves on a cure for Madmathix. Punch stood with folded arms. She had a mustache and a pair of glasses drawn on her face.

"You cannot have a relationship with a mortal. It's forbidden. I forbid it!" John nervously and frantically searched for the well-crafted argument he mentally prepared the night before. But morning did him no favors in retrieving it.

"Which John am I talking to?"

"You dare bring mortals to fight in an immortal war?!" John paced the room. "It's prohibited! You realize there are grave consequences to ah... This wasn't the plan!"

"Did you really tell James not to love me?"

"What?"

"For your sake, I hope not."

"You're introducing a level of high risks into the heart of the infernal clockwork."

"High risks?" she asked. "No, my little Oedipus. It's more like a lovely level of chance."

"Leave!"

The Aftermath 6

The key had to be jiggled back and forth in order to climb the dry and rugged terrain of the keyhole. Betty pushed open the door to her sanitized hotel room.

"They're not here," said Betty to Ticktock, who followed her. "Good." She turned the lights on. The maid had been there hours ago. Bed covers were pulled tight over the pillows like a sheet covering two halves of a cadaver. Betty noticed her team's belongings. Ticktock checked his phone. "They haven't been here all day." She pulled out her cell. "Fuck 'em." She dialed her phone while Ticktock pulled the sheets down and crashed into the bed. She held the phone to her ear. "Hey, Bitch Number 1. Just want to let you know, I have a boy over here at the room. So don't freak out." She closed her phone.

"A boy?" Ticktock mumbled, his arm over his eyes, "Next time say you have a man over."

"When I get one, I will." She lay next to him, opened the phone and dialed again.

"Who are you calling now?"

She placed it to her ear. "Bitch Number 2."

"You don't need to call 'em."

A cell phone rang from inside one of the untouched bags. Both Ticktock and Betty looked over at the bag on the dresser near the TV. Its musical tone rang again. Betty hung up. The phone rang one more time. Then silenced.

"That was her phone?"

"Yeah, that's right," remembered Betty. "Yeah. She was bitchy before our match because she forgot it here. Stupid." She kissed his lips. "--Brush my teeth." She got up, set her phone in her purse and went into the bathroom. Ticktock found a remote and turned the TV on, flipping through the channels without even looking at them.

After cleaning up, Betty, enjoying how the textured bathroom tile felt under her feet, looked across the room. She saw another Betty going through her purse and pulling out her cell phone.

"Hey-hey! What are you doing--?!" The other Betty turned. She had no face. Her hair floated on a skull of black emptiness. Betty could feel the air in her lungs pulled out and going straight, across the room, into the faceless void. Fatigue sounds of a child yelling steadily, echoed from the other woman like she was in a damp tunnel. She looked over at Ticktock, who woke up, startled at Betty's raised voice. The other Betty was gone. In her hand now, was her cell phone. Her voice, lost for a moment as she stared at it and then back at her purse. She snapped out of her episode with a couple deep breaths and Ticktock's sleepy voice of concern.

"What happened?" he asked as he looked at the door, then back at her. She shook her head, placed the phone on the counter and crawled into bed.

* * * * *

The wallpaper in Gus's room was over a hundred years old and still held together strong. White and sage green with floral patterns. It was neutral gender. At one time, John Rackle used this room to accommodate his workers and guests. Afraid to leave for the hotel and miss the return of James and Aster, Michelle, asleep in the only bed, was accompanied by Shard and Gus, both asleep on the floor. They went to sleep with melancholy moods. Shard couldn't hate Gus for long. It was Aster who had volunteered, after all. Killaovski stood at the foot of the bed, her big eyes watching Shard down on the floor. She stood so still, she almost went unnoticed. Shard glimpsed her only as she left, his mind playing catch up before her presence registered with him. That she was standing in the room, watching him. A red peripheral dancer caused him to turn his head.

* * * * *

Wes pulled out a bowling pin from his duffle bag, shiny red with black duct tape for the rings on the neck. This provided a non-slip grip. He swung it around as if he was a batter warming up.

"That could be construed as a deadly weapon," said Jeff from his bed.

"Shit, man. You wanna talk deadly weapons? After what we've seen--?" Wes set his pin down, bedside. "Shit. I'm more than a little disturbed."

"I feel a little off too," agreed Jeff.

Toto reached into his bag and pulled out a black bowling pin, the *anarchy* symbol painted red on its belly. He swung it around. Steve lay in bed, his back to the boys.

"Steve!" shouted Wes. "You haven't said a word all night..." He lay still in quiet protest. "Oh--, I see. The silent treatment. Cuz I know you're not sleepin'. Yeah, we're being punished. Cuz we didn't get your permission to leave. That's right Steve... no, you just lay there. If that's why you're ignoring us. That would be very stupid, dog."

Everyone looked over. Steve could feel it. His silence drew more attention, clearly revealing his hostile state of mind. As he was about to open his mouth, Toto dropped the bowling pin on his own foot.

"FUCK!!!" Jeff and Wes laughed. Toto grabbed his foot and fell on the bed. Steve turned off his light. It was the easiest way a mute could compete against a throbbing toe for attention.

"I hope that's not your pivot toe," said Jeff.

"Fuck! It really hurts." Toto couldn't bring himself to touch it. He laughed maniacally at his misfortune.

"Now you're gonna have a black toenail," said Wes. "It might even fall off."

"That's what he wants to hear," said Jeff. Wes grabbed ice from the mini fridge and placed it in the plastic wrapper that covered a disposable cup from the bathroom.

"Here," Wes handed Toto the bag, which he used to carefully cover his injury. Wes turned towards the TV. The blackness of the screen pulled him.

"Something is burning..." said Wes as he saw his reflection in the TV, standing next to somebody he didn't recognize-- shoulder to shoulder with somebody not in the room. He froze as his own

words echoed back in an unclear, crashing ocean wave sound.
Something was burning...

"Fuck! What do we do?!" Jeff jumped out of bed and grabbed
Wes by the head. Wes lay on the ground, convulsing in a seizure.
Everyone gathered around.

"Don't touch him!" Steve shouted.

Wes stopped and returned to consciousness.

"Turn him on his side," continued Steve. Jeff turned him.

"Wes. Are you okay, man?" asked Jeff.

"Yeah, yeah-- who was that guy?"

"What guy?"

"I'm cool--"

"Do you know where you are?" asked Jeff.

"Yeah. The hotel room."

"I don't think we need to call 911," said Steve. Wes tried to get
up. "Stay down." Wes smiled as he lay back down.

Wes smiled. "I liked you better silent. You had more
personality."

* * * * *

Little envelopes with per diem meal allowances and two nights
hotel expenses were distributed to all the remaining dart players
for an extension of their stay without tournament activity. Also
included -an invitation to a party that night at Rackle's Tub.

Shard was back at the hotel. He folded the envelope and put it
in his jacket pocket. Ticktock put on his socks.

"This buys us time," said Shard.

"So no word yet on James and Aster?"

"I'm gonna kill her."

"No, it's not like that," Ticktock reasoned. "She was really
protective of him. I'm sure he's in good hands."

"So what are we talkin' about? Where did you guys go? I don't
get it."

"I don't get it either. It was abso-fucking-lutley nuts! I've
never-- ever seen or been anywhere like it. We were all gathered
in that room one minute and the next, we were puking our guts

out in some dark field. We were in another world, mate! It's done something to me brain."

"You stoned?"

"I told you it's done something to me brain."

"Fuck. I feel useless." Shard sat on the bed. "I don't know what to do."

"I'm afraid there's nothing we can do at the moment."

"Is Killaovski like Punch?"

"Cute? I think so." Ticktock grabbed the remote.

"Yeah, I wouldn't kick her out of bed."

"No. She'd kick you out of bed, horrorshow-like!" Ticktock found the porn channel.

"I can't watch that shit."

"I know, they don't show enough men," said Ticktock. "Camera's always on the girl. It's pathetic."

"Yeah--"

"Hey, Fag-a-tron, what's wrong with you?" Ticktock made robotic, mechanical noises, singing the theme to the Transformers cartoon with altered lyrics. *"Tranny-formers, male bots in disguise..."*

"Porn just doesn't do anything for me anymore. I've seen so much of it. I think it's numbed my senses, because I'm finding it takes kinkier shit to turn me on. Before, all it took was a photo of a chick in a thong. Now, a movie of a chick, tied up and getting pissed on by a black, albino, midget who in turn is getting raped by a rabid rottweiler... on the side of the freeway during rush hour."

Ticktock laughed. "I prefer down-syndrome porn."

"You would, you sick fuck." Shard got up. "You always take it to another level."

"Oh I did? No-no. We're neck and neck. Taking it to the next level would have everything you said, replaced with down syndrome talent, including a down syndrome rottweiler... eyes crossed." Ticktock shut off the TV. He slipped his boots on.

"Always love our little chats," said Shard as he opened the door.

Shard and Michelle, Ticktock and Betty, walked past various eclectic shops on the way to Rackle's Tub. Shops that they would've loved to explore had they been in better moods.

Shard noticed walls and light posts, sidewalks and mail drop offs were spray painted with the mathematical expression for Rackle's Tub. "She owns this whole town, doesn't she?"

Ticktock touched the wall. "Funny, it looks like a smile."

* * * * *

Party night, strobe light, Rackle's Tub was dynamite- out of sight! The lobby was full of gyrating bodies, dancing to a nice mix of new and old music. No Doubt's *Bathwater*, a tub-themed song played.

Gus isolated himself in Punch's study. He sat on the floor, back to the wall and his knees propped up to support his arms, his hands over his ears. He waited for Aster, James, Punch...anyone or anything to push away the sadness that pressed him to the corner.

Having had a few drinks, Shard, Ticktock, Michelle and Betty shared a booth with the Zeros. Shard and Steve avoided eye contact as they sat at opposing ends of the long table.

"You've got your pendulum, that's you," Wes drunkenly counted his fingers and looked to Shard. "And your second hand, Ticktock. So all you're missing is your hour hand, James. And your minute hand, Aster." Wes laughed.

"Profound," noted Shard. "And your team, all present, still adds up to...zero."

"Yeah!!!" Toto raised his arms in the air.

"Ooohh, clever," said Wes. "Yo, they'll be back. Just chill out and have another drink."

"Don't tell me to chill out."

"What, you gonna kick my ass?! Please, bitch!" Wes got up. "I'll slap yo ass--" Wes's face was as red as a stop sign. Shard got up, took a sip of his drink and nodded.

"Let's go."

"No-no mate..." Ticktock grabbed Shard as Jeff grabbed Wes.

"I want him to bitch-slap me," Shard struggled with Ticktock. He looked at Wes, "Just once and I will show you pain. I will drop you now."

"Shut the fuck up! I'll punch slap ya, bitch!" Wes struggled from both Jeff and Steve's grasp. "Fuckin' right now!"

"Shut the fuck up you shit brain..." Betty chimed in.

"You shut the fuck up!" said Wes.

"Grow up," added Michelle.

"Sit the fuck down!" shouted Steve at Wes. "You drunk fuck!"

"I can't believe you guys," said Jeff. "Who saved us when the bullets were flying the other night?! Huh?! How can you just forget that? The dude saved us..." Jeff shoved Wes back into his seat. "Come on guys, what the fuck? He's got two friends missing in action, give him his space."

Ticktock raised his glass to Jeff.

"Very diplomatic of you. Thanks, mate." Ticktock downed his drink. Shard got up.

"All right. You guys want to show friendship? Come with me." He left the table. Everyone paused, confused. "Come on."

Shard led the group down the hall to Punch's study. He opened the door and found a depressed Gus lying on the floor. Gazing weary-eyed at the entourage that gathered in the room.

"Are you all right?" said Shard as he helped Gus to his feet. "Those who went through..." he pointed at the portal. "...that thing. I want you to show me how you did it."

"Shit, I dunno..." Wes searched his cloudy mind.

"I need you guys to reenact it for me. You at least remember how it happened, right?"

"We climbed in bathtubs that were in here," said Ticktock, noticing no tubs in the room.

"Punch had James draw a hot bath that was connected to that wall." Betty pointed at the wall where the invisible doorway was. She approached the wall and opened a wooden panel where a water pipe showed itself. "Here. I don't know how she did it."

"Remember there was a ton of steam from the hot bath?" said Michelle. "And then, suddenly, from that wall, was a large green door that we sort of rode into. We were in these tubs that moved. And we just rode inside... like the wall opened."

"Yeah, that's right," responded Jeff. "It sounds crazy, huh? But, it was weird, the wall opened and then we traveled to Purgy-pully, that other world... you know?"

Shard folded his arms and stood back, trying to piece it all together.

"Man, let me get this straight." Gus jumped in. "So you guys just waited until the portal opened and took you in?"

"Yeah, pretty much," said Michelle.

"The lights were off," said Wes. "She told me to turn 'em off."

"And that's when the green light of the door appeared and that's when we rode in," finished Jeff.

"Green light...?" Gus wondered. Shard had heard enough.

"Okay. I-- I don't know what to do with this information," laughed Shard. "You understand? My friends are out there. How do you make the green light appear? And the door to open?"

Everyone just stared.

"You gotta ask Punch." Wes slid with his back to the wall, down to the ground where his tired bones sat him. "I don't know how she did it..." He rubbed his sleepy drunk eyes. "It was like a dream."

Shard ran and kicked the wall. "Fuck!"

The Devastating Weapon of Ridicule

The front page of the National paper boldly stated:

New Territory Expansion For Purgalapudlia!

Maps from before and after the country's enlargement were displayed alongside two political cartoons that James had drawn. One cartoon depicted an extremely overweight angel, multi-eyed and slurping soul juice with his grotesque tongue from a dripping Rackle faucet. The second cartoon was of a two-headed John Rackle divided and controlled by two women in opposite corners, pulling on his puppet strings. Punch had John waving the Purgy flag while Mother had John wave an Angel flag and a Diangle flag, while sucking on her tit, which was labeled *Purgalapudlia funding*.

John threw the paper down at Killaovski's feet.

"Yeah. I read it," she said. "If she catches you pretending to be her, she'll kill you."

"No," said John imitating a female voice. "She'll have a good laugh." John was dressed like Punch. He wore a wig of long curly auburn hair, red lipstick, a dress and one boxing glove on his right hand. "Don't you feel any threat to your ego that she was able to accomplish this?"

"No. Because I helped her with the fighting. You obviously feel threatened."

"You are right. I do."

"This is foolish! It's childish. I can't talk to you, my ruler. How can I? You're the Indift of Purgalapudlia! Take off that wig!" demanded Killaovski.

His voice faded from its softer female register. "I find some comfort and safety in it." She reached for his wig and grabbed a handful of hair while he held on against her tugging. His voice turned more male than ever. "NO! Listen to me!" he shouted. She let go. "I'm appointing you as my right hand bitch-- blood angel, assassin, imperial pirate of the souls... whatever the Hell you and Punch have become." He adjusted the wig on his head. "You will take over her post."

"She's made you an empire, majesty. Angels are now taking you seriously," she said. He took off his wig.

"They're taking her seriously."

Killaovski raised her eyebrow. "You don't have a blonde wig somewhere, do you?"

He slipped off his glove. "You have no charisma, darling. She's visceral!"

* * * * *

The lab was a mix of old and modern gadgetry. James lay on an operating table with Punch by his side.

"I need to contact me mates. Let them know I'm alright." James held Punch by the hand. She nodded. "Is this gonna hurt?"

"No. You'll be asleep." Punch caressed his hair before whispering into his ear. "I'm so in love with you." She landed a kiss on his forehead. The doctor arrived.

"Don't worry, James. It's a procedure similar to donating blood. We're going to extract just a tiny sample of your soul. Which will replenish itself in full. Side effects...minimal. You'll feel an absence of the present, but it's nothing to be alarmed about."

"Well, I'm happy to donate. If a cure comes of it that would be great," said James.

"That's the spirit." The doctor hooked up a small glass vial wrapped in a chrome ring and attached its tube where a large, black floppy cover was placed over his chest. The vial hung from a hook on a metal pole on wheels. A tiny soul magnet, half part tungsten and the other half with native ingredients, was encased in a cap on top of the vial. This would help draw in the soul.

"I heard you were quite the warrior," said the doctor as he placed adhesive pads on both sides of his temple. Black and white wires, spiraled like a candy cane, were attached to the pads.

"No. Not really. I stayed behind Punchy here. She did all the fighting."

"That's not what Punch said," said the doctor.

"James, you were quite the fighter out there," said Punch. The doctor turned his attention to a machine that resembled a face floating in front of a porous ball assembled to a tripod. He turned one of the eyes and with the turn of an ear gear, parted the lips. An eyebrow raised. The wires were hooked up to some casing on the side of the "face". What looked like vacuum tubes were behind the sphere and they glowed into an absinthe green and with another switch flicked on, turned cloudy by the louche of soul's guard cells. The doctor placed a dark cloth over James's eyes.

"Haha, you're too kind--" James floated in and out of the moment. "All I'm saying is-sssss..." James closed his sleepy eyes. The glass vial was filling with an intense bright light.

* * * * *

"James?" said the doctor. "Are you with us?" He lifted the cloth from his eyes.

"Wha-" James awoke to find himself back in his resting quarters. Punch and the doctor were hovering over him.

"Welcome back, James," the doctor said.

"Done are we? Already?" asked James. The doctor smiled and nodded. "Hey brotha, got soul?"

"Yes James, we did." The doctor smiled. "Thank you for your cooperation."

"Oh, yeah." James looked to Punch. "Hey doc, doesn't she look so adorable?" They both laughed.

"Yes, she does, James." The doctor jotted some notes on his clipboard. "There may be some mild side effects like I mentioned. Certainly nothing permanent."

"Like what?" James was starting to feel sleepy.

"Well, you may experience a sensation of feeling like you're in two places at once."

A pause.

"If this happens, please let me or Punch know."

"Yeah. Sure." Then James closed his eyes and went to dreamland.

* * * * *

John, now dressed like a gentleman, with a shirt and tie. He brought the ink to the page and began to draw another cartoon. He had already labored tireless hours to perfect his response to the James cartoons. The hate fueled him. He couldn't draw well. The proof lay on the floor, sprouting wads of crumpled paper like little mushrooms in a damp forest. Punch entered in the midst of his toil.

"Hi." She startled him, noting his shoulders contracting. "Sorry. May I come in?" She noticed the wads of paper on the floor.

"You're already in," murmured John returning to his sketching.

"James is doing well and I'm feeling really good about finding a cure." She looked over his shoulder.

"Of course," he grumbled.

"What are you doing?" she amusedly asked. She laughed at the clumsy drawing of her with a face full of freckles. "Is that me?"

"Leave at once!"

"That's me!"

"Please leave."

"Wow, you've been busy." She grabbed a piece of paper from the floor and pried it open. On it, a crude attempt to portray Punch as a puppet that John controlled. John stood.

"I said out!" He slapped the page from her hands.

"The cartoon stated what everybody already knew about your loyalty to the women in your life, and your position of neutrality for our nation."

"Why print it then?"

"To piss the angels off."

"Those cartoons in the paper were an absolute horrific portrayal of me! How dare you print that, that damnable ... shit! My character is tarnished with this mockery against--"

"You have no character," Punch stated boldly.

"What?!"

She walked to the door. "You're just an empty vessel that once housed a heart," she felt only a pang of sadness. "Don't forget... I own your balls. You just wear them."

* * * * *

John visited James in his resting quarters. Sure enough, James was up and drawing more cartoons.

"Busy doodling I see," John said, his voice strained by the constriction in his heart. "Very much liked your cartoons, silly though they were. All for a laugh, of course at my expense. See? I can take a joke as well as any happy-minded fellow can. I do understand I'm fair game..."

James returned to his drawing with a smile.

"After all, I'm king of this country. You wouldn't draw such rubbish in the White House, in the company of the president or the Queen of England, now would you?"

"Mmmm-yeah. Sure I would." He never looked up at John. "Punchy just sent another batch to the printer."

"Really?" John sunk deeper into his bitterness. "You're very industrious. Perhaps I could commission a cartoon or two from you."

"Perhaps."

"How's your soul mending?"

"A little off-kilter at first. But, feeling much better now." James pulled out a fresh sheet. He studied John for a moment. "Hold still." James drew a quick sketch of John... exaggerated nose, tight lips, stiff neck, nervous posture and bulging, angry eyes. "Here you go." He handed the page over. "Your first commission." John stared at the drawing. Not pleased. "It's just a silly cartoon, you know. All for a laugh."

John bit his tongue.

"How's your mum?" James continued doodling.

* * * * *

The chains around his waist and the shackles on his wrists made Aster heavier by twenty pounds. The place was dark and smelled of angel ejaculation, which smelled like human ejaculation set on fire. Welcome to Hell in Heaven. Aster noticed his human legs and feet and his hands returned. He felt his face. Being human again overshadowed his fear and discomfort of being a prisoner in this damp dark cell. He smiled. At least he was no longer prisoner in a household appliance. He didn't know how long he'd been down there, but he did discover his voice was gone as if he'd been screaming all night. Only, he didn't remember.

<u>Blueprint For The Heartstorm</u>

Shard's cell phone rang on the lamp table and rattled the keys to his Cadillac. Shard grabbed the phone.

"James?"

"Morning," James greeted from the other end. "I'm a little dizzy to walk, could you pick me up? I'm at Rackle's Tub."

Shard immediately piled Ticktock, Betty and Michelle into the Cadillac. They pulled to the curb where James waited groggily, waving a salute. He climbed in the back as the two girls scooted over. The car headed out.

"Poor Aster. I had no idea." James dropped his head back on top of the seat. "We have to go back for him."

"I don't trust Punch," said Shard.

"There's a shindig tonight." James closed his eyes. "I'll let her know."

"We went to the first one," Ticktock said. "It wasn't bad."

Michelle looked out the window. A similar car pulled up beside them, the male passengers somber and dressed in black. A young woman stared at her from the back seat of the other car. Michelle made eye contact and was startled to see her mirror image reflected back at her. But it was no mirror. The other Michelle, also in black, leaned back into her seat and disappeared from view. The Cadillac turned down another road before she could tell the others.

* * * * *

They didn't look friendly as they marched down the hall. Four new giants, who called themselves the Rephaim, followed Killaovski. They were determined to find Punch at Rackle's Tub.

Punch was downstairs in the lobby helping to set up for the shindig that night. She climbed a ladder with a staple gun, and stapled streamers, all sparkly, when Og approached her.

"Punch," Og called down to her from the balcony above. "Killaovski is here with Zamzum and the Rephaim. They're looking for you."

She smiled. "Thanks Og." Punch stapled another streamer. "I was expecting them."

The penthouse suite had no windows. Six card tables were pushed together to form the large "conference" table. Zamzum and the Rephaim sat on one side while Og and the Nephilim sat on the other. Killaovski sat at the head of the table while Punch sat opposite, with a cigar in her mouth. Killaovski knew what John meant when he called Punch visceral and she proved it over and over again with her unyielding drive. For the first time, Killaovski felt threatened by Punch. John's words were the fingers that laid the needle down on the turntable, playing her jealousy in stereophonic. She had never had a problem with her before. Now that she was made aware, it became stifling for a moment. Thankfully she had a big enough ego of her own.

"We're gonna attack Hemlothson," Punch said. She puffed away and then removed the cigar to watch the reaction to her announcement.

"That's an angel establishment," Killaovski reminded her.

"On Purgy soil," answered Punch.

"You're not suggesting we..."

"Yes. I am." Punch got up and leaned on the table. "I'm bringing war to the angels. We're taking all of Purgalapudlia back." The giants cheered.

"I know you thirst for them as I do, but is that wise to start a war with angels?" Killaovski stood up. "They're not like diangles."

"No. They're worse. They're diabolical by choice. They don't belong in the fourth dimension. At least not in Purgy territory. They only came to take souls. And in the process, they've destroyed any hopes these giants had for a future generation."

Everyone in the room exchanged glances. Og smiled. Punch reached for a tube behind her and pulled out a map.

"How sad is it that I've gathered what remains of an entire civilization and managed to fit them all in this dinky little room. The Nephilim and the Rephaim," said Punch as she rolled out the map of Purgalapudlia on the table. "Diangles were a warm-up. The objective was always angels. Strategy with a map may prove useless. We already know where our land is. I propose, not a conquest and occupation of little towns, because occupying places isn't the solution. But rather, a policy of attacking wherever the enemy is. As long as angels are on Purgy soil, we will also be there. Bringing the fight to them! I believe we need to take bolder steps in securing our independence."

The giants were grunting amongst themselves in favor of her strategies. Killaovski struggled to swallow when Punch looked her in the eyes and waited for a response. Then, sensing her silent insecurity...

"Killaovski and I and a few others will lead a campaign of swift attacks with a sweep of our flanks across our land. No hesitations." Punch sat back down and stuck the cigar between her lips.

"The objective is a healthy, normal and realistic one," Og said.

"To see Purgy become its own country," added Zamzum. "To see her stand on her two feet."

"I'm in!" stated Og and in agreement, so did the rest of the Nephilim. Zamzum and the Rephaim looked to Killaovski for approval. She looked away, mind not fully convinced. Whether it was an issue of ego or for good reason, she was reluctant to make a decision.

"John has agreed he will no longer manufacture tubs for the enemy. Before deployment, we will have a specialized training course in understanding our enemy," said Punch. "We'll call it Angel Bashing 101. They have a weakness or two. Not only will we intimidate them, but should they retaliate, we will know how to entrench our defenses and have the proper security to prevent any further occupations. This is our home. It's time now to kick the unwanted tenants to the curb and remodel!"

"Okay!" Killaovski answered. "Let's do it." Zamzum and the Rephaim threw their fists in the air with a cheer.

* * * * *

James slept all day in the hotel room. Night came for its shift. James woke to the sound of keys and muffled chatter outside his door. Shard and Ticktock saying goodbye to Betty and Michelle turned the lights on.

"He's up." Ticktock collapsed on the adjacent bed.

"I'm up." James stretched. "You guys go to town?"

"That we did." Ticktock closed his eyes.

"You got a good rest, son?" Shard put his wallet, phone and keys on the counter by the TV.

"Yeah. No Aster, huh?"

"Nope," Shard sat and kicked his feet up on a chair.

James shuffled into the bathroom. He turned the light on, the sink's cool water feeling good to the touch. He splashed his face awake and pressed the towel to his brow, then gazed at a reflection he did not recognize. He blinked and rubbed his eyes, getting the same result.

"Fuck."

He touched his face and touched the mirror.

"What the fuck?" He looked at the others and then back at the unfamiliar someone in the mirror, mocking him. "Fellas..." James whispered. "Fellas..." They didn't hear him. The TV turned on. Ticktock searching for porn. James shut off the light, faced the mirror and turned the light back on. His reflection became blurred, the eyes stretching over his forehead. Face melting. He ran out.

"Guys! Guys! Check this out!" James brought the boys into the bathroom. He pointed at the other man in the mirror. "Look!" Shard and Ticktock weren't sure what to look for.

"What?" asked Ticktock. To the boys, James had a normal reflection except that he had his eyebrow raised as to compensate for something that felt out of balance.

"I can't recognize myself! That's not me!" The boys stared at his reflection and then back. "You see it?"

"Your eyebrows look kind of funky," Shard noted.

"You don't see it?" panicked James. "That's not my reflection." He stepped away from the mirror. "That's not me."

"Maybe if you take a shower, he'll wash off," suggested Shard.

"Right." James looked at the shower.

"I bet Punch did something to you," Shard continued.

"She did. It's her world. I'm still hung up on it I guess."

"Is this new fella better looking?" asked Ticktock. "Do you want me to keep you company?"

"While I'm showering?"

"Cause I can do that, love. I haven't showered. I mean, it's not a gay thing if we don't point our shafts so they touch. I mean, if I turn me back to you while you soap..."

James shut the bathroom door on him.

* * * * *

That night's party at Rackle's Tub was even grander than the night before. The dark atmosphere pulsated with strobe lights, and perfume. The pond in the center of the lobby with the floating bathtub seating, sparkled from reflecting lights.

A live band rocked behind a glass wall looking like mannequins on display at a storefront window. Each musician wore a price tag. Big flashy sales signs and discount signs and save big splashed in star bursts and markdowns were on all over the drums, guitars and even on the musicians themselves. The drummer had a price tag and bar code on his neck. The guitar player had a tag hanging from his wrist. Between songs, they froze like mannequins in the latest fall fashion. Then they broke out in the next number.

Moving from room to room and snaking out into the bar area was an unusual marching band of brass players, accordion players, violins and drums. Dressed in a theme of black, red and white colors, they wore masks covering only the top half of their faces. And a few adorned 18th century powdered wigs. The music, predominately a classic sound, became modernly unpredictable. Somewhat like a Scriabin piece. It was as if you were chasing a jack rabbit. You anticipate it turning right and it suddenly jolts left. After they collected in the bar and played a couple Purgy numbers, they paraded through the lobby and up the stairs with a group of people following and dancing.

The Clocks along with Michelle and Betty arrived just in time to see the band climbing the stairs. They met up with the Zeros, already there and they were relieved to see James back among them. Shard was slightly withdrawn until Steve and Wes made things right with a warm handshake.

"I'll be at the bar. If you see Punch, let me know." Shard didn't wait around for a response. Michelle grabbed James by the hand.

"Let's hit the dance floor."

"I'm not in the mood-"

She didn't waste any time in pulling him through the crowd of people. As they made it to the dance floor, James found himself searching the crowd for Punch.

* * * * *

Gus could hear the thundering pulse of music, faint through the high ceiling of the basement. He was on a quest to learn the layout of his employer's estate. The kettle room was just ahead, guarded by the copper soldiers standing room high like rusted robots in a salvage yard. They peeked, half-faced from the doorless doorway. The damp air had a barley high note. Navigating through this room was easier than he expected. For one, his eyes adjusted to the darkness. Two, it wasn't total darkness. Light from outside sprayed its blue hue upon the kettles and stone floor. And the kettles were in rows. At the end of the long room, not exactly hidden, but unadvertised, a door was tucked behind wine barrels and falsely promised storage no bigger than eight by ten. Gus leaned his leg against a barrel and saw it was nailed to the door. A peculiar, yet brilliant, decoy. He pulled open the door, its handle of hammered steel and was hit with a draft of frigid air from behind it. Stairs, descending, would require slow and careful footing. It was darker than dark. Gus produced a tiny flashlight, its beam a quick snack for the abyss below. But that didn't matter. All Gus needed was to illuminate the steps in front of him. He climbed down the spiral stairway. So humorous, he thought, the stairs being just like those found in all the horror movies with castles and dungeons. One step at a time. The stairs soon straightened and dumped him upon a large knobby-wooden door. It awaited him like a snapping turtle in the muck of the mud, head cocked into its shell, mouth open, tongue wavering like bait. The knots on the lumpy wood resembled drunk eyes. Silence felt like waves bumping at him from both sides. After he scanned the door he slipped his light into his back pocket and with the use of his body, pushed open the cold, wet door. Behind a wall of crated bathtubs, untouched since the turn of the last century, was a sight barely made visible by a couple of lit torches, clawed against the brick wall like sleeping bats. A large catacomb with rows upon rows upon rows of bathtubs, frozen to the brim with ice tainted with stains from shit, piss and blood. Encapsulated in each tub, a single human body, a large black tube nestled over the nose and mouth and hanging limp out of each tub. Gus could see his breath stop at the sudden realization of what lay before him. He drew closer. All the dart players, now solid and stiff in their porcelain sarcophagi. But they only provided a small fraction of the victims. Who the Hell were the rest of these people that went on room after room in this charnel-house? A terrified Gus, with madness clanging in his heart, turned and ran out the room. He slammed the door behind him and scrambled back up the stairs. In his haste he slipped and cut his shin, but clawed his way back into the kettle room where he shut the door and all its attached camouflage moved with it. When someone went to the detailed trouble to hide a door as so, terror didn't begin to describe such a mind.

"You there!" Og bellowed. Gus, thinking fast, faked drunk. He turned to him with his penis in his hand.

"Where's the bathroom, man?" asked Gus. Killaovski approached from another direction.

"There is no bathroom down here... Gus," she said as she drew near. She looked at his now shrinking penis. "Put that away." Gus tucked it in and made his way for the exit.

"Sorry. Man, this place is confusing. Shit. And I work here." Gus turned to Killaovski as he got farther away from her. "Sorry for that. We haven't officially met. I've seen ya. I'm normally a gentleman in the presence of ladies. Sorry--" He climbed out of the stairs of the basement and disappeared. Once he was in the main floor, his demeanor returned. Scared shitless and sober.

* * * * *

"Punch, have you accepted Jesus Christ as your Lord and savior?"

A Christian dart team had been working the nerve to approach Punch about Jesus Christ. They didn't like her foul mouth and everything she seemed to represent. Punch watched James and Michelle on the dance floor. The dart team surrounded her. She looked at the Christian with the question and then the rest of them.

"No." She looked back out at the dance floor at James.

"Bitch," he said. This caught her attention. She laughed.

"That was sweet," she replied. "Well, you won't get an argument from me there."

"Jesus died on the cross for you," he continued.

"I used to be Christian. I know all the propaganda."

"It's not propaganda--"

"I'm sorry boys. You know, I don't want to talk about your neatly wrapped package of faith. The truth is, you need to throw it all away. Release yourself and you shall be free."

"How dare you talk about Christ and his teachings in--"

"I understand religion does some people good," Punch interrupted politely. "It gives people structure, hope, moral responsibility and all that shit. But, like training wheels on a bike, you remove them once you've learned how to ride. No one keeps riding with them on. If you do, it will suddenly work against you and hinder your growth. It prohibits healthy movement and gets in your way when you want to turn corners sharply, go off jumps and do other adult things. It's extra weight you don't need. So why carry it? I mean, rather than have faith in God, shouldn't you have faith in yourself? You're real. He's not."

Two of the boys ran away.

"Hey, I want you guys to enjoy yourselves here," she placed her hand on the Christian's arm. "Are they going for back-up?"

"...No..."

"You don't need to convince me of anything..." she noticed he was avoiding eye contact. She placed her finger gently under his chin. "Look at me. I've already accepted you all." The third man took off. She found it rather amusing. "Where's he going?"

He shook his head. "I'm not perfect. Nor do I strive to be." She squeezed his shoulder. "One round of drinks on me. For you and your boys." She pulled out a business card. A black boxing glove was printed on one side. She flipped it and wrote the dart team's name, the date and one round. She handed the card over to the mesmerized Christian boy. He looked at the card now between his fingers and her. He couldn't move. She winked at him and left.

Punch positioned herself on the outskirts of the dance floor, watching the dancers as a lioness would a herd of wildebeests. James spotted her from across the dance floor and ditched Michelle in the sea of dancers. Punch turned away attempting to disappear in the crowd.

"Punch!" James caught up with her.

"Hey."

"I was lookin' for ya," said James.

"You guys make a cute couple," she said. He shook his head and kissed her.

"I need your help. Aster was sucked up by the portal!"

"Really? When did this happen?"

"I'm not sure." He had to shout as the music was getting louder. "It was when we were still up there!" She grabbed his hand and led him back to Michelle. "What are you doing?!"

"Michelle," she called out. "Will you watch James while I'm gone?"

"Gone?" James asked.

"Oh, you're that confident that he won't stray?" Michelle pulled James in. "Of course I'll watch my man." Michelle kissed James good and long. Punch was taken back by her sudden domination. Michelle's knees rattled with fright.

"I'm sorry things got off on the wrong foot between us," said Punch. "I do feel threatened by you. Can you blame me?" She gave James a once-over. "He's beautiful." As she left, James followed.

"James!" pouted Michelle.

"Punch!" shouted James. She turned. "I'm coming with."

"No, James. You're not." He clapped his hands on her shoulders.

"I don't have a thing with Michelle! I love you." He kissed her. When he pulled away, he stared into the gravity of her eyes.

"I know." And with that, she left.

Shard sat alone at the bar when Killaovski sat next to him. Her huge blue eyes stared at him as if she was memorizing for an exam.

"You're Killaovski," he said without looking.

"Yes, Shard. What are you drinking?"

"You want to join me?"

She nodded. He could feel her staring. He caught her as she turned her face away, her eyes still glued to him. She smiled.

"You're different," he said.

"Is that a good thing?" she inquired.

"Yeah. Good."

"Do you also like woman fighters like your friend, James?"

"Oh. You mean Punch. Yeah, um, I never thought one way or the other about it." He took a quick sip. "A pretty girl is a pretty girl. I don't hold any prejudice against what a woman does. Maybe I guess if she whores around..."

"Good answer."

"You're a fighter too?"

"Yes. Champion." She placed the knuckles of her fist delicately under his chin.

"If you're like Punch, take me through the portal to find Aster."

"That's why I'm here," she smiled. "And my drink?"

James found Shard and Killaovski at the bar.

"Punch went to go look for Aster."

"Really?" Shard asked.

"Yeah." He noticed Killaovski grab Shard by the hand as she got up. "Hey, there." James nodded. She smiled.

"James," she greeted. She looked at Shard who was now on his feet. "Come with me." Shard followed her.

"Keep an eye on Ticktock," he said as he left. James nodded and looked over at Ticktock making out with Betty.

"Oh, I'd say Betty has that covered."

* * * * *

It came on unexpectedly, and terrified her as Punch passed a
tavern in the city of Pearley. The deep hunger derailed her mind
enough that she steered her vehicle down an alley and smashed
it against the wall. She tumbled out, laying in the throes of a vast
mental and physical strain diminishing her humanity. A couple
purgies and angels, walking by didn't notice her until she made
her way out of the alley, breathing hurriedly. Agony apparent in
her face, she was on the verge of tears. She ran inside the tavern,
its darkness the perfect place to hide her painful muscle spasms.
Slouched in a booth in the back, clutching her arms and looking
to see if anyone was watching, her elbow glued to the table, she
slammed her finger joints to her forehead and held them there,
shaking her head. A curious pleasure, now on the edge of pain
manifested as her teeth slowly became tiger-like. Her wet eyes
stinging shut only to open in a violent darkness expanding over its
surface. She couldn't fight back the changes and slid under the table
as her shirt began to rip. White claws, filling in black, tore free from
her feminine skin. Her moans and suppressed screams became
deeper growls. Her body contorted and she bucked the table, her
back knocking it over, with a solid thud, its edge hitting the ground.
Struggling to her feet, she searched for a way out, but too many
drinkers blocked the front door. Down a narrow hall, the back door
was locked. A drunk Purgy man amusedly wiggled his tongue at
her. She grabbed him by the neck and slammed him inside a storage
closet then tore him to pieces and drank his soul.

An old rickety watchman heard the commotion and crept up
to the now silent closet. He carefully pushed open the door and
hearing a heavy panting suddenly stop, he shined a soul light into
the small room. Punch sat bloodied on the floor, the twisted body
of her victim lay dead on her lap. Her mouth, gaped, cheeks of
gold, murderous eyes sparkled, with a hold on the old man. His
heart palpitating as he could feel the tug on his soul. He closed
the door, stumbling out into the hallway. He had never seen such
a beast. They had always been an elusive type of immortal. Blood
angels, angelivore, animavore-- Latin for soul devourer, angel
assassins, false angels... many names for what is essentially a soul

vampire. The old man gathered others and ran down the hall to what was now, an empty closet save for the shriveled body of the victim. The back door, lock busted, hung from the frame.

A pack of vandals descended on Punch's abandoned tub, smashed open the chrome drain plate inside and attached a black tube, draining the vehicle's soul energy into tin jugs.

* * * * *

Shard lay back, sick and clutching the side of the moving tub. Killaovski rode the tub through vast fields in Purgalapudlia, hopping over gullies and streams, it climbed and maneuvered over the terrain.

"So, you own my soul?" asked Shard, the breeze through his hair reviving him.

"Soul type B neutral to the infinity. That's your soul type."

"Really?"

"It's like you have a favorite musician or actor and all your life, their posters hang on your wall. Their music plays on your record player. Their pictures play at your cinema. And then you meet them in person. This is what it's like to own a soul. And that's why I'm attracted to you. I'm sorry... my English is... hard to express myself. So, yes to your question."

"That's ah, very upfront of you."

"I know. I'm sorry. This is maybe, too much. Too soon."

"No. No, I really love a woman who is direct. It's a nice change for once."

She grabbed his leg, squeezing it. "Good." He reached for her hand and held it to his lips where he kissed it. She blushed and turned back to the road ahead, her butt jiggling to the bouncy ride.

* * * * *

Aster awoke in his prison cell sensing that someone was with him. Too many shadows to hide in. From the corner, a newspaper flew like a startled bird and landed at his feet.

"Your friend has been manipulated to draw *innocent* cartoons," spoke a deep male voice from the shadows. "Your friend with the positive soul type to infinitum or whatever he's made of. Punch keeps him in her pocket. She's dangerous company to have." An angel stepped into the light, wings spread outward and his multi-eyed body all stared at the petrified Aster. Aster's eyes bulged in disheartened apprehension.

"Who are you?" Aster barely audible. "You're an angel?"

"An angel named Mickeyoiliver. You mortals have no reason or experience to be up here. Mankind has always been obsessed with imperialism. You can't apply laws of that nature to this world. Punch is not even a real soldier! Where does she suddenly come off as a military expert and self-appointed leader, trainer of Purgy men, who need permission to wipe their own asses! She's a fool who has gotten in over her head!" He squatted in front of Aster. "Don't worry, your soul type is B negative. Everybody has that one. And poor Mr. Rackle. He has no business in politics." His wings shook, creating little dust circles on the floor as he grabbed the paper and stood. "She runs a clever little brewery. Do you really want to drink ales made from the bath water of angels?"

"I--I don't know what that means." quivered Aster.

"I'll spell it out for you." Mickeyoiliver rolled up the paper and leaned in. "She's a killer." He swatted Aster's head with a hollowed pop-sound. Aster covered his head the best he could while still chained. Mickeyoiliver slammed the paper under his arm and walked back into the shadows. "Oooh-- she gives me chills." He laughed. "Don't like her kind. And most, under normal circumstances, would never have anything to do with her. You can't have a normal relationship with a murderer. The public is all too willing to forgive her blunders. She hits hard, I'll give her that."

"What is this place?"

"Heaven."

"What do you want with me?"

Mickeyoiliver landed on Aster and beat him violently with the newspaper until it shredded.

"Chew on a million paper cuts!" joked Mickeyoiliver, stuffing the pieces in Aster's mouth. The angel leaped into the air and flew through a doorway up near the ceiling, his laughter fading behind the shut door.

* * * * *

A large booth at Rackle's Tub occupied the Zeros on one end, and James, Ticktock, Michelle and Betty on the other end. Gus ran alarmingly at the table getting their attention. He was pale and anxious as if his life were stuck elsewhere, trying to get home.

"Where's Punch and Killaovski now?" asked Gus as he eyed an untouched glass of ice water at the center of the table.

"They left looking for Aster," said James.

"I desperately need to talk to you all, man," after he caught his breath, "I don't know if I should call the police. It might not do any good." He grabbed the water and gulped it down.

"Dude, what's going on?" asked Steve. Gus put the empty glass down.

"Hey, that was me water, that was," joked Ticktock.

"You know those giants you see at every match? They've been collecting the losing teams and then we never see them? Right?"

Michelle and Betty looked to one another, fearful of where he might be going.

"That's because," continued Gus, "She's got them all frozen in the basement! She's got everyone laid out in those bathtubs, man! We're her petri dish in those water coffins!" He looked over his shoulder and back. "I saw it, man! I swear! And now I don't know what to do..."

"Wait-- what exactly...?" Michelle became frightened.

"What the fuck are you talkin' 'bout?" asked Wes.

"There's dead people...in the basement?" Steve was puzzled.

"If you're fuckin' with us..." Wes looked elsewhere.

"I'm terrified, man! This is no joke. I'll show you," hissed Gus. James put out his cigarette. The girls sucked in air. It made sense. They never heard back from their friends.

"You're saying, Punch and Killaovski, put bodies in the basement? Am I understanding you...?" asked James.

"Yeah, man. I mean, I don't know who exactly did it, but damn it! It was so fuckin' weird, man. I left quick. But whatever it was, it didn't look good at all. I'm tellin' you."

James looked away. Ticktock looked at James and then at Gus. "If there's dead people as you say-" questioned Ticktock, "Every losing dart player... that's a lot of fuckin' dart players. Do you realize what you're saying? That would be like a genocide."

"We need to call the cops," said Jeff. "This is some serious accusation."

"You stoned fuck. Do you really expect us to believe you? All this nonsense." James's eyes danced around everywhere, but at the table. "I don't know. I don't know about this. She wouldn't..." He couldn't breathe. "That's heavy, mate. Real heavy."

* * * * *

A completed war tub ran off to join the ranks of waiting tubs, already completed. John's factory was in full swing as bathtub war machines came off conveyor belts. Purgy workers were assembling in a frenzied state. Claws, feet and legs for each tub were bigger, longer and stronger than before. The Purgy nation's flag and seal were stamped on each tub. Colors of black, red and white. At the last stop of assembly, a tube was connected into the drain plate in the tubs and a soul was pumped into the tub, giving it animation. One tub however, recieved a contaminated soul. Madmathix caused the tub to jolt out of line like a panic-stricken stallion, legs kicking and scratching the air. Purgy workers tried to grab the tub but it became too dangerous.

"Euthanize that tub!" John's voice came from a loud speaker.

Shard, Killaovski, Mother and John watched through windows high above, overlooking the factory.

"Shit-" John held a letter with which he swiped the air with.

Down below at the factory, Purgy troopers rode in on tubs of their own.

"Back!" yelled one of the soldiers.

The Purgy workers scattered from the infected tub, now dotted with dark splotches. The troopers surrounded the tub, which behaved like a rabid dog with a low sustainable hum sounding like a growl. It jumped onto one of the troopers who luckily countered with his own tub by catching the rabid tub and throwing it back in the center where it was quickly dismantled by the other tubs. John, still watching out the window at the dead tub heard Killaovski grunt as a reminder to get back to their former discussion. John turned away from the window.

"If her intent is to eliminate angels from acquiring souls here in Purgalapudlia, I fear it will upset the natural order of things. And thus, could have upon us, a devastating effect." John explained. "I knew she wasn't fond of angels, but I had no knowledge that this was her intention. She simply stated to me that these tubs were for a lovely victory parade, downtown."

"You are so blind to her, you puppet man!" Killaovski dared to be bold. Mother smacked her across the cheek.

"Mother!" shouted John.

"You have the final say, not Punch. Or is she running your factory too?" said Killaovski as if Mother wasn't even in the room.

"Shut it! Or I'll cut your serpent tongue!" yelled Mother.

"Mother! Please!"

"Yes 'Mother', listen to the Indift of Purgy," said Killaovski.

Mother pointed to Killaovski, "Your hands are better ministered squeezing your neck, so the only words--"

"Mother...!"

"...Out of your foul mouth are sounds of gagging and choking!" Mother continued.

"How theatrical of you. You should write children's books. You've already written his," pointed Killaovski. As Mother charged, John grabbed her.

"Mother! Enough!" He carried her towards the door. She jumped to her feet.

"You choose the worst women," and with that, Mother left. Shard stayed glued to the window and away from the friendly chat. John turned to Killaovski.

"How dare you illuminate me and Mother on how to do my job! How dare you show such impudence!"

"Your majesty, I'm looking out for your best interest. The truth is, your mind is still clouded with Punch," said Killaovski. "You assigned me to this position... if I'm not 'visceral' enough, then simply discharge me from this post and find another."

John caught Shard looking back out the window, pretending to be invisible.

"You see Shard," John lightened his tone. "Women. They're all the same." John stood shoulder to shoulder with him. Flapping the letter to his lips. Shard couldn't respond. He felt like a child stuck between feuding parents. "Maybe you and I should have a go and leave the wildcats be. You seem well behaved and agreeable." Shard didn't flinch. He scratched his brow and made his way to the table and sat. John looked at Killaovski. "No. I want you to remain as I instructed. You have done good work. You're dependable." He approached her waving the letter. "I have some information here as to why I haven't stopped her advanced order." John grabbed a seat at the table, as did Killaovski. He gave the letter a long sniff. "I smell ransom. This letter, from archangel Mickeyoiliver, requests a simple trade off. Aster...for Punch."

Shard leaned in. Finally something worth his full attention. "Aster?! He's okay?"

"Let's hope so. He's been captured. His value increased the moment Punch took interest in him. And you have James to thank for that. I'm sure you'd be pleased to have your mate back. Normally, under other circumstances, I wouldn't indulge in such barbaric terms. But at last! We know his whereabouts."

Ground Zero

At the hotel room, Toto pulled out his signature bowling pin from his bag. James, Gus, Ticktock, Betty and Michelle next noticed Wes reach from under his bed to also pull out a bowling pin. He held it in the air as if he were Conan the Barbarian raising his sword, victorious. Steve peeked out of the closed mini blinds and then drew the curtains shut.

"You guys bowl, too?" asked Betty as she cleared her wet eyes.

"Yeah," joked Wes. "No. It's to bash heads in. I gotta be honest with you. I'm a little frightened this is all gonna be true."

"If it's true there's bodies down there, then we need to get out and call the cops. Let them do the dirty work," said Jeff.

"Well suppose while we're down there, we get jumped. I ain't going down without a fight." Wes swung his pin. "You wanna end up like the rest of them?"

"I'm saying we *never* go down there. Let Gus take them down there," said Jeff.

"I don't think that's a good idea," said Gus.

"Unless you're lying," said Toto.

"I'm not lying--"

"Cops aren't gonna do shit," reasoned Wes. "We're talkin' about angels and demons and all that supernatural shit. You guys should know."

James felt sick to his stomach. "I don't feel good about this," he said.

"There's nothing good about it if it's true," said Wes as he pulled out a bag with blue bowling pins. "A'ight. These are your weapons." He handed everyone a pin.

"Mob mentality is not the answer. We could get ourselves killed," said James, refusing his bowling pin. Michelle refused to, but Betty grabbed one and felt its weight.

"What do you suggest then?" demanded Wes.

"Fuck." James turned to the window. "I don't know. I love her."

"I know you love her," noted Wes.

"Where do you draw the line?" asked Steve.

"How can I answer that? We don't even know what Gus saw. Of course I condemn murder, but shit." James could feel tears on the verge.

"That's why we're going in. To make sure. Let there be no doubt about it." Steve patted James on the shoulder.

"Man, for your sake James, I hope I just had a massive hallucination." Gus felt the grip of the pin, heavy in his hands. "But you all need to see this."

"Bowling pins can't stop angels," said Jeff while he tossed his pin on the bed.

"And cops can't do shit!" shouted Wes.

"And you think you can?!" shouted James. "Are you serious?! How?! If there's any jeopardy to our safety, I will be the one to risk it! There's no use in having us all get killed. I know her and her world better than anyone. I will be the one to face this."

"Glad to hear you say that," said Gus. Wes handed James a bowling pin.

"Get that away from me."

"I'm going with you, regardless of what you say." Steve pulled a gun out of his bag. He checked the chamber and popped the loaded clip in place. "In case we run out of bowling pins." He tucked it in his coat pocket. Michelle and Betty embraced each other while the guys prepared.

"We're staying here," Betty said as she tossed her pin on the bed.

"Me too," responded Jeff.

"Okay." Steve made his way to the door. "That's fine." James stopped Steve with a gentle touch to his arm.

"Let's not get carried away with that thing," James said, "please."

"All right, James." Steve patted him on the back. "Just a precaution."

"Thanks, Steve."

"That's his girl," Ticktock felt another reminder was needed. "She means a lot to him."

"I know." Steve opened the door for everyone.

* * * * *

It was a wonder that there was nobody around the kettle room. Especially since Gus was caught wandering around that area, when fragile exhibits, only meant for a privileged party, were so close by. Gus led his platoon, James, Steve, Toto, Wes and Ticktock, retracing his steps around the large kettles, looking like sleeping guards for the disguised door. After seeing such a clever door,

James felt a slight congealing of his blood. The group quietly followed Gus down the stone stairs. Ticktock, the last one in, made sure to close the door behind them.

Once at the bottom, Gus, with help from James, pulled open the door to the catacombs. It was worse than Gus had remembered, and terrible to the others that what they'd been told was true. The disturbing sight had lent itself room after room of bathtubs neatly sitting in rows. These tubs held people from far back as the 1960's. All with a criminal-looking element to them. Some, mean-looking, tattooed, others looking more like men from mob families. All the victims were nude and had a rubber tube over their mouth and nose for air. The tubes lay long over the rim like a turkey's neck on the cutting block. The temperature didn't buy the boys much time to explore. Frost covered the walls, floors and ceilings. James could feel his tears freeze to his cheeks. He didn't know what to think. And neither did the rest of the boys. A concussion of the senses rammed them with stupefaction. If Punch did it or didn't do it. It was her place. She's the type of person that didn't let things escape her. Always aware, so of course she would've known about this. You couldn't keep something of this magnitude hidden from her. Which led to a conclusion that sickened James beyond words. Gus vomited in the corner.

The frost on the ground caused Toto to slip and fall on his back.

"Fuck."

"Shh!" Steve helped him up. They wandered down the aisles examining the frozen cadavers, all purple and white.

"Suspended animation," uttered James, teeth clacking. "Which means they could still be alive! You don't kill someone and give 'em a snorkel!" Each tub had a date written on the front. The farthest rooms had empty tubs dated from the early twentieth century. There was still some ice in them, a quarter filled, browned and stained from holding bodies which had been long ago removed. James, seeing tubs dated from 1965 filled him with sudden hope Punch had nothing to do with the horror. These people had been placed here long before Punch was ever born. But if John was over a hundred years old, who's to say how old Punch really was? His spark of optimism went out. His gut sank with betrayal and so many other emotions onboard. In his heart of hearts he wanted to believe she wasn't capable. He now felt as if he carried guilt just for having had a relationship with her.

Wes spotted rows of empty tubs up front. Dated...and current.

"Are these for us?" shivered Wes. He got colder than he'd been before. Any colder and he'd be frozen like the poor occupants in the tubs. Unbearable, "Fuck! I'm out of here," the others followed. As Wes turned to run, his flashlight's beam caught the glint from strings in the air. James saw the silver threads attached to each victim disappearing into the ceiling.

"H-hey, th-they're all um-bil-bilically connected to w-what looks like another p-p-portal," shivered James. He turned to find everyone but Ticktock already gone. "Let's get out."

Ticktock didn't respond. He was staring at something down the corridor.

"Hey-" James tried to rouse his friend to leave. Still no response. James saw Ticktock, neck crooked, still watching something. Ticktock, as if under a spell, watched himself down one of the aisles. He stared at himself staring back with sadness about him. The other Ticktock tied a rope around his neck and threw it over a rafter. Ticktock could feel the bristly rope as if it was around his own neck, scratching.

The sound of another door opening threw James into Ticktock. He grabbed him and headed out. A peripheral hallucination forced James to turn and look. Four young men in dark suits, marbled in thick ice, lay inside the bathtubs. His dart team. He pushed Ticktock through the door then looked back. The disheartened visual disappeared.

"Someone is coming," said James as he pushed up the stairs. The group hurried. Another sound, coming from their opposite direction, drew nearer.

"Wait -shh," Gus said, "stop!"

James, Ticktock, Steve, Toto and Wes heard the sounds too, rambling down the stairs. Too late to run, Wes, Toto and Steve readied their bowling pins.

ZamZum, the giant Rephaim crashed and rolled onto James, Gus and the rest of the boys, each swinging wildly. ZamZum bellowed out in anger. The Zeros continued their bashing.

"STOP--!" yelled James.

They bludgeoned the giant to death. His skull caved in, penetrating his brain. He dropped down the stairs. The sickening silence that followed sobered them like quicksand.

"Ah shit, you guys." James knew there was no saving him.

* * * * *

Shard fucked Killaovski in one of the private chambers at J.R. Industries. He fucked her hard and good. His hips made a flapping sound against her ass cheeks. Both were of the disposition of fucking first, to get any awkwardness out of the way. She then brought him into a large bath already drawn and bubbly. They both entered naked and relaxed.

John, in a robe, walked into the room with an irksome smile.

"Simple mathematics," said John, as his Mother too entered in her silk robe. Nipples erect underneath. "I see you've already introduced your ass to my marble. Now, you take one pretty damsel and add her to the tub and you take another pretty damsel and add her to the tub..." Mother dropped her robe and slipped into the tub. "How many people would you have in the tub with you?" John disrobed. Shard was a little uncomfortable sharing the tub with another man. "Four! You must always count me." He slipped into the tub. "The phantom variable, hiding beneath the suds!" He dived under and popped up alongside Killaovski. Shard watched him kiss her. He looked across at Mother, smiling. She pushed herself over to him for a taste of his tongue.

* * * * *

By the next morning, sleep didn't do much to rid the morbid feeling Wes, Steve and Toto felt having murdered the night before. Tonight was tournament night. Shard hadn't returned and Aster was still missing. James had tossed and turned all night. No matter how he lay, the hurt in his stomach and brain stabbed him repeatedly.

A knock at the door woke James and Ticktock, who felt heavy with regret and guilt.

"Yeah?" James got up to answer it.

"Hey." Gus had bags under his eyes. "We need to talk."

They gathered in the Zero's hotel room. Trashed from their restless slumber, nobody needed coffee -their nerves and adrenaline kept them wired.

"I suggest no one plays in the tournament tonight," said Gus.

"Well, we can't on account of we're two players short," said Ticktock.

"No," said Gus. "We stage a protest and get the proper authorities involved. I'm going to warn all the other teams to stay away from those giants. And if they play, avoid capture if they lose."

"Proper authorites?" asked James, "Police? We're murderers now."

"She probably owns the police," said Ticktock.

"Is there a rescue plan?" asked Steve.

"What if we find the switch to kill the freezer?" asked Wes. "And bring torches to melt ice and fight off giants."

"Do you think it'll be that easy?" wondered Steve.

"Who said it would be easy?" said Wes.

* * * * *

Tournament night at Rackle's Tub was a ghost town. Gus bussed dishes from one of the tables and carried them to the kitchen. Through the window on the door he saw Punch. He backed up. Punch headed straight to the kitchen. Gus, backtracking, dashed out the back door. Gus ran across the courtyard trying not to slam his feet to the pavement. He pulled out the keys to his van and unlocked the door, dived in and shut the door. Silence broken by his wide-eyes throbbing from his heartbeat and the air hitting his teeth on the way out of his mouth. He lay low on the van floor, ear crumpled against the thin carpeting. The door handle on the front driver's side clicked and snapped open.

"Gus. Are you avoiding me?" Punch leaned in to find Gus lying flat on his stomach. He slowly raised his head. She elbowed the horn.

"FUCK!" screamed Gus and got up. He shook as he scooted towards the back. "Don't do that."

"Sorry. Where is everybody?" She started to unbutton her tunic. "It's tournament night. Where's James?" He struggled to get his words out.

"I--I don't know." Gus shrugged his shoulders. She studied him.

"You don't know, or you won't tell me?"

"No. I--I don't... I've been feeling sick. I've been here."

Gus spotted Og and a couple giants come out of the kitchen and point to Punch. She turned her attention to Og and then back to Gus.

"I hope you feel better." Punch closed his door and joined Og. Gus lifted his head for a peak. He couldn't make out the conversation but based on Og's body language, it didn't look good.

* * * * *

The next morning James and Michelle found a large pond nearby and leaned against the railing of the boardwalk, trying to calm their minds. James watched the water pat the shore. Not speaking, Michelle touched his arm. He meant to push her off when the sun landed on her just right. She wore black go-go boots and a tasteful navy-blue mini skirt. Her conscious choice of '60s fashion grabbed James for the first time as he looked at her differently than he had before. Beautiful. Loyal. James didn't realize a lot of things about Michelle until that moment and she might be all he could handle about now.

"What-?" she blushed.

"Nothing." James leaned in closer, eyes transfixed on her parting lips. The two kissed. James pulled away while Michelle, eyes closed, went in for another one. A longer kiss felt just right.

The familiar sound of the Cadillac's motor drew their attention. Expectation of seeing Shard back, they turned to disappointment. Punch was behind the wheel. Michelle swallowed the air as if it was her last. Punch waved and parked the car.

"It seems I always find you two together." Punch came near them. "Can we talk?" James steadied his nerves. He turned away. "You saw the catacombs. Will you look at me?" She grabbed his arm. He pulled away and regained his strength on the railing. It became his crutch. "You're not going to talk to me?"

"Where's Aster and Shard?" He still avoided eye contact with her.

"That's what I need to talk to you about. Shard is back at the hotel. Aster is in trouble." She placed her arms around him and hugged him. He pushed free from her embrace and stepped away, finding a new spot in the pond to stare at.

"James."

He shook his head.

"Take a walk with me." She started down the boardwalk. "Come on."

"No," said James. "I'm-- I'm not... Just leave me alone."

"I obviously have some explaining to do, as do you." She got closer to him. "Will you listen to me?" He raised his hand in defiance. "James, please."

"Just go."

"Just like that." She searched for a response. "I guess you're done with me then," Punch lamented.

"You terrify me! Okay Punch?! I can't even look at you." James hissed. She looked away as a well of tears began to rise within her.

"No..." her cheeks reddened. She turned to him. "No, don't say that...James, please?" She gently touched his cheek. He smacked her arm away.

"I can't even find the bloody words for you!" He was colder than the catacombs and she wished their eyes would connect. "The car keys," he ordered.

She just stared at him. He looked at her.

"Are they in the car?!"

"My pocket," she whispered, barely audible. She pointed her hip to him. Any physical contact would be better than nothing. He looked at her hip, then at her wet eyes. A drop of gold landed on his sleeve as he dived his fist into her tight, warm pocket, fishing for the keys, jerking her around, all the while, her eyes never leaving him. Grabbing the keys, he pulled away.

"You liked that, didn't you?" said James. He knew he couldn't look at her for long or it would be the end of him.

"James-" Punch lost her voice...

James grabbed Michelle and put her in the car.

"Please, don't run away from me-" her breathing became difficult, "please-?"

He looked over at Punch. "You touch my friends--" He raised his fist and then got in and shut the door. Punch hung her eyes on a flower that had grown through a crack on the boardwalk, its leaves shaking in the light breeze. Or it may have shaken from fright - Punch's eyes began their change.

As James pulled away he watched Punch through the rearview. She had covered her face with both hands and slouched her head down. He felt as if he was leaving his heart behind. With every passing yard he could feel himself falling apart. "Shit, I still love-," he stopped his confession. Michelle knew it was best to let him be.

* * * * *

Shard waited outside the hotel room, smoking and a bit nervous. James pulled up and jumped out of the car. The two mates embraced each other tightly.

"Oh fuck, you're safe," James breathed into his neck.

"Let's go inside." Shard with his arm around him, opened the door and the three of them entered.

A buzzing noise behind a closed bathroom door didn't distract Shard as he sat James down.

"Where's Punch? Did you talk to her? Aster was taken prisoner by these angels. They have negotiated his safe return if, in exchange, they meet with Punch in person. It's a set-up for her capture, and she will knowingly take the bait. If all goes accordingly, we will have Aster here by tomorrow."

The buzzing stopped. Bathroom door opened. Ticktock and Betty came out with shaved heads. They clutched each other tightly and walked out the front door as if no one else was in the room.

"Betty," called Michelle. The front door closed behind them.

PART 4

Flight

<u>Save Me</u>

If they're funny, should one laugh at the mentally ill? On the dock of his factory, John Rackle, dressed as Punch, had planted himself in one of the war tubs. He rocked back and forth, while passing his hands over the smooth rims. Then pointed forward as if conducting a charge and then appeared, suddenly, to be swatting mosquitoes. His dialogue, a mixture of female grunts and crying. An audience gathered across the way. Their laughter braved the risk into greater volume when John didn't seem to hear them.

"Silence!" Mother marched her way over to "*Punch*". The two could be observed exchanging words before she spanked his head. Then hit him again and ripped off his wig, throwing it far. One couldn't help but laugh. She grabbed him by the arm, bringing him to his feet. Another swat landed on his butt. He noticed some of his men across the room laughing. He straightened up and grabbed Mother by the wrist.

"You lay one more finger on me and I'll break it!"

* * * * *

Disguised over her black armor, Punch wore a royal blue, wool, single-breasted, standing collar greatcoat with an over cape to her elbows. Her black leather gloves were tight and elegant. Killaovski dressed in her usual armor. Their tubs led a small squadron on the beach. Punch was in a tub, completely black. Although it was glossy, it proved to be invisible in the ocean water. The rest of the tubs were standard white with black tribal patterns painted on the front extending around both sides.

"Killaovski," Punch called while parking at the water's edge. Killaovski pulled up along side her. Punch produced two autoinjectors in chrome casings. "This should suppress our urges long enough." She handed one over.

"I already took mine," Killaovski said.

Punch injected the serum into her forearm, then placed the extra autoinjector away. Punch sped off into the ocean, her squadron, right behind her and made their way for calmer waters.

The oceans on Purgalapudlia were black and deep. Soon enough, angel escorts flew overhead as Punch and her small army reached their side of the ocean.

An angel guard, large eyes painted on the backs of both wings, like a peacock's tail feathers, found Mickeyoiliver in his main chamber, flapping his wings, pacing the room, his many eyes, racing from one end of the socket to the other.

"She's here," said the guard.

With a deep breath, "Good. Good." Mickeyoiliver smiled. "Let's show her in." He rubbed his hair back. "How do I look?" The guard was caught off-guard by the question.

"Sir--?"

"How do I look? Am I looking-- altogether sharp?"

"You never cared how you looked before."

"How do I look?!"

"You look great. The hair is just... you know... it's great. You washed. I can tell. You washed it today. You did, didn't you? There's a shine, that's... great. Great shine. I mean, it's reflecting in my eyes. I didn't know hair like that was possible. But it is. Obviously. I'm looking at it. And it's there." Mickeyoiliver pulled out a blade. Sensing his life would be lost, the guard left.

"I'm just a little nervous!" He threw the blade at the door as it shut. "She's actually here. In my home. Here! The infamous Punch!" he laughed. "Oh dear, dear, dear, dear, dear, DEAR!"

Mickeyoiliver awaited her arrival in the dinner hall. He sat at the head of the table. Armed angels stood at doorways behind him. In front his guards brought in Punch, two Purgy guards accompanying her. Mickeyoiliver stood up, bumping his leg on the table, causing the silverware to clank against the plate.

"Punch. You look like a little doll in that uniform." He approached her for a handshake. She shook his hand.

"Is Aster alright?" she said while looking at his hair.

"Yes. Please. Have a seat," he offered while patting his hair down.

"Nice hair," she sat. "Forgive me for being forward, but, which eye should I look at when I'm addressing you?"

He laughed as he sat at the other end. "Everyone's a comedian today," he smiled. "I love it. How about the ones on my face?" She scanned his face.

"Well, you've got quite a few up there."

"Pick a few then. Did one of my guards say something to you about my hair?"

"Let's get to the reason why I'm here."

"Yes, of course. Have you ever had real angel food? I mean authentic..." he picked up a bowl of something already on the table.

"I already ate, thank you." She pushed aside her plate. "Can we bypass the formalities?" He set the bowl down.

"Oh?" His hand trembled. "Sure. That's what I like about you."

"Mickeyoiliver, you're not gonna like anything about me."

* * * * *

A swarm of Purgy troopers disrupted the sky with another fleet on the ocean. All headed straight for Mickeyoiliver's territory.

* * * * *

"That's not true," reasoned Mickeyoiliver. "I like a lot of things about you--"

Punch erupted like a volcano sending the chair scattering behind her with a kick. Not enough serum in her blood to restrain the change, her pupils enlarged and glittered. "I don't think your extortion would require us to be seated! Bring me Aster right now unharmed!" She pointed to his guards "GO!"

"You've got the halo eyes!"

"YES! And these fucking eyes on my face will be the last eyes you FUCKING STARE AT! I will BURN THEM into you!" She punched the table and swiped her plate and silverware, shattering it against the wall. The guards drew their weapons. Mickeyoiliver nervously nodded to one of the guards who then left to fetch Aster. She strutted over and planted her ass next to his plate. She folded her arms and stared into the eyes on his face. Mickeyoiliver could hear the leather of her uniform stretch as she tightened her muscles. The other angel guards approached with blades pointed. She didn't flinch. She didn't care. Her eyes stared right through him.

Locked. Mickeyoiliver felt paralyzed. The two Purgy guards stood by Punch, ready for an altercation. And with her, it wouldn't be the first time.

"Please--" Mickeyoliliver found breathing difficult, his nerves melted down to the wire. How quick she made him bare and vulnerable, despite having protection in the room. As if he were alone with her.

"Punch!" cried Aster. She jumped to her feet. The angel guard unchained him, but laid grip to his arm.

"Aster!" She approached him. He was startled by her eyes. "Are you hurt?" He shook his head.

"No," he said as she rubbed her fingers through his hair. "Your eyes!"

"Allergies," she said with a smile.

While Aster wondered what the fuck she was allergic to, Punch nodded to the guards. They released him from their grip.

"Take him to Killaovski," she said as Aster exchanged hands. They escorted him out. Mickeyoiliver flagged in more angels. They grabbed Punch by the arms and one grabbed hold of the back of her neck.

"We need more men in here!" shouted Mickeyoiliver, jumping and clapping. He flew up to the ceiling and back while other angels flew in.

* * * * *

The Purgalapudlian army drew closer to Mickeyoiliver's headquarters. Silcher led the air fleet.

* * * * *

"Let me see to it that he leaves safely," said Punch. "I've kept up my end of the deal." Mickeyoiliver nodded and they escorted her through the darkened corridor. Claws growing pushed at the leather gloves that covered her knuckles. The darkness worked to her advantage as her teeth sharpened and muscles painfully tightened. The two angels that held her arms could feel her muscle tissue hot and expanding. She panted, looking pale. She grabbed at her throat, ripping her coat open. The claws, longer, had now

pierced the leather surface of her gloves. She dropped against the
wall in agony. She shed her coat. More angels grabbed her.

Killaovski, eyes of halo, grabbed Aster and loaded him into one
of the winged tubs. She turned to see a flock of angels struggling
with Punch as they brought her out. The struggle quickly turned
into an ugly fight. Aster saw Punch in assassin form, tearing open
angels. She seemed entangled in white flapping wings as angels
fought her. A red fox in the hen house with a bleeding mouth and
chin. A few Purgy fighters joined in the brawl. Claws emerged
from Killaovski's knuckles. She kicked Aster's tub and it took off.
Killaovski next, strutted to Punch, grabbing her head shoving her
against a rugged wall. Punch, almost speechless...

"What are you doing--?"

Killaovski buried jabs into her stomach and ribs. Then grabbed
her, the two grappling until Punch knocked her legs out from
under her sending her down. Killaovski returned to her feet with
split-second timing and connected a blow to the back of her skull
as Punch tried to avoid the hit, lodging one of her claws behind
her ear. Punch dropped to the ground. Killaovski delivered more
rounds of beating and all Punch could do was embrace Killaovski's
legs. Punch wasn't used to being on this end of a beating and felt
true fear.

They wrestled amongst the circle of angels and disloyal Purgy
fighters who watched. When they got the chance, the angels took
cheap shots at Punch. A hit to her head, a kick to her back. An
angel stepped on her hand, crushing it, while the two assassins, like
queen bees, rolled around the ground. Killaovski wrapped her well-
built legs around Punch to secure her then found openings for her
assault of claw-armed punches. More gashes to her head, Punch
blocking with only one arm, finally freed her other hand. A mixture
of blood and gold ran from her eyes. Her fear, close to crippling.

Another angel grabbed Punch by the boot and held her leg
down. Killaovski got up to her feet, grabbed a gun and fired a shot
just above Punch's hip. The burning pain curled Punch into a ball
burying her face to the ground, dirt embedded onto her wet cheeks.
Killaovski put away her gun and reached for Punch, grabbing her

by the belt. Punch kicked her in the groin and painfully struggled
to stand, wounded, but not defeated. She saw Aster's tub in the
air getting farther away. She touched her wound, her palm red and
dripping. Her determination cracked her fear.

Killaovski felt the stun of a right hook from Punch. Her
quickness made it look like it came out of nowhere. Killaovski
returned fire, proving she was better at sparring and connected
more jabs to Punch than Punch could connect to her. Adrenaline
numbed the pain just enough for Punch to stay in the fight, but
soon it didn't matter. The blood pouring out of Punch made her
dizzy and Killaovski knocked her to the dirt where she stayed, the
pain even more unbearable.

A Purgy fighter pulled a gun and shot Killaovski in the leg.
Angels scrambled to wrestle the weapon from him. Killaovski shot
him dead, then collapsed to the ground next to Punch who had
managed to climb on her hands and knees. Killaovski held the gun
to Punch's stomach.

"Why--?!" Punch could only whisper.

The angels pushed Punch to Killaovski as she shot the gun, but
the bullet barely grazed Punch's arm as it whizzed by and took out
an angel behind her.

Punch disengaged the gun by slamming Killaovski's arm to the
ground. The gun tumbled free under some heavy vegetation. Punch
dug her knee into Killaovski's fingers, breaking them. Killaovski
rolled her off, getting back to her feet. She screamed, giving it all
she had, kicking Punch's wounded hip area over and over with her
good leg. Punch covered herself as the life was pounded out of her.
Killaovski dragged Punch's body and shoved it off a cliff where it
ensnared in a mesh of barbed wire below. Her safety net. She hung,
crown pointed to the ocean, still alive. Blood leaving her body like
water over the falls.

Mickeyoiliver clapped excitedly. Killaovski, with help from
her men, climbed into her war tub. She didn't care to listen to
Mickeyoiliver's congratulatory statements. She took off with the
rest of her squadron, half to the sky, half of them to the ocean.

Aster, in tears, had witnessed the assault from a far vantage point. His pilot, who had ignored his request to turn around, finally turned in his seat and bludgeoned Aster over the head. He fell unconscious.

Mickeyoiliver patted one of the angels. "Bring her up! I want her body, dead or alive!" he looked over the edge of the cliff into the darkness. The loud ocean disapproved by slapping the rocky shore and crashing against it. "PUNCH! Your heart still beats?!"

Killaovski approached the oncoming fleet in the sky. She raised her bloody hand to stop them. Below her, the rest of her squadron on the ocean, did the same.

"I bring good news!" she shouted, exhaustively. Her squadron fired shots in the air to grab their attention. "I bring good news-!" She collapsed in the tub. Her pilot turned to her - "Tell them," she whispered...

"The fighting has been called off!" he said.

"Punch... is negotiating... a truce," whispered Killaovski to her pilot.

"Punch is negotiating a truce at this very moment!" shouted the pilot to the men.

"What happened to Killaovski?!" asked Silcher. "Why is she bleeding?!" The pilot turned to Killaovski.

She whispered, "A simple disagreement, we now work out good." She fainted. The pilot turned to Silcher.

"We need to get her to sickbay! She had a little disagreement, but now everything is good! There will be no war! The angels will be our friends! Let's go!" He led his squadron past Silcher's men.

"I don't believe you!" shouted Silcher.

"I didn't believe it either!" The pilot shouted. "But I'm glad for it! No more bloodshed!"

"Where's Punch?!"

The pilot raised his hand and shouted. His squadron all did the same. A joyous shout! They headed back to J.R. Industries. Silcher noticed the fleets below were also turning around and heading home.

* * * * *

James couldn't understand the sudden dizziness that overtook him. The light-headed feeling left him anxiety-riddled his hearing coming and going from his left ear to his right ear, like a pulsating stereo. Back and forth. Heart, palpitating and then fluttering. While the rest of the boys were asleep at the hotel, he trembled and shivered himself awake. James stumbled to his feet and felt a strangely coherent longing for Punch, as if he had been addicted to her all his life. He wanted her back. But she was a murderer. He wanted to forgive her and just hold her in his arms and fill her with unconditional love. He wanted to breathe her in.

Blood dripped from his nose. James ran to the bathroom, hit the lights and turned the shower on. Before the water had a chance to warm up, he stepped inside still in his sweat pants and t-shirt. He had never felt these sensations and they explored his body. Every pore. Every cell. Every nook and cranny from his scalp down to his toenails. He could feel the gangrenous line from the fourth dimension creeping up to poison his soul. He gripped the shower curtain, pummeled with strong emotion and longing. The shower curtain couldn't hold his frigid body. The plastic rings snapped. James fell out back first, wrapped in the curtain. "PUNCH!" he yelled. "Punch!"

* * * * *

John Rackle came to the sickbay for a visit, but from the looks of him, he appeared sicker than the patient.

"You did not kill her?"

Killaovski was in bed with bruises and bandaged up, her right hand and arm in a cast.

"I had to leave in order to stop the oncoming attack. I left her dead." She delicately sat up. "If, for some miracle, and it would be a miracle, she is not dead, Mickeyoiliver will make sure she is."

"Is that so?" he grunted.

"After I pushed her off the cliff, I didn't go back to check for a pulse," she snapped.

"Damn it!" he alarmed. "She will come after me and you."

She laughed. "You give her more credit than God." She smiled. "Let her come back. This I have to see."

"I know her well," he said. "She's a mastermind. And a crafty little devil."

"I did not enjoy hurting her, you know."

He looked to her sad state as if for the first time. His voice uplifted by a sudden wave of hope.

"Get well, my sweet. We have history to expunge and re-tailor for a waiting customer named Purgalapudlia!" He kissed her. She flinched. "I am proud of you in all honesty and humility!" He started to spin in circles around the room. "Proud!"

"Stop it."

He kept spinning.

"STOP IT!" He bumped into a medicine cabinet, laughing. "What's the matter with you?"

"Mother will be happy."

"Okay. Please. Just go." The overwhelming sensation of shame leaking out of the anesthetic like sober rays of light. When John left and she was sure she heard his footsteps echo farther down the hall, she cried. Tears of gold.

* * * * *

Bookshelves for fossils, the oceanside cliff had many outcrops and pockets. The old barbed wire that entangled Punch came from the days when angels fought angels and diangles. The sounds of the ocean crashing below proved to her that she was still alive. So did the flapping wings of an angel guard landing next to her. His stench tickled her nose. The angel pulled on the wire as it cut into her, then placed his hand on her neck and felt her to be alive. Carefully, he untangled her of the mess. As he pulled her into his arms she clenched the barbed wire behind him and wrapped his neck. She sunk her teeth into his shoulder and rode him down the cliff side like a bobsled, using his head as a steering device, her knee into his sternum. His wings tore and the skin pulled off his back like the peel of a rotten banana. The wire, more like a noose, halfway decapitated him. It lodged into his vertebrate and stopped them from reaching the bottom. She yanked him off his wedged head, snapping the bones clean. They fell the short distance into the ice-cold water. Her black tub paddled beside her. She pulled herself up and got in, then fished the cadaver out and brought it in with her to finish draining him. The tub drifted away from the shore. The angel's head, still hanging on the cliff, watched them disappear into the blackness of the horizon.

* * * * *

The front page of the National newspaper read:

Punch With Angels, Has Fallen Ill And Is In Their Custody And Care. Will Recover Soon! Aster Returned Safely. Peace Negotiations Continue.

Silcher shook his head and handed the paper to another purgy soldier. John Rackle raised his hand from behind the podium to the gathered crowd.

"When we can find a window for peace, shall we not pursue it? If an enemy shows their loyal intentions for our people, should we not listen?" John paused to build momentum. "My fellow patriots, we have come to find a true ally amongst our angel neighbors. They have welcomed our dear sweet Punch to their most hospitable capital and with differences set aside, have decided to help her. We have learned that we are more alike than we first realized. They have finally recognized that we are a new nation and that war will not solve anything that a small friendly chat would. Let me be clear with you today... angels are and always will be, our allies!" John stood back to absorb the applause. Then, what started as a couple voices turned into an entire congregation chanting,

"Punch, Punch, Punch, PUNCH, PUNCH, PUNCH...!" John smiled and nodded.

"Yes, yes of course! She is doing well among the angels! I assure you! Our own Killaovski had just spoken with her this morning." He turned to Killaovski who sat behind him amongst a panel of diplomats and officials. She was dressed impeccably, despite the casts on her hand and leg and some bandages elsewhere.

She stood, and with encouragement from John, took the podium.

"Hello. I am not much of a public speaker. Because I am not a politician, but a fighter. A protector. This is my job. But I need to tell you that after Punch took sick, she tells me the angels are treating her well. She even joked about wanting to live there for a while. You know Punch. Always a comedian." The crowd applauded. Silcher shook his head. He and a few of his men had left. The smell of bullshit tarred their lungs. "In the meantime, I will assume her duties. I know I can't live up to her shoes, but will do my best in her absence in securing our nation. Thank you and good day." She returned to her seat, sweaty from her nerves. The crowd applauded again.

* * * * *

A morning knock sounded so distant in a head still heavy with sleep. The knocking and doorknob jiggling became persistent. Shard and the boys awoke from an exhausting night caring for James. James got out of bed and looked through the peephole.

"Oh shit!" he unlocked the door and threw it open. Aster, well worn, stepped in.

"Ah fuck it's good to see you guys," he said. James embraced him as the others jumped out of bed for a group hug.

"Aster!" Shard yelled.

Aster was dirty, bloody and in much need of a shower. While he cleaned himself up, the boys ordered room service.

"...Punch saved my life! I owe her big time!" said Aster while stuffing his face. "She's in big trouble. Her own men attacked her! Killaovski beat the shit out of her and left her with the angels. When I saw the attack I started yelling at the Purgy that I was flying away with to turn around to help her when he hit me over the head! And when I woke up, I pretended I didn't remember what I saw so they could let me go. I just hope she's not dead." He guzzled orange juice. "If she's not, we gotta do something. She freed me! She fuckin' rescued me!"

James shook his head. "Aster, you haven't seen the catacombs have you?"

"What catacombs? What are you talking about?"

"She bloody killed people mate," Ticktock offered. "She's devil-hearted--"

"She's killed people?" Aster said.

"That's what we're trying to tell you," said Ticktock. "There's a roomful in the basement of her restaurant!"

"Shut up."

"Would you listen to me," insisted Ticktock.

"I haven't seen it. Only heard about it," said Shard. "But Punch brought us Aster. She's a hero. She knew her life was on the line."

"She has rooms down there with bodies! James and I saw it! The Zeros saw it! Gus saw it! It's bloody disturbing!" continued Ticktock. Aster looked at James, who looked elsewhere.

"What are we gonna do then?" asked Aster. "I mean, why did she save my life if she's a killer?"

"What proof do we have that she, in fact, killed them all?" asked James. He remembered she tried to explain herself to him, but he was too terrified to listen.

"Her eyes changed. It was scary, but she saved me. She's an angel though. They're supposed to be-- weird."

"What have I done to her?" said James. "Fuck. I need to get her out of there."

"If we're gonna do this, we better stick together," said Shard. "I don't want us split up again."

"What about the catacombs?!" shouted Ticktock. "Who's fuckin' crazy now?!"

"We're gonna need a lot of help and a lot of know-how if we're gonna bust her out," said Aster.

"You're gonna get yourself fuckin' murdered helping her," said Ticktock.

"Are you in, Ticktock?" asked James.

"Well fuck! I'm not gonna sit around while me mates are in danger."

* * * * *

James's journal entry:

Notes on the virus Madmathix: The fruit, with the weight of its contamination, was brought to the Purgy soil. Madmathix had turned this once healthy soul, into a tar-like servant to gravity. While other clean souls floated away, this one left a greasy mark where it landed. It became unrecognizable and acidic. The devil's own feces wouldn't have extended to this degree of foulness. This soul became unusable for energy use and the risk of contaminating other souls into a similiar useless state caused panic with every life force that depended on it. But for some reason, madmathix couldn't dial wormholes into my soul type. I don't know why. But I do feel partly responsible for restoring peace up here if I can.

* * * * *

"She's a killer James," said Steve. "You're not!" The Zeros had invited the Clocks into their hotel room for what turned out to be part two of the same debate. Gus had also arrived. Michelle and Betty were purposely left out.

"And she's probably always thinking strategy. Even when she's not thinking it," said Gus.

"She's using you," said Steve. "Hate to say it, but she doesn't love you. I mean this is all part of her big plan. We're just pieces to her puzzle."

"Her plan for what?" asked James.

"I don't know. You don't think she has a plan with all those bodies, neatly laid out and dated?"

"That would take calculated thinking," said Gus. "Plus the orchestration of this tournament. To gather people for some twisted reason."

"We could all die," said Jeff. "We are out of our league fighting up there. We're dealing with things that we're not even supposed to be seeing! She's already violated whatever rules by bringing us into that world."

"Dude, and saving her kinda goes against our plans to stop her," Wes said. "Most of you've seen the revolutionary shit she's tangled in up there. That alone is reason to break off ties with her. And now, that shit in the basement? Come on dude. She's fuckin' scary."

"She might be dead already," Aster brought on silence from everyone.

"Killaovski can't be trusted either," said Shard. "At least with regards to Punch."

"So," said Wes. "Let 'em kill each other."

"Why would Punch rescue me if she didn't have some love for us? For James?" asked Aster.

"She's absolutely unpredictable, man," said Gus. "You've been watching too much TV thinking the bad guys are so obvious."

"Well gentlemen, I didn't come here for your permission or approval," said James. "I came to let you guys know what I'll be doing. I'm going in and regardless of how sound your arguments are, and I do appreciate them, my mind is already made up. I'm gonna get me into the biggest brawl ever. I'm determined to save Punch. And Purgalapudlia."

"Why?" asked Jeff.

"I love her," said James. "Here, I'm just a dart player. Over there, I may have a chance to make things right for an entire civilization. People I know nothing about or never met-"

"Are you insane?! How can you ignore what we saw?" asked Gus. "Was it so horrific, your mind totally blocked it out? You're delusional. You're not in the right frame of mind to make judgments like this. She's got you emotionally wrapped!"

James nodded. "Yes, it's true Gus. I'm emotionally wrapped. I'd be a fool if I said I wasn't. But you know, I've learned... we're privy to something no one has seen. And it's up to us, or me, to do something. In fact, I think it's best I go alone. I've come to the realization that she's been nothing but upfront with me, about everything. Trust me. I'll tell you about Punch. She's a great girl. A great girl who needs another chance." He opened the door. The urgency in his eyes was laser sharp. The rest of the Clocks got up and followed him out the door. Gus and the Zeros looked at one another. Toto got up and dug through his army green duffle bag. He pulled out his bowling pin and nodded to his friends while going out the door.

"Anarchy, hee-hee," he kissed his pin. "Nil or nothing."

* * * * *

The Clocks, Zeros and Gus waited outside a drug store as James came out with a box of Dramamine. He opened the package and proceeded to hand out the little pills to each player. They gobbled them like candy.

James took his new army right into Rackle's Tub. Og wasn't too hard to find.

"Need to talk to you." James walked past him and headed for the study. "Let's go."

"You guys want blood?!" Og pulled out a club of his own.

"Yes I do," said James. "But not yours, my friend." He climbed up the stairs. "Come on, Og. We need your help." Og looked at the others who drew their pins as they followed James up the stairs. They gathered on the landing.

"There was an assassination attempt on Punch. She's in serious trouble and may even be dead. We need you to get us through that portal to save her. Simple as that," said James. The rest of the Nephilims had gathered with clubs out, ready for a bashing. Og turned to them.

"WAIT! Punch is in trouble!" Og shouted.

"We're running out of time," pushed James.

"Follow me!" said Og. He led them down the stairs and straight into the kettle room.

"Wait, you're taking us to the catacombs?" James panicked. "We've been down there, you know. We know all about it. Are you trying to--"

"There's a portal down there that leads straight into the capital, near J.R. Industries. The city of Pearley," said Og as he pulled another door open to the catacombs. "If we're buying time, this is the portal to use." They and the Nephilim entered a new stairway, this one went straight down. "Who was trying to kill Punch?"

"Killaovski," said Aster.

"No. That can't be," Og said. "Punch is with the angels. Killaovski is back."

"I just came from there."

"You're Aster? The man that was with the angels?"

"Yes. And Punch came with Killaovski to rescue me, then it went horribly wrong."

Og opened the door at the bottom of the stairs and brought everyone into another frozen room full of empty bathtubs. Beyond it, an open door led into the main catacombs.

"That's them!" shouted a Rephaim from the other room. "They killed ZamZum!" The three Rephaims ran, one slipping on the icy floor and crashing on his back.

"Stay here!" shouted Og to the boys as he and his Nephilim stood outside the door and shut it.

"Punch has been attacked!" Og shouted at ZamZum's men.

"Clear the way!" shouted back the Rephaim.

"STOP!" cried Og. The Rephaim stopped in front of Og and his men. "Answer me this... Killaovski... assassination on Punch? Is this true?"

"Clear the way." the Rephaim ordered. He shoved Og, but was pushed back by the other Nephilim.

"Is it true?!" Og persisted and grabbed the Rephaim by his shoulders. "IS IT TRUE?!" The other Rephaim pulled out their clubs. CLACK! The quick hit of a club over a Rephaim's head by a Nephilim was the first of many blows in the brutal fight.

James and his boys could hear the commotion from the other side of the door. They sat freezing to death, each in their own tub.

"What now?" asked Shard.

"I don't know," answered James as he looked at the door, hoping it would hold back the barrage on the other side.

"Wha-what if this was p-part of the plan?" shivered Gus. "T-to trap us here?" Everyone was turning blue.

"Th-that would s-suck," quivered Wes. He noticed something white clawing at the air. He turned his eyes to find it now floating in another part of the room. Toto followed another one climbing up the air near the ceiling. Jeff and Steve looked toward one another because in between them floated a white centipede-type of hallucination. Ticktock and Aster tried to reach out and grab what looked like liquid smoke, floating towards the wall in front of them. Depth perception slid in and out of focus. The hallucinations made their way to the wall, forming a large circle. It glowed and a portal emerged. It was large and from the center came a green light, which lit their faces. Og slammed open the door. On the floor at his feet, were the wicked Rephaims, all three, dead. Og's eyes shined green like the portal light. Unfortunately, one Nephilim was dead too. The tubs started to move on their own towards the portal.

"We're coming with you!" Og ran through the portal with his two giants.

* * * * *

The black ocean carried a small fleet of angels in war tubs, a terrified Mickeyoiliver among them. All night and all day they searched with soul lanterns.

"Those Purgalapudlians don't play fair," Mickeyoiliver said. He was in a tub with two other angels. "Killaovski probably aided in her escape!" One of the angel guards pulled up a floating wing, shredded and dotted in blood. Mickeyoiliver turned away. "Oh DRAT! Call in the big boys! We're gonna hit them hard!"

* * * * *

The Brothers Nil, as they were now coined for the mission, were in town at the poorly lit pub where only days ago, Punch committed murder. Toto thought of the name. They sat in the shadows and kept to themselves. Quiet. Awaiting word from James and Og, who had sneaked over to J.R. Industries. One round of a local, bitter drink would help ease them for the fight. They raised their glasses without clinking and said not a word before drinking.

* * * * *

Silcher met Killaovski in her private chamber, where she was removing the cast from her arm. "Much better. Could you help me undo my leg?" She sat on a chair and raised her cast-covered leg at him.

"Certainly," Silcher carefully grabbed at the cast. He pulled out a knife.

"Our two best doctors are gone," she said as she clutched the arm rests. "Inconveniently."

"Lunch hour perhaps," he worked the blade up the cast. "I'm going out on patrol now. I will check on the soul wells up north, make sure diangles haven't returned."

"They won't return."

"Nevertheless, we will return by morning light." He gently peeled off her cast. They both looked at her bullet wound. It left a tender scar. "You do heal quick."

She smiled, "I'm strong that way."

* * * * *

James wore the Purgalapudlian military uniform. The two doctors were also disguised. Og and his giants knew it was pointless to hide under uniforms so they positioned themselves by the exit, ready to jump in the soon passing war tubs. Silcher and his men entered the hangar.

"James," he said. "You and the doctors will ride with me." James nodded. His men all climbed into the war tubs and fastened themselves in. They loaded their weapons.

* * * * *

Killaovski had joined John and Mother in his quarters for cocktail hour. She was enjoying the perks of her new position. The room overlooked the runway, where Mother stood enjoying the view. Her hand, raising her glass to her lips, stopped short.

"John..." said Mother, eyes drifting from the runway to the sky. "Why is half your army leaving?"

"Don't be silly, Mother. It's probably nothing to be alarmed about," smiled John. "When it comes to these matters, you're so... motherly." Killaovski approached the window. She spotted Og and his men taking off in war tubs of their own.

"What is this?" Killaovski put her drink down. "No, no-- this is a rescue mission!"

"What?!" John came to the window. The last of the tubs had taken to the air. He slowly shook his head. "This can't be. I thought she was dead!" he looked at Killaovski, "Who are they rescuing if she is DEAD?!" He didn't know where to step next. Panic gave him an ultimatum. "An arrest shall be made! ALL OF THEM! You must stop them!"

"Silcher must have gotten a tip," said Killaovski as she left the room.

"You failed me," he paced the room. "I knew it! I bloody hell KNEW IT!" He threw his glass at the wall.

* * * * *

James entered the pub in town.

"I have escorts to take you home," James tried to reason with his friends. "You've all proven to be friends beyond any measure. I love all of you for that."

"Fuck the escorts!" said Wes. "No dude, we're in. Period. So save your little speech."

"Don't be foolish. Why risk everyone's lives?"

"Sorry, James," said Shard. "We're in. All the way." They all placed their hands together in the center.

Outside, the Brother's Nil ran to the waiting squadron of tubs. A crowd gathered in awe of the army parked in the street.

* * * * *

Flying just above the ocean's reach, Silcher led his men in search of Punch, headed for Mickeyoiliver's territory. A storm pouted in the distance, getting ready for a full blown tantrum. Fog, thin at first, scattered about as if a cloud had sneezed. A small cluster of islands just ahead of them stood dangerously near a *chaos crier*. Every so often great marvels could be seen such as the unpredictable *chaos criers*, a multi-dimensional storm. Colossal, tornado-shaped portals to many dimensions all jumbled together connecting the ocean to the sky. It was best to avoid them, for one could be dissolved into pieces and scattered into different dimensions at the same time. Or, should you remain in one piece, where you ended up, you might never be able to return. They weren't impenetrable and with risk one could travel through them by spotting the intended dimension at a big enough interval and going through it at that instant. Again, at such a risk! Fortunately, *chaos criers* moved slow enough and could be spotted miles away. The ocean was usually violent around these crystalized mammoths.

The multi-dimensional storm lurked two miles away, but getting close. Something caught James's attention. Lodged in the rocky shore of the island, a black war tub. James pointed.

"There!" cried James. He could see Punch, not moving. "Oh God-- that's her!" Silcher raised his arm in the air. Splash! The wings folded in and the feet began to paddle. James's heart raced as he edged to the brim of the tub, head and body out far enough over the edge to resemble a figurehead to a ship. The rest of the army landed in the water behind them. "PUNCH--!" It began to rain. Once Silcher's war tub drew close enough, James jumped into the shallow end and ran. Og, also jumped out. "PUNCH! PUNCH!" cried James. She painfully and slowly turned around, eyes half closed. "Punch!" James looked blurry to her, when he finally arrived by her side.

"James-?" she slurred. She wasn't dreaming. It really was James. She hid her face.

"She's alive!" James reached for her. The doctors crowded behind him, their kits open. They checked her body for wounds. James grabbed her cold hand but she pulled away, ashamed and embarrassed. James glimpsed what looked like claws and thought they were part of the armor from her torn leather gloves. He was mortified to find the tub a couple inches filled, not with ocean water, but blood, splashing red on the doctor's legs. She fainted. James discovered infected slashes all over her body as he lifted her from the tub and carried her to a new one. The army sat in silence.

Their fearless leader, completely far from the inspirational being she had once been. Nothing could have prepared them for this shock. All spunk and vitality, now gone. The rain let up as if to salute a fellow force of nature.

"I love you," whispered James into her wet ear. Silcher spotted the *chaos crier* drawing closer.

"James," he said. "Give the doctors room. We're heading out." James climbed into another tub.

The fleet, wings open, took to the air. Thick fog engulfed the island. James sat back. He could only hope for a speedy recovery.

* * * * *

Mickeyoiliver and a portion of his mighty ocean fleet came upon the island just as the *chaos crier* tore at it from the opposite corner. He spotted the black war tub bouncing on the waves and crashing against the rocks.

"It's one of their specialized Imperial war tubs," he said steering to it. His guard grabbed his shoulder.

"Don't go near it!" cried the guard. "The storm could swallow you!"

"Not if you're quick enough," said Mickeyoiliver. "Go." He stood to get a better view.

"It's too close to risk."

"She will not escape me a second time. Now go. Fetch her."

"We don't even know if that's her's."

He turned around and grabbed him. "Well go find out!" The *chaos crier* bit into the island, chewing rocks at some instances while leaving others untouched. Its behavior was unpredictable. The Imperial war tub jammed in the rocks. Towing it out with a line would be difficult.

"It's too dangerous!"

"Are you defying an order?!" Mickeyoiliver pulled out a blade. The guard flew into the air just avoiding the tip of the blade. He cautiously approached the bobbing bathtub. The rest of the fleet waited some good distance behind them. The storm cut across the island, moving quickly toward the black war tub. The angel guard, despite having multiple eyes, couldn't see if the tub was occupied. He had to fly even closer. Fog drifted by, blinding him. He considered returning to safety and lying that he had not seen her. He was now upon the abandoned vessel.

"She's not here!" he shouted.

Mickeyoiliver nodded and waved him back. Fog evaporated with a giant lift of its curtain, revealing the *chaos crier* on stage, crashing into the rocks and lifting the black tub. The angel guard muscled his wings, feeling the pull as if hands gripped his ankles and cement poured thick over his wings. Screams went unheard, swallowed whole by the funnel. His body twisted like a Cubist painting, then his molecules dissolved into different dimensions. The image of his body hovered like the shadow from a nuclear blast. But it soon faded.

"LET'S MOVE!!" shouted Mickeyoiliver to his fleet. They steered away in the opposite direction. The island was pulverized.

* * * * *

A quickly moving cloud in the distance turned out to be not a cloud at all. Silcher's alarmed reaction let James know it was Killaovski and her bigger fleet coming right for them. They hastily surrounded James and his rescue squad.

"Silcher!" Killaovski called out. "Take your men to sea at once!" She escorted his fleet like geese coming in for a landing. She spotted James, Shard and the others, eyes searching until she found the two doctors shielding Punch, as she slept. Killaovski's heart beat with a dire pulse at the discovery.

Killaovski shouted to Silcher. "You found her?!" She bumped her tub against Punch's, grabbing one of the doctors by the shoulder for a closer inspection. "Is she alive?!"

"Barely," said the doctor.

"She's alive! How miraculous! How did... where did you find her?" Killaovski turned to Silcher. "You knew about this, didn't you?! You lied about the wells up north."

"I checked the wells--" Silcher began to explain.

"You're under arrest!" she confirmed. She looked at the rest of his fleet. "All of you!"

"On what grounds?!" asked Silcher.

"Deceit, for one!"

"You appear to be disappointed in our having rescued Punch," Silcher said.

"Enough! Let's bring her home for the proper care she needs. Poor thing." She rode to the tubs that carried the Brothers Nil. "James. Aster. Nice to see you again." She rode her tub up to Shard's. "Shard. Hop aboard. I want you near me."

Shard grabbed her hand and kissed it. He then shook his head. "I can't," he calmly spoke. "These are my friends. I belong with them." After an awkward moment of silence, she nodded and rode her tub to the front of her prisoners. With a wave of her arm, the massive army moved as one collective group.

Above Killaovski's fleet, Mickeyoiliver flew silently. More angel troops had joined his army. With the raise of his hand, the entire fleet slowed to a hover directly above the Purgalapudlian army below. Clouds provided perfect cover. A glowing grey matter materialized from his hand. It was small and growing. Bombay doors on the floor of the tub opened. Every angel had produced these glowing grey matters, placing them in the dock that fed unto the bombay doors.

"Let them each have a pocket of sadness." And with those words, Mickeyoiliver and his army dropped the spheres of grey matter upon the Purgy army. Killaovski sensed the magnetic fluctuations and looked skyward.

"ANGELS! ABOVE!" she shouted. Everyone's spears aimed upward in unison as Mickeyoiliver and his army of flying tubs lowered themselves within shouting distance. The pockets of sadness planted themselves over many Purgy heads. Depression began its work, their minds feeling slow and numb. Energy sapped, in a slow gulp, filling the pockets that floated above them.

"It was agreed that Punch would remain my property! Dead or alive!" Mickeyoiliver landed his men, positioning them on both sides of Killaovski's army. "A deal is a deal."

"You arranged for Punch's assassination!" Silcher shouted to Killaovski. "Didn't you?!" She looked at him and then addressed Mickeyoiliver.

"You couldn't even hold onto her! You fool! The deal is off! She is coming home with me! And I will look after her!"

"Who's the fool now? You were supposed to kill her! Or maybe I smell a horrid scheme from a rotting cunt!" said Mickeyoiliver. "You played it off to kill her. Only, you and your troopers would retrieve her later. Very dexterous of you two." His tub bumped alongside hers. "Well, I hate being taken advantage of. It leaves a terrible feeling in the gut..." He spit on her. "My emotions have their seasons and you've reached me dead of winter." She laughed and wiped her face.

"How poetic. Should I write that down?"

"I am here for Punch, *and* the James fellow, for added interest."

"You're crazy."

"Just hand them over and you can be on your way."

"And risk Punch coming back? No!"

"Let us remedy this now then." With his heel, he pushed his tub away from hers and rode straight to Punch's. James grabbed the steering from his pilot and drove his tub at Mickeyoiliver's, who had produced a large sword. He leaned on it as if it was a cane. "Perfect soul James."

"You want me? Slow down," said James.

"Let me kill Punch first."

James stood on top of the seat. "You don't need to do that. She's already gone." James leapt from his seat and tackled Mickeyoiliver. The Brothers Nil, and their bowling pins jumped from tub to tub, as angels and Purgy fighters followed, until they arrived at Mickeyoiliver's tub. Mickeyoiliver and James felt the weight of the dog pile pressing them to heavy panting. The tub tipped over dumping the aggressive occupants. The underwater silence and blackness terrified James. He didn't want to stick around searching for an enemy in these conditions. He popped his head from the surface and swam to Punch's tub where he stood in her defense. Mickeyoiliver and some of the angels flew into the air.

The Brothers Nil swam to other tubs close by. Killaovski pulled out her gun and shot at Punch, but missed. The rest of her army took aim at Silcher and his men, who quickly returned fire to her Purgy soldiers. The Brothers Nil joined Silcher in the fight, firing shots. Silcher shoved James and Punch's tub away with his own.

"Get out of here now! My men will escort you and the Brothers Nil to safety!" Og and his giants joined them and rode away, speed climbing, wings unfolded. The doctors lay like blankets over Punch who drifted from half asleep to half awake. The first tub lifted off. Killaovski yelled as her halo eyes appeared and this triggered her body to change into the assassin form, claws punching through her skin. Mickeyoiliver and a dozen angels gave chase to James and the fleeing squadron. Toto's tub couldn't outpace them as they rode parallel to one another. Toto swung out his bowling pin and cracked it over an angel's head, splitting his skull and sending him to his watery grave. Another angel tackled the Purgy pilot pulling him overboard. Three angels descended on Toto lifting him out of his tub ripping his body as if it were made of old cheese. Arms, legs, everything to shreds. The rest of the Zeros, as they rode higher and higher into the Heavens, watched helplessly. Wes screamed and threw his bowling pin at one of the angels, taking him out of the air. Toto's sacrifice bought the Brothers Nil and company some time, and distance. They got away. Eardrums popped and the turbulence jolted their adrenaline to exhaustion. Punch tried to get up, but the doctors leaned her back down. Mickeyoiliver gave up the chase and returned to the battlefield-below.

* * * * *

Through the hallways of J.R. Industries, James carried Punch, following the doctors. John Rackle trailed them like a vulture.

"She's alive!" John reached for her hair.

"Don't touch her." James rushed her to intensive care. John stopped at the door. He could still feel the wisp of air going by after the door slammed in his face. The salivary glands under his tongue climbed with an ache up both sides of his mandibles, overproducing saliva as his stomach acids burned their way up to a sudden eruption out his mouth. It spilled through his fingers and onto the floor.

James sat at Punch's bedside, gingerly reaching out to touch a claw, which he now realized were a part of her.

"Why does she look like this?" he asked, frightened.

Punch heard him but kept her eyes and mouth closed as to not reveal her other changes. She turned her head away to speak, her voice faint. "I don't look pretty when I'm around angels."

"Punch--"

Two Purgy guards brought in an angel, cuffed. All of its eyes were red, its wings clipped. One of the doctors wheeled another bed alongside Punch's, the angel strapped into it.

A doctor looked to James. "Why don't you go see your friends." James nodded. He got up. When he placed his hand on the door...

"James?" Punch called him. He looked at her. "Thank you." She was a little choked up. Light reflected off her blood-stained neck and cheeks, golden tears in her eyes.

"Take care of her." James felt the tears welling up as he left

James joined his dismal Nil. They were planted solid in their coats like barnacles on beach-carved rocks. Gus, Steve, Jeff, Wes, Shard, Aster and Ticktock.

John, a bit shaken found the brothers huddled together.

"James, old fellow, it appears we have drawn closer to a cure." He patted his shoulder. "May I have a word with you?" James hesitantly got up and followed.

"Punch will remain safe here in our custody." John explained. "We have the proper facility to house her."

"No. She'll come back with me. I'll look after her."

"I'm afraid that is not an option to explore, my dear boy. She is a threat and needs to be locked away. She wanted a genocide! Do you understand? Her irreverent nature will be the end of us. Otherwise, should you take her back, you will have the full wrath of the angels descend upon you! You've seen the beast she's become. I am currently having a cell prepared. I am her home. Leave her, James! I implore you!"

James looked over at his brothers, before turning back with a response.

"We were in a fight. I lost a friend."

"I am truly sorry, James."

"Will you take good care of her?"

"With the utmost warmth possible. She was my lover once too, you understand."

James nodded and returned to his brothers. Og and his men stood guard at Punch's door.

"John!" cried Mother. "I have soup for you." He followed her voice.

"Yes, Mother." He made a quick glance at the boys to catch a reaction. There was none.

* * * * *

They faked sleep in the lobby, waiting for John to leave for the Grand Prison of Purgalapudlia. The Brothers Nil rose to their feet once he did. James had no intention of surrendering Punch to John. The Brothers prepared the escape vehicles. One doctor smuggled Punch outside, covered in a dark cloak, her face hidden in the darkness of the hood, yet the jewel of her eyes sparkled at moments when she gazed at her entourage. Gus and the others, still terrified of her, periodically checked the lock on her caged tub. Too weak to protest, she accepted her confinement. Nightfall helped in concealing her from their probing eyes. At times, James could feel her staring at him until he turned to her. It startled him to see her eyes reflecting a little moonlight white. She sunk deeper in her hood, eyes still shining. They traveled quickly by tub, cutting through a forest, and then a trail into town. Only one doctor joined Og and his Nephilim and the Brothers Nil; they traveled as silently as possible. Shots from a distant battle could be heard. The angels brought the fight to Purgalapudlian land.

* * * * *

John hobnobbed with his high council in the lobby of the Grand Prison of Purgalapudlia, giddy that arrangements for Punch's cell were complete. Every detail, complete... except the prisoner. A winded guard threw open the door.

"Your excellency!" he said with urgency. "James has taken the prisoner! I found them all gone!" John took a moment to lose sanity... then rushed out the door.

"I should have stuck with mathematics!" He pulled out his penis and pissed as he walked. "I have no business governing anyone..." He cut through a field mumbling. "...Ants live a simplified life. Each one is born into a job and they do nothing else but that job. They know their place. Some ants provide security. Some, engineering. Some, childcare. Some, livestock farming, earth movers..." He wandered farther away. "I'm a physicist and it is foolish of me to go beyond what I know in all heart of hearts to do. I never cared for politics. How in Hell did I get roped into this? Mother!"

* * * * *

The Brothers Nil and associates arrived at the portal. James, Ticktock, Punch, the Doctor and Og were the first to go through.

"FUGITIVES!" Killaovski arrived with her army blocking the portal from the remainder of the Brothers Nil. "I believe you are all my prisoners." She stepped out of her tub, as did her men, grabbing their respective prisoners and cuffing them.

"Why are you doing this?" Shard asked. She smiled at him.

"I like you better in cuffs."

Quarantine My Love

"Where are they?" Ticktock had to keep moving. He was a bundle of nerves. In contrast, James stood like a statue, eyes on the area where the portal would be, near the ceiling in Punch's study.

"I don't know." James looked at the door.

"Something's happened to our mates, James."

"They should've been back by now."

"What are we gonna do about Punch?" Ticktock was coming to grips with reality, while James had an internal conflict to sort out with Punch. James sat on the desk. "James, did we do the right thing? I mean, I know she's your girl, but..."

The door opened. Og stood behind it.

"Punch wants to talk to you," he said.

"She's alright then?" asked James standing up from the desk.

"She's a little weak, but has made a remarkable recovery since we first saw her." Og gleamed with hope. The portal opened briefly enough to dump Shard to the floor. James ran over to help him up.

"Next time we should each carry our own box of Dramamine," said Shard.

"Where is everybody?" asked James.

"Not good." He paused to compose himself as Og left. "We ran into Killaovski." He vomited on the floor.

"Well-?" James pressed.

Shard waved Ticktock over. "This is getting so repetitive. We save one, only to lose another."

* * * * *

James, alone, ran down the hall to a more isolated wing of the building. Og waited for James, opening the door to Punch's room when he arrived. Punch stood in the shadows, her back to James.

"Punch?" James proceeded with caution. "I hear you're feeling better." She stayed with her face to the wall. Her bandages bleeding through.

"Why did you rescue me?"

"You're still my girl." He crept a little closer. "Right?"

"Are you sure?" She brought her clawed hands against the wall. She closed them into fists. He stopped.

"Of course I'm sure." She kept her back to him. "Why are you still hiding?" He dared to walk closer. "Come here." He placed his hand on her shoulder. She gave him her profile. "The claws don't bother me, love." He turned her around. Her eyes and mouth were shut as he embraced her and held her.

"Careful." Punch was still sensitive from her bullet wound.

"Sorry--"

"That little bitch." She pressed her claws into his shoulder and gently started digging. He pulled away and grabbed her hand. "Sorry. I--"

"Wow, these are sharp." She grinned apologetically.

"James--" Punch looked at the ground. "I need to constrain myself around you."

"Why?"

"I love you so much-" She opened her halo eyes to him, and the parted lips, unsheathing her sword-like canines... James stepped back.

"Shit..." he held his arm out in defense. She looked away. "Why are you like...this?"

She shook her head and after a moment, started to cry. "I don't know." She looked up to gain the courage to ask him a question. "How could you ever love something like me?" James slowly backed away. She wiped her face, and sniffling, turned elsewhere. "It was always my intention for you to see me like this."

"You forget, I'm still getting used to all this." He carefully grabbed her hand. "It's not everyday I experience someone like you. Like this place. Like this whole world of yours." He rubbed her claw with his thumb. "I lost a friend in the fight. And my other friends have been captured."

"James, I'm so sorry--"

"And the catacombs..." continued James. "Your soul-splicing research. Any sane person would lock you up." Her silence was loud with guilt. "Well?"

"You should, in all honesty." She looked away from his interrogating stare. "Lock me up. This is the dirty work that angels do."

"They're not...dead?" James had to find some redeeming quality in Punch. "How long were you planning to keep them like that?" She withdrew from his hands. "You have tubs down there that date back decades! Their lives will never be the same, even if you do bring them back. How can you justify that?" Punch still wouldn't look at him.

"What did you have planned for me, hmm...? If my team lost. Was Og gonna march us down to the basement, throw us into tubs and freeze us alive?!"

"No, James!" She closed her fists then loosened them. "You've witnessed a side of me that is detestable, cruel and unforgivable. Those bodies... I feed on souls, James."

James backed himself to the door. Punch quickly followed. As he opened the door, Punch blocked it with her leg, closing it.

"You *feed* on souls-?" James grabbed the door knob again. Punch took his hand into hers while she then leaned her body and head against the door.

"It's a source of food I can't live without," said Punch, "Angel souls aren't enough for me anymore. The catacombs are a soul bank John and I created because we didn't want to risk contamination from any pestilence. I own those souls because I killed their angels. I'm sorry James, I hate what I've become. I saw you as my last hope! My salvation from all of this. I swear to you, I was protecting you because I need you."

"Protecting me from what? The way it's looking, I'm the one needing protection. From you." The door knob turned from the other side. Punch backed off. The door opened.

"Excuse me." The Doctor stood at the door. "It's time for an injection." At her nod he came in and set his leather bag by her feet.

"I think James wants out," said Punch.

"No," said James.

The Doctor grabbed her left arm and wiped the vein to a shiny exposure. A syringe with a purple solution pricked her vein and pushed the contents into her arm. She closed her eyes.

"This is angel blood," the Doctor told James. He finished with the injection and wiped her vein, taping a cotton ball over it. "It looks like you need another bandage." He pointed at the bullet wound by her stomach. Her claws began their return back inside her knuckles. Her teeth and eyes returned to normal. James watched the change.

"The claws and stuff...does it hurt? When it comes out of you?" James asked.

"A little," she looked at her stomach.

The Doctor peeled away her old bandage and replaced it with a new one. "There we go." The Doctor replied. "You're looking much better." The doctor left the two alone.

"Have you been journaling?" she asked.

"I quit."

"You quit?" She made her way to the door. "That's not like you." With both hands she rolled her hair into a long ponytail. Then nervously gripped it, like a rope. "Am I still your girl?"

James couldn't pull away from her unfairly beautiful stare. He nodded.

* * * * *

The blood splattered everywhere like a Jackson Pollock painting. Ticktock carved the theorem for Rackle's Tub into his arm, the knife blade outlining its curves in red. Tears, not from physical pain, but mental anguish had him locked in a trance. James and Punch discovered him sitting in the hallway just as he pulled out his tongue and pinching it between his fingers, brought the blade to it.

"NO! DON'T!" James shouted, running to his friend. He grabbed the knife and tossed it away. Punch ripped a large piece of her shirt and wrapped the bleeding arm. Punch closed her eyes. When she opened them, her eyes had shifted to halo and she could see the large pocket of sadness hovering above Ticktock's head, crippling his will to live.

"Hold still!" She pulled out a mini faucet gun from her holster by her ankle and aimed it above his head.

"What are you doing?" James feared for the worst. She blasted at the depression, destroying it. They both watched Ticktock's emotions bleeding back into his existence. Og and the Doctor ran in. "A knife wound to his arm!" explained James. Punch stood and braced herself against the wall, eyes returning to normal.

"What happened to me?" Og brought Ticktock to his feet. He could feel the throbbing of his arm. Og carried him off. Punch reached out for James and reeled him into her embrace.

"I'm sorry--"

"He lost it," James found comfort in her. "They're not going to freeze him, are they? What did you shoot at?"

"They're called pockets of sadness. An angel weapon filled with positive ions which has a negative effect on people. The magnetic impulse stimulates the brain and brings people to suicide. It just saps all your energy and fills you with a desperate, quiet pain in your heart. Angels plant them on people. Then, they collect their souls."

"John told me of the mass suicide here at the brewery."

She nodded. "Let's go." She took his hand and led him to the study.

"It sounds like you're no different than the angels," James pulled his hand away. "You're both after souls. It's just your methods of killing are different. I don't know which one is more humane."

"I'm not above being a hypocrite. You still don't trust me." Punch handed him her gun. "Here."

"Jesus, Punch, it's not that--"

Punch opened the study door and they both entered, shutting the door behind them. "That gun you hold? It can kill me. It's yours."

He tossed it on the desk. "I don't want to kill you," said James. Punch grabbed her side as the pain competed for attention.

"Are you okay?"

"Hold me-" She stumbled over and braced herself against him. Behind her, Killaovski, Shard and an army of Purgy soldiers, weapons drawn, grabbed her shoulders and shoved her to the ground. They double cuffed her wrists behind her back.

"Nice work, James," said Killaovski. Punch looked at James, betrayal in her eyes. The rest of the Clocks, Gus and the Zeros entered through the portal, dazed as Punch was brought to her feet. The remainder of Killaovski's men left the room in search for Og and the Doctor.

"The tournament is officially over," said Killaovski. "No declared winner." She grabbed Punch by the arm and looked at James and Shard. "You tell this to everyone." The Purgy soldiers returned with Og and the Doctor in cuffs. Punch hung her head down, avoiding their stares. Gold droplets fell from her cheeks.

"I'm sorry, love," James softly spoke. She didn't respond. Killaovski and her men escorted Punch, Og and the Doctor back through the portal. The Brothers Nil gathered around James for an embrace. It was a bittersweet moment for him and he couldn't wrap himself wholly with the idea of never seeing her again. But it had to be done.

* * * * *

With a heavy heart, James and the Clocks packed to leave. None of the boys were on the happy side of conversation. Michelle and Betty had already left for home without saying goodbye.

A knock on the door. Shard opened it. Gus had been running. His breath was heavy and wheezing.

"Hate that feeling of being left behind while others have moved on, grown and reached new heights." Gus said. "And you're still stuck. They've made new journeys. They're not coming back to what they once were. They've tasted a new level of success, or just a new level, and found things in life that closes doors and opens new ones. Only the doors they closed is to the room you're still in. And there is just no turning back when things like that happen. You just don't see them anymore. You can't relate to them. They're no longer in the same dimension." Gus caught his breath. "I'm talkin' about everybody that's been in my life these past several days. Rackle's Tub is shutting down. I don't know, man."

"Fuck--" Shard felt his nostalgia strongly. "You sure make it hard to be a man around you."

"It's not easy," said James, while giving Gus a hug. "Events sometimes are beyond your control." He returned to his bag on the bed. "Honestly, I'm devastated. I don't want to leave. But what are we going to do here, right?"

"What's going to happen to Rackle's Tub?" asked Aster.

"I don't know, man. I just don't know." Gus slid his hands into his pockets. Ticktock, awfully quiet, went into the bathroom. As he stood over the toilet pissing away, a bullet blasted through the wall from next door -followed by the sound of a body dropping. His heart beat loud in the silence. His pissing stopped as his prostate painfully cramped up. Shard opened the door. The sounds of people staggering, cussing and screaming behind the wall brought the Clocks out and pounding at their neighbor's door. It was unlocked. They entered to find Jeff on his knees on the bathroom floor, lifting Steve's bloody, lifeless head into his lap. Wes was on the phone, red-faced and teary eyed.

"He shot himself, man-"

* * * * *

The police arrived at Rackle's Tub. Already the place had changed. Dust and cobwebs everywhere. The busy bustle of people gone. Gus led the police down to the kettle room where he found the clever door to the catacombs already open. The temperature was not as chilled and the smell of mildew was strong. Probing flashlights and doubtful minds descended the stone stairs into the catacombs. Once there, Gus blanched at the sight. Nothing. No bodies. No bathtubs. No signs of foul play. Nothing.

* * * * *

Gus packed his things into his van. He unplugged his computer. He discovered an old bong hiding behind it. He checked to see if it was clean. A slap to his window startled him, the bong crashed to the floor. John Rackle, bug-eyed, was pressed against the glass.

* * * * *

The Clocks sat in their hotel room with Jeff and Wes when the desperate knock banged at their door and Gus entered with a bewildered John.

"James!" cried John. "You need to come back!" He stumbled over and grabbed him by the arm. "You have to come back. There is social unrest to such a degree. I need your help to calm the people down. I will offer you residency in Purgalapudlia!" James shoved him, he fell on the bed.

"Don't touch me," growled James. John just lay there.

"Please, James--"

"What about Punch?" asked James.

"This is beyond her now," said John as he stood and straightened himself. He wasn't behaving like an Englishman. "I assure you James, she is safe. In our custody, where she'll remain." He looked at Shard. "Killaovski wishes to see you."

"Where are all the bodies, man?!" Gus pulled John forward in his direction. "I want answers. I want straight answers, man!"

"Bodies?"

Wes grabbed John by the jacket and slammed him against the wall.

"You dare to come here--" Wes pulled him back only to slam him against the wall again, cleaning it with his back until he hit the TV. "To ask for our fuckin' help--" he pulled him back and slammed him once more and shoved his hand over his mouth, cracking a tooth. "I lost two friends, you shithead! You think I'm gonna fuckin' risk losing more, MOTHER FUCKER?!" Wes threw John across the room and then reached for a bowling pin. Jeff grabbed it from him.

"No," Jeff said.

"I didn't kill any of those boys," said John, feeling his tooth, blood dripping from his mouth. "If anyone's to blame, it's Punch." James grabbed the bowling pin from Jeff. "Whether you realize it or not, you are all part of this now. History has been written. James, please. You understand." James looked at the others.

"Hold him," said James.

"Right!" Ticktock grabbed John by the ankles. "It's time for a bashing with full-hearted tolchocks!"

"Let's soften his gloopy guttiwuts," said Shard, he and Aster grabbing John by the shoulders.

"What are you doing?!" panicked John.

"Never fear," quoted James. "If fear thou hast in thy heart, O brother, pray banish it forthwith."

"Please!"

"Let's go bloody horrorshow on his litso!" Ticktock said. Wes stepped on his hand and kneeled down over John. James swung the bowling pin in the air to get a feel for it. Then he leaned in.

"Mr. Rackle," said James. "The Brothers Nil work for no one." Jeff secured John's other hand. Gus stood over John.

John's voice changed to that of a little girl's, "Please, James. Pretty please? Don't hurt us. I come for your help. John is not right in the head. Please save us. Make it right."

"He's lost it," said James.

"It's true," continued John with the child's voice. "John's lost it. But an entire civilization needs you to help them find it."

"Stop with the silly voice," said James as he leaned the bowling pin on John's gut. "or I'll bash your teeth in." John nodded and passed out. James handed his weapon to Gus and then reached into his bag, fishing for a box of Dramamine.

"Get up," grunted Shard. He poked John with a boot to his ribs.

* * * * *

Running down narrow trails in the woods, the silent slapping on the ground by the hands and feet of the stealth tubs provided a smooth ride for John and the Brothers Nil. Four tubs carried two passengers each. James rode with John. The trails, like cow pathways, were worn packed and solid. Where a man upright wouldn't fit, a man sitting in a bathtub found the tunnels of peculiar sage and scrub a perfect camouflage from skyward enemies. Thus, an easy fit. The twists and turns of these paths and the in and out of the underworld of the brush brought the team to a dirt slide that dipped down the hill into a small river. Like otters, the tubs slid, one after the other into the water where they floated downstream. Branches above their heads hid most of the night sky. Moths that glowed like distant stars, flew in clusters throughout the brush and reflected off the water when near it.

"The most peaceful route for our return," said John. "I think with word from you and the news of a cure, perfected, from me, will help simmer the people and the angels down."

"A cure?" asked James.

Mirrors Of Midnight

If anywhere was a home for sadness and madness, it would be here, the Grand Prison of Purgalapudlia. A hopeless inferno, its large stone walls, ash grey and tomb-like. A pile of gothic, twisted volcanic rock. James, alone, rode up to this mastodon of a building. Guards brought him inside. Either the occupants forgot to pay the electric bill or they were allergic to light, but the stale hallways, barely lit from lanterns flickering on the walls, dimly displayed the main walkways. James followed his guard closely. As they passed the iron doorway of each cell, he found them surprisingly quiet. Their little caged windows so high up, one needed a chair to stand on for a glimpse inside. James couldn't bear to think of Punch inside. These cells must have been built during the age of the Rephaim and Nephilim. Elsewhere, modified doors attached at a lower height must have been built during the decline of the giants. The guard escort brought James deeper into this labyrinth of cells. As the guard slowed to gather his keys James felt his heart kicking at him with new boots. The guard banged on her door, his lantern reflecting from the moisture on the iron. He placed the key in and turned a large handle with both hands to open the door. The room was as black as tar. The guard lit a lantern and James spotted Punch, awake. The guard left as soon as James stepped inside, shutting the door behind him. Punch wore a tunic with long grey sleeves that bound her hands in front of her body. Chain around her waist was leashed to the wall. Her ankles were cuffed and her hair was loosely tied back.

"Um, room service?" James's voice was small. "Hey, love. Sorry. I, ah..." He could hardly muster a thought. He couldn't stop his body from trembling and hoped it wasn't noticeable. She gazed at the ground. James took that moment to get closer.

"I know why you're here." She looked at him. He stopped. "I forgive you."

"I had to--"

"It's okay."

"My friends were in trouble. I had to stop you. You're dangerous." The word *dangerous* blocked her continued pardon.

"Have I ever hurt you?" asked Punch.

"I don't even know what you're capable of. And it terrifies me."

"You're lying to me. You obviously care, or else why would you keep coming after me?"

"I just wanted to set things right and let you know--"

Her stomach nudged with slight laughter. "James. If I were free right this very moment--" she pulled on her chain, "This chain broken. Suddenly..." He stood back, creeping to the door. "Would you feel safe? Would you trust me, that I wouldn't hurt you? Look at you, you're already out the door." She yanked at her chain. He flinched. "That hurts. I opened up to you-"

"You manipulated me with my soul!"

"I took care of you, before we ever met. But now, you no longer need to worry. I've surrendered all of my assets. They've stripped me of everything. Your soul is now under the care and protection of John and Killaovski."

James chewed on his finger. "Shit--"

"They've jailed half my army here. All my supporters." She cocked her head back, eyes still on him. "Sit with me." She tested him. She sat down. He crept close and sat in front of her, with a little distance still between them. His loud breathing didn't convey courage.

"I can't do this--" he said.

Punch turned away. She brought her nose to her sleeve and covered her face. James stayed seated and calmed down.

"But, I'm not going anywhere," he said. She lifted her head.

"It must be trying, not knowing how you feel about me," reasoned Punch. "There was never a question in my heart. I love you now, more than ever. I've committed to you and have never budged. I only wished you were so sure in your heart as I am in mine." Tears, clear, spilled down her cheek.

"Punchy-"

Punch quickly threw her loop of an arm around James's shoulders and brought him in close. He wrestled to lift her arms up. She didn't fight him, only held him close and tight. He continued to violently struggle at her grasp. She took a hit, lips bleeding. He finally surrendered like a mouse tucked in the embrace of a python. Her face pressed against his ear.

"You never used to be frightened of me," she said as she tasted her blood.

"I used to think you were normal."

She brought her swollen lips close to his neck. "Am I hurting you?"

"Please, Punch."

"James, look at me--" She tried to meet his eyes.

"Punch-"

"You're safe in my arms." She almost planted a kiss, when he pulled back.

"No. Please!"

She stopped. "Ouch," she whispered. The blood dripped off her chin. "That hurt worse than your kicks." She lifted her arms to free him. He escaped from her lap and jumped to his feet. She too rose only to plant herself in the corner of the room, facing away from him, eyes closed tight. The cell door opened. Visiting time was over. James turned to the guard.

"Wait!" he said. "Give me another minute." When James looked back at Punch, he had tears in his eyes. The guard left, shutting the door.

"Punch. I'm so sorry." James brought himself close to her, grabbing her arms and placing them over his shoulders. She kept her face away from him so he gently tugged her chin towards him. He wiped her lip with his thumb. "I'm still crazy for you."

He kissed her. He pulled away to look at her, eyes now open and drenched. She closed her eyes for another kiss, then lifted her arms up from him.

"Thanks to you, there's a cure for the epidemic," she smiled.

* * * * *

Gun fire and rioting in the distance disturbed James and the Brothers Nil as they stood in the lab listening to John.

"A type of cell encapsulation," John said, "We've studied your soul type James and constructed an impermeable membrane. A code in cells that makes the cell look like a virus to other viruses, preventing it from injecting the cell and thus floating around, until scared enough of its own reflection, it dies. I worked vigorously on the cure. It wasn't until midnight the remedy was perfected." John held up a small bottle of clear liquid, which at certain angles, resembled mercury. "Thanks to your soul-type James. The top note for this final solution."

"No side effects?" asked Gus. "What if a normal cell replicates itself as a virus? Since it looks like one? Or what if other cells attack it, thinking it's a virus?"

"Impressive Gus. First of all we're not talking about simple mitosis," said John, "these are cells to souls. A little different in nature than the cells you and I are composed of. It's all a magic trick. The normal cell only appears to be a virus to the virus cell. To itself and all other cells, it appears normal."

"Ok. Neat," said Gus.

"James's soul-type has a peculiar way of dissolving the capsid to madmathix, destroying its genomes, the reproduction segment of the virus. The Mirrors of Midnight have a twenty-four hour shelf life in which they then shatter," explained John, "right off the host cell."

"Seven years bad luck, mate," said Ticktock.

"The timing is so perfect isn't it, John?" wondered James. "Now that Punch is put away and there is social unrest, this cure is the perfect Band-Aid."

"It's a mystery how things unfold," said John as he made his way to the cabinet. "Time is a little irrelevant here."

"How long have you been sitting on her cure?" asked James. John locked up the serum and gave James a look.

"*Our* collaboration has been nonstop," said John. "And as such, this batch will not be the final one. We are done here. Ceremony awaits!" He walked to the door. "You, James, have the intrinsic nature to be a born leader. Perhaps you'll consider the position of the Indift of Purgalapudlia."

"I'm not a politician."

"That makes two of us."

War And Love: Two Sides To The Same Heart

A thousand white-winged angels, armed with soul-plated swords and shields landed on a soul mining establishment in Purgalapudlia. They met with little resistance as they stabbed and beat their way to the sensitive mining machines, ripping into the equipment and pipes. The transection on the pipes caused the current of soul to spill upward into the sky forming a splendid display of fireworks. With their soul absorbing equipment and soul vents on the sides of their tubs, they drank from the artery. Mickeyoiliver's 'big guns' were now in war mode.

* * * * *

James couldn't sit still during the ceremony to be "knighted". To be an official resident of Purgalapudlia meant nothing to him. He didn't want to live here. Gus on the other hand didn't find it foolish. He was, in fact, more than delighted. The idiocy of the ceremony tested patience. John made loud chicken noises into both ears of the honorees. He next placed his right hand over their forehead and with closed eyes, raised a dagger to the sky with his other hand.

"I hereby, duladuladuladula--do!" He switched hands, covering the forehead with the left and raising the dagger with the right. "I hereby, duladuladuladula--do!" He placed the sword on a purple pillow held by a Purgy priest. "The two hemispheres of the mind here, do enter the gates of Purgalapudlia." He next made a buzzing sound which then abruptly silenced with the snap of his fingers. "Welcome and congratulations! Next."

"Are you kidding me?" asked James.

"No, James, I'm not. Who's next?"

"What a fuckin' waste of five minutes," said Wes.

"And what would you have done with your five minutes?" asked John.

"Let's see," Wes thought aloud. "Killing you would take one minute. And with four minutes left, any fuckin' thing would be better than 'bokbokbokBAK! DuladulaDO! Bokbok! Duladula, bokbok!'" He snapped his finger. The Purgy priest laughed until John gave him an unsavory look. He then walked away with the pillow and dagger. A Purgy diplomat scurried to John.

* * * * *

After conquering parts of the northern territory, Mickeyoiliver headed straight for J.R. Industries. There wasn't much of a Purgal army to stop them. Killaovski was tied up in the south fighting protesters and thus unaware that Mickeyoiliver had fetched a bigger army. The Brothers Nil armed themselves with faucet guns and suited up for battle in Purgy uniforms. They anticipated the fight would be brought to their door. Cannon blasts, as distant as they were, had been growing louder. The barricade against protesters on the perimeter of the factory wouldn't hold up against an angel assault. But there was no time to reinforce it. Flashes of light zoomed over the building. The heavy artillery made an explosive impact on the upper level and surrounding areas. John was quickly escorted to an underground bunker. James could already see angels out the window, landing in the yard. Some on their own wings, others in winged tubs. Their bodies looked like Swiss cheese until eyes emerged from all the holes. James threw open the balcony doors and raised his hands as he stepped out. Mickeyoiliver landed, without tub, on the other side of the balcony.

"James," he called out. "Are you choosing to be smart about things this time around?" He looked through the window from a protected angle. The Brothers Nil stood inside, their hands in the air. "This is just a taste of what I'm capable of." He looked back at James. "I can crush you and this entire civilization."

"I know."

"My demand is simple. I want Punch."

"And I'm prepared to give her to you."

"You know where she is?"

"I will gladly take you to her. The violence has gone too far. I'm sick of it. I'm sick of you. I'm sick of Punch. I'm sick of John. I'm just sick of this place. And I want you to promise that you'll let me and my friends go. Promise."

"Promise," smiled Mickeyoiliver. "Oh, and ah...I'll actually be needing you too."

* * * * *

James and the Brothers collectively rode in bathtubs with Mickeyoiliver, following with his men, flying tub free. James took roads that weren't too obvious as to where he was going so the angels wouldn't pass him to get there.

The Grand Prison opened her doors to the Brothers Nil. They entered as Mickeyoiliver landed.

"Hold it, boys," Mickeyoiliver and his men stood around the front. He pointed to one of his men. "Take the first squadron around the back." James and a Purgy guard opened the doors and secured them. "You had her locked up."

"I didn't," said James. "John and Killaovski did." Mickeyoiliver stepped in with his men. James led them down a hallway.

"Where's your small platoon?" asked Mickeyoiliver.

"Out of the way," said James. As they turned down another hallway, standing at attention, one at each cell door, the Brothers Nil imitated Imperial guards. James didn't even look at them. "At ease," he said as he passed.

"So now you're a military leader?" Mickeyoiliver laughed. "And what rank have you appointed yourself?"

"I just want to put an end to this." James took Mickeyoiliver to the guard at Punch's cell door. He waved to the guard. "I'm handing over Punch. If you refute me, there will be war." He

pointed to the cell door. The guard grabbed his keys, unlocked
and opened the door. He lit the lantern inside. Punch was asleep.
James grabbed the keys from the guard and walked over to Punch.
Mickeyoiliver stepped in and watched James unlock and unfasten
her restraints.

"James?" Punch could barely open her sleepy, *halo* eyes.

"Not so fast," cautioned Mickeyoiliver.

"I'm turning you in, love," said James as he brought her to her
feet.

"Whoa there--," said Mickeyoiliver. "Cuff her. Leave the cuffs
on!" The guard shut the door.

"What the fuck?!" shouted James as he ran for the door. "Hey!"
Then, with the quickness of a shark, he turned on Mickeyoiliver
and tackled him to the ground. The two wrestled. James knew
he was out of his league, but he also knew it would buy time for
Punch to attack. And attack she did. James could feel the weight of
Mickeyoiliver hoisted from him as Punch dragged him off by the
neck. She had a glint of madness in her eyes. Claws pushed through
her skin and muscles tightened. Mickeyoiliver struggled and the two
curled into each other in a death roll. A tarantula hawk stinging her
spider prey.

In the hallways, every cell door opened and out poured Punch's
army and supporters, including Silcher and Og and another woman,
a blood angel by the name of Kimkixle. They attacked the angels.

James had to turn away from Punch as she tore grotesquely
into Mickeyoiliver. The sounds of breaking bones and tearing
membranes terrified James. Her orgasmic noises and tribal
screams, the blood on her face and hands and long sharp teeth was
unbearable. James banged on the door.

"We're good in here now. FUCKIN' OPEN THE DOOR!"
There were peripheral movements of blue and white light twisting
in the room until the white light was completely gone. Her throat
swallowed large heaps of light from Mickeyoiliver's soul. The door
opened and James fled with one last look back at Punch. As she
used her jacket restraints to wipe her face and hands clean, the
Brothers grabbed James, stepping over the bodies of fallen angels.

The fighting now extended to the front gate.

"James!" Punch called out. The Brothers stopped. She stood in the center of the hallway behind them. Her monstrosity gone. She was beyond beautiful and dangerous. Her hair -untied. She saw the bodies in the hall. "Come here." They all looked at one another, not sure if Punch could be trusted. She stood with her legs on either side of a dead angel. "What -are you going to force me to come after you?"

James carefully made his way over. The Brothers stood back, intimidated. James turned to them. "Go on, fellas. I'll be alright."

"How do you know that?" she asked. He shook his head.

"I guess I don't."

"I need to have a word with you, in private," she said while pushing open the door to a cell across the hall. She punched the wall, grabbed James and shoved him into the darkened room, slamming the door behind her. The dying torch on the wall almost went out from the draft of the door. James got up.

"What are you gonna do?" he trembled, and scampered to keep his distance.

"You're not going to get away from me here, James." She stalked him, closing the gap between them.

"You're going to change."

"Something like that."

"Shit, Punch-"

She dashed at him, dismantling his hits, pinning him to the wall with her body. She looked into his wide eyes "Why do you make me so angry?" She kissed him quick, pulling away from his lips to gaze at his reaction. She cleared his bangs and looked into his eyes. James laughed. "It's not funny."

"If this is angry--" he said. She grabbed him from behind the neck for another kiss. This one was long and turned violent, her teeth bumping against his. She threw him to the ground. He nervously looked up at her circling him, the muscles in her legs ripped to perfection. Her stare was penetrating.

"Punchy?"

"Yes, James."

"I love you," he confessed. "I'm scared of you, but-" She silenced him, continuing to toy with him by sitting on his feet, ankles trapped under her crotch. She clamped her hands over his legs. He tried to get up.

"Don't fight me."

"Okay," he winked at her.

"Your little boy charm won't work." She stared right into his soul. The world went silent, he could feel the life resonating out of his body, only to return when she broke out of her trance and moved closer to him.

"I know where your heart is."

He took a moment to catch his breath, nodding. "Next to the lungs, behind the rib cage last time I checked."

She smiled. "You don't like my idea of foreplay?"

"That's what this is?" He dared to land a butterfly kiss on her nose.

"From now on, no more betrayal," she demanded. "Because from you, it cuts me so deep."

"Me too Punchy, me too."

* * * * *

Punch led her men to a wooded area outside the Grand Prison. They managed to defeat the angel escorts that Mickeyoiliver brought to the prison, but there were thousands more fighting all over Purgalapudlia. She confiscated the angel's weapons and war tubs and whatever else she could gather for her army. The Purgy guards at the prison armed the rest of her troops with their weapons and vehicles. Once her hodgepodge of an army was formed, she led them out, past one village after another. The revolutionary zeal, like a new perfume, had already reached the people, and at her sighting, they began to cheer uncontrollably. With tears in their eyes, as Punch waved to them. She was now with a council of war, and ready to fight the fight!

Punch and her men wouldn't have to wait long. Outside the village, an army of angels were raiding a soul mine. She quietly brought her flank as close as possible and waited for them to get drunk with their own complacency. Because of her feast of Mickeyoiliver's soul, Punch didn't change into that blood angel beast. Once the angels laid their weapons aside, she charged them. This attack proved swift and powerful. They never expected an army of opposition to have formed so quickly. The angels didn't even have time to scatter. She tore into them. Shots blasted. Kimkixle jumped on the wings of an angel and rode him to the ground. Gus watched her with lust and love in his eyes. She knew he was watching her, as was Punch. She eagerly wanted to prove to them her skills and earn their respect.

"Who is she?" asked Gus. He had been keeping a healthy distance from Punch because he still thought her wicked. But his curiosity for the new girl overrode his fears.

"Kimkixle," said Punch. "My protégé." Gus watched as much as he could stomach, as she tore an angel apart. The Brothers Nil blasted with their faucet guns. As one angel drew close, Wes clubbed it with a bowling pin. James closed his eyes and threw a spear right through the heart of another angel.

After the victory, they marched onward to the next squadron of angels. And yet again, they proved to be victorious. They fought two more skirmishes before dark. Punch rode past the country cottage that she had showed James on their first trip to Purgalapudlia. She turned to observe James, hoping his reaction conveyed not just the memory of the place, but perhaps a fresh interest. James looked at the place as they rode by, his face less curious, not realizing he was studied from afar. He did look over to Punch, catching her warm eyes on him. She smiled.

Punch and her army camped in the woods. Her men ate well, the dinner provided by a local village. James sat against a hillside, writing in his journal. A little lantern hung from a nearby branch casting a glow like a small campfire. Punch was happy to see him writing again. She walked over.

"Care if I join you?" she asked.

"No." He cleared a spot for her to sit. She sat near. "What a difference you make in the fighting. You're only one person, and yet you come across as an abundant and graceful, encouraging, and secure source of energy for everyone. Being around you is like being around the company of many friends. You lift the morale so anything is possible."

"Wow...are you writing that?" She laughed.

He looked at her. "Yeah." She grabbed a stick from the ground. "Remember that country cottage?"

"Saw it earlier today."

"I bought it."

"You bought it?"

She nodded with a tight-lipped smile. "It needs a man's touch."

"Does it now?" said James. He closed his journal.

"Maybe you could...be that man." She nervously looked down. "If you want to live with me. If you think you could." She steeled herself and looked at him. "Do you think you could?" James looked at her, stone-faced. She laughed out of apprehension. She looked back at the ground, her tongue pressing her jaw open. "You're not answering--" She used the stick to scratch the earth. "I'm sorry-- it's too soon."

"No. I'm a little," James searched for the right words. "I'm a little stunned at the proposition. That's all." He paused. She nodded. He couldn't exactly imagine spending the rest of his days in Purgalapudlia. "I'll have to think about it."

"Of course." She touched his cheek. "I love you, James. I want you to know that."

"I do know that."

She kissed his lips, then got up. James watched her crawl into the bath. Truthfully, he was still scared of her. But he loved her like no other. He looked up at the night sky, twinkling over him. He finished up his journal entry and made his way over to her, slipping inside the tub, under the blankets. He wrapped his arm around her, kissing her exposed ear.

Nearby Gus slept in his own tub. Only instead of sharing his blanket with Kimkixle, he shared it with Aster.

* * * * *

Word had got out that Punch was on the war path. News of Mickeyoiliver's death was her battle-blowing bugle. The angel High Council felt the effects of her sting and prepared to counter it. Punch knew it was only a matter of time before the angels would catch on that she was teaching them lessons in warfare that even they couldn't comprehend. Who was she to suddenly come out of nowhere and make a laughingstock of immortals who had fought wars since the beginning of mankind? Could it be heart? Could it be she understood her enemies? And could it be she knew no other option, than to win? She shepherded the masses with an omniscient touch.

Punch managed to expand her army. Volunteer fighters in their own tubs joined in each passing town. Atop a ridge on a hill, an army of angels stood in formation. Many of their tubs, black splotches growing all over them, jerked against a chain keeping them in place. They waited for Punch and her army. With their jousting spears pointed up, the angels lowered them and their tubs, chains cut, began the charge down the hill. Punch and her Purgy army had just entered the clearing below the hill. Her army spotted the oncoming cavalry and noticed, flying above them, the angel's army of flying war tubs. The Brothers Nil looked on with fear. There was nowhere to run. Punch turned to her men and twirling her finger in the air shouted...

"CIRCLE FORMATION! CIRCLE!" she jumped from her war tub and lifted it on its side, belly facing out. She unhooked one end of the seat and swung it around so it acted like a kickstand and held the tub secure on its side. Another row of tubs climbed on top of the first row and locked hands with the other tubs. This reminded James of how army ant workers form a wall or bridge by also grabbing each other's legs creating a net for the rest of the colony to walk on. Punch's men followed suit and with faucet guns loaded, waited in the safety of the barricade. Her army formed three separate impenetrable circles of upturned tubs. Pockets of sadness and soul-plated bullets rained down.

On top of the hill, a platoon of angels wore weapons that resembled a large marching tuba called sound canons, which produced a low, bass sound when fired. It caused deafness from afar. But near, it dismantled people. They fired the soul-plated soundwaves, but were out of range. They ceased fire and dismounted the heavy weapons. It was another product from the minds of J.R. Industries.

Most of the angel cavalry reached the circles, stabbing at the tubs with such force the impact echoed across the land. A couple angel tubs however, strayed elsewhere with erratic movements. Punch wondered why those tubs behaved strangely.

Both sides fired upon each other with faucet guns and stabbed into each other with swords. The circles slowed the enemy. Angels that made it inside the circle, were met by Purgy soldiers. Silcher was in another circle holding back the angel assault. Kimkixle had formed the third circle. Several enemy tubs shattered, their souls airborne and collected by the vents on the Purgy tubs.

Punch noticed the black splotches on the attacking tubs. "Shit, their tubs are contaminated!" shouted Punch. "Shut off all soul ventilators!" She reached into her tub and pulled a chrome handle. Silcher, Kimkixle and the other tub pilots followed her orders.

From atop the ridge, the angel commanders looked on. Like a dog trying to kill a turtle, Punch's army was too impenetrable to defeat. Angels were easily picked off. With the blow of a horn, the cavalry retreated.

Punch looked to her men. "They have sound cannons!" She upturned her war tub. "I hate John for that!" she muttered under her breath and rode out to the front of the three circles. She held her sword in the air. "CHARGE FORMATION!" The three circles broke up.

"CHARGE FORMATION!" yelled Silcher to his line.

"CHARGE FORMATION!" screamed Kimkixle to her line of men.

The circles formed three separate lines. Punch swung her sword to the enemy. "CHARGE--!" And all at once, they exploded into a high speed chase up the hill.

The angel commanders positioned their sound cannons closer only to find the Purgy army mixed with the retreating angel cavalry. Punch rode their coattails, fighting midway up the hill with the angel army bringing them to the ridge. The sound cannons fired a couple shots, causing enemy ears to bleed, but were soon eliminated due to the close range fighting. The angels sent their winged tubs out again, but a little too late to make a difference. Punch and Kimkixle took on the commanders in a sword fight. The commanders didn't stand a chance. Not only did Punch and Kimkixle sink their swords into angel flesh, they bit their throats open, swallowing their souls, preventing a full blood-angel change. The winged tubs landed and attacked the Purgy soldiers. The Brothers Nil threw the quill weaponry along with blasting their faucet guns. Souls from the dead floated away.

Punch led her army to another victory. But it was a painful and exhaustive one. She collected more weapons and headed out. Her army marched to Pearley. Punch enjoyed the breeze on her face. The soul light in her tub flickered, making a low buzzing sound. Punch turned her attention to the light, now darkening. She looked at another tub running along side hers, splotches forming on its side. Just then, her tub bucked. She grabbed the sides of her tub. The soul light turned black and dark splotches slowly appeared on her tub.

"Hey-!" shouted the Purgy riding next to her. His tub bucked and rammed against Punch's tub knocking her around. She raised her sword which stopped her army. Most of them anyway. The rest wandered out of control in their contaminated tubs. Punch pulled on a lever to brake. It didn't work. James, in his healthy tub, went after Punch. He sped right up to hers. Already, a couple of Purgy soldiers had flown out of their bucking tubs.

"Punch!" James shouted from behind, pulling next to hers. "Jump in!" As Punch unstrapped her seat belt, her tub shoved James's tub off course. James steered back towards Punch, both tubs bumping. "Jump -!" Her tub attacked his, clawing it.

"No James-!" Punch tried to steer away, but her tub didn't obey. Both tubs locked into a fight while still running... full speed.

Kimkixle's tub suddenly jerked and bucked. Gus and Aster, sharing a tub quickly rode over to her tub.

"Get in!" shouted Gus. As Kimkixle climbed aboard, her tub grabbed her by the leg. Wes pulled up and blasted at her tub, setting Kimkixle free to jump in Gus's tub.

"Thanks," she hugged Gus.

James's tub grabbed Punch's tub on the back rim. "Hang on!" His tub worked it's forefeet down until it grabbed the hind legs of Punch's tub, forcing her tub with a hard left while braking. Her tub slowed enough, its left leg snapped off and Punch crawled out from her tub and jumped into James's embrace. At that moment both tubs parted with a shove. James returned to the waiting army, now loud with clapping and whistling. Punch kissed James long and good.

The Brothers Nil stayed close to Punch and Og at a tavern. They sat around a large round wooden table. Gus tended the wound on Kimkixle's leg. She found great comfort in his patting it with a healing ointment.

"I feel like I've gained a third and fourth wind," said Jeff. The adrenaline turned their bodies and demeanor into painless vessels of athletic warriors.

"It's like when you play football," said Shard, "and by the fourth quarter, finally learning how to manage your energy so you don't over exhaust yourself. To keep a healthy momentum."

"And then squeeze it when it counts," said Punch, "like boxing. When you strike, strike hard and lightning quick. It's good to use your anxiety and to not become overly confident."

"You hit so much harder than anyone I've fought and I've fought many," said Silcher, laughing.

"Yeah, you don't want to piss her off," said Kimkixle, "because she'll deliver the cannons right then and there. No joke."

James reached for Punch under the table, affectionately squeezing her leg. Smiling, she leaned and nestled her tired head against his chest.

"My hero." Punch spoke softly and happy in James's arms. Everyone agreed with a cheer.

"It was easy," joked James. "Nothing to it, really. It's just a simple problem every suburban, homeowner faces from time to time-runaway bathtubs."

That night in the tavern, upstairs, Punch and James cuddled in a comfortable bed. She lay on the warmth of his stomach. The contrast of this moment from the brutal fighting, just hours ago, only made this moment merciful and sweet and much needed. This was the happiest James felt. Punch too, glowed.

"What am I going to do with you?" she whispered, "my sweet, beautiful, little, James."

Grounds Of Contention

Killaovski waited with her army in front of J.R Industries. She had that advantage, among many others. A distant rumble reached the ears of her and her army. They settled into position and waited. She, too, heard news of Punch on her enemy-annihilation tour of the country. She made a point not to clash with her on the road, but to position themselves at home base. The rumble grew louder and closer. She was grateful she got there first.

Punch slowed her army as they arrived near the gates of J.R. Industries. She spotted Killaovski's army waiting for her. James noticed strangely-shaped bathtubs, bent up like a boot.

"What kind of enemy is that?" asked James.

"A dead one," responded Punch. "Let's park right here." She brought her army to rest at a healthy enough distance from Killaovski's reach. She slouched over to Silcher, bluffing exhaustion for Killaovski's benefit, "Hide the sound cannons." She winked.

He saluted and brought the weapons down low. Kimkixle did the same. The rest of her army followed Punch's cue and lolled about.

Killaovski nodded. "Just as I suspected. She suffers from battle fatigue. Well, Punch. No rest for the weary. Not here."

The new war tubs were dispatched. They were the remnants of the catacombs. Most of them anyway. A half-man, half-bathtub, fighting machine. There was a similarity to centaurs in form, but encased in a porcelain body, the front end bent up with a face in the front. They operated independently, and therefore, required no passenger to steer them into combat. In addition to their standard four legs, they had two arms that could claw, punch and hold weapons.

The Brothers Nil stayed close to their guns. "She's testing us," said Punch. The enemy tubs kicked into a mad dash towards Punch and her army. "FIRST BATTALION! SPEARS!" screamed Punch. They drew out their long pointy spears and lowered them towards the oncoming cavalry. "CANNONS TO THE FRONT!" The Purgy soldiers wearing the sound cannons stepped up front and held formation.

"SECOND BATTALION!" shouted Silcher. "LOAD GUNS!" Like a machine, they all at once loaded their faucet guns. "POSITIONS!" They all lined up behind Punch and her first battalion who were in a line formation. "FIX YOUR TARGET!" They took aim at the fast approaching enemy.

"THIRD BATTALION!" shouted Kimkixle. "SWORDS OUT!" The remaining men drew their swords. "POSITIONS!" They reared behind the second battalion.

"James," said Punch. "Take your friends and fall back."

"No."

"We're staying here for the fight," said Jeff, gun drawn.

The thunder of the enemy tubs running closer to her waiting army was like a jolt to the brain. Punch stabbed the sky.

"CANNONS! FIRE!" her sword sliced through the air.

The Purgy soldiers blew into a trigger valve. A loud bass sound, similar to a foghorn, shot out of the bell over their heads, followed by a *wawawawaw* sound as it flew past the enemy. Clods of dirt fanned into the air from the hits. Almost like a continuous ripple effect, one soldier moved forward and fired, then he moved back while another moved forward to fire a shot. With this formation of a back-and-forth rhythm, they successfully blasted at the enemy tubs.

Killaovski watched as pieces of her new troopers exploded. But there were many still untouched and getting closer.

Within 50 feet, Silcher threw his sword down. "FIRE!" A wall of explosion from his second battalion sent a direct hit at the oncoming war tubs, but that didn't stop them, however, A few of the enemies lost limbs as a result.

"CANNONS! FALL BACK!" shouted Punch. The cannon men ran behind the third battalion to drop their sound cannons for lighter weapons.

"FIRE AT WILL!" Silcher shouted. A couple of tubs shattered like thrown plates, but the advancement was now upon them. Enemy tubs crashed against spears, some impaled while others broke through. It became a hand-to-hand ordeal. War tubs of old were fighting war tubs of new. Both clawed at each other. The third battalion joined in the fray, their swords out. With the tub's extra limbs, they were able to grab the Purgy soldiers and pull them out of their tubs and tear them into pieces.

Killaovski watched the progress from afar.

Punch jumped inside one of the enemy tubs and stabbed her sword through, tearing out of the face in front. Og wrestled one like a rodeo rider bringing down a bull for branding. Jeff and Wes pulled out their bowling pins and cracked a tub to pieces. Shard and Aster wrestled against an enemy tub impaled at the end of a spear. Shard pulled out his gun and fired at its face until it stopped moving. Punch jumped inside another tub and stopped it with a blast to the face. Having found their weakness, soldiers jumped inside the enemy tubs and blasted them in back of the head.

With the last enemy tub destroyed, Punch jumped in her old tub and raced towards Killaovski. Her troops followed. Both armies, now within spitting distance, stared, face-to-face and silent.

"Don't let her get away!" said Punch as she hopped out of her tub and defiantly walked through Killaovski's men.

Aster nodded. "You don't want to mix it up with Punch," he said to Shard. "I've seen her inflict Mike Tyson type of damage for someone her size. Now that's scary."

Killaovski stepped down from her tub. "I'm impressed," she commented.

"Spare our men what you and I can settle alone," said Punch. Punch wasted no time and began the assault on Killaovski with a jab to her lip. Blood exploded from her face. She followed with more hits as Killaovski scrambled to keep away long enough to counter. Both armies gathered around, shouting. Killaovski was quick to put up her defenses and both girls circled each other, giving and taking hits. They were evenly matched. And they weren't talkers. They both were well aware that fighting each other was a deadly business.

Killaovski grabbed Punch by the neck but she knocked her arm away and at the same instance, snapped a punch to her face, followed with a punch from her other hand and didn't let up, forcing Killaovski to take the defensive position. At every opportunity for an offensive, Killaovski only managed a couple hits as Punch machined through them, putting her back on the defensive. A swift kick to the gut sent Punch to the ground. Killaovski jumped on her, pounding her head. Punch sat up, clinching her body to hers, trapping an arm. They rolled over, grappling one another. Punch's cheek was shoved against the dirt. With an eruption of fury, Punch escaped the human knot and got back on her feet. Killaovski tried to bring her back but was whiplashed by a direct hit between the eyes. It was another square-off, the two exchanging blows. Killaovski grabbed Punch and picking her up, slammed her inside one of the tubs. She then leaned in throwing jabs into the tub while Punch, clawing at the air, tried to block her. The tub started to move, but that didn't matter to the fighters. Punch's legs kicking, she instantly curled her entire body around a trapped arm. The other arm continued hitting, but Punch, now with both hands free returned fire on Killaovski's face, her head bouncing up from repeated hits. Punch pushed her back, hopped out of the tub and wrangled her to the ground.

The armies joined as they pushed and followed the two wherever they landed, dirty, bloodied and bruised. The girls held onto each other. They could feel their hot and desperate breath against each other's faces. Sting of sweat in their eyes. The skin of their knuckles grazed off. Exchanging hits that no human could ever live through.

Punch broke up her timing, making it difficult for Killaovski to find a pattern. One instance she was there, then appeared elsewhere, almost like Killaovski were fighting a double. Punch moved that quickly. Dropping hits seemingly out of nowhere. She stayed light on her feet, feinting and blocking kicks with her meaty thighs. Even catching a leg and ramming Killaovski backwards to the ground. But Killaovski grabbed her and wrestled with her again. She could overpower Punch on the ground and soon had her in an arm lock. But before her arm was broken, Punch head-butted her in the face and escaped. Punch was faster with the strikes and slippery on the hold.

Blood poured down Killaovski's nose. She got up and once again faced Punch. The two, gasping for breath now, continued boxing. Punch raised her intensity to a new level. She pulverized with precision as she tapped into her last resources of energy. This machine-like focus made Punch a better fighter. Every opening she encountered, she connected with solid brutality. A left hook, dislocated Killaovski's jaw and ruptured her eyeball. A jab further fragmented her nose. An uppercut shattered a rib. Another cross ruptured an eardrum. Killaovski couldn't connect with any shots. Hit after hit landed on her like atomic bombs. It became impossible to defend against. Pain all over her face and body distracted her. And that's when it happened. Quicker than a bullet. Punch delivered her infamous, coma-inducing right hook to the temple, dropping her dead. Punch screamed, tears diluting her bloody face as she continued punching the air, nearly collapsing on top of her opponent's body.

The Punch supporters cheered with tears of their own as Punch stood over Killaovski. Killaovski's men were emotionally torn, as some shouted others were saddened.

"No shit they call her Punch," said Wes. Shard ran over to Killaovski's limp body and lifted her arm, looking at her face.

"I'm sorry, Shard," Punch said catching her breath. He didn't need to close Killaovski's eyes. They were swollen shut.

"Yeah. Me too."

He got up. Punch turned to the crowd. "We are now one!" She addressed Killaovski's men. "As we were. And always will be. Undivided--" Punch sat at the rim of a tub, still winded. "Make your peace with it and shake hands." She got up and both armies stepped away from their tubs and shook hands, welcoming each other. Punch, feeling faint, wended until James grabbed her and carried her. "Whoa, hello, stranger," Punch smiled with sleepy eyes. "See? I need you."

"You need a doctor," said James.

"Changing the subject? I'm fine."

"You take my breath away. You amazed everyone," said James.

Og, Kimkixle and everyone gathered around James and Punch, celebrating her victory with shouts. Punch grabbed Silcher by the arm.

"See to it that Killaovski gets a proper burial," she told him. He saluted her.

From Mother's view out the balcony window, it looked like a whirlwind of activity. The event horizon! They followed James into the building as he carried his love. The doctors rushed over to treat her wounds. She got to her feet and crossed the lobby. And with a gesture of her hand, stopped everyone following her.

"This is where it's going to get ugly," said Punch, grabbing Kimkixle and Gus. Everyone laughed. "I want you two to stick together." She looked to Kimkixle. "Show him the hangar."

"Okay," said Kimkixle. "Be careful, Punch." She grabbed Gus by the hand and left.

"Silcher," spoke Punch. "Dismiss your men. Take a holiday. You all deserve it. You and your men are the greatest men I have ever had the privilege to fight alongside."

"The honor is ours!" cried Silcher. He and his men pulled off uniforms and removed helmets.

"My Brothers Nil," Punch called out. "Follow me."

* * * * *

James's journal entry:

Punch explained how John Rackle and his tyrant of a mother were able to live for so long. It's called a live wire. This was a method where you utilize another's soul to sustain you. But it's important that the other chap be alive as well, like in a state of suspended animation. It made one seem immortal like Punch, until you cut the line. That explained the frozen lads in the catacombs. The ones that Punch didn't feed on anyway. And the rest? Well, you've heard of solar energy to run a place. Like solar power, soul energy was just another form of alternative energy Punch used to run Rackle's Tub.

* * * * *

It was a dark room. Only a few bodies lay in bathtubs of suspended animation. The Brothers Nil stood with swords made of neutrino star, soul and tungsten. Just by merely holding the sword out, over the bodies, the umbilical lines of the soul, illuminated. Even the Brothers glowed slightly.

"Let's do this," said James. And he took his sword and cut the live wire which connected the frozen body to a portal above.

"Yeah!" Shard cut another line.

"Keeya!" shouted Ticktock as he too ran to another body and sliced the line.

Aster approached another tub, "Oh line, be gone!" He sliced.

"Down you go, mother-fucker!" Wes sliced yet another line.

"No more!" Jeff cut the last line.

* * * * *

The moment Mother informed John of Killaovski's death, he returned to hiding in a bunker room used for storage. His heart palpitated and a tiredness hung over him like he never felt before. He carried a loaded faucet gun in his coat. But, it was too late to retrieve it. As soon as the door opened and closed, he heard the familiar click of a gun, cocked. He froze in hopes that Punch wouldn't spot him. But in his peripheral vision he could see her standing there. Watching him. He could barely breathe, or so much as swallow, to clear his throat. The waiting and waiting turned him blue and proved to be a harsher punishment than to just face her. He turned to see her only to discover -that she wasn't there, only a plastic sheet, taped to a ladder. A deep breath to reoxygenate his deprived brain tingled his vision. A hooded diplomat whispered from behind him.

"Sir."

John, startled, turned.

"Oh Heavens! You trying to kill me?" John wiped the sweat off his head.

"Sorry," the diplomat whispered. "Your chamber awaits. Mother will join you."

"She's here. In the building. It's not safe."

The diplomat, hunched in an arthritic display, shuffled to the door. "I know. Follow me." The diplomat opened the door and John followed.

John entered the chamber first. He noticed her bleeding hands closing the door behind her. Her posture straightened. He turned to see Punch disrobe.

"You could have killed me down there." John surrendered. She aimed her gun at him. He looked like he aged ten years in ten minutes, hair grey, skin sagging. "You were always one for theatrics."

"Empty your pocket," said Punch. "I can see the bulge where your gun is." She approached him as he carefully handed it over. John noticed his own hands, as if for the first time -all bony, pale and curled. Punch slipped both guns into her hip-hugging holsters, then sauntered to his mini bar where she leaned over, hanging her eyes on the cocktail glasses he first offered her when he rescued her from a life of solitude.

"You cut my line." John felt his face.

"You tried to have me assassinated." She looked at him.

"My dear. You are a danger to everyone," he confessed. "I was jealous of you. I wanted-- I wanted to become...you."

Punch looked away with confusion. "You wanted to *become* me?"

"I felt threatened by you. And I wanted to draw James close, not because of his soul, but because I wanted to kill him. He knew how to turn you on in ways I didn't." As he drew closer, Punch cautiously watched him with her palm over her holster. "You are the very pith of strength and when you approach your dreams, it is always on a seismic level. This tireless energy and effort...even when you've been knocked to shit, leaves me paralyzed at the attempt to even try to realize and endure my own passions!"

"That's close enough."

"As you wish." He cleared his throat. "Could you fix me a scotch, darling?"

"I didn't come here to play bartender."

"No. You came here to arrest me." He held up his wrists to her.

"Do you see me carrying cuffs?"

"Punch, I love you. You are everything I would ever strive to become."

"No, I'm not. Everyone has an over-inflated view of themselves. I know I do. I speak in such absolutes. It's like a fortress for my truly flawed kingdom. I've become good at the hustle of my product." She pulled out her gun. "When you've lived as long as we have, you can't help but become a genius at something. Even if it's nothing."

"Spoiling the illusion for me, are you?" John bent down to his knees for forgiveness. He slowly and subtly pulled out a small blade from his sleeve while she checked her gun for bullets.

"An illusion, once realized, is like losing a friend." He lunged for her. She shot him in the head. His brain matter and skull splattered while his body fell. "That's for being a --mother-fucker."

The door opened and Mother, grey and shriveled, aimed a gun at Punch. Both women stood teary-eyed. A bowling pin smashed over Mother's head as the round she fired blasted the ceiling. She dropped. Jeff stood at the doorway.

"Jeff. Your timing is impeccable."

Farewell

"I am really, really, really pleased to make this next announcement." Punch stood behind a podium in front of a gratified audience. "The unveiling of who will be our next leader. The next Indift of Purgalapudlia!" She turned to look at the panel of people behind her. Among them, the Brothers Nil. She turned to the crowd, "I give you...Gus Dillard!" The crowd applauded as Gus stepped up to receive a hug from Punch. He waved to the crowd. Punch pinned a medal in the shape of a boxing glove on red ribbon to his jacket. She faced the audience. "You will be in good hands," she spoke. The crowd applauded. Og stood guard at the end of the stage, in a new Purgy uniform. "As you all are aware, I have officially stepped down from my post." The crowd saddened. "But, you will have a new protector. I have personally appointed Kimkixle as my replacement." The crowd clapped. "Love her as you would me." Kimkixle waved to the crowd. "I'd like to personally thank a group of boys I've had the privilege to know." She looked back at the Brothers Nil and waved them over to stand beside her. "And I can say this...excuse me." She looked down at the podium for a moment to choke back tears. "What a complete and total honor it is to have known these fine men who risked everything in securing our nation. They have shown me what it is to be loyal, sincere-- what it is to have a true brotherhood. They may claim nil; they are everything but." She pointed at them individually. "Shard. Aster. Ticktock. Jeff. Wes. Gus. And James. And the fallen, Steve and Toto. The Brothers Nil." The crowd roared with approval. She went to each brother, shook their hand and kissed them on the cheek until she got to James. She grabbed the back of his neck with her left hand and reached her right hand under his arm and planted a kiss for all to see. The crowd whistled and cheered. Gus grabbed Kimkixle by the hand.

"Hey, everybody!" shouted Gus. "Let's hear it for our gal, Punch!"

* * * * *

Gus and Og stayed behind in Purgalapudlia while Punch took the rest of the boys back home to Rackle's Tub. Abandoned tables, unswept floors, silent halls... The Clocks, Jeff and Wes and Punch gathered in the quiet lobby.

"Is the bar open?" asked Ticktock.

Punch reached over the dusty counter and pulled on one of the taps. Beer flowed. "I still have inventory." She climbed over the bar and tested a few more beer taps. They were all on and working. "Take home as many bottles as you can carry."

"What?!" shouted Ticktock.

"I'm closing shop," she said.

"Really?" asked Aster.

"Until next year," said Shard.

She looked at her bar proudly. "For good." Everyone rushed to the bar, grabbing bottles.

"Thanks!" said Jeff. She smiled and noticed James standing next to her. She reached out her hand and he grabbed it.

Aster glanced over. "What are you gonna do with this place?"

"Nothing."

"And the fighting?" asked Shard.

"I'm sick of fighting." She pulled on James's hand to follow her. "I'm done with it."

"You're one hell of a fighter, Punch," said Ticktock as he brought a box full of booze to the counter.

"Mind if I borrow James?" she asked. "Goodnight, everyone." She kissed her finger and waved to them. They stood motionless and watched as the couple went up the stairs, hand in hand.

"Where are we going?" asked James as they passed Punch's study.

"The attic."

Arriving at a small landing, Punch walked up the narrow stairs to the attic door and opened it. She reached for a box of matches inside and lit a lantern before entering. James followed her up.

"Punch." He dropped to one knee and grabbed her hand. "Will you marry me?" She reacted as if she held her breath underwater and had just come up for air. She sadly pulled away and removed a white sheet that had been covering a wooden trunk. James looked perplexed.

"This is where I say goodbye," she mumbled.

"What?" He got up.

"My Achilles' heel." She looked at the trunk.

"What are you talking about?"

"James, I want to die." She spoke softly. He grabbed her and turned her face to his.

"Don't be so fucking selfish. Okay? Stupid idea. Don't be so fucking selfish. I'll move to the cottage with you. We'll live together!" The lump in his throat grew, squeezing his voice box shut, eyes on the verge of flooding. He knew her mind was made up.

She grabbed his hands and squeezed them, "Come here," then reached her arms around him in a tight embrace. He cried into the curve of her shoulder. She held his head to her.

He pulled away wiping his eyes.

"I love you, James. You are the greatest love I've ever known. But when I saw you with Michelle, it hit me that you two were meant to be--"

"What?! Hell no! Punch, it's not too late--"

"Let me finish." She rubbed his wet cheeks. "I keep thinking, how dare I come in from a generation long dead, with hopes to nurture or relive love by robbing the fruits of this new one. Look at how many lives I've already fucked up. Including yours."

"Who's counting?"

"What I'm trying to say James, is I've had this feeling hanging over me for some time. I should've been gone yesterday."

"I've only known you for a week or two and look what you've bloody done to me," his voice strained.

"I'm sorry, James. For any sort of normal life, we missed each other by a hundred years." She reached into her blouse and pulled out her key necklace. "Open that trunk." She yanked the key off her neck.

"I can't open it," he weakly protested. "I won't open it." She looked away, eyes shut, nodding her head emphatically, fighting her own nagging sadness. She took a moment to repose. Tears building, her lashes barely held them.

"James... do this one last favor for me." She handed him the key. "Let me find peace with my generation. It's time to let me go, sweetie." He turned to the trunk and dropped to his knees before it, placing a hand on the lid. "Leaving you is my one regret." She wiped her cheeks red as she stood watching him. He gave her one last look. The key entered the lock on the trunk. It clicked as he turned it and lifted the lid open. Inside, the skeletal remains of a woman sat nestled in her Victorian bridal gown. James turned to where Punch stood. She was gone.

"PUNCH! NO! NOOOO-!" He shouted and jumped to his feet. His head throbbed as the blood shot to his brain all at once. Eyes exploded tears like broken bottles of wine. His spinal column, decalcified, knees buckled and he collapsed. He couldn't breathe, as though kicked in the gut by steel-toed boots. An earthworm left out in the morning sun, he withered in his useless emotions, the one solution he wanted was the one he could never have.

* * * * *

Before Gus was officially named Indift, Punch had taken all of her assets and rewarded those who remained from the tournament: The Clocks, Jeff and Wes, Betty and Michelle. Gus was granted ownership of Rackle's Tub. The winnings were placed in an envelope that was discovered on her desk in her study by Shard. In addition, there was money set aside for Steve's memorial. And with nothing left, her account was closed.

They stayed in town just long enough to hold a memorial for Punch. The only people present were the Clocks, Jeff and Wes. James had her remains cremated and laid to rest at a nearby cemetery. She appeared in the local paper's obituary as Mary Tabitha Lilybell "*Punch*". After the service, Jeff and Wes hit the road.

James sat in a booth at the library, searching through a microfilm machine. Colorado newspapers from a hundred years ago flicked past enlarged on the screen as he scanned through them, searching. His heart sank when he came across a photo of Punch taken somewhere between 1888 and 1890. She had won a writing contest and with the warmest smile, posed with her ribbon. It was a heroic story of how she saved a stray dog wounded by a porcupine. It was published at the time of her award.

Brotherhood

"Dad! There's a naked man in our bathtub!" The two children were up against the window overlooking the front yard of their farm.

Outside in the yard, James gripped the rim from both sides and leaned forward as if he were flying. His hand twitched, holding an imaginary faucet gun.

"Hey! Sir!" The farmer shouted from the house. "This is private property!" He made his way over. "You're gonna have to leave or I'll call the police!"

"I see her when I close my eyes. Pressed against my eyelids." James rocked back and forth.

"You're gonna have to leave." The farmer thought if he sounded a bit more clear it would cut through the babble coming from James.

"How did this tub get out here?"

"Where are your clothes, boy?" He noticed the newspaper photo on his leg. "Are you high on drugs?"

James grabbed the photo and stared at her, then turned away from it. "I'm just hurting, sir." The farmer grabbed the picture for closer inspection. His family waited out on the porch.

"Honey, get my robe."

"Have you seen her?" The farmer looked at the photo once more before handing it back.

"No." The farmer met his wife half-way with the robe. "Here. Put this on." He threw the robe into the tub. "I've got my wife and kids here. You understand?"

James nodded and slipped into the robe. He was beyond the realms of sanity for brief moments and then back. He thought he could enter her world by merely sitting in a bathtub. He was in pursuit of reconciliation as he fought to restore equilibrium from the hit he took. He shivered as if the robe were made of ice. He stared at the photo, touching it lovingly with his finger.

"She's not here anymore." James began to cry. "I buried her today." He fell limp to one side of the tub. "My love. My life."

"Come on. Let's get you inside." The farmer understood his pain. Still, he tried to lift him.

"Could I just stay here? For a little bit?" The farmer straightened. He sighed.

"Is there someone we could call for you?"

* * * * *

Shard's Cadillac arrived twenty minutes later.

"There he is," pointed Ticktock. There he was. Sitting in a lonely claw-foot bathtub out in the open field. Shard and the boys got out of the car. The farmer waved as they walked past.

"He's hurtin' in a bad way," said the farmer.

"Thank you," said Shard. It was terrifying to see a friend he'd known for years to be such a rock, suddenly collapse and disintegrate before his very eyes.

"James," Shard called out as they got closer. He didn't budge. "James--" he grabbed his shoulder.

"Hey guys," James looked at them, trying to regain his strength.

"You alright, mate?" asked Ticktock. James nodded. "What happened?"

"You know that feeling when someone you adore is here?" explained James. "You can never seem to get enough of them. And whatever you're doing... the moments without them around are just anxiety filled depression. A restless depression that robs you of appetite and prods you into a dull motion. No matter what you engage yourself with, it's empty headed and hollow hearted because all you can fucking do is think and think and think about her! She fucking bleeds me! Do you understand? She fucking bleeds me!!! Fuckin' shit! It's over. What am I gonna do?!" James broke down into Shard's arms. He held him. "What am I gonna fuckin' do?! I still love her so much and she's gone! All this love, still pouring out of me for that girl and it will never be returned." Shard cried silently with him. Aster grabbed the picture and placed it in his wallet for safe keeping. He and Ticktock joined Shard, holding onto James.

The wind blew at them, jackets wavering, as their bodies stood motionless in a tight huddle.

The Clockbrothers

James sat with ink-stained fingers in a bookstore in Los Angeles. A line of his readers clutched their own copy of his best seller. Once enough time had passed that he could open his journals, painfully reliving the early moments of the entries, he vigorously finished them and found Punch to be very much alive in the pages he wrote. And once he wrote, the healing began. After typing his 400 page manuscript, his friends, each with a copy to read, added their critique and perspectives which he included in a final draft that went out for publication, illustrations and all. He loved sharing Purgalapudlia and introducing Punch to a new generation. Michelle sat next to James and looked over at him. He finished signing a book and looked at her with a loving wink.

* * * * *

Shard sat behind his desk in his new office while Ticktock, swiveling back and forth, tested the limits of a chair.

"Your very own classic auto shop," Ticktock pulled out his wallet.

"It pays the bills."

"I guess you can afford to turn down those pesky reality gigs since you've got the big name clients," said Ticktock looking at the stained glass window of Shard's office made from colorful bottoms of various wine bottles and beer bottles. "Very appropriate for an auto shop." He pulled out some cash. Shard glanced at the bottles.

"The Clockbrothers-" said Shard grabbing a set of keys from his desk drawer, "-problem is, you've got one letter too many. Remove the L and you've got yourself a dart team."

Ticktock handed over the cash. "Oh yeah? Why don't we just fuck and get it over with?"

Shard handed over the car keys. "Still reliving that summer? You guys kind of lack the talent, don't you?"

"I'll show you *talent*... nine inches of talent! No, but we're getting better."

Shard's lobby had a theme decor, inspired by Rackle's Tub. A wooden ship chandelier glowed from light inside, coming forth out of the cannon doors, decks and captain's quarters. And on his walls, album covers and famous quotes. Shard followed Ticktock out the door. Parked out front, the Clock's Cadillac. The two stood in admiration of the car.

"Take care of her," said Shard, "she's been a good ride."

"Yeah, mate-" Ticktock shook his hand, "thank you. Will do." He opened the door.

"Hey," said Shard, "good luck."

* * * * *

The Cadillac sped past a sign that read highway 70. Ticktock felt good behind the wheel like he always imagined Shard would feel. His eyes, red from lack of sleep and boozing the night before, didn't help his driving. The Clockbrothers wore white t-shirts and patched-up dress slacks and drunkenly sang to keep Ticktock awake.

"Hey wankers, whose got the scotch?"

One of the brothers passed him a flask. Ticktock connected the end to his lips where it rested before he raised its warm contents collecting on his tongue, then swooshing down his throat.

Somewhere between Utah and Colorado the horizon turned white and that was the last thing Ticktock saw before his team drove into a ravine.

1892

His employees found him lying on the ground, elbows jutting outward like the spokes from a broken wagon wheel, a half-empty bottle of whiskey near. It was morning and too early for flies to hum requiem music in his ears. His men lifted John, who still wore the tuxedo from his wedding. Everyone knew about his runaway bride. It was killing him. He hadn't showered or eaten in days.

His body began the decaying process.

"I'm just not feeling well." John's sleepy eyes felt the sting of daylight. "My heart has lead anchors. I can't move to live and I can't live to die... I'm just a stagnant, empty shell, still moving out of memory to move." He covered his face from the sun.

"You'll get through this, Mr. Rackle," a worker reassured him.

The next day, John went missing. He was last spotted by a chambermaid. She watched him gallop away on horseback never to be seen again. The factory, as a result, shut down. No one dared to touch it, fearing it was cursed. Somebody, however, did. Mother made sure the factory wasn't disturbed.

Viscosity Of Time

One day, Gus had hoped someone from the tournament might return to Purgalapudlia for a visit -but they never did. Then again, crossing over wasn't as easy when you didn't have angelic escorts. Order in Purgalapudlia wasn't completely restored when Punch left. The country soon fell into war with the angels once again when word got out that Punch was gone. The angels were hoping to take advantage of the new leadership and bite the soft underbelly of a mourning nation. Their disdain for her was still fresh. Punch had left plans for securing the nation's independence in the care of Silcher and Kimkixle. They, with Gus and his high council, led the campaign against the angels. The fighting soon came to an end. Sovereignty restored. Purgalapudlia, a nation, once again! Gus married Kimkixle.

The cure for madmathix, mirrors of midnight, proved successful and this greatly helped ease tension between the nations. Gus introduced soul stations which were very much like gas stations in concept. He expanded on soul banks, making them accessible to everyone. Angels and diangles included. There were new checkpoints at every soul drilling station. The soul drilling equipment was updated from John Rackle's designs. Gus led a team of bioengineers to build better machines. He pored over John Rackle's notes and theories.

"Having a math equation with a symbol representing God in the formula," Gus inhaled, lungs filled deep in a wisp-berry tobacco called *wicklewisps*. He held his breath, still, until the buzz transcended his body. Then he blew the smoke out. "I think someone said the laws of nature may seem hard to understand, but with reason, can be solved. If only you knew what questions to ask. God might present hard problems, but he never broke the rules by presenting unanswerable ones." Gus flipped to the next page of John's journal. "I think this is the closest we've come to having a great, mathematical expression for a *'unified theory'*... Rackle's Tub."

The End

Bull's-Eye

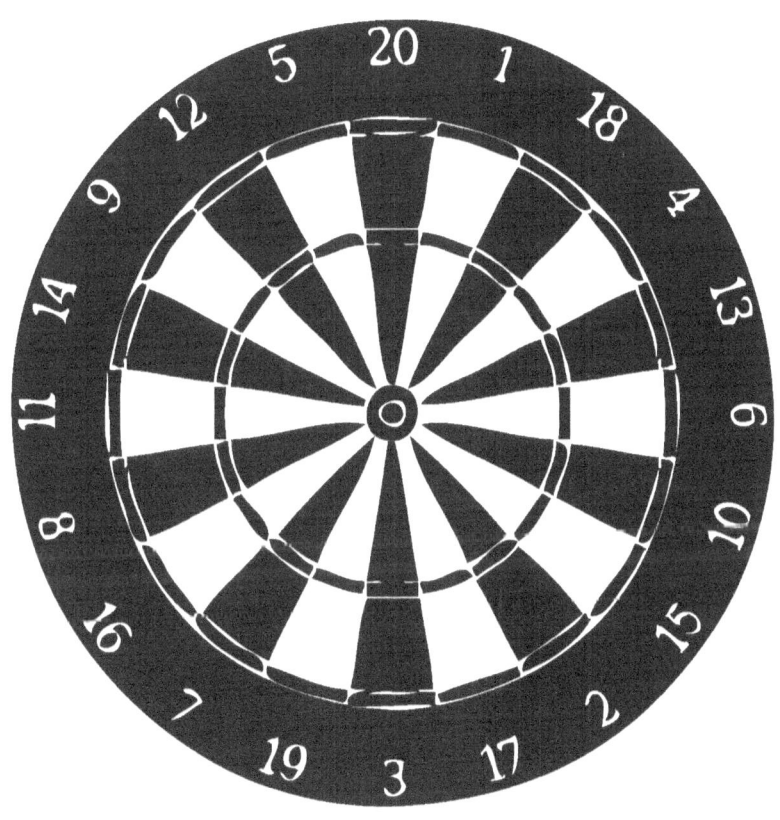

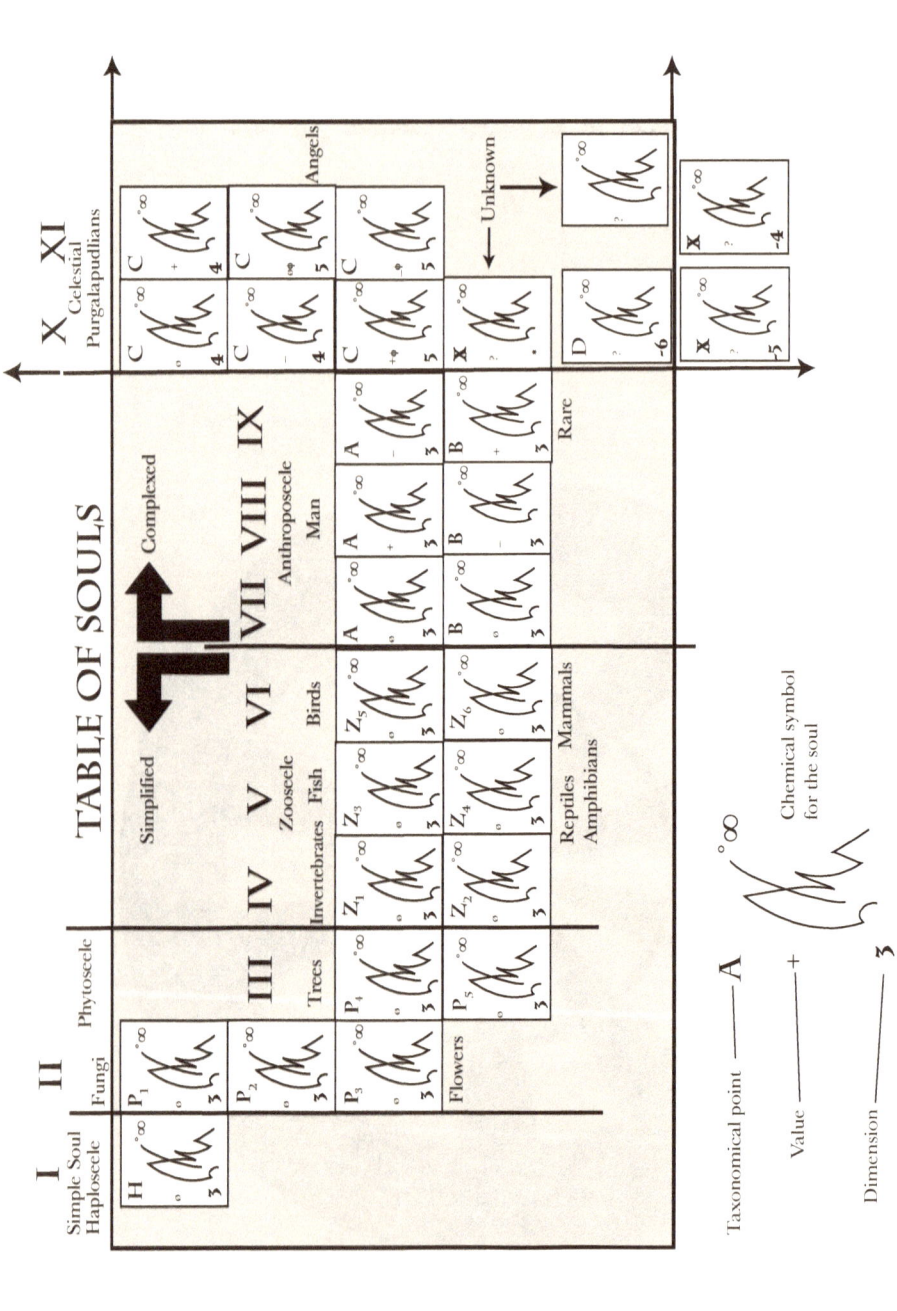

TABLE OF SOULS

I	II	III	IV	V	VI	VII	VIII	IX	X	XI

Simple Soul · Phytosele · Zoosele · Anthroposele · Celestial
Haplosele · Fungi · Trees · Invertebrates · Fish · Birds · Man · Purgatapudlians

Simplified ⟷ Complexed

Reptiles · Mammals · Angels
Amphibians

Rare

Unknown

Taxonomical point ——— A

Value ——— +

Dimension ——— 3

Chemical symbol for the soul

What soul type are you?

1) If you prefer salty things.
And strangers feel compelled to share secrets.
And street lights go out when you're near them.
And you enjoy the scent of lavender.
And green makes you happy.
And you get dizzy and puke when spun in a circle.
And you feel you should have been born with extra
appendages and holes.

Then you are a:

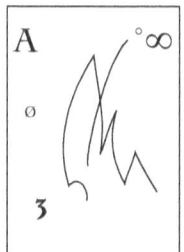

2) If you have more emotions to cover than vices available.
And you feel as tall as a Holy Warrior.
And dumpster diving at the end of a semester excites you.
And no one appreciates your gallows' humor.
And your kitchen fills with grey sunshine.
And you're never bored even when you are.

Then you are a:

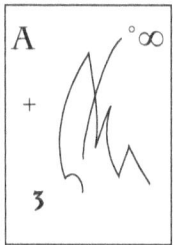

3) If you inhale your farts quick so as to not let on
that you stink around others.
And you avoid mirrors in public.
And you are without words when pressed on political issues.
And winter is your favorite season.
And light makes you sneeze.
And you find you misunderstand people a lot.
And you often feel trapped in a perpetual motion
of not knowing where to begin.

Then you are a:

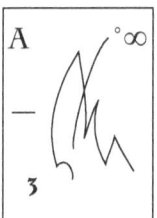

4) If you are aroused by handcuffs.
And wait to do laundry until you realize you're buying
new clothes to replace the dirty ones.
And you sing best when alone in your room.
And the sounds of the gardener's aluminum rake,
sweeping makes you feel Zen.
And you love the smell of old books.
And you're an insomniac.

Then you are a:

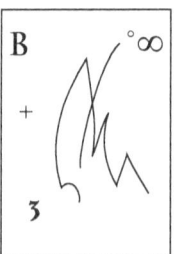

5) If you wonder too much about how dead people lived.
And you have nervous ticks.
And you enjoy the taste of chewed finger callous.
And you pretend to be bipolar so people will think
you're a sick genius.
And you see yourself as Steve McQueen when the sun
hits your eyes. (Even if you're female)
And no matter the season, you always feel hot.

Then you are a:

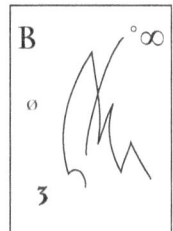

6) When birds follow you.
And your fecal matter flushes away cleanly.
And you fake laughter to be socially closer.
And you like minor chords to follow major chords.
And you have a hidden birthmark that should be checked
to be sure it's not cancerous.
And people always look like an opened can of ugly stuff.
And you feel compelled to talk even when you have nothing
to say.

Then you are a:

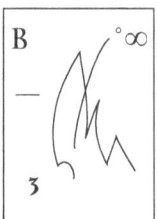

7) If you excel in learning.
And people often compare you to the statue of David
or a painting of Venus.
And your health couldn't be better.
And you just got a promotion.
And you won a new car from a radio contest.
And the police always let you off with a warning.
And sex is a daily habit.
And people worship you because you are so fucking
charming, brilliant, talented, good looking, Goddamn perfect.

Then you are a:
No soul! You're a fucking robot, computer, bullshit! You're
just shit coming hot out of a bull. Okay?! Loser. Whatever!
Just close the book. We're done here. I'm not jealous.
I know it looks it. But I'm not.
Okay, fine, maybe a little.

A James sketch from his journal.

The cartoon of Punch drawn on the wall of Rackle's Tub by James.